Also by Tarah Benner

Bound in Blood

The Defectors

Enemy Inside

The Last Uprising

Recon

Exposure

Outbreak

Lockdown

Annihilation

Book Five of The Fringe

By Tarah Benner

Printed in the United States of America
First Edition
Cover design by Slobodan Cedic

ISBN 978-1534806030

www.tarahbenner.com

To my wonderful beta readers.
I couldn't have built this world without you.

one

Harper

There's nothing as dark as the desert at night. This far from the compound, there is no florescent glow bleeding onto the sand. There are no searchlights hunting for wanted men.

Before Death Storm, this street would have been lit by porch lights and street lamps, but all we have now are the moon and stars to guide us through town.

We're driving at a snail-like pace with our headlights off, squinting through the darkness for any sign of movement. To my right, Sage has her head cocked out the open window. She's dressed in high-waisted jeans, a cutoff coral tank top, and a studded white jacket that's been rolled to the elbows. Her long hair is whipping out behind her like a flag, and whenever we hit a pothole, her silver bracelets clink against the butt of her rifle.

I barely know Sage at all, but I know she must be worrying about Owen. We all are.

Eli is sitting in the driver's seat, scanning the dusty road with his brows crinkled in worry. His right leg is pressed against my thigh, and I can feel the nervous energy popping off him like static.

We left the compound to look for a cure to the virus that killed everyone at 119, but when Owen was shot, that mission was scrapped. Owen came to the compound looking for Eli, and Eli won't stop until he rescues his brother.

He hasn't said a word since we left Owen's house, but I know he's thinking of all the horrible things Constance has done to make people talk. If Owen is still alive, that's where he'll be.

There's no use going back to the compound tonight — not with Recon on high alert. Instead, we're headed for the abandoned pawn shop Malcolm has been using as the Desperados' base to get our hands on some heavy-duty weapons and explosives.

Breaking out of the compound is no easy task, but breaking *in* will be nearly impossible. To have a chance, we'll need much more than the two M-4s we brought with us.

After a few minutes, we reach a fork in the road, and a loud *bang* on the roof makes me jump. Eli presses the brake and glances into the side mirror. Jackson is sitting in the bed of the truck, signaling Eli to turn left. Eli gives a barely discernible nod and turns, slowing to a crawl until he hears another *bang* from Jackson.

To our left is a used-car dealership that's been picked over by looters; to our right, there's an overgrown junkyard filled with old tractor tires, car batteries, and oil drums.

Eli turns into the weed-choked gravel drive and parks the truck behind a pile of twisted scrap metal. He kills the engine, and Jackson jumps out of the bed with a gun in one hand and a pair of bolt cutters in the other.

I'm not as familiar with this area as he is, but I know we can't be too far from the pawn shop. Based on our experience with the Desperados, Malcolm will have lookouts posted all around the base. And the closer we get, the greater the risk of coming under fire.

Eli opens his door, and I hop out after him. I check my rifle for what feels like the hundredth time and wipe my sweaty palms on my borrowed jean shorts. We follow Jackson through the inky blackness, and the sound of our feet crunching on gravel fills me with dread. I know we're going to have to kill whoever stands in our way, but the thought of pulling the trigger makes me feel sick.

We pass a run-down Mexican restaurant, a laundry mat, and the dilapidated shell of a filling station before reaching an area that looks stark, poor, and industrial. We *must* be getting close.

Suddenly, Jackson freezes and throws out an arm to stop us. Eli finds my wrist and gives it a squeeze, and I hear a rustle over my shoulder as Sage draws her weapon.

Jackson points across the road, and as my vision sharpens, I can just make out the shadow of a man lurking under a decommissioned streetlight. If it weren't for the tiny orange glow emanating from his cigarette, I might have missed him entirely.

Jackson signals us to stay put and hands Sage the bolt cutters. He stows his gun in the waistband of his frayed khaki shorts, pulls a knife out of his holster, and starts walking purposefully across the street.

He cuts around an abandoned car and soon disappears from view. Eli lets out a long breath, and we wait for Jackson's signal.

Ten agonizing seconds later, the cigarette hits the ground, and I hear the sound of a struggle. A sickening gurgle echoes across the street, and the lookout's body hits the pavement with a dull *smack*.

Jackson lets out a low whistle, and I clench my fist to try to pull myself together. Eli's finger finds my belt loop, and he pulls me forward to the spot where the cigarette's glow disappeared. My heart is pounding in my throat, but I manage to hold my gun steady as I scan the road for threats.

We step up onto the curb and cut around the sagging chain-link fence running between the buildings. An overflowing dumpster on our left throws the alley into shadow, and I hold my breath as Eli leads me toward the door of the pawn shop.

Suddenly, my toe catches on something — or someone — sprawled across the alley. I pitch forward, but Eli's arm shoots out to catch me.

Holding in a gasp, I squint down at the ground to see what I tripped on.

It's a body.

I can't make out the dead man's face, but I can tell he's wearing a cutoff T-shirt, frayed denim shorts, and bright white sneakers.

The man on the corner wasn't the only one guarding the base, and Jackson dispatched him with the silence and efficiency of a trained assassin.

Shaking with nerves, I force myself to breathe normally and step aside to let Sage pass.

She doesn't look down at the body. She doesn't even blink. She just crouches down next to the door, pulls a flashlight out of her bag, and hands it off to Jackson.

There's a loud *zip* and a soft clatter of metal, and when Jackson shifts to the left, I see Sage rifling through what looks like a lock-pick set.

She inserts a thin metal rod into the lock and an even thinner pin over the top. Then her delicate cinnamon hands begin coaxing the pins into place. Her long dark hair falls across her face like a curtain, and I can tell she's completely absorbed in her work.

Eli glances over his shoulder, checking and rechecking for approaching drifters.

After about a minute, Sage lifts her head with a satisfied smirk and pushes the door wide open. Eli's eyebrows shoot up into his hairline, but Jackson takes the lead without a word as if he's seen Sage do this a hundred times before.

Taking a deep breath, I raise my rifle and follow Eli into the pawn shop. Jackson shines the beam of Sage's flashlight onto the opposite wall, and I hear him whisper a quick "clear." Then Sage slips inside and closes the door behind her.

In the wavering pool of light dancing over the walls, my brain constructs a scattered snapshot of the pawn shop. The front windows are covered with cardboard and plywood, and the dusty shelves are mostly bare. All that's left is a busted guitar, a dusty toaster, an ancient television set, and a few old movies.

The clatter of the beaded curtain makes me jump, and I hold my breath as Eli glides into the back to look for drifters.

"Clear," he calls.

All my muscles tense as I follow Eli and Jackson into the cramped control room, but I feel myself relax as the shadows of a dozen sleeping computer monitors come into view.

Eli and Jackson head straight for the metal cabinet in the corner, which the Desperados have converted into a makeshift gun safe. Jackson's bolt cutters make quick work of the combination lock, and within seconds he and Eli are pulling out the weapons we came here for.

Sage is standing guard just inside the beaded curtain, so I wander over to examine the bulletin board hanging on the opposite wall. When I shine my stolen interface over the papers, I immediately recognize the rumpled map of the town we're in and the surrounding desert terrain. There are a few more markings than last time, indicating Recon activity in the area, and a large black X drawn over the restaurant that used to serve as the Desperados' base.

Next to this map is a larger aerial image of the Southwest, dotted with a symbol that most closely resembles a tower. Next to each tower is a number: 112, 113 — all the way up to 121. My eye is immediately drawn to number 119, which is one of about half a dozen towers marked with an ugly black X.

"No," I whisper, following the map up to the next closest X: 116. Judging by the rough semicircle fanning southeast from Salt Lake City and cutting into the corners of Colorado, New Mexico, and Arizona, the Desperados have been working to eradicate all the compounds near their base.

"Is this . . .?"

Eli's voice makes me jump. I glance over my shoulder and see him standing behind me with a horrified expression on his face.

I nod, too numb for words.

"What is it?" asks Jackson.

When I don't answer, Sage wanders away from her post and comes to stand beside Eli.

Sage, like Jackson, isn't from the compounds. She has no allegiance to the people who live there and no reason to care about the thousands of deaths those Xs represent. But when I glance over at her, I'm startled to see that her almond-shaped eyes are shimmering with tears.

"I can't believe Owen was involved with this," she murmurs. "I can't believe —"

"What is it?" asks Jackson.

None of us responds, so he steps forward with his arms full of guns to see what we're all staring at.

I know when he finally gets it, because I hear his sharp intake of breath and the sound of several guns hitting the floor. "*Ho-ly shit.*"

Eli runs a shaky hand through his hair. "One-nineteen wasn't the first."

"But 112 is next," I choke.

"Malcolm's been picking them off as the Desperados migrate west," says Sage.

"He isn't going to stop," I whisper, looking up at Eli.

He lets out a long, angry burst of air. "No. He isn't."

For a moment, I forget all about Owen. I forget my guilt over leaving him and our responsibility to Eli's only living relative.

All I can think about is Sawyer. She's lying in the medical ward right now, dying from a virus that no one can control.

Since we left the compound, I've managed to push all thoughts of her out of my mind to focus on the more immediate threats, but seeing those black Xs of death spanning across the Southwest makes it impossible to ignore the choking dread I've been suppressing all day.

I can't banish the grisly memories of 119 — the stench of death, the remnants of innocent lives cut short, and the devastating emptiness of those tunnels. When Malcolm's virus ripped through 119, it didn't leave anyone alive. It killed with the raw, indiscriminate power of a nuclear blast.

I understand Eli's determination to rescue Owen, and I feel the pain of the lie he told his brother to gain his trust. But as much as I love Eli, I can't justify going back for Owen when we're this close to the only man who can control the outbreak.

If there is a cure, I have to find it. I have to find a way to end the killing before Malcolm's virus destroys my home and kills everyone I've ever met.

"We have to do something," I murmur.

Eli doesn't say anything, but I can tell he's shaking his head. He knows what I'm going to say next, and he's preparing to fight me on it.

I open my mouth to head off his argument, but I never get the chance. Behind me, I hear the clatter of a rifle and the soft *click* of a safety. Somebody behind Jackson and Sage clears his throat, and all the hairs on the back of my neck stand on end.

two

Eli

"Don' move," growls the intruder in a harsh Southern drawl.

Every muscle in my body tightens. We didn't hear him enter the pawn shop, but there's someone in this room who wants us dead.

"Don' move," he repeats.

I've heard that voice. I *know* that voice. It belongs to Gunner — the bleached-blond stoner with the lip ring who used to guard the pawn shop.

Gunner is one of Malcolm's men, but I always thought he lacked the killer instinct to make it as a Desperado. Maybe I was wrong.

"Easy, man," says Jackson. "You're outgunned here."

"'S'at right?" pipes Gunner in a strangely high-pitched voice.

He definitely sounds panicked at the thought of having to shoot someone, but that doesn't mean he won't.

"I-I got a clear shot at the pretty brunette, so unless you want her brains splattered all over that wall there . . ."

My stomach drops to my knees, and it's all I can do to stop myself from wheeling around and kicking Gunner's teeth in. I don't know if he's talking about Harper or Sage, but the threat is enough to unleash the monster inside me.

"Hey," I choke, trying to keep my voice calm despite the heavy weight pressing down on my chest. "Go easy, man.

Nobody has to die today."

"*Owen*?"

Gunner sounds almost as surprised as I feel. I completely forgot that he knows Owen and that I look and sound exactly like him.

"'S'at you?" Gunner asks.

"Yeah," I say, trying to sound normal.

It's possible the Desperados already know that Owen split town, but I'm banking on Gunner's loyalty to help get us out of this mess.

"Take it easy," I say, fighting to keep my voice steady. "That's my girl you've got your gun pointed at."

There's a loud rustling sound behind me, and I glance over my shoulder. Gunner is putting down his weapon.

"Shit, I'm s —" He breaks off, suspicion coloring his features. "Hang on . . ."

The beam of a flashlight ripples over the wall, and when it lands on Jackson, the tension in the room seems to mount.

"I know you," says Gunner. "You're Jackson Mills."

Panic and dread wash over me. Jackson fled Malcolm's gang soon after Nuclear Nation was absorbed by the Desperados. And when Owen was captured and interrogated at Malcolm's old base, he unequivocally denied any knowledge of Jackson's whereabouts. Getting caught with Jackson now isn't going to help ease Gunner's suspicions.

"It's not what you think, man," I say, trying to draw his attention back to me long enough to come up with a believable story.

"Really?" asks Gunner. "'Cause it looks like you're helpin' him steal our plans."

"Come on . . ." I mutter. "You know I would never do something like that."

"I don't know *nothin'* for sure no more."

I take a deep breath, gathering up the courage to do what I know I have to. "Just put the gun down, and I'll explain everything."

"No!"

"Gunner, listen —"

"Don' try to confuse me with your lies."

"I'm not *lying*," I say in an exasperated tone. "Man, I thought we were friends."

"We are," he says, sounding as though he's trying to reason with himself. "I'm just doin' my job."

"I know, I know. Just don't do anything stupid, okay? Nobody has to get hurt here . . . Just let me explain."

There's a long, heavy pause.

I still have my back to Gunner, but I would bet money he's shaking and sweating, weighing the odds that I'm a traitor.

"Turn around," he mutters.

I let out the breath I've been holding and prepare to tackle Gunner to the ground.

"Real slow!" he yells as I pivot on the spot.

I slow my pace, my mind still working a mile a minute.

"Not you!" he yells, and I hear a sharp intake of air.

A dark cloud of distress wells up inside me, and when I'm finally facing Gunner, I realize that he's got his gun trained on Harper. She's still facing the wall, and her bottom lip is trembling with fear.

"Don' try anything," he warns, taking a step toward her.

Every muscle in my body is screaming at me to tear Gunner apart, but I force my feet to stay planted on the floor.

Harper flinches at the sound of Gunner's footsteps.

"Don' move!" he yells.

Now that I'm facing him, I can see the beads of sweat

sliding down his upper lip and the way his hands are shaking.

This guy definitely hasn't shot many people in his life, and I can tell he doesn't want to kill any of us. He's scared shitless.

Unfortunately, experience has taught me that the jumpier someone is, the more dangerous he is with a weapon.

Gunner glances over at me, and I send a mental plea to Sage and Jackson not to do anything stupid. If nobody spooks him or says the wrong thing, we might all get to walk out of here alive.

"Start talkin'," he says.

I swallow twice to wet my parched throat. "Malcolm is preparing for another attack."

"Yeah, no shit," says Gunner, brushing back his overgrown swoop of bangs.

I glance at Jackson, thinking fast. "Well . . . did Malcolm tell you the compounds have basically doubled their boots on the ground?"

Gunner doesn't reply. He's still staring at Jackson with deep suspicion.

"Where did he come from?" Gunner asks.

"None of your goddamn business," mutters Jackson.

As the former leader of Nuclear Nation, I can tell he's not used to taking lip from guys like Gunner.

"He's been away," I add, shooting Jackson a shut-the-fuck-up sort of look.

"So what are you doin' all the way out here?"

"Me and Malcolm drove by earlier," I say. "We didn't see the lookouts out front, and he got nervous . . . Asked me to check things out." I nod to Jackson, Harper, and Sage. "I brought them with me as backup. I'm sure you can understand why."

Gunner follows my gaze to the others. His eyes linger on Harper for longer than I like before snapping back to me. "So you just came by to check things out?"

"Yeah."

"'Cause somethin' didn' look right . . ."

"Yeah."

"And Malcolm sent you?" he asks.

I nod. "Turns out he was right. We found two of our people dead — stabbed to death outside."

In the bluish glow from Harper's interface, I see Gunner's mouth tighten into a hard line. He shakes his head, and when he speaks, he sounds upset. "See, that don' make much sense to me . . ."

Suddenly, it feels as though all the air has been sucked out of the room. My mouth goes dry, and when I finally find my voice, I don't sound like myself at all. "Why not?"

Gunner raises an eyebrow. "'Cause I was just with Malcolm. He sent me over to take Trent's place, but he didn' say nothin' 'bout no missin' lookouts."

My stomach drops.

"I found Craig and Trent," he says.

My heart is pounding in my throat. We all know the jig is up. The only question is how long we have before Gunner puts a bullet through the back of Harper's head.

"You're lyin'," he murmurs in an accusatory tone.

My hands tingle on my rifle. I'm about two seconds from shooting Gunner in the head when he takes a sudden step forward. Harper jumps.

"Don't!" I yell.

"You move and I shoot," he says, clear panic in his voice. Gunner is sweating heavily now, and I can tell it takes every shred of courage he has to close the distance between him and Harper and place the muzzle of his gun against the back of her head.

Harper drags in a shaky breath. She looks as though she's just barely holding it together.

"Tell the truth," says Gunner, glancing from me to Jackson. From the tone of his voice, it sounds as though he's begging for an out so he doesn't have to shoot Harper.

My brain is running on overdrive, gaming out every plausible story. Unfortunately, every scenario that comes to mind puts Harper at risk. I just don't know what I can say to make Gunner believe that we're on the same side.

"You're not here for Malcolm, are you?"

I glance at Jackson, whose expression is unreadable.

"*You* killed Craig and Trent! Didn't you?"

I open my mouth without knowing what to say.

"*Didn't you*?" Gunner demands.

Before I can answer, a flash of light squeezes through the crude cardboard window covers and darts across Gunner's face. He sucks in a startled gasp but quickly refocuses on his hostage.

He's working up the courage to pull the trigger, but the brief distraction gives me a chance to raise my rifle slightly. At the same time, a flash of movement catches my eye.

The movement was so small I could have imagined it, but I know I saw Harper's shoulder twitch.

A second ago, she was facing away from Gunner. But as his eyes followed the beam of light, she pivoted twenty-five degrees to her left.

Harper has taken matters into her own hands, I realize. She's going to try to disarm Gunner, and she's going to get herself killed.

"We need to move," I say suddenly.

I don't know who's outside, but convincing Gunner that they could be hostile is our best chance to escape.

"Yeah, you'd like that, wouldn't you?" he spits.

"Did Malcolm *tell* you he was sending backup?" I ask.

Gunner doesn't answer, and I can tell that he isn't sure whether the people outside are Desperados or Recon.

"You said Malcolm sent you to relieve Trent," I reason. "You didn't say he was sending anyone to take over for Craig."

"Shut up while I think!" he splutters.

"You don't know if those people are Malcolm's or the compound's," says Jackson.

"They gotta be ours," snaps Gunner. But his voice is wavering with uncertainty.

"Those aren't Desperados," I say, more insistently this time. "We need to get the fuck out of here!"

"Hey! We aren't goin' *nowhere* 'til I say we are," says Gunner, sounding genuinely worried.

"You can't shoot her," I say. "Not until you know who's out there."

Gunner shifts nervously from one foot to the other. In his distracted state, he doesn't notice Harper taking another small step to the left. I watch her chest rise and fall, and everything seems to slow down.

Harper whips around and slams her arm into Gunner's with all the force she can muster. Shock flashes in Gunner's eyes, but I don't see anything else. I dive toward the floor as Harper knocks his aim askew and brace myself for the blast of a gun.

It never comes.

Gunner's weapon hits the floor with a heavy *thud*, and when I finally look up, I see Harper standing in front of him with her rifle pointed at his chest. Her breathing is ragged and uneven, but her sharp gray eyes are calm and deadly.

"Not so fun when it's pointed at *you*, is it?" she snarls.

"Please," whimpers Gunner, looking as though he might wet himself.

"Tell me where the fucking cure is," she says.

"W-what?"

"Harper, we have to go," I say, glancing out the window. Whether the people outside work for Malcolm or the compound, it's gonna be bad news for us if we're caught. But Harper is laser-focused on Gunner, and she gives no sign that she heard me.

"Malcolm has been using that virus to wipe out the compounds one by one," she says. "There *has* to be a cure. Now where — the fuck — is he keeping it?"

"I don' know nothin' 'bout no cure!" blubbers Gunner, his wild eyes darting from Harper to me and back to Harper.

In that instant, I know Gunner is telling the truth. The kid looks absolutely petrified. And when someone that green crosses over from scared to scared shitless, any ability to lie convincingly flies out the window.

Harper isn't having it. She releases her safety and steps forward until the muzzle of her rifle kisses Gunner's chest.

"You better start talking," she whispers.

"Hey!" Jackson hisses, interrupting their drama to flash his light over an emergency exit sign. "We have to go."

"Harper!"

But Harper is completely checked out. As I watch, her lips tighten into a scowl, and she pushes her weapon harder into Gunner's sternum. He squeezes his eyes shut in the exact same expression Harper was wearing two minutes before, and I can almost hear the frantic loop of prayers playing in his head.

"You have three seconds to tell me what you know about the cure," she mutters.

"I don' —"

"One . . ."

"Harper —"

"Two . . ."

I don't know what to do. Judging by the stone-cold look in Harper's eyes, I can tell she isn't thinking about our escape right now. She isn't thinking of herself or me or Owen or the people outside who want us dead. She's thinking of Sawyer lying in the medical ward with a deadly virus coursing through her veins. She's already weighed the value of Gunner's life against hers and decided she'd have no trouble ending his.

I know it. She knows it. Gunner knows it. His already pale skin has gone stark white, and he's trembling like a dog left out in the rain.

"Three."

I drag in a deep breath and prepare for Gunner to drop to the floor. But before Harper can pull the trigger, I hear the sound of breaking glass out front. The disturbance pulls Harper out of her trance, and I seize the opportunity to restore some sanity to the situation.

"We have to get out of here," I say, crossing behind Gunner and pointing my rifle at his back. "We'll finish this later."

For a second, I worry that Harper is going to fight me. But as we stare into each other's eyes, I see all those murderous intentions slip away.

"Fine."

Sage lets out a breath of relief, and the three of us follow Jackson out the back door. He spins around to clear the alley with one of Malcolm's AK-47s and jogs a few feet ahead of us to search for hostile gunmen.

"You make a sound, and I shoot," I whisper, shoving the end of my rifle into Gunner's back.

He doesn't say a word.

Harper dashes out ahead of us, and I can practically see her trying to shake off the demons that temporarily hijacked her senses.

It's awkward and slow moving down the alley with a hostage, but I manage to get us several blocks away without losing Gunner. I can just see Harper out of the corner of my eye, and the sound of footsteps tells me Sage must be right behind us.

"There!" yells a voice about fifty feet away.

"I see them!" yells another.

I glance over my shoulder, and when I turn back around, I realize I've lost sight of Jackson in the dark.

Panicking, I lower my weapon and grab Gunner by the collar. Dragging him along, I lead Harper and Sage back behind another building and down the second side street.

"Hurry!" I gasp, turning over my shoulder to make sure the girls are still with me. Harper is right on my heels, but Sage is nowhere to be seen.

My stomach drops. I squint up ahead and back the way we came. Neither Sage nor Jackson is anywhere in sight, and I realize they must have gone down another side street.

A skid of gravel a few yards ahead makes me freeze on the spot. I see the outline of three individuals, but I can't make out faces or uniforms.

Suddenly, a gun goes off, but I don't hear an accompanying scream.

"Drifters!" someone yells.

It's Recon.

Another shot fires — the bullet whizzing past my head — and I realize they've got us hemmed in on both sides. Our only option is to get out of the alley and hopefully draw them away from the others.

In a moment of desperation, I hunker down and heave Gunner's slim frame over the low fence. He hits the ground in a dusty heap, and Harper hops over after him. I shoot blindly into the darkness — careful to aim over the heads of any Recon operatives — and clamber over the fence after them.

Gunner is already trying to make his escape, but his legs are slow and clumsy.

"Hey!" I yell, shooting again and causing him to freeze on the spot.

My right hand finds Harper in the darkness, and I use my left to snatch a fistful of Gunner's shirt. Half running, half stumbling, we whip around the corner and reach a wide-open stretch of road.

We're less than a quarter of a mile from the truck, but we're completely exposed.

Harper takes off at a sprint, and I follow her with Gunner in tow. But then my foot catches on something lying in the street, and I feel my grip on Gunner loosen.

I pitch forward, unable to stop my fall, but I somehow manage to take Gunner down with me. Dirt and gravel scrape my arms, and I catch a boot to the face as Gunner tries to get away.

"No!" I yell, groping in the dark to pull him back down. My hand closes around his ankle, and he aims another kick at my head.

Fortunately, he's scared and uncoordinated, and that motion is all it takes for me to pull him back down. He hits the ground with a heavy "Oaff!" and I get a whiff of sweat and cigarette smoke.

Then I hear another gunshot. Someone lets out a horrible yell, and then the streets go quiet.

three

Celdon

There are days when you wake up, take a look at your life, and wonder how the fuck you got to where you are. You wonder how you made so many wrong turns. You wonder how things might have gone differently.

This is not one of those days.

I know exactly how I got here. I am the architect of this fucked-up shit castle that is my life. The weird part is that I don't completely believe that it *is* my life. Today it's felt more like a nightmare than reality.

A few hours ago, I watched Devon Reid choke Jayden to death. I watched her realize that her life was over just before her eyes went blank and her head fell forward. Then I wrapped her up in half a dozen garbage bags, tossed her onto a cart, and wheeled her to the incinerator chute.

Jayden seemed heavy for such a tiny woman. Wrangling her corpse onto a file cart and hauling her ass to the incinerator wasn't easy.

The awkward, sweaty struggle felt like an out-of-body experience — as if someone else stood in that room with Devon and helped him clean up the mess.

Only it wasn't. It was me. It's still me. Only now I'm watching a man writhe in pain as Watson sends 50,000 volts through his body.

The man is Owen Parker, and Watson has been working him over for the last hour — demanding the whereabouts of

Malcolm Martinez, Jackson Mills, Eli, and Harper.

Watson is a slim man with tan skin and the emaciated look of a long-distance runner. He's got blindingly white teeth and the most boring haircut I've ever seen.

Publicly, he goes by *Dr.* Watson and spends his day terrorizing interns. But behind closed doors, he's known only as the Answer Man — a member of Constance whose job is to think up creative ways to exert control through cruelty.

Watson is Constance's best interrogator because he has stamina. He'll work on someone for hours or days until they crack, but it hardly ever takes that long. Most of his interrogations last less than an hour.

But Owen has stamina, too, and like his younger brother, he's throwing Watson off his game. So far, he hasn't responded to the pain at all except to string together a few unimaginative obscenities.

"I'm going to ask you one more time," says Watson, licking his lips and whipping the shock collar's fob around on his finger. "Where — is — your brother?"

"Go to hell," snarls Owen.

A fake smile flickers across Watson's smooth façade, but I can tell by his flared nostrils that he's growing frustrated.

Without blinking, he hits a button on the fob, and all of Owen's muscles seize in unison. He buckles on the table with a strangled yell, and his lower back arches as he strains against the straps.

When the convulsions subside, Owen shudders and gasps for air. A fat drop of sweat rolls down the side of his face, and he clenches his fists together to keep his hands from shaking.

It's hard to watch. I *wouldn't* be watching, if it were up to me. But after I disposed of Jayden's body, Devon told me to meet him here. He hasn't shown up yet, and I'm about ready to leave.

Watson and Owen have been at this for hours, and Owen looks as though he doesn't have much left in him. I'm amazed he's held out this long, actually.

After three rounds of electrocution, people usually lose control of their bowels. At five, they almost always lose consciousness. Owen's already taken four rounds of shocks.

"I don't understand why you're protecting him," says Watson in a smooth, compassionate voice. "Eli *left* you. You broke in to help him escape, and he left you for dead at the first sign of trouble."

Somehow Owen manages to produce a crooked sneer. "You don't know what the fuck you're talking about."

"I know Eli doesn't care about you — not really."

Owen's crazy grin expands, and I feel something inside me snap. I can't take much more of this. No matter how good people are — no matter how determined they are to do the right thing — Constance always breaks them.

"People like Eli are users," Watson continues in that silky, disgusting voice of his. "They'll help you and tell you what you want to hear, but the second you aren't useful to them . . ." He snaps his fingers and opens his palm to show all of Owen's hopes and dreams scattering to the wind.

I have to hold back a snort of disgust. Using people is what Constance does best.

"And you're *what*?" Owen chokes. "My friend?" He shakes his head. "What happens to me, then, huh? As soon as I tell you what you want to know, you're just gonna kill me, too."

"You're mistaken," says Watson calmly. "I have no interest in you. As I said before . . . my only interest is in your brother, Harper Riley, Jackson Mills, and Malcolm Martinez."

Owen lets out a bark of incredulous laughter. "Yeah right. You'd kill any one of us the second you got the chance. The only reason I'm still alive is that you think I'm going to talk."

Watson doesn't say anything, but I can almost hear his wheels turning as he decides which manipulation tactic he's going to use next. Owen is still panting and sweating from his last round of electrocution, staring up at the swinging florescent light strip with eyes full of hatred.

Finally, Watson seems to make a decision. He sniffs deeply and stalks out of the room, leaving me and Owen alone. For a moment, I think he might be taking a break, but that's not Watson's style.

The room falls silent as we both wait for him to reappear, and Owen's eyes snap onto me. "Who the fuck are you?" His voice is hoarse from holding in his screams.

I jump. "Nobody."

Owen studies me for several seconds with harsh, unblinking eyes. He looks as though he's staring right through me, but I know he's searching for signs of weakness. And even though he's the one strapped to the table in Constance's torture chamber, I feel a prickle of unease.

"You're scared," he says finally. His voice is low and even, but it has a quiet confidence that says he's certain.

I freeze. *Is it really that obvious?*

I try to roll my eyes, but it's surprisingly hard to fake it with Owen.

"You're in over your head, and you don't know what to do," he continues, turning his head back to the ceiling. "I've known guys like you."

I swallow, trying to keep my expression neutral. I can't have him outing me to Watson. I clear my throat and get up to go, but then I hear a harsh "Wait!" that stops me in my tracks.

I don't turn around, but I feel every hair on the back of my neck stand on end.

"Eli escaped?" Owen asks. "He's really gone?"

Deep down, I know I should ignore him. I should keep walking as if I didn't hear a thing and leave him to suffer in uncertainty. But Owen Parker isn't long for this world, and he deserves to know the truth.

"He escaped," I croak. "Eli's gone."

Owen doesn't reply.

I take a step toward the exit, but then the door flies open and Watson strides back through. He's holding a bottle of clear liquid in one hand and an eye dropper in the other.

I stop and turn reluctantly as Watson approaches Owen.

"Weren't you headed out?" he asks in an irritated tone.

"D-Devon told me to wait," I stutter, too horrified to move.

It doesn't make any sense for me to leave, since Devon gave me orders, but Watson is too absorbed in his work to care.

"I know your type," he says to Owen as he unscrews the bottle. "I've spoken with your brother, you know."

Owen doesn't say a word.

"It took a long time, but Eli and I came to an understanding . . ."

Owen lets out a bark of disgust.

"See . . . what I've learned is that no matter how determined . . ." He pulls out an eyedropper full of liquid. "No matter how noble one may be . . ." He holds it up to the light so he can examine the contents of the glass tube. "Pain — always — prevails."

Watson flicks his wrist, and the room is filled with the sickening hiss of burning flesh. Owen lets out a scream of anguish, and I grind my teeth together in disgust.

I feel the burn of vomit in the back of my throat as Owen arches up on the table. I can see the acid burning his flesh — see the skin bubbling up and withering before my eyes.

Watson watches the spectacle with a look of cool indifference, and I feel the puke hit the back of my throat.

My vision narrows to a point as I stagger toward the exit. I pound in my code and fumble through the server room, pressing my lips together to hold in the vomit.

I barely reach the dark Information tunnel before the contents of my stomach splash out onto the fake granite tile. I choke and wretch until there's nothing left in my stomach and my throat is sore and scratchy.

I stand there for several minutes, staring down at the pool of orangish liquid as my stomach squeezes and flutters.

I'd give anything to think about something else, but my brain keeps replaying Owen's torture session and the sounds he made as the acid burned his skin. The hiss, the gurgle, the strangled yell of pain — as long as I live, I'll never forget those sounds.

four

Eli

The crack of gunfire lingers in the air as I stagger into a standing position. I whip around frantically, searching for the source of the noise, but it's impossible to tell where the shot might have come from.

Harper is standing about ten feet in front of me, breathing so loud I worry she'll give us away. Gunner pulls himself to his feet, and I grab his shirt to make sure he doesn't try to escape again.

When I stumble over to Harper and get a good look at her face, I know she's thinking the same thing I am: That bullet could have been meant for Jackson or Sage.

We listen carefully for several seconds, waiting for the patter of footfalls or the sound of breathing nearby. But now the streets are quiet and empty, and there's no way to tell if the bullet hit its intended target.

For all we know, the Recon people may have fired off the shot and fled. Or they could be lurking a little farther down the alley, waiting for us to walk by.

Either way, we can't stay here.

"Come on," I murmur, putting a gentle hand on Harper's back.

She starts walking, but she doesn't say a word as we move down the dark alleyway. I coax Gunner forward with the muzzle of my gun, and we slowly make our way around the block and down the road toward the junkyard.

When the saggy fence and mountains of scrap metal come into view, every muscle in my body tightens like a tripwire. I'm ready to fight at the first sign of trouble, and my finger is practically humming on the trigger.

Halfway across the yard, something hard and sharp locks around my ankle. Metal teeth poke into my flesh, and I bite down hard to hold in my yell.

Panic flashes through me, and my whole body flinches. But when Harper shines her interface down on my leg, I see that I just caught my foot in an old coil spring trap. Heart racing, I pry it free, and we continue through the maze of tires, engine parts, and broken beer bottles.

Owen's old teal truck is parked right where we left it, but there's no sign of Sage or Jackson anywhere.

Harper and I exchange a concerned look but make a silent agreement to put our worry on pause. Harper turns her weapon on Gunner to make sure he doesn't try to escape, and I focus on clearing the immediate area around the truck.

There aren't any drifters or Recon people waiting to ambush us, but by the time I return to Harper and Gunner, I can no longer ignore the mounting sense of dread in my gut.

"Let's just give them a minute," I say. "They might have led the shooters away so we could get back to the house."

"Maybe," says Harper. But she sounds even less convinced than I feel.

She lets out a heavy sigh and wipes her brow with the back of her hand. I know she's imagining the worst. She probably feels responsible since we dragged Sage and Jackson along on our mission.

There's no use reminding her that those two have probably weathered more attacks in the past month than we have in our entire lives. She knows as well as I do that experience can only take you so far out here. Simply being in the wrong place at the wrong time can have lethal consequences on the Fringe.

"Let's go," I say after several minutes. "They're probably waiting for us back at Owen's."

Harper doesn't look hopeful, but she gives me a strong nod and walks around to the passenger-side door. I wait for Gunner to climb into the middle seat, but he's looking at the truck as if we're about to haul him to his death.

"What's your plan?" he asks in a panicked voice.

"Shut up and get in," I snap.

Gunner obeys, but I'm beginning to think that bringing him along was a bad idea. Harper seems convinced that Gunner knows something about a cure, but taking a hostage adds a whole other layer of risk to an already dangerous situation.

The drive back to Owen's place seems to take forever. In my nervous state, every shadow is a drifter lurking behind a building, and every breeze is the rustle of an approaching enemy. But my eyes are just playing tricks on me, and soon the row of run-down houses comes into view.

I want to call out for Sage or Jackson, but I don't make a sound in case they were followed. I let the truck coast through Owen's patchy yard and kill the engine when we reach the back. Harper jumps out first and starts combing the yard for signs of trouble while I hold my rifle on Gunner.

"Clear," she chokes, lowering her gun and heading for the door.

But before she reaches the house, I hear the low murmur of voices echoing down the street.

"Harper!" I hiss.

She freezes. I turn my head toward the road, but it's impossible to tell if the voices belong to Sage or Jackson or someone else. I can't see anything in the dark.

After a few seconds, the speakers draw nearer, so Harper turns and jogs back to hide behind the fence running along Owen's yard. I follow more slowly with Gunner in tow, forcing him down onto the ground behind some banged-up garbage cans.

By now the voices are clear enough to distinguish. Both of them belong to men, but neither sounds like Jackson. The intruders have reached the far corner of Owen's yard and are headed right for us.

Luckily, a few clouds are rolling in, blocking bright slivers of moonlight that would be shining down on Owen's street. As long as they don't look too closely at Owen's neighbor's yard, they won't be able to spot us.

Squinting through the fence posts, I see the two men approaching Owen's front door. The taller one is pale and scrawny with lots of tattoos and a sandy-blond beard. He's carrying a flashlight and wearing faded camo shorts and a cutoff gray T-shirt. The other man is a short Latino dressed in an oversized black hoodie and baggy cargo pants.

They have to be Malcolm's men, which means they must be looking for Owen.

"Wait here," I whisper.

"No!" she hisses. "You can't go over there!"

"They're looking for Owen," I murmur. "If he doesn't answer the door, they're gonna know something's up."

Gunner looks confused. Harper shakes her head once, communicating a silent no with those steely gray eyes. She holds my gaze for four long seconds, but once she sees that the men have no intention of leaving, she lets out a resigned sigh.

She still thinks pretending to be Owen is a stupid idea, but she turns her rifle on Gunner and shoots him her most intimidating look.

"You make a sound, and you're dead," I growl.

Gunner nods, and I take off toward the street at a crouch. Malcolm's men are fixated on Owen's front door, so they don't see me dart out into the street and slow my pace to a brisk walk. I let out a low whistle to get their attention, and they both wheel around with their guns in the air.

"Hey!" shouts the Latino.

"Who's there?" yells the guy with the beard.

"It's me," I call, hoping they'll recognize my voice as Owen's.

"Parker?"

"Yeah. What? Were you gonna blow me away?"

"Where the fuck have you been, man? Compound rats busted the base. Craig and Trent are dead. Gunner was suppos' to be fillin' in for Trent, but no one's seen that little pussy for hours."

I take another few steps forward, trying to keep enough distance between us that they can't get a good look at my face. I know Owen and I are practically identical, but I always worry that someone who knows him well will be able to tell the difference.

"Gunner's missing?" I ask.

"Yeah," says the bearded guy. "We gotta move. Malcolm wants everybody at the bar in ten."

"Shit."

"You comin'?"

"Yeah. Just give me a sec."

The bearded guy moves his flashlight, and I see that he's about my age. The Latino looks several years younger — maybe eighteen or nineteen — but he's probably been roughing it out on the Fringe for most of his life.

"What the hell's goin' on?" he asks in a harsh voice.

"Nothing."

The two men exchange a suspicious glance, and the bearded guy raises the flashlight to get a closer look at me.

"Hey . . . I know what's going on here," he says slowly.

I freeze, trying to figure out how to shoot them both before they shoot me.

"You gotta check in with your woman," he says with a grin.

I practically collapse in relief but let out an embarrassed scoff. "*No.*"

"Yeah, that's it," he says, breaking into a hazy smile.

"She in there?" The Latino guy asks, gesturing over his shoulder. "Sorry, man. We probably scared her."

"Yeah. She's been really worried lately . . . what with all those fucking rats sniffing around."

The Latino gives me a terse nod. "Aight. Just don't take too long. You know how Malcolm is."

"Yeah."

I slap hands with both men as they pass. The tall bearded one is still grinning in a way that says he thinks I'm whipped, and once they're a few paces away, I hear them joking about Sage having me wrapped around her finger. I have this nagging feeling that Owen would command more respect from those guys, but I'm just relieved that they bought my act.

I wait for the men to disappear into the shadows and then cut across the yard to Harper. She's got her back against the fence and looks as though she's holding her breath.

"It's okay," I hiss. "They're gone."

She lets out a sigh of relief. Then her gaze flickers over my shoulder, and I see a flash of panic in her eyes.

"Get down!" she cries, jumping to her feet and pointing her gun behind me.

I duck down and aim my rifle in that direction, but it's too dark to see anything. Blood pounds in my ears as I scan the shadows for the threat, and for a split second, I wonder if Harper imagined the intruder.

"Don't move!" she growls suddenly.

"Hey, hey! It's us!" calls a familiar voice.

I squint harder. This time, Jackson's stocky frame materializes out of the darkness, and Sage's silhouette appears right behind him.

"Oh, thank god," whispers Harper.

"What happened to you guys?" I ask, waiting for my heart rate to return to normal.

"We had compound people hot on our asses," says Sage, lowering her weapon and pulling a few strands of damp hair off her face.

Both of them are sweaty and out of breath, and I realize that it really must have been a close call back at the pawn shop.

"Why are you hiding out here?" Jackson asks, glancing over the top of the fence.

"Malcolm's men paid Owen a visit," I say. "The Desperados know the base has been compromised. They're meeting in ten."

"Wait, what?" asks Gunner.

Everyone ignores him. It's only a matter of time before he figures out who I am, but it seems wise to keep him in the dark as long as we can.

"You have to go to that meeting," says Harper.

That catches me off guard, and judging from the look on Jackson's face, he's confused, too.

"*What?*"

"Getting close to Malcolm is the only chance we have of finding the cure," she says.

I open my mouth to argue, but she cuts me off.

"Sawyer only has a few days. This might be our only chance to get close to Malcolm."

I shake my head and try to come up with a tactful way to shoot down her plan. As much as I want to help Harper find the cure, my top priority is getting back to the compound to rescue Owen, and the only thing I need to do that is more fire power. Now that the pawn shop has been compromised, we're going to have to find another way to get our hands on those weapons.

"No . . . Look," I say, squeezing my eyes shut and pinching the skin between my eyebrows. "I know this is important to you, but honestly . . ."

"It's a long shot," Jackson finishes. "If there is a cure, Malcolm's gonna be pretty secretive about it. He's not just gonna go spewing all his secrets at a meeting like this."

"I know it's a long shot," says Harper. "But we should still go. We need to know what the Desperados are planning. We know they're going to attack the compound, but we don't know *when*. Maybe we can find a way to warn Lenny and Miles so Recon can be ready."

I let out a long sigh and glance at Jackson. He thinks this is a bad idea, too.

"Don't you think it's gonna look suspicious if Owen blows off the meeting?" Harper splutters.

She does have a point. Owen was already treading on thin ice with Malcolm, and I'm not laboring under any delusions when it comes to my brother. If we do manage to save him, he's not going to want anything to do with me. He's gonna run straight back to the Desperados, which could be a death sentence if Malcolm thinks he's a traitor.

I start to nod, but Jackson's still not convinced.

"What are you gonna do when Malcolm realizes you're not Owen?" he asks.

"Eli's passed as Owen before," says Sage. "It should work."

It's the first time Sage has weighed in on the debate, and I'm a little surprised that she's in favor of a plan that could delay Owen's rescue.

Jackson lets out a groan of resignation. "Fine."

"One question," says Sage, shifting her gaze to Gunner. "What are we supposed to do with *him*?"

I turn to Harper, and we have another one of our silent conversations. I know she wanted to drag Gunner along in the hope that we could extract some information from him, but it's clear to me that he doesn't know anything about a cure. Right now, he's just slowing us down.

"I think we *know* what we have to do," says Jackson pointedly.

"Don' kill me!" Gunner begs, looking frantically from me to Harper.

Harper catches my eye, and I can tell her natural compassion is duking it out with the cold reality of the situation. She knows that Gunner is a liability, but killing him would destroy her.

"Please," says Gunner. "I'll tell you anything you want to know. Just please, *please* don't kill me."

"Where's the cure?" asks Harper.

"*I don' know*," he says with a look of genuine desperation. "Honestly . . . I don' know anything about that. I swear!"

Harper and I exchange a dubious glance.

"But if there *is* a cure," he chokes, "I know a place it might be."

Harper straightens up.

"There's another base," he says in a nervous voice. "In Arizona . . ."

"*Where* in Arizona?"

"I'll show you!" he says. "Hell, I'll take you there myself. Just please don' shoot me."

"How do we know you're telling the truth?" I ask, turning to face Gunner head-on. Normally I can spot a liar pretty easily, but Gunner is so terrified that it's masking any obvious tells.

"I'll take you straight there," he says. "If I'm lyin', you can kill me then."

"*Fuuuck*," Jackson moans. "Just kill him now! He's lying to us, and we're wasting time."

"Yeah we are," I say. Malcolm's meeting will be starting any minute.

I give Gunner one last hard look before making up my mind.

"We'll hold off on killing you until we see if this intel of yours pans out," I say finally.

He lifts his eyebrows in a hopeful expression.

"But right now, you're with me. You're gonna take me to this meeting, and then you're gonna tell us how to get to that base."

"I can't go to that meeting!" cries Gunner. "Malcolm will have heard I wasn't at the pawn shop. He'll think I'm a traitor!"

"No, he won't," I say. "You're going to tell him exactly what happened — leaving out the part about us breaking in. You got to the base and saw Craig and Trent dead, so you went inside to investigate. You saw the lights from the compound people, so you ran out the back and came looking for me."

"What if he don' believe me?"

"He will," I say. "And if you go rogue and mess up the plan, I'll kill you myself."

Gunner is still breathing hard, but he seems to realize that there's no way out. After a moment, he gives me a shaky nod, and I signal Harper to lower her gun.

For this to work, we're going to have to trust each other. We're about to walk into the lion's den, and I need Gunner to sell his story. If he doesn't, Malcolm will see right through it, and we'll both be as good as dead.

five

Eli

As confident as I sounded laying out a cover story for Gunner, I begin to feel real panic as we make our way to the drifter bar.

My palms are sweaty on Owen's steering wheel, my throat feels scratchy, and my heart is beating so loudly that I'm sure Gunner can hear. I've got Jackson's handgun sitting in my lap, but I feel naked without my rifle.

"You're not Owen, are you?" asks Gunner. It's more of a statement than a question.

I shake my head.

"You're from the compounds."

I nod. "Owen's my brother. We got separated when we were kids."

"*Seriously?*"

"Yeah."

"Damn," says Gunner. "You two could be twins."

"That's what I've heard."

There's a long pause, and I sense him chewing on his next question. "Where . . . Where is he now?"

I let out a slow breath. "He got shot outside compound 112. Harper and I think he's alive, but they've still got him."

Gunner's eyes grow wide. "And you're trying to rescue him?"

I let out a huff of irritation. I don't know why I'm telling Gunner the truth, but I can't seem to shut up. "I have to," I say.

"He's my brother. And it's my fault he was there to begin with."

Gunner's eyebrows scrunch together in confusion, so I add, "He came to warn me that Malcolm was going to attack the compound. He wanted me to join the Desperados."

Gunner quirks an eyebrow. "Would you have?"

I shoot him a cold glare, which kills any more follow-up questions. It's not that I'm sick of talking about it. I'm just ashamed.

Gunner stays silent for the rest of the drive, and the lights from the bar appear about a mile down the road. If one didn't know about the compounds, one might think McNally's was the last shred of civilization left on earth. It's the only building illuminated for miles around, and it stands out like a glowing beacon on the horizon.

Up close, the place is much less impressive. The tavern's brown clapboard siding is chipped and warped, and the dingy beer posters in the front windows are so sun faded they're almost unreadable. Several beat-up trucks and SUVs are parked haphazardly around the parking lot, and I can hear the low rumble of voices as we crunch through the gravel toward the battered aluminum door.

As soon as we step inside, the stench of cigarettes, pot, and body odor nearly knocks me over. It's unnaturally hot with fifty or so drifters packed inside the tiny bar, and I can tell by the excited timber of their voices that Malcolm must be planning something big.

I catch several slaps on the back as we push our way toward the bar. There's a tight knot of people crowded near the end, and they're the rowdiest of them all.

I can't see Malcolm, but I'd bet money he's seated in the middle of that group, soaking up the attention and whipping up the crowd as much as possible.

I hate Malcolm with a passion, but even I have to admit the guy has charisma.

I haven't even reached the bar when the sound of a knife on glass rings out over the room. The crowd quiets down, and the roughneck guys all turn to look at the man calling the meeting to order.

Malcolm Martinez has dark hair, mocha skin, and a ratlike face that seems to be frozen in a constant sneer. He's standing on the lower rungs of a rickety barstool, holding a glass of whisky and a cigarette in hand.

His eyes hover over me for half a second as he scans the crowd, and then his harsh gaze lands on Gunner. Suspicion flickers across his face, but he doesn't say anything.

"Hey!" he calls, silencing the last few people talking by the door. "Let's get started."

The big guys next to me shuffle uncomfortably, clearly uneasy about the break-in at the pawn shop.

"As you all know . . . we have succeeded in weakening compound 112. We've infected their people, and we attacked their soldiers stationed near the border."

The men break into rowdy applause, and I clench my fists to keep my rage under control. They're celebrating the deaths of fifteen innocent people and the infection of dozens more. I want to knock that smirk right off Malcolm's smug face, but kicking his teeth in would *definitely* blow my cover.

Malcolm continues. "Now, naturally, we expected some sort of retaliation, didn't we?"

He pauses, and there's a low grumble of agreement.

"Let's not forget . . . we've grown our ranks tenfold in the past year and built up our artillery in preparation for this attack." He pauses for a beat to let that sink in. "Unfortunately, the compound rats we've risked life and limb to exterminate have managed to sniff out our center of operations in the area."

My ears perk up at those last few words, and I glance over at Gunner. Maybe he *is* telling the truth about there being a base in Arizona — one that's large and secure enough for Malcolm to store weapons, supplies, and a cure.

The crowd falls silent, and a few men nearby exchange uneasy looks.

"Does anyone have any idea how our base was compromised?" asks Malcolm. His eyes linger on me for a little longer than everybody else, but I meet his gaze unflinchingly.

This asshole can't intimidate me. I've been dealing with gangsters like him since I was a kid.

"I have an idea," he says.

Nobody moves or speaks.

"Does anyone want to know what I think?"

The men begin to shift nervously from side to side. Everyone knows what he's about to say, and everyone is dreading it.

"I think," he says, drawing out the words to build suspense, "that we have a rat hidden in our ranks."

A wave of anxious chatter rumbles over the room. A few men near Malcolm look around and mumble variations of "not me" that sound more cowardly than convincing.

"Who is it?" pipes the tall bearded guy I spoke to earlier.

"I have an idea," says Malcolm, shifting his gaze in our direction.

The mumbling in the crowd grows louder, and my hand slowly inches toward my belt. When Malcolm calls me out, I'm gonna have about two seconds to draw Jackson's handgun and shoot my way out of here.

"Young Gun . . ." snarls Malcolm.

At first I'm not sure I heard him correctly, but when I glance over at Gunner, I see a look of horror spreading across his face.

The crowd around us splits in two, leaving me and Gunner standing alone in the middle of the room. Young Gun must be a nickname, I realize, and Malcolm just accused Gunner of flipping.

"I didn't," Gunner chokes, his eyes darting to me. "I swear."

A ghost of a smirk flashes across Malcolm's face, and he licks his lips as though he's getting ready to dig into a Porterhouse steak.

I clench my teeth together to keep my fury from spilling out. Malcolm has no idea whether Gunner turned or not, but he's throwing him under the bus anyway.

"I heard something interesting from the boys who went by the base earlier," says Malcolm, rubbing his pointed chin as if he has all the time in the world. "When they showed up, a couple of compound rats were tearing the place apart . . ." His eyes dart around the room. "Rafee and Coop found Craig and Trent . . . dead."

Gunner swallows.

"You were *supposed* to be there," Malcolm growls. "I sent you to take over for Trent *hours* ago."

The crowd is good and whipped up now. I'm waiting for Gunner to jump in with the story we prepared, but I'm worried he might not get two words out before these guys start tearing him limb from limb.

"I'm curious . . ." says Malcolm. "How is it that Trent and Craig both wound up dead while you skated out of there without so much as a scratch?"

Gunner opens his mouth to speak, but he just flounders silently in a puddle of his own sweat. He looks as though he's going to be sick. He certainly doesn't look *innocent.*

In that moment, I seriously consider letting him fry. He doesn't have the balls to stand up to Malcolm — even if doing so is the only way to save his own skin. Gunner taking the blame would draw suspicion away from me/Owen. And for all I know, he could have been lying about the Arizona base all along.

But when I look at Gunner, I don't see another hardened, ruthless Desperado. I just see a scared, stupid kid who bummed his way from Georgia or the Carolinas or wherever, only to get caught up in some shit he couldn't handle.

I can't let him take the fall for this — even if it throws the spotlight on me.

"It wasn't him," I say quietly, stepping up so he and I are standing side by side.

Malcolm's gaze narrows. He wasn't expecting this, and by the look on his face, he doesn't like having his theories questioned.

"He was there when the compound people broke into the base."

Gunner nods quickly, still too pale and terrified to look convincing.

"Tell 'em," I say.

Gunner opens and closes his mouth twice before actual words come out. A couple of men near the back snicker, which causes a deep flush to bleed through Gunner's pasty complexion.

"I went to the base to take over for Trent like you said," mumbles Gunner, addressing Malcolm directly. "But when I got there . . . they were both dead."

Gunner stops and swallows again, and I know he's working up the courage to sell the big lie. "I went inside to see if the bastards had broken into the base. Next thing I know, I was surrounded by rats."

Gunner's story seems to be calming the crowd, but Malcolm's eyes have narrowed into slits. He doesn't believe him, and he knows I'm covering for the kid.

"I went out the back," Gunner continues, picking up speed

as he gains confidence in the story. "They didn't see me. I ran straight to Owen's house to warn him, but . . ."

"I wasn't home," I say. "When I found out, I came straight here."

There's a brutally long pause as Malcolm turns our story over in his head. Judging by the look on his face, he's not deciding whether or not he believes it — he's deciding whether it would be in his best interest to get behind it or call us both liars.

"That's how it happened?" he asks finally, cocking one thick black eyebrow.

"Yeah," says Gunner in a hoarse voice.

Malcolm drags in a deep breath and nods slowly. "Well . . . if anyone has any more information, you come straight to me." He cocks his head in my direction. "I want to handle this personally."

"What about the compound people?" asks a chubby bald guy near the front.

Malcolm nods. "They're weak right now. It doesn't matter that they're still on the offensive. They took a big hit during our last attack." He looks around the bar at the crowd of bloodthirsty men. "They've been picking us off one by one for years. I say it's time for them to feel what we've felt."

There's an enthusiastic rumble of agreement.

"We attack while they're *weak*."

A few men near the front nod.

"We have the manpower . . . We have the fire power . . . We have — every — advantage."

The crowd is growing restless now, and I feel as though the entire place might combust with violent energy.

"*Who's with me*?"

The men burst into enthusiastic cheers and whistles, and I

feel the bile rise up in my throat.

This is their life, I realize. The Desperados aren't just trying to survive. They live and die by how much damage they can inflict.

"All right, all right," yells Malcolm, trying to calm the crowd with a gratified sneer. "We'll meet back here tomorrow morning at eight. Bring whatever weapons and ammo you have. If you've got a vehicle that runs, drive it here. I've called in some reinforcements from the south, but I'm going to need every one of you with me. We attack strong with *everything* we've got!"

The crowd erupts into a renewed storm of cheers. The men are slapping each other on the back, and the group seems to condense as everyone flocks toward the door.

As the bodies press closer together, our escape route narrows, and I start to get a slight itch of panic in the back of my throat.

While the Desperados are still celebrating, I grab Gunner by the collar and yank him toward the door. The men are too worked up to notice our exit, and we make it out to Owen's truck without getting stabbed or shot.

"Where are we —"

"Get in," I murmur, jumping into the driver's seat and turning the pocketknife Owen keeps jammed in the ignition. The truck roars to life, and I back out of the parking lot in a spit of gravel.

We fly down the center of the road back toward Owen's house, my heart pounding in my throat the whole way there.

Gunner mumbles something I don't quite hear, but I don't bother asking him to repeat it. All I can think about is Miles and Owen and all the other innocent people trapped back at the compound.

The Desperados are coming, and they have no idea what

they're up against.

I drive the truck up over the curb and throw it into park right in the middle of Owen's yard. I head straight for the house without closing the door, and Gunner stumbles out after me.

Harper meets me halfway and throws her arms around my neck. Sage and Jackson appear behind her and start bombarding me with questions, but none of them manage to reach my brain. I have one important message to deliver, and that's the only thing on my mind.

"It's happening," I choke, struggling to fill my lungs with air. "Malcolm is attacking the compound."

six

Eli

Harper stares at me for so long that I start to wonder if I actually said it out loud. Several seconds pass before she manages to choke out a response.

"Wh-when?"

"First thing tomorrow morning."

Sage shakes her head. "What?"

"Malcolm's calling everyone in. He's going to attack the compound, and he's bringing a fucking *army* this time."

Harper looks as though she might be sick. "Eli, the compound isn't prepared for something like this."

"I know," I say, dragging a shaky hand through my hair. "We still haven't recovered from the first attack . . . and that was just a few drifters with automatic weapons."

While the compounds themselves were built to withstand bullets and bombs, the people on the ground were not. The devastation will be unimaginable, but that's not our only problem.

The looming attack also fucks up our rescue plan. I'd counted on having the cover of nightfall, and with so many people out hunting for me and Harper, the guard would be lighter around the perimeter.

But as soon as those bullets start flying, Recon will call in all available operatives and rush to secure the area. Covering that much ground in broad daylight with an army on either side makes a smooth escape next to impossible.

"Eli . . . we can't do this," Harper whispers. "Not with the Desperados declaring war on the compound."

"We don't have a choice."

Sage and Jackson exchange a troubled glance, but I take a step closer to Harper to keep her eyes on me.

"What do you think they're going to do to Owen once the drifters attack?" I ask.

Harper shakes her head.

"He's a hostage."

"I know, but —"

"He's the *only* leverage the compound has over the Desperados."

"Which means they aren't just going to *kill* him," says Harper, trying to be reasonable. "They're going to keep him alive to use as a bargaining chip."

"Bullshit," I whisper.

"They won't want to risk pissing off the Desperados."

"We have *no idea* what they're going to do!" I snap. "But I can tell you what they did to *me* when I was held by Constance!"

Harper grimaces, and I get an automatic twinge of guilt. I know it isn't fair to bring up my imprisonment, but I'm starting to panic. Harper's having second thoughts about our rescue plan, and I can't abandon Owen.

"I won't leave him," I growl.

"I'm not saying we should leave him," says Harper. "I wouldn't do that, Eli. But we need to be realistic."

"I am being realistic!" I yell.

"You were the one who said it was too dangerous with Recon looking for us."

"That was before Malcolm decided to attack."

"You're talking about blazing into a war zone where both sides want to kill us!" cries Harper.

"Do you have a better idea?"

"We should wait. We should —"

"We can't!" I yell. "There's no time."

"Then what's the plan?" she asks. "How are we going to get past the Desperados *and* Recon? If somebody sees us —"

"I know it's risky . . ."

"Risky?" Jackson breaks in. "It's fucking *insane*."

"It's a suicide mission," whispers Sage.

"Like I haven't heard *that* before," I mutter, suddenly furious at Sage for being so quick to give up on Owen. "I thought you and my brother had a thing," I snarl. "Or were you only fucking him so long as it was convenient for you?"

"Eli!" Harper yells, her eyes flashing with rage.

"You need to calm the fuck down," says Jackson, taking a step forward and giving my shoulder a hard push.

"Don't touch me," I growl, throwing Jackson a sharp glare.

He doesn't shove me again, but he doesn't back down. "You can't talk to her like that."

"It's okay, Jackson," says Sage in a weary voice.

"No, it's not."

"He's just looking out for Owen," she mumbles.

"Yeah," I snap. "And it seems like I'm the only one."

"I'm sorry, Eli," says Sage. "But Harper's right. The timing is terrible. And we aren't any good to Owen if we're *dead*."

"I agree," says Jackson.

I toss him a murderous look, and he shuts the hell up.

"Besides," says Sage. "Ever since we left the pawn shop, I keep thinking —"

"*What*?"

She takes another fortifying breath. At first I think she's trying not to cry, but she uses the breath to draw herself up and meet my gaze dead-on. "I keep thinking about how disgusted I am that Owen helped Malcolm kill all those people."

Judging from her guilt-laden voice, she feels terrible even admitting she's angry with Owen, but she isn't going to change her mind.

"I love Owen," she adds quickly. "But I can't just do nothing while thousands of people die." She swallows. "I don't know how big a part he played in all this, but it makes me sick to think we were even involved."

"You *weren't*," I snarl in exasperation. "Owen might have been, but you said you didn't even know what Malcolm was planning!"

"But I should have," she says. "I knew Owen and Malcolm were up to something terrible, but I didn't ask because I didn't want to know."

I stare at her for several seconds, torn between anger and admiration. On the one hand, I think it's fucked up that she'd turn her back on Owen now when he's in trouble. On the other, at least *someone's* taking some goddamn responsibility for the Desperados' shit.

"What about you?" I ask Jackson.

"Sorry, man. I can't." He shoves his hands into his pockets and looks down at the ground. "I made Owen a promise."

"Was that before or after you left him high and dry the first time?" I ask.

Jackson blanches, and for a moment, I think he might deck me.

"Before," he admits, clenching his jaw. "He made me swear that if anything ever happened to him, I'd take care of Sage."

Sage jerks her head up to look at him, and I can tell that this promise is news to her.

I shake my head and circle back to Harper, already dreading what she's going to say.

When I meet her gaze, I know I'm fighting a losing battle. Her eyes are soft and full of compassion, but she's already made up her mind.

I suddenly wish we didn't have an audience for this discussion. Harper's refusal is going to kill me, and I don't know what I'm going to say.

"Did you ever plan on coming with me to rescue Owen?" I ask quietly.

Harper looks as though I reached out and slapped her, and I feel like a piece of shit.

"How can you even ask me that?" she whispers. "I wanted to go back the *second* Bear fired that shot. *You* were the one who made us run."

To keep you safe, I think to myself. *Because it would kill me to lose you.*

In that moment, all the pent-up anger inside me spills out and disappears.

Harper is right. Charging up to the compound to rescue Owen in the middle of the Desperados' attack is way too dangerous. I can't postpone Owen's rescue, but I can't take her with me. I wouldn't be able to live with myself if she died.

I nod furiously to relieve the crushing weight of disappointment that just slammed down on my chest. I know I must look deranged, but I'm so — fucking — tired.

Every turn we take, we hit a dead end. Every time I try to do the right thing, something goes horribly, horribly wrong.

"I have to try to save him," I murmur. "No matter what he's done . . ." I sigh. "Owen's my brother. If there's any chance he's still alive . . . I have to try."

"I know," says Harper, her eyes filling with tears. They collect in little pools on the lower rims of her eyelashes and ripple as she shakes.

I hate seeing Harper cry. It feels like a punch to the liver every time.

"I know you have to try to save Owen," she says, taking deep breaths to maintain her composure. "But I have to try to save *Sawyer*."

That knocks the wind out of me, but suddenly her refusal makes sense. Harper is no coward. She's never backed down from a dangerous mission in her life, and she wouldn't abandon our rescue plan unless she had a very good reason.

"Sawyer's running out of time," she adds. "So is everybody else."

She glances over at Gunner, who's been completely silent throughout this conversation. "He knows where the Desperados' base is. If there's even a *chance* Malcolm's hidden the cure there —"

"We don't know if he's telling the truth," I say. "And even if he is, you don't know if there *is* a cure."

"You're right," says Harper, giving her shoulders a heavy shrug. "But we both know that if we try to break into the compound now, we aren't all going to make it out alive."

I don't know what to say to that. I never expected this to happen. Harper has been by my side nonstop for the past six months, but it wasn't until this moment that I realized just how much I've come to depend on her.

After our time together on the Fringe, I just assumed that if I was running through a storm of gunfire, Harper would be right beside me. I never prepared myself for the possibility that we might have to go our separate ways.

Finally, I clear my throat and look over at Gunner. "What about you?"

"I'm in," he says. His voice betrays no hint of hesitation, but I'm not sure that I heard him right.

"What?"

"I'll go with you to rescue Owen," he says. "I ain't scared."

I blink several times, still shocked that the one person I'd written off as nothing but dead weight is the only one willing to come with me.

"I'll tell you guys everything I know about the base," he says. "Then tomorrow I'll head out with you."

I don't know if Gunner's willingness to go along on my rescue mission is a sign of loyalty to Owen or just general stupidity, but at this point I'm in no position to refuse the help. Harper looks just as shocked and devastated as I feel, but I nod stiffly and turn my attention to Gunner.

"Let's hear it, then," I say. "Owen's got a map in the den."

Gunner looks simultaneously satisfied and panicked, but he nods once and turns to lead us back to the house. Sage and Jackson turn and follow right behind him, anxious to exit this uncomfortable conversation.

I can see Harper staring at me out of the corner of her eye, but I can't talk to her right now. I can't even look at her.

I *hate* this plan. I hate the idea of her going to Arizona without me, but I know there's no use trying to stop her.

I follow Gunner and the others inside, and we all crowd into Owen's living room. Whoever owned this house before him must have been either old or blind, because the decor is hideously outdated. The room is decked out in wall-to-wall shag carpet and dark wood paneling. The couches are a hideous yellow-and-brown paisley, and creepy cat figurines are tucked into every nook and cranny.

I take a seat on the couch where Harper and I once spooned, but she crowds onto the beat-up paisley loveseat with Sage. Jackson perches on the edge of one of the high-backed armchairs, and Gunner kneels down beside the coffee table with Owen's old road atlas.

Holding the marker cap between his front teeth, Gunner traces a route to the base in red, making notes off to the side about potential threats and the nearest Recon checkpoint.

"I've only been there once," he says, capping the marker and examining his work. "But I remember where it is."

"How far of a drive is it?" asks Harper.

"About six hours . . . if you don' run into any problems."

"Six hours?" I repeat incredulously.

"It's a casino out in the middle of the desert — very isolated . . . very secure."

"How secure?" asks Jackson.

"We're talkin' twenty-four-hour surveillance. Armed security, cameras . . ."

"Cameras?"

"They are *set up* out there," he says, a note of awe in his voice. "The entire place runs on wind and solar, so they never lose power. It's Malcolm's fortress in the Southwest, so it's always occupied."

"So you're saying it's a death trap."

Gunner raises his eyebrows. "A base that heavily guarded . . ." He nods. "Yeah, it'll be tough to get in — but not impossible."

"How do we do it?" asks Harper, purposely avoiding my gaze.

Gunner sighs. "They have lookouts posted a half a mile in every direction. They're looking for blacked-out license plates. That's their signal to hold fire."

"Then what?"

Gunner produces another piece of paper and begins to sketch a rough outline of the building. "Your best bet is to act like you're there to make a supply drop. Supplies go in and out of there all the time, so it would be easy for a shipment to slip through the cracks. Even if they're not expectin' you, they'll have a hard time refusin' the supplies."

"How do we do that?" asks Sage.

"You need to go around on this side." Gunner draws an arrow and makes an X on the diagram. "There's a loadin' bay here."

"So we just drive up with some supplies and we're in?" asks Jackson in disbelief.

Gunner shrugs. "I don' know if that will be enough to get you inside, but it will at least buy a few minutes while they do inventory. Most of Malcolm's men will be here, so the base should be fairly quiet — essential personnel only."

"And where would Malcolm keep a cure?" Harper asks.

"I have no idea. All I know is that the place is *wired.* There are cameras everywhere." Gunner pauses and looks from Harper to Sage to Jackson. "If you're goin' in, you better *blend.*"

"We can do that," says Harper. But she's staring down at the diagram with an overwhelmed expression on her face.

I can tell this is going to be a lot harder than she originally anticipated, and the entire situation smells like ten miles of bad road to me. I still don't trust Gunner completely, but there's no way I'll be able to convince Harper to scrap this mission — not when she sees it as her only lead on a cure.

"All right," says Jackson, picking up the atlas and folding Gunner's diagram inside. "I know where we can get some stuff for a supply drop. It's just down the road."

"I'll come with you," says Sage quickly.

I can tell both of them are anxious to get away from me and Harper, so I don't offer to help. Gunner follows them out to get some sleep before the mission, and Harper and I are left alone.

"We should get some sleep," I mutter, staring down at my hands as if I've never seen them before.

"Eli . . ."

"Big day tomorrow."

"Will you *look* at me?" she yells.

I meet her gaze against my better judgment and instantly wish I hadn't. Harper's eyes are wide with fear, and I realize she hates this plan as much as I do.

"I'm not abandoning you," she says in a firm voice. "You have to realize that."

I nod, even though that's *exactly* what it feels like.

"I just can't go along with this," she continues. "Not when my friends' lives are at stake."

"My *brother's* life is at stake," I remind her.

"I know," she says, looking at me with intense love in her eyes. "That's why you have to go . . ."

She doesn't finish the thought. She doesn't have to. I hear the rest of that statement plain as day: *That's why she has to go to Arizona.*

I can't argue with her. I'm terrified I might lose her, but there's not a single scenario that *doesn't* terrify me.

I could die trying to save Owen. She could die trying to break into the Desperados' base. If we go along with the plan and I lose her, I'll spend the rest of my life wondering what would have happened if I'd stayed by her side. But if I persuaded her to go and she died in the crossfire, I'd never forgive myself.

Staring at her from across the room, I realize that this could be the last night we spend together. She seems to realize it, too, because a second later, she's standing right in front of me, silently begging me to forgive her.

"Come here," I murmur, reaching out and grabbing her around the waist.

Harper lets out a sigh of relief and folds herself into my lap.

As soon as I have her in my arms, every angry thought evaporates. I pull her tight against my chest and plant a kiss on top of her head. I inhale deeply, trying to commit her scent to memory, and she sighs against my neck.

"I love you," she says.

"I love you, too," I choke, resting my chin on top of her head. "So — damn — much."

Harper sniffs loudly, and I pull back just enough to tilt her chin up and plant a soft kiss on her mouth. Her lips tremble a little as I work my tongue between them, but she grips my arms with strong, steady hands.

My fingers get tangled in her long silky hair, and I lose track of where we are as she grinds her hips into mine. I yank her hoodie off her shoulders, and she pulls her tank top and bra over her head.

I must be out of my goddamned mind.

I know I shouldn't be leaving her. I shouldn't ever let her out of my sight.

But before I can berate myself any more, Harper reaches down and tugs my shirt over my head. My mouth falls open as her shorts hit the floor, and soon my jeans are lying in a tangled ball next to them.

My breathing grows fast and uneven as she straddles me on Owen's couch, and when I feel her bare skin on mine, a jolt of electricity shoots through my entire body.

"Please be careful," I say, locking my arms around her waist.

"You, too," she whispers, brushing her lips against my cheek.

"Whatever happens," I say, "we meet back at the apartment above the post office in four days. You remember the place?"

She nods slowly, a serious look in those deep gray eyes.

"Watch yourself," I say, trying to stay focused as I run my

hands up her hips. "Don't — trust — *anyone*."

She nods and swallows, drinking me in one last time with lust-filled eyes.

"If someone threatens you, you shoot. If someone gets too close and makes you nervous, you shoot."

Harper nods.

"Protect yourself — no matter what."

"You too," she whispers. "Get Owen, and get yourself out."

I nod, trembling with anticipation and gripping her waist for dear life. Harper is still my cadet, and my brain is fighting to stay in lieutenant mode. Unfortunately, the rest of me is utterly consumed with the sight of her straddling me naked, and it's making it difficult to muster up any more practical advice.

With a whimper of impatience, Harper flings herself against me, and our lips meet in a clash of love and frustration. I throw everything I have into that kiss, and she responds with a low moan of satisfaction.

I lift her hips, and Harper thrusts herself on top of me. I let out a loud groan, and every worry — every thought — evaporates in an instant.

My hands lose themselves exploring her, and my body seems to overcome the need for air as one kiss bleeds into the next.

I don't know how long it lasts, but I never hear Jackson and Sage return. It's dark and silent outside the house, and when Harper and I collapse on the couch in a tangle of limbs, an odd sense of peace falls over me.

We're completely spent, but we have one last night together. I grab a blanket from a basket on the floor and toss it over both of us. Harper lays her head against my chest, and I lock my arms around her.

I stay awake listening to the sound of her breathing, trying to memorize every curve and freckle. I want to remember tonight forever because it might be all I have.

Tomorrow, everything is going to change. Tomorrow, I may never see her again.

seven

Celdon

I never had any use for a gun until the day I was hauled in by Constance. Before, I never understood why anyone outside of Recon would ever need one. But the week I spent being tortured by Devon Reid made me realize how easy it is to lose control over your life.

After I got out, I overrode Recon's high-level security, broke into the weapons room, and swiped a compact handgun. It's lived under my bed ever since, and I haven't touched it once — until today.

Maybe that's why it feels so heavy and unnatural in my hand. I have no business with a gun. I have no business knowing what I know. I was supposed to be just another overpaid hacker. I was supposed to feel satisfied reporting to Systems every day, doing my work, and spending my weekends getting burned in Neverland.

But I never wanted a life in Systems the way Harper did. I didn't want to be just another drudge. I keep telling myself that I only joined Constance to find out what happened to my mother, but maybe I joined because I felt trapped — trapped in the compound, trapped in my life.

I didn't want to hurt anybody. I just wanted something *more*, but instead Constance took the only things that truly mattered.

Turning the gun over in my hand, I examine the smooth black muzzle and the heavy, grippy handle. I fiddle with the safety and point the gun straight at my head.

I don't feel anything — not sadness, not fear, not even self-pity.

I lean back against the wall and rest the muzzle against my scalp. There's already a bullet in the chamber. All I have to do is pull the trigger, and all this shit will finally be over.

Living is hard, but dying is easy.

I contemplate for a moment what it would be like to end my existence. What would it be like to shut off like a light? No more thoughts, no more fears, no more consciousness.

I've never been afraid of dying. But oblivion? Oblivion is scary as hell.

I sit there so long that my hand starts to cramp. Then my bicep wobbles, and soon my entire arm is quivering. Maybe I'm just out of shape, or maybe it's my body's last-ditch attempt to save itself. The instinct to survive is strong — perfected over millions of years. Even my crushing misery is no match for evolution.

With a hard gasp, I let my arm drop to the floor, and I feel immediate relief as the blood rushes back to my hand. I stare down at the deadly weapon with a mixture of surprise and self-loathing. Then I lean back and bang my head against the wall.

What kind of person just stands by as an innocent man is tortured? What kind of person stays silent as people are murdered? What kind of person doesn't fight to keep his best friend?

A fucking coward, that's who.

I can no longer blame Constance for all my problems. I'm part of Constance now, and I can't hold myself blameless. That's the worst feeling of all.

Laying the gun on the floor, I pull my knees up to my chest and try to figure out what my next move should be. I can't leave Constance, but I can't just pretend these things aren't happening.

I might not be able to avoid oblivion, but I'm not taking the coward's way out.

Galvanized by my almost suicide, I get to my feet and stagger over to my computer. I wake up the sleeping monitor, pound in my password, and immediately click over to the security portal.

A tingle of excitement shoots up my spine, followed by a sobering dose of reality. What I'm about to do could have dire consequences — not just for me, but for the board, as well.

Since the outbreak, no one except a private security detail has been allowed up to the board members' suites. And after the murder of Sullivan Taylor, Walter Cunningham asked Systems and Control to shore up security.

The suites are nearly impenetrable — unless you're me.

Each board member's compartment is protected by a six-foot-tall beefcake guard and a steel-plated door — not to mention a passcode, a card-access lock system, a thumb print ID scanner, and a secondary passcode. Each compartment is connected to the board member's office on the level above. Those offices are protected by the same authentication settings, minus the human guard.

I take a quick inventory of all the risks and then get to work undoing all the extra security measures I helped put in place. Within a few minutes, I've overridden the electronic security and unlocked President Ferguson's bunker remotely via the office door.

Plucking the least wrinkly blazer off my bed, I leave my compartment and take the emergency stairwell to the uppermost Systems level. The main tunnel leads to Systems headquarters, but it also branches off to another wing housing the board members' offices.

Fortunately for me, the main tunnel is completely deserted.

The security cameras mounted along the walls track my every move, but as far as anyone is concerned, I'm just another penetration tester going to finish up some work.

When I turn down the tunnel leading to the offices, I flip on my interface and act as though I'm video messaging someone.

I stop in front of President Ferguson's office and key in my temporary access code. The little light on the keypad turns green, and I hear a friendly *beep* as the bolt slides back.

Ferguson's office is huge — roughly four times the size of my compartment. The front room has two luxurious white sofas, a reception desk, and a tall glass table accented with a vase of orange calla lilies. The back area branches off in two directions: Ferguson's private chamber to the left and a large conference room to the right.

As soon as I step into his private chamber, the automatic lights illuminate another couch and two cushy armchairs. Behind the sitting area is an enormous glass desk supported by a fake mahogany frame. The ceiling-to-floor exterior windows are auto-frosted for privacy, but if it were daytime, the president would have an unimpeded view of the tier-three workers huddled on the Fringe.

On my second scan of the room, I find what I'm looking for: a narrow door off to the right that leads to the president's compartment.

Taking a deep breath, I pad across the soft white rug and turn the handle. The door opens easily, and I step out onto a landing at the top of a narrow staircase. I can hear the faint murmur of voices drifting up from the president's living room, and I get a tingle of discomfort.

This was way — too — easy.

I tiptoe down the first few steps and strain my ears to hear the conversation going on down below. Both speakers are men, and I recognize one voice immediately. It belongs to the president.

I can't make out exactly what he's saying, but he and the mystery guest seem to reach a conclusion, and then the room falls silent.

The president is on his own.

Seizing the opportunity, I take the stairs two at a time and emerge into a compartment nearly identical to the one Harper and I visited at compound 119. It's got a large open floor plan, and the furniture is classic Systems decor. The common area is accented with teetering glass tables, fresh tropical flowers, and weird marble sculptures.

Ferguson is the only president in compound history who's never been married, so the expansive compartment is all his.

"*What in the hell?*" yells a familiar voice.

I freeze on the bottom step. When I look up, I'm startled to see the president staring right at me.

Lane Ferguson is a tall, paunchy man in his late fifties with waxy-looking skin, a wide forehead, and hypnotic hazel eyes. As long as I can remember, his hair has always been more gray than brown, but it still lies thick and unruly over the top of his head.

Right now, he's standing in his kitchen holding an empty coffee cup and looking as though he's seen a ghost. He's wearing a pair of silky cream pajamas under a burgundy robe, but it's his bare feet that make me pause.

"Uh —" I stammer, thrown off by the excitement and weirdness of it all.

"I'm calling security," says Ferguson, his mouth tightening into a hard line. "My man is right outside, so —"

"I wouldn't do that if I were you," I say, trying to sound ballsier than I feel.

Ferguson freezes. He doesn't look panicked at having an

intruder in his home. He's staring at me as if I'm a pest rather than a threat.

"Since you're not Information, I'm left to assume you're not a paparazzo . . . If it's money you want, you should know our policy on —"

"I don't want your money," I say. "And I'm not here to get a picture of you in your jammies."

At those words, all the blood drains from the president's face.

"I'm not here to hurt you," I add quickly. "But if you don't listen to what I have to say, you're going to regret it tomorrow."

Ferguson doesn't say a word. I can almost sense his fingers itching for his panic button, but I'm more familiar with this compartment's security than he is. The only panic buttons in this place are under the mantel and next to his bed, and he's got a lot of ground to cover to get to either one.

Suddenly, the water heating on the stove begins to boil, and the high-pitched whistle of a kettle echoes through the compartment.

"Who are you?" he asks finally.

"Celdon Reynolds."

For a second, he seems to forget that there's an intruder in his home. His mouth twitches, and I catch a flash of superiority in his expression. "Am I supposed to know who you are?"

I snort. "You should. I'm one of maybe five people in this whole compound who knows exactly how to get to you anytime I want." I fake a modest shrug. "I helped develop the security."

Judging from the stone-cold look on Ferguson's face, he isn't impressed.

"Why are you here?"

"I'm a penetration tester in Systems. I'm also Constance's newest, uh . . ."

Ferguson's face goes slack with panic. *Now* I have his attention.

"What do you want?"

"I just wanted to fill you in on a few things Constance has been up to lately," I say.

Based on the look that flashes across Ferguson's face, he has a pretty good idea what Constance has been up to.

"Did you hear we captured one of the drifter leaders?" I ask.

"I am aware of the situation . . ."

"So you know James Watson has been torturing him all night with a shock collar and a bottle of acid."

Ferguson blinks. "We don't need to discuss this."

"Oh, I think we do," I snap. "Because a little while ago, I had to watch him torture my best friend's boyfriend. Eli Parker?"

Ferguson lets out a deep sigh and runs a hand through his thinning hair.

"You don't seem surprised."

"Why are you telling me this?"

"So you can step in and *do* something! Constance is out of control."

"You shouldn't be here," says Ferguson, setting down his cup and walking over to the door.

"Well, I am."

"You should go."

In that moment, I realize Ferguson knows *exactly* what's going on in Constance. But whether he's let it continue out of fear or because he's in cahoots with them, I'm not sure. So I push harder.

"Yesterday I watched Devon Reid kill Jayden Pierce," I say in a rush. "I helped him dispose of the body."

"Stop talking!" grumbles Ferguson.

"Did you hear what I just said?" I ask, raising my voice. "Constance is *killing* people."

"Shut up!" yells the president.

"*Why*?"

Ferguson looks as though he might be sick. For a moment, I don't think he's going to answer me, but then he takes a deep breath and begins to speak.

"If you know the extent of Constance's reach, then you also know that they do what they do for a reason."

"Are you *serious*?"

Ferguson doesn't reply.

"Constance doesn't need a reason!" I cry. "They'll kill anyone who gets in their way! They'll kill anyone who threatens their agenda."

"And yet you're still here."

"Look, I know it's not like you people to care what happens to tier-three workers — even a commander — but maybe you'd be more interested if you knew that Constance killed your old buddy Sullivan Taylor!"

At the mention of the Undersecretary of Vocational Placement, Ferguson's face drains of color. He seems genuinely shocked. It's the first *real* emotion I've seen from him besides anger, but it doesn't last long.

"You should go," he repeats, swallowing several times.

"Did you hear what I said?"

"I heard you!" he says. "And if what you're saying is true — and I don't have any *proof* that it is . . ."

"What proof do you need?" I shout. "Did Control ever find out who planted that bomb?"

"It doesn't matter," says Ferguson. "The fact is that I couldn't do anything about it even if I wanted to."

"You're the president!" I yell. "If you can't do anything,

who can?"

"Oh, grow up," he snarls. "Look around you. You think I have any real power over Constance? Do you think *any* board member can control what they do?"

"If they knew —"

"Oh, they know!" he spits. "People disappear in this compound and no one asks questions. People turn up dead, and yet there's no Control investigation. Do you think those things go unnoticed?"

"You're just a fucking coward!" I yell. "You'd be impeached if people knew —"

"And what good would that do?" he demands. "If I were gone and another man sat in my place, Constance wouldn't go away. It's existed since the compound's inception. The founders built our system so that Constance could protect humankind at all costs. They weren't thinking about checks and balances. They weren't thinking of equality. They were thinking about survival."

"*Survival?*" I repeat incredulously. "Have you seen what's going on out there? They're *killing* people!"

"I don't pretend to understand their methods," says Ferguson. "But Constance has a bird's-eye view — always has. And the hard truth is that bureaucracy doesn't always work. Sometimes it prevents us from making the hard decisions."

"Hard deci —"

"Look at everything that happened before Death Storm," he continues. "Government can't protect people, Mr. Reynolds. Sometimes we have to color outside the lines to keep our species alive."

"That's bullshit."

Ferguson shakes his head. "It's ugly, but that's reality."

I roll my eyes. The whole "survival of humanity"

rationalization is such a cop-out. I'm fucking sick of it.

Somewhere behind Ferguson, I hear a soft *click*. My eyes scan the compartment for an intruder, but it's still just the two of us standing there yelling at each other.

"If you won't do anything . . . I will."

For a moment, Ferguson just stares at me. Then he breaks into a sardonic grin and lets out an annoying huff of laughter. "No, you won't." He lowers his voice to a whisper. "If you try anything, you're going to get yourself killed. If you try to blackmail me or expose me . . . I won't have to lift a finger to make you disappear."

There's a long drawn-out pause. In that moment, I realize that this entire mission was futile. I was naïve to think that everything could be solved by exposing Constance. Ferguson always knew what Constance was up to. He just didn't care enough to stop it.

Shaking with rage and disgust, I brush past the president and head straight out the front door toward Systems headquarters. I half expect to be tackled by Ferguson's security guard, but nothing happens. Maybe his security guy left to take a piss.

It's just as well. Ferguson is a complete waste of space. Any biped with a firm grasp of the English language could easily stand in front of a camera and do what he does.

I'm already halfway to the corner when I hear a soft voice drifting down the tunnel.

"I know you," calls the voice.

I freeze on the spot and turn, my hands already itching to flip the security guard the double bird. But instead of some overpaid Control douchebag standing outside the president's compartment, I see a tall black man in a crisp taupe suit striding toward me with purpose.

I know this guy. It's Remy Chaplin — Undersecretary of

Reconnaissance. He has a seat on the board overseeing the deployment of all Recon operatives within the compound.

"*So*," I say lamely. "I know who *you* are, too."

Remy doesn't seem put off by my rudeness. His expression is grim, but I sense his concerns run deeper than insubordination.

"If you know who I am, then you know why I'm here," he says.

I shrug.

"I came to talk to the president about finding a replacement for Commander Pierce."

I take a few steps forward, drawn to Remy purely on curiosity. He looks extremely uncomfortable for such a tall, imposing man, and I suddenly wonder how much of my conversation with Ferguson he overheard.

Thinking back, I recall hearing a sound that could have been the front door snapping shut, and I realize that Remy must have been listening the entire time.

"Did you hear?" I ask.

"Yes," he says in a grave voice. "In fact . . . I've been aware of Constance's dealings for far longer than I'd like to admit."

I don't say anything right away. I'm too busy feeling out Remy to determine if his regret is sincere. He's stood silent like Ferguson, but he seems genuinely disturbed by Jayden's murder.

Remy takes a deep breath. "Truthfully, I'm ashamed that we've allowed it to go on for this long."

"So why have you?"

"The president is correct," he murmurs. "Constance has enormous reach."

"But if people knew —"

"That's just it. People don't *want* to know," says Remy matter-of-factly. "People want to believe that everything is fine because it absolves them of responsibility. When people can blame ignorance, they don't have any reason to intervene. Yet I would imagine that people who've been around for any length of time remember that things weren't always like this."

"Like what?"

"We haven't always used the tier system," he says. "We didn't need to. Recon itself is a fairly new section. The compounds were built before there was ever a need to secure the outside world."

I never thought of that, but it makes sense.

"So what do we do?"

Remy takes a deep breath and glances up and down the tunnel. I know he's probably thinking of all the various ways Constance could be spying on us: his interface, the security feeds, somebody listening to our conversation on the other side of a door.

But I'm having a hard time mustering up an appropriate level of concern. I'm a dead man walking no matter what I say from here on out. I won't attend another torture session, and I already blew off one assignment tonight. I'm done being Devon's little bitch.

"Look," says Remy, lowering his voice to a whisper. "You don't stand a chance trying to take Constance down from the inside. They — will — crush you."

I roll my eyes before I can stop myself, but Remy keeps going.

"Look what they did to Commander Pierce. She was one of the staunchest pragmatists Recon ever turned out. She'd been groomed for Constance since she was your age, and she was among the best they ever had. But they disposed of her just like *that*."

Remy snaps his fingers in the air, and I resist the urge to say, "Yeah, I was there."

"If you step out of line, Constance will put you down," says Remy. "Plain and simple."

"So what are you suggesting?"

Remy starts walking down the tunnel back in the direction of the megalift. He gestures for me to follow and begins talking in a rapid whisper. "Based on what I know about Constance, the only way to take them down is from the outside."

There's a long, heavy silence as I turn that statement over in my head. Suddenly I stop, positive he can't mean what I think he said.

"You want me to go *public* with this?" I ask incredulously. "Go over the president . . . Tell people everything Constance has done?"

Remy shrugs as if I just came up with the idea all on my own, but his eyes are telling me that going public is *exactly* what he's suggesting.

"You have access to the media."

"*Are you out of your fucking mind?*"

"It's the only way."

"It's also the fastest way to get myself *killed*!"

"Maybe so," says Remy, touching the button to call the megalift. "But the truth won't die with you." He steps inside the lift and raises both eyebrows. "You can't kill the truth once it's out."

eight

Eli

I awake the next morning to the smell of vanilla and sex.

I don't want to get up, so I roll over, pull the blanket tighter to my shoulders, and burrow deeper into the couch. When I finally peel my eyes open, I see Harper hovering over me with the sunlight flickering through her long dark hair.

"Morning," she whispers, brushing her thumb down my scruffy jaw.

I smile and run my hand up her bare leg until it hits the cuff of her shorts. "You're dressed," I grumble.

"Sage and Jackson are back. They just pulled up."

"Shit," I mutter, lifting Harper's right leg and dumping her gently onto the couch.

She chuckles as I hunt around on the floor for my pants, and something soft hits my face.

"Thanks," I chuckle, pulling on my boxers.

A heavy silence falls over the room as Harper watches me get dressed. We don't say it, but both of us are thinking it: This might be goodbye.

Once I'm decent, I turn around to look at her and instantly wish I hadn't. Her eyes are full of worry, and her mouth is tight — the way it is when she's trying to hide her grief.

"I love you," I whisper, reaching for her hand and pulling her against me.

"I love you, too."

I hold her tight and breathe deeply, trying to commit her

scent to memory. I don't have long.

Half a second later, somebody is pounding on Owen's front door. It has to be Sage or Jackson, telling Harper that it's time to go.

The morning sun is blindingly bright when I step outside. Jackson's Explorer is idling in the yard, and Gunner is pacing in front of Owen's truck. He has heavy bags under his eyes and looks as though he didn't sleep at all.

Harper drags in a deep breath, and her hands shake a little as she double-checks her rifle.

"Remember what I said," I murmur, leaning in on the pretense of a kiss. "Don't hesitate. And don't trust anyone."

She nods. "Be careful."

Harper kisses me one last time, but I'm lost in a haze of dread. She jumps into the middle seat of the SUV, and I watch them drive off with a tight knot in my chest.

"We're really doing this?" Gunner asks as I climb into Owen's truck.

"Yep," I mutter, loading my rifle and sliding it down to rest between my foot and the seat.

Gunner eyes it warily. His bangs are stuck to his forehead with nervous sweat, and he's worrying his lip ring between his tongue and teeth.

"Okay," he chokes.

I want to smack Gunner for being such a basket case, but he's not the only one who's scared shitless. My knuckles are white on the steering wheel, and my foot feels clumsy as I press the gas.

The plan is simple: We'll move out with the Desperados to attack the compound and try to reach the perimeter without getting shot or blown up. If we can get close enough to locate Miles or Lenny, then we'll have a chance of getting over the electric fence and into the compound. Once inside, it's just a matter of finding Owen and getting us all back out alive.

The plan has way too many ifs for my liking, but there's not exactly a *safe* way to go charging through a war zone full of people who want to kill me. Still, it blows my mind that anyone would agree to go along with this — especially someone like Gunner.

"Why are you here?" I ask, my curiosity getting the better of me. "Why did you *really* decide to come with me?"

Gunner shrugs. "I don't have a lot of friends."

I wait for him to elaborate.

"Owen and I weren't exactly *friends*, but he's the only person around here who didn't treat me like dirt."

That pitiful statement tugs at my heart, but I shove down my sympathy and study Gunner critically.

Gunner is a drifter. He might be young and a bit of a pushover, but that doesn't mean he hasn't done some pretty terrible things to stay alive. The cold, logical part of my brain says he could be playing me, but I know in my gut that he's sincere. Gunner's had a hard go of it, and he probably doesn't feel as though he has anything to lose by risking his life for Owen.

My analysis is cut short when we pull into the dusty gravel parking lot of McNally's. Malcolm is already standing outside next to a white pickup truck, leaning in to talk to the passengers. Judging by the enormous rifle strapped to his back, he's battle ready and hungry for blood.

I throw Owen's truck into park and idle on the edge of the lot as Malcolm delivers a few final instructions.

A moment later, he pounds on the hood, and the driver pulls out with a two-finger salute. A few more cars follow the white truck, and the small caravan heads down the road in the direction of the compound.

"This is it," I breathe just loud enough for Gunner to hear.

He swallows, and I can see my own anxiety reflected in his terrified eyes.

I'm about to throw the truck into gear and join the caravan when Malcolm waves at us and starts walking toward the truck. For such a scrawny man, he moves with an unusual amount of swagger, walking at the pace of someone who's accustomed to making other people wait.

"Stay cool," I say to Gunner, who looks as though he's about to wet himself. "Just . . . try not to say anything."

Once Malcolm is within earshot, I crank down the window so we can talk. "What's up?"

"Why don't you guys hang tight for a second?" he calls. "We're heading out in two waves. You're gonna follow the first wave about an hour behind."

My breathing speeds up. "You don't want me on the front lines?"

"Nah," says Malcolm, his dark eyes boring into mine. "I want you with me."

I nod as if this makes perfect sense, but my gut is telling me to abort the mission. Malcolm hates Owen with a passion. Why wouldn't he want him where the fighting is most dangerous?

I don't have long to wonder.

Malcolm waves the next cluster of vehicles forward, and the remaining Desperados pull out to join the caravan. Pretty soon our vehicle is the only one left, and Malcolm walks over and throws open the passenger-side door.

"What's going on?" I ask.

"We're meeting the rest of the guys at the old base," he says, elbowing Gunner into my lap.

"The pawn shop?" I ask, shoving him away to reclaim an

appropriate amount of space.

Malcolm shakes his head. "The restaurant."

"Oh."

Alarm bells go off in my head as I press the brake and put the truck into gear. I can't think of any reason for Malcolm to get us on our own like this except to kill us.

"I can't believe it," says Malcolm as we pull onto the road.

"Believe what?" I ask, trying to come up with some excuse to reach for my rifle.

"I can't believe today's the day we're finally going to crush those filthy compound rats."

"It's about time."

Malcolm shakes his head. "It's overdue, brother. I can't tell you how infuriating it's been . . . losing men year after year and not being able to do anything about it." He leans forward and props his elbows on his knees. "These guys . . . They look to me as their leader. You know what it looks like when a leader sits by and appears to do *nothing*?"

I nod slowly, not sure what he wants me to say.

"I mean, obviously we haven't been doing *nothing*. But people only see results."

I keep nodding, but Gunner is frozen in panic.

"It's humiliating . . . demoralizing . . . like when your friend Jackson ran off," he adds.

It's a loaded statement. I know Malcolm is just testing me to see where my true loyalties lie. Either that or he's hoping that I'll snap and give him an excuse to kill me.

"He left his people with *nothing*," Malcolm continues. "Me, I would never do that — not with people depending on me for protection."

I grit my teeth and grip the steering wheel tighter. Even though I don't feel Owen's strong loyalty to Jackson, simply understanding the root of Malcolm's manipulation is enough to make me want to bank hard to the right and crash into the dilapidated gas station on the corner.

I wonder what would happen if I just killed Malcolm right now. If he never turned up at the restaurant, would the rest of the army still attack?

I never get the chance to find out. Just past the abandoned filling station is the rustic-looking restaurant the drifters once used as their base. It has an enormous wooden porch that wraps around the front and a bunch of old license plates mounted to the siding.

Two dozen cars and trucks are idling in the parking lot, waiting for Malcolm to give them the go-ahead. The men waiting outside are rowdy and impatient — just waiting for the signal to rain hell down on the compound.

I slow down and coast into the parking lot, and another red SUV appears behind me. At least five drifters are crammed inside, armed to the teeth with automatic weapons and explosives.

Even if I turned around and made a break for it with Malcolm in my front seat, I wouldn't get half a mile before the Desperados took out my truck with a flamethrower.

Malcolm hops out before I've even put the truck in park, and Gunner shoots me a wide-eyed look. I know he's thinking what I'm thinking: With all these people, it's going to be nearly impossible to slip away unnoticed, and it's going to be a thousand times harder with Malcolm riding shotgun.

"He's not coming with us," I say to Gunner. "We'll just make sure we're at the end of the caravan so we can split off when they open fire. No one's even gonna know —"

My thought is cut short by the crack of a gunshot.

I duck down on instinct, and another bullet whizzes through the air. Shards of broken glass rain down on my back and get lost in my shirt.

The bullet shattered Owen's rear windshield, but before I can even grab my rifle, another blows out the passenger-side window.

Gunner yelps and throws himself onto the floorboard. Drifters are swearing and shouting as they try to locate the shooters, and bullets are still flying.

Heart pounding, I scoop up my rifle and lift my head over the edge of my open window.

A volley of shots echoes over the street, and another bullet pings off the side of Owen's truck. I swear as another rips clean through the door and lodges somewhere in the filthy backseat.

"Move!" I shout to Gunner, crawling over him to get to the door. I fumble for the handle, and we fall out of the truck in a tangle of limbs.

Gasping and swearing, I pull myself into a crouched position and run for cover. I hear Gunner stumbling along behind me, and my brain absorbs the scene in a patchy array of details: car doors thrown open, bodies sprawled across the ground, and a dotted line of blood trailing behind a drifter. Some of the men have taken cover behind their vehicles, but most are running toward the filling station.

Diving behind the corner of the porch, I glance around wildly to see who's shooting. That's when I catch a flash of gray moving behind a dumpster.

Recon.

I swear again as Gunner slides into home beside me. His face is red from exertion, and his eyes are wild with fear. He's still too shocked and breathless to shoot, but I'm glad he made it.

"How the *fuck* did they know we'd be here?" growls a voice from behind me.

I jump. Malcolm is crawling toward us from the back of the restaurant, shoving a new mag into his gun.

He stops beside me and opens fire, aiming for a corner of the parking lot where the operatives must be hiding. His bullets punch out a dozen holes in the side of a dumpster, but I don't hear anything except the return of gunfire from a new location.

I can't tell how many people are shooting, but all those bullets definitely didn't come from a single pair of Recon operatives. If I had to guess, there must be six or eight people shooting, but I still have no idea where they are.

"What now?" I pant, hoping Malcolm will decide to delay the attack.

"Now we make them pay," he says, gritting his teeth as he shoots off another round.

I hear a guttural moan from across the parking lot and a muffled scream as he makes contact.

My heart stutters. I don't know who he hit, but they have to be one of our own.

"Those fucking pussies," snarls Malcolm.

In my dazed state, I can't tell if he's referring to the Recon operatives or his own men. Across the street, a couple of drifters who fled are making a break for the abandoned body shop down the road.

"This changes nothing," says Malcolm, elbowing his way forward to find a better position.

I reload my gun with shaky hands and take my time searching for a spot where I know I won't hit anyone from Recon.

What was I thinking? There's no way in hell I'm going to get past Recon *and* the Desperados on my way into the compound.

"Let's get the hell out of here," says Malcolm. "I don't have time for this shit."

I nod. I don't like the idea of running back across the parking lot to the truck, but at least I won't have to shoot any of my own people.

"Now!" he cries, tearing out from our hiding place at a sprint. "Cover me!"

"Okay!" I yell, glancing at Gunner.

Despite my racing heart and scrambled brain, I know what my next move has to be.

I rise into a standing position and watch Malcolm run across the parking lot, just waiting for a bullet to rip into his back and pierce his heart.

In a few seconds, the Desperados will be an army without a general. In a few seconds, the greatest threat to humanity will be dead.

I wait, but the shot never comes.

Halfway to the truck, Malcolm turns to look over his shoulder, and several things happen at once. A Recon bullet zings past my head, missing me by an inch or two. Then one of the Recon operatives leaps out from behind a parked car and takes a shot at Malcolm.

"Parker!" he yells, raising his rifle a second too late.

I panic, torn between protecting Recon and protecting my identity as Owen. But then I catch sight of two wide blue eyes and a head of white-blond hair. Two child-sized hands are holding a semi-automatic rifle, and they're attached to one of my own.

Kindra.

For a split second, we just stare at each other. Even though I'm dressed in jeans and a dirty T-shirt, I know she recognizes me. She has her gun pointed at Malcolm, and the only reason she hasn't killed him yet is because she's still in shock.

Then a shot cracks the air, and Kindra dives back behind a rusted burgundy car. It takes me a second to realize that the shot came from Malcolm, who's already climbing into Owen's truck and throwing it into gear.

Gunner jabs me hard in the back, and I manage to stumble across the parking lot without getting a bullet through my head.

Shaking and sweating, I climb in behind Malcolm, and we peel out of the parking lot in a thick cloud of dust. Gunner is hanging off the side of the truck with one foot on the runner, and he summersaults through the shattered window as we pull onto the road.

Malcolm slams his foot down on the accelerator, and my stomach clenches automatically.

I don't hear any more gunshots, but I'm too shaken to feel relief. Neither Gunner nor Malcolm has said a word, and when I glance over at the driver, I see why.

Malcolm is wearing an expression of fury mixed with grim delight. He saw me hesitate when Kindra exposed herself. He knows I spared her on purpose.

nine

Eli

Horror washes over me when I see the knowing look on Malcolm's face. His mouth twists into a contemptuous scowl, and his dark eyes narrow in satisfaction.

Malcolm never trusted Owen. He knew Owen was Jackson's man through and through, and I just offered up the last shred of evidence that Owen is a traitor.

I take a deep breath and glance over at Gunner. His head is twisted over his shoulder, watching the restaurant shrink in the distance. He's panting and sweating, but he seems oblivious to the silent showdown going on between me and Malcolm.

I focus on the road ahead. Judging from the small fleet of vehicles in front of us, more than half the drifters fled during the shootout. There's one last truck coming up behind us, but we've lost a lot of manpower.

Suddenly, Malcolm slams on the brakes and pivots the wheel sharply to the left. He pulls into the parking lot of an abandoned storage facility and whips the truck around to face the way we came.

"What're you —"

"Just a little experiment . . ."

I look over just in time to see the fiery glint of vengeance in his eyes.

"We're going back?" squeaks Gunner, all the blood draining from his face.

"I just want to try something," says Malcolm, not taking his eyes off the road.

"Are you crazy?" I yell. "We can't go back. We barely made it out of there alive!"

"Is that right?" snarls Malcolm, finally turning his head to look at me.

At that moment, we pass the last truck to make it out of the parking lot, and I catch several confused looks from the drifters inside.

"What are you doing?" I ask again, unable to control the fury in my voice.

"Are you questioning me, Parker?"

I don't respond. Malcolm isn't listening anyway. He's wearing the crazed expression of a man bent on destruction. He presses down harder on the gas, and I watch the odometer creep toward sixty.

I know what Malcolm is doing. As soon as we get back to the restaurant, he's going to put a bullet through my head and tell everyone that I died at the hands of the compound.

He isn't thinking about the driver behind us, who pulled an abrupt U-turn to follow Malcolm into the fray. He doesn't care about the men he's leading into an ambush. Malcolm is a madman, and he's going to get us all killed.

Before I have a chance to rethink my decision, I dive across Gunner's lap and grab the steering wheel. I yank it hard to the right and brace myself as the truck swerves off the road.

Malcolm wasn't expecting that, but a second later, he knocks my head back with an elbow and twists the wheel to the left.

I'm seeing stars, but I still have one hand on the steering wheel. I pull it back toward me, and Malcolm's eyes grow wide.

I crane my neck to look at the road, and my heart stutters. I barely have a chance to register the telephone pole looming up ahead before the truck veers off the road and everything goes dark.

When I open my eyes, I'm staring directly into the blinding sun. My entire body is stiff with agony, and I'm lying spread-eagled in the dirt.

"What's the matter, Parker?" croons a nasty voice from above me. "Have you grown a soft spot for those fucking rats?"

Malcolm's dirty, distorted face appears above me, blocking out the sun. He's hungry for violence, and I don't have time to defend myself.

Before I can get to my feet, Malcolm throws out a kick. It lands hard in my ribs, and I roll onto my side to protect myself.

"Or maybe you just wanted me *dead*!" he yells.

He kicks me again — this time aiming his boot directly at my exposed back. A white-hot flash of pain shoots up my spine, jolting my entire nervous system.

I swallow down a moan of agony and try to get to my feet, but Malcolm kicks me in the head. I go down hard, and this time I'm too dizzy to get back up.

Somewhere off in the distance, I hear a squeal of tires and the sound of truck doors slamming. Heavy boots crunch over the gravel shoulder and rustle into the ditch.

"What the fuck happened?" yells a man I don't know.

"This motherfucker tried to *kill me*!" bellows Malcolm.

"What? Parker?"

Malcolm hawks up a wad of spit, and I feel the warm wetness splatter the side of my face. "He's a fucking *rat* is what he is!"

"He did this?"

"Well, I didn't drive the truck into that pole myself, asshole!"

Malcolm lets out another grunt, and I feel a renewed surge of pain as he kicks me under my shoulder. I grit my teeth and suck in a burst of air.

The pain is reverberating throughout my entire body, but the shock from the crash is starting to fade. With a huge amount of effort, I pull myself off the ground, and somebody grabs me from behind.

Two strong arms latch on to my biceps, and my shoulders scream in protest as the man yanks my arms behind my back. The stench of tobacco and body odor fills my nostrils as my sweaty captor pivots me around.

The crash did a number on Malcolm. He's got a three-inch-long cut running down his neck, his left arm is shredded, and his scalp is oozing blood.

To my left, Owen's truck is still crunched around the telephone pole, the front end all bent to shit. The windshield is shattered, and there's a sharp odor in the air that tells me the truck is leaking fuel.

Looking around, I spot a disheveled heap of bones lying several yards away. The body is pale and scrawny, and the messy hair confirms what I already know: It's Gunner.

His body is bent at an odd angle, which means he was probably killed on impact. A gnawing sense of guilt rises up in my throat, mixing with my despair, but I can't think about him right now. Four more drifters are standing behind Malcolm, looking as though they're hungry for blood.

"Any last words?" snarls Malcolm, his bloody nostrils flaring in delight.

"Go to hell."

Those are the last words I manage to get out before an ugly

drifter with a scruffy face lays into me with two strong hooks to the body. I clench my core to protect my organs, but I still feel each punch like the stab of a bayonet.

A minute later, another drifter with shaggy brown hair elbows his way in and cracks my temple with a sloppy overhand right. The impact rattles my brain, but I just grit my teeth and brace myself for the next blow.

Scruffy and Shaggy take turns hitting me, and I feel myself fading. Soon I'm hanging limp in the big drifter's arms, drooping toward the ground as I inch toward unconsciousness.

Hot blood is trickling down my face, and the cartilage in my nose feels loose and crunchy. My vision narrows in on the two drifters delivering my beating, but a few minutes later, I hear Malcolm's voice drift over their grunts: "That's the one."

The strikes stop immediately. My face throbs as blood rushes to the surface, and the short break gives me a chance to take stock of my injuries: cracked ribs, a busted nose, and possible internal bleeding.

The drifters in front of me shift to the side, and Malcolm appears in my peripheral vision. The two other men are swaying behind him, holding a second prisoner in their arms.

The captive is pale, blond, and petite. At first I think they're holding Gunner, but as the blood clears from my eyes, I realize they've got Kindra.

She's struggling against the drifters' grips, but when she sees me, she freezes and stares up at me with those chilling aquamarine eyes.

Kindra's got streaks of dirt running down both cheeks, and a spot near her temple is battered and bloody. Her air filtration mask is hanging from its strap, and she's panting with fear as she sucks radioactive dust into her lungs.

"You two know each other?" Malcolm asks in a casual

voice, stepping between us and grabbing a fistful of my shirt.

I don't say a word. I'm staring past his eyes to the point where I know Kindra is standing.

The big guy holding my arms has relaxed his grip. He probably thinks I'm too weak to move. But with Malcolm's hands at my neck and my cadet trembling between two thugs, I feel a surge of invigorating fury.

Summoning all the strength I have left, I lunge toward Malcolm like a tiger bounding from its cage. I manage to break my captor's hold, and Malcolm and I hit the ground in a clash of knees and fists.

I know I only have a few seconds, so I focus on inflicting as much damage as possible.

My fist connects with his mouth — then his nose and then his chin. Malcolm lets out a guttural moan and shoves his hand into my face, but I lay into him with everything I've got.

The fight doesn't last long. I only get four or five good strikes in before somebody gets me in a choke and pins me against the side of Owen's truck.

I look over at Kindra, who is staring at me in horror.

"I'm sorry," I choke, wishing I could communicate just how wretched I feel.

If it weren't for me, Malcolm would have let her escape. If I hadn't hesitated, he wouldn't have singled her out to torture me.

He's not going to let her walk away. He's going to kill her and make me watch.

To make matters worse, I have no way of knowing what might have happened to the other people she was with. I heard the gunshots. Those bullets could have been meant for any of them: Bear, Lenny, Miles . . .

It takes a moment for Malcolm to recover from my attack. The Desperados are staring at him with a mixture of shock and concern. I'm sure none of them would ever dare to pick a fight with him — no matter how much they might want to.

A line of blood is dribbling from Malcolm's chin, and his lip curls in loathing as he wipes it away with the back of his hand.

"You've got some fucking balls, Parker," he growls, spraying me with blood and spit.

I just glower at him. It's no use trying to lie my way out of this. He knows I'm working against him, and he's not going to let me live.

"I never really trusted you after Jackson left . . . but I never guessed you'd have a hard-on for some filthy compound rat."

Of course he still thinks I'm Owen. He has no way of knowing who Kindra is to me. He doesn't know she's one of the cadets I was charged to protect.

Malcolm works up another ball of phlegm and spits it at my feet. "If there's one thing I can't stand . . . it's treachery."

I barely hear him. My blood is pounding in my ears, and my breathing is shallow and ragged.

"What should we do with her?" Malcolm muses, his voice trembling with barely contained glee.

Tears are leaking out of Kindra's eyes, running down her face and dripping from her nose. She's trembling with fear, but she hasn't stopped trying to get away.

"Please," I choke, staring up at Malcolm with a pleading look in my eyes. "Do whatever you want to me . . . Just let her go."

"Aww," says Malcolm, cocking his head in mock sympathy.

His men let out a rumble of derisive laughter, and I feel the blood pump harder in my head.

"What — a — sacrifice!"

I glare up at him in silence, hoping that if I just don't say anything, maybe he'll grow bored with Kindra and decide to hurt me instead.

"Aren't you a goddamned hero!"

I grit my teeth together, shaking with rage.

Kindra is still crying and fighting to get away. She knows this isn't going to end well for her, and she's giving it everything she's got.

"You want me to punish you instead?" Malcolm asks, looking at me as though he's never heard of such a thing.

"Go ahead."

Malcolm laughs. "No . . . I don't think I will."

My heart sinks, and I lock eyes with Kindra. I don't know how I'm going to get us out of this mess, but I have to do something.

"Well, I've got news for you, Parker," says Malcolm, sniffing loudly and spitting at my feet. "Nobody likes a fucking hero."

Before I can reply or formulate a plan, Malcolm raises his gun into the air and points it at Kindra's head.

"No!" I yell, lunging forward. The men holding on to me tighten their grip, but I manage to free one of my arms and swing my elbow into a drifter's nose.

He lets out a strangled moan of pain, but before I can fully extricate myself, a shot rings out over the desert.

One minute I'm staring into Kindra's terrified blue eyes, and the next, her pupils are blank and unfocused.

I suck in a burst of air, but I can't seem to get any oxygen to my lungs. My ears are ringing from the blast, and everything seems to slow down.

As I watch, Kindra's face goes slack, and she slumps in the drifters' arms — just a shell of a girl with a hole in her head.

"No!" I yell, fighting and straining against my captors.

"Such a *waste*, Parker . . ." Malcolm's smile fades. "I really thought you were smarter than this."

I know Malcolm is trying to command my attention, but all I see is Kindra. She was alive and fighting just a second ago, and now she's dead.

"I'll make you a deal," he says. "You can die like the traitorous little rat you are, or you can tell me where the rest of your little friends ran off to."

"Fuck you," I growl.

Malcolm's lips tighten into a hard line. "Have it your way."

I don't reply. I can't even think. All I feel is agony and disbelief.

"Finish him," Malcolm mutters.

I don't notice my captors moving, but then a fist flies toward my face, and my knees hit the dirt. Another punch jostles my skull, and I let out an animalistic howl of pain.

Something hard and unforgiving connects with my head, and my chin hits the pavement — hard.

Someone else kicks me in the side, but I don't feel anything. I'm staring across the ditch at Kindra's crumpled body, watching a line of blood drip down her face like tears. It falls onto the ground and seeps into her gray fatigues — staining the uniform I would have given my life to protect.

This is how it ends, I think. *This is how it has to end.*

I couldn't protect Kindra, and I couldn't protect Blaze. I left Harper's side the moment it counted most. I'm just grateful she wasn't foolish enough to follow me.

I had *one* job to do, and I failed miserably. In the end, I couldn't protect myself — much less my five cadets.

Darkness closes in around me as the scruffy drifter jumps down and continues to pummel me into submission. I keep my bleary eyes focused on Kindra as I lie there waiting for it all to end.

The physical discomfort of the drifters' strikes eventually subsides, but I feel no relief. There is no peace at the end of a war. All that's left is suffering. All that's left is pain.

ten

Harper

The ride to the drifter base is the longest of my life. I'm sitting alone in the middle row as we speed down the deserted highway. Jackson is driving and Sage is riding shotgun, twisting a long piece of hair between her fingers.

The sun is climbing in the sky, heating the blacktop and beating down on the cracked leather seats with excruciating intensity. We roll all the windows down, but the howl of the wind whipping through my hair isn't loud enough to drown out the deafening silence.

I should be focused on the mission ahead, but all I can think about is Eli.

Part of me already regrets my decision not to go with him. I can't stand the thought of him being out there on his own, and I hate myself for abandoning him when it mattered most.

But despite how terrible I feel, I know in my gut that it was the right thing to do. Even if Eli manages to infiltrate the compound and rescue Owen, the time it would take to get there and back is time Sawyer doesn't have.

I know the Arizona base is a long shot. I know the odds are stacked against Sawyer. But I would never be able to forgive myself if I didn't try.

Sage is sitting with one leg propped against the dashboard, staring out the open window. I can't see her face, but I can feel the despair radiating from her and know she's thinking of Owen. Maybe she's regretting her decision to come with me, or maybe she's still thinking about the fallen compounds and hating Owen for his involvement.

I know exactly how she feels. It's how I felt when I learned that Celdon was part of Constance. All of a sudden, my world turned upside down, and I felt as though everything I'd ever known had been a lie. The instinct to love is still there, but it's muddled by crippling disappointment and shock.

Then there's the agonizing helplessness that comes with not knowing if the man you love is alive or dead. If Owen is alive, he's suffering at the hands of the enemy, and there's nothing I can say to ease the burden of that reality.

I don't know if Owen was born with Eli's sense of loyalty, but I know that he's just as stubborn and ten times more abrasive. It won't help him in the end. It will only prolong his suffering.

"He'll make it," says Sage out of nowhere.

I jump in my seat, wondering if I spoke out loud.

Jackson doesn't say anything, but I can feel the tension pouring off him.

I nod before realizing Sage can't see me. "Owen's tough," I choke.

It's about the nicest statement I can muster up to comfort her. I don't know Owen well, but my brief interactions with him haven't left me with a stellar impression. Owen has all of Eli's flaws and none of the redeeming qualities that made me fall in love with the younger Parker brother.

Eli is the only reason I care about Owen. Eli would never forgive himself if he didn't do everything in his power to save his brother. It's the sort of thing I love about him, but it's also the reason I might never see him again.

Feeling sick, I push the thought aside and stare out the window to distract myself. Miles of empty desert stretch in front of us — nothing but dark-brown dirt, sandstone rock formations, and scrubby little bushes in muted shades of green.

There's no civilization — no water or fuel for miles. More than once I catch Jackson eyeing the fuel gauge nervously and glancing down at the highlighted route on the map, but it doesn't do anything to shorten our journey.

Jackson's Ford Explorer runs on the same algae-based biofuel that the compound rovers use, but his pre–Death Storm vehicle is years older and much less efficient. The only way we're going to make the six-hour journey to the casino is if we stop and refuel at an old Recon checkpoint near compound 119.

Because of the outbreak, it's been ages since there were active Recon operatives in this area. Counting on the checkpoint for fuel is a huge gamble, but we don't have a choice. Fuel is hard to come by these days, and the little that is available in the area is either guarded by the compounds or controlled by Desperados.

As we approach 119, Sage sits up taller in her seat and leans out the window to scan the landscape for drifters. Jackson pulls off the road, and we bump along on the uneven ground in search of the checkpoint blinking from my stolen interface.

When we get close, Jackson coasts to a stop and kills the engine. We all get out, weapons drawn, and Jackson opens the back hatch to fish out a crowbar.

It feels amazing to stretch my legs after the long drive, but I know it would be foolish to relax even a little bit. While the Desperados may be focused on wiping out 112, it doesn't mean that unaffiliated drifters aren't lurking nearby to steal our supplies.

Sage and Jackson follow me as I search out the checkpoint marked on the map. I alternate between staring at our blinking green dot and searching the ground for a protruding spigot.

Suddenly, I catch a glimpse of exposed metal poking through the brush.

"Found it," I murmur, bending down and pulling the weeds aside.

Sage gets down on her knees to help me clear the metal trapdoor, and Jackson wedges the crowbar under the lip. He pries the door open with a heavy groan, and the smell of earth, old plastic, and dry goods hits my nostrils.

I've never seen the inside of one of the checkpoints in person, and I'm stunned by the volume of stuff crammed in there. Jackson shines a flashlight down into the cellar, and I let out a breath of relief when I see more than a dozen green fuel tanks nestled in the opening.

"We're in business," Jackson mutters, kneeling down and lowering himself into the hole. "Looks like Malcolm's crew has been using this place as a fuel stop for a while."

"Why do you say that?" I ask.

"Checkpoints don't normally have this much fuel," he grunts, lifting one of the heavy containers and passing it up to Sage.

I feel a little foolish for not knowing that, but it makes sense. The main purpose of the checkpoints is to provide Recon operatives with the food and water they need on extended missions. Rarely does a compound rover pass by in need of fuel.

Sage hands me the first container, and I don't waste any time hauling it over to the SUV. My arms scream from the weight of the sloshing fuel, but I feel immediate relief that we're one step closer to reaching the base.

"How many should we take?" Sage calls as Jackson passes her the fifth container.

"As many as we can. We don't know if we'll be able to stop again."

Once we've got four containers, I start emptying the contents into the Explorer's fuel tank. It's hard work, but soon the tank is almost full, and we still have three containers left.

Sage takes one to load into the SUV, but then I hear an odd rushing sound coming from the highway.

I turn and squint back toward the road.

It takes my eyes a moment to adjust to the hazy scenery, but when they do, my heart rate speeds up. A white car is barreling down the road a quarter of a mile away, and it's headed right toward us.

"Uh, guys . . ."

Jackson follows my gaze to the road. "Shit," he mutters. "We gotta go."

He slams the back hatch closed, and the three of us jump into the Explorer. We peel away from the checkpoint in the opposite direction of the highway, and the white car seems to speed up.

"Fuck!" yells Jackson, his eyes locked on the rearview mirror.

Sage and I exchange a nervous look. She gives me a small nod, and we each open fire on the car.

It's tough to hit a moving target, and it's even harder to hit one in a vehicle traveling fifty miles an hour over uneven desert terrain. But Sage is an impressive shot.

One of her bullets zings through the car's windshield, and blood splatters the glass as the bullet finds its home. I take aim at one of their tires, but a second later, a bullet whizzes through our back windshield.

"Stop shooting at my car!" Jackson yells, pounding the steering wheel in frustration.

The drifters fire again, and this time a bullet pings off Sage's door frame. She yelps in panic but keeps shooting, hunkering down below the dash.

"They better not hit that fucking fuel tank," says Jackson.

I didn't even think of that, but it's just one more way for the drifters to kill us.

Heart pounding, I take aim at the car's front right tire.

I miss, and the drifters fire off another volley of shots. I hear the bullets tear through the Explorer's fragile exterior, and several get caught in the rubberized seat backs.

Finally, one of my bullets makes contact.

The effect is delayed, but after a few seconds, the car seems to be losing steam. I managed to puncture one of their front tires, and they won't be able to make it much farther.

"Was that you?" Sage calls back to me, unmistakable admiration in her voice.

"Yeah," I pant.

"Whoooo!"

I let out a long, cautious breath, too shaken to celebrate. I haven't heard another shot for nearly a minute, and the car is shrinking on the horizon.

Unfortunately, fleeing the drifters took us several miles off course, and we're going to have to make a huge detour to get back on the highway.

"Everybody okay?" Jackson calls.

"I'm fine," says Sage, finger-combing her hair and reclining back in her seat.

"Fine," I choke, much less convincingly.

With several deployments and multiple drifter attacks under my belt, I should be used to getting shot at, but I'm not. The surge of adrenaline still gets me every time. My hands start shaking, my breathing goes haywire, and my legs turn to jelly.

Jackson is staring at me in the side mirror, so I swallow down my anxiety and try to calm my expression.

"It's okay if you're *not* okay, you know."

"I'm fine."

"You're not fine," he says. "You're not used to this."

"Do you *ever* get used to this?"

"Sort of," says Sage.

"I don't know if I want to," I mutter.

Jackson raises his eyebrows and consults the map to find a path that will get us back to the highway. Fleeing the drifters will add almost an hour to our journey, but there's nothing we can do.

By late afternoon, billboards appear along the side of the road featuring happy gamblers and steak dinners from the casino restaurant. They're faded from the sun and peppered with bullets, which adds a sinister edge to the cheery images.

We stop once to switch seats, and Jackson joins me in the middle row. We don't want the drifters to notice that two members of our party have run off, so the plan is to make them think that Sage drove there alone.

We already collapsed the back row of seating to make room for supplies, so I pull a large plastic crate onto the seat beside me and cover us with a ratty old comforter.

"Here it is," Sage murmurs.

I peek out from our hiding place just in time to see a fancy-looking sign flash by the window. It's a manmade stone formation with the words "Red Desert Oasis" spelled out above a miniature waterfall.

Pulling the comforter more securely over my head, I hunker down and watch the road through a tiny slice of window.

We blacked out Jackson's license plates with duct tape the way Gunner told us to. Now we just have to hope that none of the lookouts get suspicious.

The road leading to the casino must have been well maintained in its day, because the ride smooths out the closer we get. I spot the edge of a rustic stone-and-wood archway, and we pass several more signs welcoming us to the Red Desert Oasis.

I only catch flashes of the building, but I can make out an imposing stucco structure accented by natural stone buttresses. The attached hotel is a six-story building with enough rooms to house hundreds of drifters.

My breath catches in my chest. At least we know that Gunner wasn't making this place up. Now it's just a matter of whether or not Malcolm really could have hidden a cure here.

I feel the Explorer slow to a crawl as Sage drives around the back of the building. We come to a standstill, and she parks the vehicle in the shadow of a tan awning.

"Here goes nothing," she whispers.

I force myself to take slow, quiet breaths so the drifters won't hear my nervous gasps. My body is curled around my rifle, but not being able to see what's happening makes it tough to stay calm.

It's hot and humid under the blanket with Jackson, and he bumps me several times trying to gain a better position to shoot.

Suddenly, I hear a sharp male voice coming from outside the Explorer. "Drop your keys on the sidewalk, and step out of the vehicle."

Sage unbuckles her seatbelt and removes the keys from the ignition. I hear her drop them onto the concrete, and then she opens the door.

"Slow!" calls the voice. "And keep your hands where I can see them."

Judging by how she reacted to the shootout, Sage is the type who works well under pressure. Still, I can sense her unease as she climbs out of the SUV and raises her hands above her head.

"Name?" shouts the stranger.

"Sage Bishop."

"What's your business here?"

"I'm a friend of Owen Parker. Malcolm needed him for the 112 mission, so he asked me to drop off a delivery."

There's a long pause, and I readjust my grip on my rifle. If this goes bad, I'm prepared to leap up and start shooting. The thought puts a heavy lump in my throat, but if it comes down to it, I won't hesitate to kill a Desperado. This isn't just about protecting Sage and Jackson. It's about saving Sawyer and everyone else back at the compound.

"We're not expecting a shipment for another two weeks," says the man, a slight note of suspicion in his voice.

Sage lets out an exasperated sigh. "I'm just following orders," she says. "I don't know what your agreement was, but you'll have to take it up with Malcolm."

"What did he send?"

My stomach clenches. We weren't sure what supplies would be most convincing to the drifters at the base, so we settled on items that we knew would be in high demand: clean water, ammunition, batteries, and dry goods.

Sage rattles off the list of supplies, and I can practically feel Jackson's mind working. He and I must be thinking the same thing: We might be able to shoot our way out of here, but Sage is highly exposed. One wrong move, and she's as good as dead.

"Well," says the stranger, "we weren't expecting you, but I'm not about to turn down all that ammo — not with all our weaponry being diverted to 112."

I clench my jaw to relieve the surge of aggression I feel at the mention of my home compound.

"Good," says Sage. "Listen . . . It's been a long drive. Can I grab a bite to eat and catch up with you in a bit?"

"Sorry," says the man. "I need you to check in with Carl before I can let you onto the premises. Standard operating procedure. It won't take long. Just pull forward, and we'll get you sorted out."

"Okay," says Sage.

I hear her get back in the front seat and slam the door behind her. She puts the key in the ignition and taps the steering wheel absently. To the casual observer, it would seem like an unconscious gesture of impatience, but it's our signal that the coast is not yet clear.

Sage starts the car and pulls forward, but then someone outside yells something, and she stops.

I wait with bated breath, hoping the drifters don't just throw the doors open and start rifling through the supplies before we have a chance to make our escape.

There's a loud groan that sounds like a metal door, and then nothing.

A few seconds later, Sage messes with the toggles on the side of the steering wheel, and I hear the unmistakable groan of the windshield wipers skidding across dry glass.

That's our signal to move.

Jackson pushes open the door and hops onto the pavement. I wriggle out after him, checking my pockets for ammo and blinking in the brightness as I take in our surroundings.

We're standing outside an open loading bay, waiting for someone to check Sage in. The path inside is unguarded for now, and this might be our only chance.

"Stall!" I whisper.

I don't look back to get a read on Sage's expression, but I know she will do everything she can to buy us some time. I don't know her that well, but I know she's the type of person I want on my team.

Jackson has already disappeared into the loading area, and for a second I worry I may have lost him completely. But then I spot him up ahead, waiting for me behind a forklift.

I know there must be half a dozen drifters lurking nearby who would shoot me as soon as look at me, but right now hesitation is not an option.

We have one chance to get inside and find the cure, and I'm not going to pass it up.

eleven

Harper

My legs feel clumsy and slow as I follow Jackson out of the loading bay. My heart is hammering against my ribcage so hard I can feel it in my throat, and my hands are slippery with sweat.

The storage room is dark and dusty, with endless rows of crates for drifters to lurk behind. There are pallets of food, piles of clothes, and stacks of empty fuel tanks.

Finally, we reach a heavy door that looks as though it could lead to the rest of the casino, and Jackson throws it open. We emerge into a stark employees-only hallway with a dozen or more beige doors. We pass a kitchen and employee break room, but I'm focused on locating the casino's nerve center.

Based on Gunner's description, the casino is too big for us to perform a room-to-room search. Our best bet is to find the room that houses the Desperados' computers, hack into their network, and perform a digital search to find out where the cure is stored.

From what I've seen, Malcolm runs the Desperados like a business. And to keep the gang armed and fed, they must have a system to track the flow of supplies.

Gunner's rough map of the interior is burned into my brain, but we still don't know exactly what we're looking for. Jackson covers me as I duck through every unlocked door, but we don't encounter a single Desperado.

My heart sinks when we reach the last door. I really thought we'd find the Desperados' nerve center in this area, but we've come up empty. Three of the doors we passed were locked, but unless we want every drifter within a two-mile radius to know we're here, we can't risk shooting our way in.

Feeling defeated, I follow Jackson out into the main area of the casino, and my mouth falls open.

We're standing in an enormous lobby covered with loud purple-and-red carpet. The twenty-foot ceiling stretches up into a grand arch hung with glittering light fixtures, and the entire place is outfitted in fake wood and rustic stone accents.

To our left is an enormous escalator, a shopping area, and some kind of restaurant. Our reflections blink back at us from dozens of dark screens, and Jackson explains that these aren't real computers but machines designed specifically for gambling. I find that disappointing, but at least the banks of machines provide some cover as we jog across the casino.

To the right, I spot another employees-only hallway and tug on Jackson's sleeve. He turns to go in that direction, but several distorted voices echo off the high ceiling.

Jackson leaps behind a bank of machines to hide, and I duck down beside him.

I can't tell if the voices are coming from behind us or up ahead, but a moment later, I see two rough-looking men in ripped jeans and T-shirts sidling toward us across the lobby. Judging from their casual pace, they haven't spotted us, but they're going to reach us any minute.

There's nowhere to go except back the way we came, and there's nowhere to hide in the hallway leading back to the loading bay.

Peeking around the corner of a machine, I mentally track a path to the rooms we need to access. The row of nondescript doors is halfway across the lobby, which means we'd either have to run past the drifters or cover about thirty yards of open space around the perimeter.

"You go ahead," murmurs Jackson, following my gaze. "I'll distract them and meet you back here."

"But —"

"We don't have much time," he hisses. "It won't take them long to figure out that Malcolm didn't send Sage."

I hesitate. Splitting up seems like a terrible idea, but there's no time to come up with a better plan.

"Don't worry," he growls. "I can handle these guys."

"Fine," I choke. "Just be careful."

Jackson nods, and I dart out from behind the bank of machines. I don't stop, and I don't look back — I just sprint for the row of enormous pillars along the outer edge of the lobby.

My thighs ache as I push myself forward, and by the time I reach the pillar, my legs are burning with exhaustion.

I stop to catch my breath and glance back to make sure I wasn't spotted. To my horror, I see that the drifters have changed course. They're headed right for me, and it's still ten yards to the nearest door.

Just then, Jackson slinks out of his hiding place, reaches into a shiny gold trashcan, and withdraws an empty beer bottle. In one motion, he reaches over his shoulder and chucks it across the lobby. It flies toward the ceiling in a perfect arch and shatters on the tile floor by the restaurant.

The drifters fall silent. They wheel around in search of the noise and then take off running in the opposite direction.

I lock eyes with Jackson, nod once, and dart out from my hiding place. I fly around the edge of the room toward the first fake-mahogany door and scan the little gold placards for a room that could house the Desperados' computers.

Finally, my eyes latch on to a placard marked "security," and a gunshot cracks the air.

I stumble, ducking down on instinct, and a drifter yells across the lobby. Two more shots fire in quick succession, and I look around for Jackson.

Nothing.

Men are shouting across the casino, but I reach the door marked "security" and pull it open. I run inside without bothering to clear the area, and lights flicker on above me.

I'm standing in a long, narrow room filled with computers and filing cabinets. There are no windows and no other doors — just nine or ten full-sized monitors and two dozen smaller screens.

Back before Death Storm, they must have displayed security feeds for the entire casino, but now these computers probably house data on all the Desperados' operations.

Despite the chaos unfolding in the lobby, my hands are tingling with excitement. I can only imagine how valuable this information would be to the compound, but right now I have to focus on finding the cure.

Breathing hard, I slink over to one of the computers and perch on the edge of a high-backed chair. I tap the keyboard impatiently and wait for the monitor to boot up.

A dialogue box appears asking for a password, and my stomach drops.

I should have expected this. I should have known they would protect their data, but I'd foolishly hoped that the drifters would be just as sloppy with their security as the average compound user.

Not for the first time, I get a pang of homesickness when I think about how easy it would be for Celdon to gain access to the Desperados' computers. Unfortunately, cracking passwords was never my strong suit, so I look around for a pad of paper or a scribbled cheat sheet taped to the wall.

Nothing.

Leaning back, I open the top desk drawer and push aside the pens and stapler. Again, I come up empty.

Shit. The only way to access the drifters' files is going to be a brute-force attack. At best, I have ten incorrect attempts before the system boots me off. At worst, three incorrect passwords will automatically wipe the computer's data and alert the Desperados that they have an intruder.

Wiggling my fingers, I hover over the keyboard and wrack my brain for an easy-to-remember password that would have some significance to the drifters. But before my fingertips even touch the keys, I'm interrupted by a harsh, unwelcome voice.

"Stand up and put your hands where I can see them."

My heart leaps into my throat at the sound of the woman's voice. My fingers freeze over the keyboard, and my back goes ramrod straight.

Out of the corner of my eye, I see a tan arm reach for something at the woman's belt. A weapon? A radio? I can't tell.

"Show me your hands!" she barks.

I wince and raise my arms above my head.

"Good," she murmurs, more to herself than to me. "Now stand up *slowly*."

Breathing deeply, I slide out from the desk and get to my feet.

"Easy!" she yells as I begin to turn, her voice trembling with barely controlled panic.

In that moment, it occurs to me that this woman is more scared than I am. She may be armed, but I still have one advantage.

I'm about to make a grab for my rifle when the woman closes the distance between us and starts to frisk me. Her hands skim over my hips and then brush down my legs as if she's done this before. She finds the knife I keep tucked in my boot, tosses it onto the computer desk, and then pulls me back by a chunk of my hair.

I cry out in pain and strain to escape her grip. I still don't know if she's armed, but if she isn't, my best bet is to overpower her and make a break for the door.

"Okay," she says, releasing my hair roughly. "Turn."

Scalp prickling, I pivot slowly on the spot. The first thing I notice is that the woman has a handgun strapped to her belt.

There goes *that* plan.

But as my gaze drifts up to her face, I get the feeling that my eyes are playing tricks on me.

I've never seen this woman before in my life, and yet there's something familiar about her.

She has to be in her late forties, and she looks tough as hell. She has smooth tan skin, short blond hair, and cheekbones that could cut glass, but it's her eyes that give me pause.

"Who the hell are you?" she barks.

"H-Harper," I choke, desperately trying to come up with a good excuse for walking into a room that's clearly off-limits.

"I don't care what your name is," she says with an impatient clip to her voice. "I just want to know what you're doing in my command center."

"Malcolm sent me," I hear myself say. It's a long shot, but it's the only lie that springs to mind.

The woman's eyebrows narrow in a withering look. "To do *what*?"

"Surveil the compounds," I mumble. "He and his men are headed for 112. I'm supposed to hack into the compound's network and gather intel on their defense."

"Really?"

"Yeah."

I hold my breath and force myself to act normal. I'm not sure if she believes me or not, but at least it's buying me some time.

Maybe if I stall for a few more minutes, it will give Jackson a chance to dispatch the drifters in the lobby and come find me. But then the woman lets out a musical laugh and cracks a smug grin.

"Funny . . . That's my job."

My stomach drops, and my mouth falls open. I search for something to say, but my brain is running on empty.

"You say Malcolm sent you?" she asks sweetly.

I force myself to nod. I know she doesn't believe me, but I already committed to the lie. My only hope is to really sell it.

"Did Malcolm also send the girl down in the supply room?"

I swallow and shake my head. "I don't know anything about a girl," I say, desperate to avoid implicating Sage.

"Really?" she hisses, searching my face with those icy-blue eyes.

I shake my head.

The woman doesn't say anything. She just draws her gun and points it at my head with both hands.

"So why don't you tell me why you're walking around with a compound-issued knife?"

I think I might throw up. *How does she know my knife came from the compound?*

"The *truth* this time," she adds, giving me a look that says she'd have no trouble pulling that trigger.

I let out the breath I've been holding until my chest deflates, running through all the possibilities in my mind. This woman is clearly too smart to believe any of the bullshit I've fed her so far. And now that she's caught the scent of my lie, I have a feeling she isn't going to stop until I spill my guts.

"I'm waiting," she says, releasing the safety.

My heart beats harder, throbbing against my ribcage.

Suddenly, a gunshot out in the lobby makes us both jump.

"What the hell was that?" she yells, her expression shifting quickly from cold and in control to reactive.

I shake my head, hoping desperately that it was the sound of Jackson eliminating a drifter on his way to come find me.

"Tell me what you know — now!" the woman growls.

With nothing left to lose, I decide my best option is to buy myself some time. And the only way to do that is to give this woman a taste of the truth.

"Okay," I whisper. "I'm not . . . I'm not who I said I am."

"Go on."

"I'm not here to hurt anybody," I add quickly.

"You're lying."

"I *swear*."

"Then who the *hell* is shooting out there?"

Her voice doesn't tremble or shake, but I can tell from the wild look in her eyes that she's beginning to panic. We haven't heard anyone return fire, which means either Jackson or one of her men must be dead.

"Listen," I say in a rush. "The reason I came here is because Malcolm introduced a deadly virus to compound 112. It's already infected a bunch of people. If I don't find a cure and *soon*, all those innocent people are going to die."

I hold my breath and listen to the loud *tick* of the clock behind me. The woman is staring at me with wide eyes, but she doesn't say a word.

"These aren't the same people you all have been fighting," I say in an imploring voice. "These are *innocent people.* They don't even know there are survivors out here."

The woman still has her gun pointed at my chest, but her eyes flicker in a way that tells me she's bothered by that information.

I keep going. "I *did* break in here. But I only did it to figure out where Malcolm is keeping the cure."

"That was a big risk," she says evenly.

I nod. "There *has* to be a way to stop this. Otherwise, the epidemic could spread to the Desperados. *You* could get infected. Did you ever think of that?"

There's a long pause as the woman studies my face. I can't tell if she plans to shoot me or help me, but she's definitely working something out.

"You're in Recon, aren't you?" she whispers finally.

"Yes," I sigh. "But I —" I stop. "Wait. How do you know that?"

Of all the drifters I've encountered, I've never heard one refer to Recon by name. Most don't even seem to know that there's a specific section within the compound whose job it is to kill them.

The woman lowers her gun a few inches. "My husband was in Recon."

I shake my head, sure I must have misheard her. "Your *husband?*" I repeat incredulously.

She nods.

"How did you . . . Wait, who is he?"

The woman's eyes are shining with tears, and I can tell this is something she hasn't shared with anyone in a very long time. "His name was Albert Reynolds."

"Albert Rey —" I shake my head. "Did you say *Reynolds*?"

"Yes. My name is Robin Reynolds, and I used to live in compound 112."

"*No*."

My brain is still reeling from shock. This whole situation feels too bizarre to be real.

"What is it?" she asks, her voice much gentler now.

"You're *her*, aren't you?" I ask. Then I realize she probably has no idea what I'm babbling about. Judging from the look on her face, I must sound absolutely insane.

"Your son . . ." I begin, fighting a smile. "Is your son Celdon Reynolds?"

At the mention of Celdon, her expression changes completely. Her cool-blue eyes soften, and the harsh line of her mouth goes slack.

"Y-yes," she murmurs. "How do you —?"

"Celdon's one of my best friends," I choke, utterly shocked that I'm standing across from his long-lost mother — the mother he thought abandoned him out on the Fringe all those years ago. The mother he joined Constance to find.

"Oh my god."

Robin looks just as stunned as I feel, and it takes me a moment to circle back to the original point of our conversation.

"My other best friend is infected," I say quickly. "I have to find the cure."

For a moment, I'm not sure how Robin is going to react. Just because Celdon is her son doesn't mean her loyalties lie with the compound. There had to be a reason she left and started working for Malcolm.

Robin nods and looks away. As she lowers her gun, I feel

a question that's been bothering me for years bubble up to the surface and burst out of my mouth. "Why did you leave him?"

Robin's eyes frost over almost immediately, and I hurry to revise my question so it sounds a little less judgmental.

"I mean . . . how did you end up out here? And why would you —" I break off, realizing there's no nice way to phrase the rest of my question.

"Why would I leave my infant son alone out in the desert?" she finishes.

I nod.

"Like I said . . . Celdon's father was in Recon. *I* worked in Systems."

I raise both my eyebrows. A Recon operative marrying a Systems worker is unheard of.

"I'll spare you the messy details of how Albert and I came to be married," she says in a breezy voice. "I'm sure I don't have to tell you that the Recon leaders weren't happy about it."

Her expression hardens, and her eyes drift over my shoulder. "They sent my husband out on a mission meant to kill him, and that mission succeeded."

Robin lets out a low, humorless laugh. "My marriage was deemed invalid, and they told me my son was legally a bastard. They wanted to take him away from me to be raised by a guardian in the Institute. They wanted to punish me for what Albert and I had done."

Horror washes over me as Robin's story unfolds. A year ago, I never would have believed that Recon would purposely send out one of its own to die, but now I have no trouble believing it at all.

"I did the only thing I could think of," she says. "I fled. I took Celdon to the city, not knowing that's where the radiation was the worst." She shakes her head. "He got very sick. So did I."

So Celdon *doesn't* have the gene mutations for radiation resistance. Robin must not have them either, but she had the genetic pedigree to secure her son a place in Systems.

"I started to recover when we moved out of the hot zone," Robin continues. "Celdon did not."

"So you brought him back," I whisper.

She nods. "He was just a baby. I couldn't let him die." Her mouth begins to quiver, and I can tell she's on the verge of tears. "I knew I couldn't ever go back there — not after I'd deserted. I would have been killed on sight. But Celdon . . . I knew they would want him. They were bringing in kids from the Fringe, and he had good genes. My husband had a friend in Recon who'd always looked out for me, so . . . I contacted him and made the arrangements."

"Who?" I ask.

She shakes her head. "It doesn't matter. I expect he's long dead by now. No one lasts long in Recon." Robin lets out a sigh and looks at her hands. "It's hard to believe I've survived out here for more than twenty years. But if I had to do it over again . . . I don't think I ever would have left."

"You would have stayed after Recon killed your husband?" I whisper.

"I would rather have stayed and watched my son grow up at a distance than go twenty years without seeing him once," she says. "Now I'll probably die before I can ever fix things between us."

"There's still time," I say, feeling an unexpected surge of sympathy for the woman who'd been holding a gun to my head just minutes ago.

She shakes her head. "Twenty years out here is like fifty in there," she says. "Malcolm's doctor says I have cancer . . . and there's nothing they can do about it."

My heart sinks. "Maybe if you came back to the compound . . ."

Robin fixes me with a sad, sympathetic look. "What? You think they'd treat me? After everything I've done?"

I open my mouth to speak but then decide against it. We both know how things work in the compound. We know what would happen to a deserter turned Desperado.

"I never wanted this to happen," she mutters suddenly, looking up at me with haunted eyes. "When Malcolm offered me his protection, I knew it would come with strings, of course, but . . ." She shudders. "I never thought he'd use me to murder thousands of innocent people. I never thought he'd make me a killer."

That statement feels like a knife to the heart, but suddenly I feel angry rather than sad for her. Robin may have had a shitty life, but she has made a pile of shitty decisions. And instead of trying to fix her mistakes, she's passively gone along with all of Malcolm's despicable schemes.

"Celdon gave up everything for you," I say in a harsh voice. "He joined Constance so he could find out what *happened* to you."

She looks as though she might be sick, but I push down any feelings of remorse. I refuse to let her off the hook just because she might be dying.

"You have to make this right."

"How?" she asks, her eyes shimmering with tears.

"By helping me undo all this shit Malcolm has done," I whisper. "*Please.* Just help me find the cure, and you can put a stop to all this."

For a moment, I think my words might have moved her. Robin's tears dry up, and her expression turns serious.

"It's not that simple," she whispers, biting down on the

inside of her cheek. "Ever since I found out about the virus, I've been scouring our system for any information about a cure. I've called in a lot of favors and asked questions I have no business asking."

"And?"

"If there was a cure, I would have found it." She lets out a heavy sigh. "As far as I can tell, Malcolm never had any intention of stopping this virus."

twelve

Sawyer

The worst part about being in isolation is the way one hour bleeds into the next. I have no way to mark time in the windowless room. I have no way to know when another day has slipped between my fingers, bringing me twenty-four hours closer to death.

It's fucking depressing, really.

The only thing that keeps me focused is monitoring my symptoms and making a mental note of where I am in the virus's progression. All the nurses flitting in and out of my room in their green hazmat suits are doing the exact same thing, but some egotistical part of my brain is holding on to the idea that they're going to miss something and fuck up the data they're using to put a timeline on the outbreak.

So far, I've only experienced the wheezing and coughing and a body-numbing fatigue that keeps my limbs glued to the bed. With every nurse's visit, my head seems to sink deeper into my cheap foam pillow. It's only a matter of time before my entire body turns to mush.

I hope I don't look as bad as Caleb. His normally ruddy complexion has turned the color of oatmeal, making his strawberry-blond hair look practically orange. He talks less and wheezes more, and we spend most of the day in tired silence.

Only his vibrant green eyes look exactly the same. In the days we've been quarantined together, my only joy has been making him laugh. I've only done it a couple of times — both at the expense of the nurses — but those little comments made his eyes light up and sparkle the way they did before we were sick. I miss that laugh.

I'm about to fall into a light sleep when a knock on the door shakes me out of my stupor. The sound is muffled by the airtight door, but it gets my attention.

"Come in," I croak, shocked by the raspy quality of my voice.

The door swings open slowly, and a petite woman in a hazmat suit shuffles in. Her face is blurred by condensation on her mask, but I can tell she has dark skin and delicate features.

Ignoring the weakness spreading down my arms, I press the button by my pillow to raise the top of my bed to a sixty-degree angle. With an enormous burst of effort, I hoist my butt half an inch off the bed and scoot it toward the crease in the mattress.

"Good afternoon, Miss Lyang," says the woman. Her voice is clear and friendly — the voice all Health and Rehab workers use to talk to patients — but I don't recognize it.

"Hey," I murmur, squinting through her face shield to get a better look.

The woman has a smooth ebony complexion, full lips, and beautiful brown eyes. She's got her hair done up in six or eight braids that snake along the side of her head, and she's gathered them together in a neat updo to accommodate the hood of the suit.

"My name is Angela Starks. I'm a specialist working in Progressive Research, and I'll be overseeing your treatment from this point forward," she says.

I feel a pang of dread in my stomach. If they're changing up my care, that must mean I've passed the point of no return.

"I'm not dead yet," I mutter, blinking back a small annoying trickle of tears.

I look over at Caleb, who's still fast asleep, and get an overpowering sense of hopelessness.

"Exactly," says Angela. "I'm actually here to discuss some options you have for the rest of your time with us."

"Is *not dying* an option?" I ask bitterly.

Angela takes a deep breath. When she speaks next, her voice is low and careful, as if she's worried she might say more than she should. "Miss Lyang . . . given your position in Health and Rehab and your . . . *specialized knowledge* of this virus . . . you know better than most patients what the progression and outlook are."

I want to roll my eyes, but the phrase "specialized knowledge" instantly piques my interest. It sounds as if she knows about the records from 119 — and she knows that *I* know, too.

"It isn't good," I say, purposely keeping my language vague to force her to reveal what she knows.

She doesn't take the bait.

"Exactly. You and the rest of the staff members afflicted with the virus are in the unique position of being able to weigh the likely outcome against the risks of some more . . . *experimental* treatment options."

I narrow my gaze, unsure what she's getting at. "Caleb's Health and Rehab, too," I say quietly. "He should hear this."

"Of course."

I turn around and reach across the space separating our beds. I can't quite touch him, so I hoist myself out of bed and sink down next to him. As my weight shifts the mattress, Caleb stirs and slowly opens his eyes.

He blinks several times before focusing on me. "Hey," he murmurs, breaking into a weak smile.

"Hey."

He's still oblivious to the fact that we have company, so I clear my throat and glance over at our visitor.

"This is Angela," I say. "She's from Progressive Research."

"Hey," says Caleb. His tone is friendly enough, but I can detect a note of unease in his voice. Judging by the look on Caleb's face, he doesn't recognize Angela, either, but he sits up in bed as if he senses the importance of her visit.

"She came in to talk to us about our treatment options," I say.

"Options? I thought we only had one option."

Angela looks extremely uncomfortable, so I decide to cut to the chase.

"If you read the same files I did, you know Bartrizol didn't do much to slow the virus down or alleviate the symptoms," I say quietly.

Caleb nods. "I'd rather not spend my last few days nauseous, itchy, and constipated, if it's all the same to you."

"Bartrizol is one option," says Angela in an even voice, unfazed by Caleb's snarky tone. "But you're right. We haven't seen much success with that treatment, and some people do experience nasty side effects. I'm sure you're aware that the main reason they kept administering it was to reassure the public that they were trying *something*."

I let out an exasperated sigh. So far this woman isn't inspiring much confidence.

"Another option is one they didn't try at 119. Progressive Research has been working on it for some time, but the treatment hasn't undergone the necessary clinical trials."

I sit up a little straighter. It may be a long shot, but this sounds much more promising.

"What is it?" I ask, careful not to betray my small surge of hope.

"It's a new form of immunotherapy," says Angela.

"Like the cure for ebola?" asks Caleb.

"Not exactly. More like the treatment for HSV-1."

"How does it work?"

"By stimulating your immune system, we hope to get your body to fight off the virus on its own. The goal is to induce your immunological memory so that you'll have continual protection after we've stopped treatment."

I nod and look at Caleb. We both understand the basic theory of immunotherapy from higher ed, but it sounds almost too good to be true.

"It's the most promising treatment option we have," says Angela. "But you should still prepare yourselves for the possibility that you'll get worse before you get better. And of course there's a chance it may not work at all."

"Well, it's gotta be better than not doing anything," says Caleb, sounding more enthusiastic than he has in days.

I expect Angela to nod, but she hesitates. "I have to warn you: There is a chance that your symptoms will get drastically worse. And you may develop a host of new symptoms as well." She pauses. "To do this, we'd need to introduce another virus to your system that's similar — one that your body knows how to fight. Our hope is that it will begin to recognize the 119 virus as that familiar virus and fight it as well."

"We can handle it," I say, meeting Caleb's gaze.

Neither one of us has much time if we don't do *something*.

Angela seems satisfied with our answer, but then Caleb asks the obvious question that's been bouncing around in my head. "Why didn't they ever try this at 119?"

Angela shifts uncomfortably. "The board wanted to keep news of 119's troubles under wraps."

"But you knew," I say sharply. "Progressive Research *knew*."

She gives a noncommittal nod. "We were approached by the board once the situation turned dire."

"And you didn't *do* anything?" Caleb snaps.

"This particular therapy was developed under lock and key in our branch of Progressive Research," says Angela slowly. "We share a lot of medical knowledge among the compounds, but proprietary drugs and treatments are not included under that umbrella."

"Why the hell not?"

Angela sighs. "When any compound develops a new drug, it sells that drug to the other compounds. The profits from those drugs all funnel back into Progressive Research, which is where we get our funding to develop new treatments."

"And 119 wouldn't buy it?"

"It wasn't ready to go to market. And by the time we realized the severity of the epidemic, most patients at 119 were too immunocompromised to benefit from the treatment anyway."

I let out a snort of derisive laughter and shake my head, hands trembling with rage. "You guys wanted to wait to release the drug until it was most *profitable*?"

"We wanted to wait until we knew it would work," says Angela.

"But you still don't know if it will work," says Caleb.

"Which is why we are only offering it to those who can truly appreciate the risks," she says. "I'm sure you both realize that springing an untested treatment on a desperate public goes against every oath we take in Health and Rehab. An adverse reaction on that scale would be *disastrous* for our reputation. When our reputation suffers, we lose funding, and people die."

"People have already died," I say angrily.

"Miss Lyang, we are *all* desperate to stop this virus. But we simply cannot move forward with this treatment until we've done the proper tests."

She takes a deep breath, looking from me to Caleb with clear frustration in her eyes. When she speaks again, her voice is softer but still fierce. "You two could be a part of something *big* — something that saves lives."

I let out an infuriated huff and fall back against Caleb's pillow. I've wanted to be in Health and Rehab all my life, and as soon as I learned about Progressive Research, I had to earn a place there. But finding out that all the researchers I admire stood by while thousands of people grew sick and died is more than I can handle.

I don't know if I believe in that dream anymore. It seems to be less about saving lives and more about turning a profit.

"Should I take it that you're willing to undergo treatment?" asks Angela.

"Sign me up," I grumble, too disgusted by my own naïveté to be truly angry at her.

Caleb nods and meets her gaze with a look of cool resolve. "What else have I got to do?"

thirteen

Eli

I don't know how long I've been lying unconscious in the dirt.

The aches in my body throb in and out, and every bruise and abrasion feels as if it has its own heartbeat. Blood oozes from my wounds and then hardens to a crusty coating.

A bird of prey rustles nearby, and then I feel the prick of a beak on the back of my neck. I shift just enough to shoo the bird away, and a sharp burst of pain erupts in my side.

Even the birds think I ought to be dead.

I squeeze my eyes shut to block out the blinding sun, but a moment later, all my senses are awakened by the slow shuffle of approaching footsteps.

It could be one of Malcolm's men who fled in the shooting, or it could be someone from Recon.

Somewhere in the back of my mind, that old sense of urgency stirs. I'm ready to die — ready to surrender — but my body is still hardwired to survive. I need to move.

Gritting my teeth against the pain, I pull myself into a seated position and prepare to fight with whatever strength I have left.

Suddenly, the footsteps stop. A shadow passes over my above-ground grave, blocking out the worst of the sun.

"Shit," says a voice from behind me.

I whip around to face the intruder, and my injured ribs scream in protest.

"Fuck!" I hiss.

A pair of legs appear in front of me: bony knees, frayed jeans, and a pair of scuffed white skater shoes.

"Jesus," says the intruder, bending down to inspect my injuries.

Gunner's face swims slowly into view. His eyes are wide and horrified, and his hair is plastered to his forehead with blood. He's got a nasty cut over his right eye, and his lip is split where his piercing used to be.

"I thought you were dead," I choke.

"You thought *I* was dead?" he splutters. "How the fuck are *you* still alive?"

I shake my head. It doesn't matter. Somehow I'm still here, and the Desperados are waging war against the compound.

As Gunner helps me into a standing position, my mind goes automatically to Kindra. Her body is lying just a few yards away, crumpled in the dirt like a soggy newspaper.

It wasn't me the vulture was after. It was her.

With Gunner supporting most of my weight, I stumble over to where Kindra fell and drop to my knees beside her.

Kindra's skin is already pale and lifeless, and her hair seems too bright to be real. Her eyes are half closed, and her mouth is soft and open.

Kindra's child-sized feet are stuffed into the smallest pair of combat boots Recon stocks, and her hands don't even look large enough to hold a rifle. If it weren't for the line of dried blood running from the hole in her head to her chin, one might think she was just daydreaming.

"Who was she?" Gunner asks.

"Her name was Kindra," I choke, not really sure why I'm telling him. "She was one of my cadets."

But she wasn't just my cadet, I think. *She was my responsibility.*

I was supposed to train her. I was supposed to teach her

everything I could and make sure she was prepared for battle. And if I ended up out on the Fringe with her, it was my duty to protect her at all costs.

I failed her worse than I failed any of my other cadets.

"Malcolm killed her?" Gunner whispers.

I nod.

"Shit. I'm sorry."

I shake my head, wishing there was something I could do to make her death a little less gruesome.

Kindra didn't deserve to die like this. She wasn't cut out to fight drifters. She had no business being out here in the first place.

Kindra grew up watching her grandmother do palm readings in the commissary, and that's what she'd planned on doing until Bid Day. At least that's what Harper told me. I never heard it from Kindra herself because I never really tried to get to know her.

Struck by a strange, desperate surge of inspiration, I scoop my hands under her arms and try to get us both off the ground.

"Help me with her," I gasp.

Gunner is looking at me as though I've gone insane, but he helps me lift Kindra off the ground and carry her away from the road.

There isn't much out here — just dirt, rocks, and desert plants for miles. So we carry Kindra to the nearest clump of sagebrush and lay her down on the ground.

It isn't a perfect grave, but it's peaceful. And when night falls, she'll be gazing up at real stars for the first time in her life.

"We have to go," I say, swallowing down the lump in my throat and tearing my eyes away from Kindra.

"Go?" repeats Gunner. "Go where?"

"To the compound," I say in a low voice. "The plan hasn't

changed."

Gunner's eyes bug out for a second, and he makes a show of looking me up and down. "Um . . . I think it has."

I shoot him a cold glare, silently daring him to try to stop me. "I'm going after Owen," I say. "And I'll kill any Desperado who gets in my way."

"You want to go chase down the guys who just beat the shit out of you?" Gunner lets out an incredulous bark of laughter. "You can hardly *walk*."

I jerk my chin up in defiance, trying not to show how much that tiny movement pains me. "I can walk."

"You're gonna get yourself killed."

"Well, who gives a fuck?" I snap, moving gingerly to start the impossibly steep trek back up the hill to the road.

"I'm sure Harper does!"

"Shut up!" I yell without looking back.

"What are you gonna do if Malcolm's guys see you?"

"I guess I'll be like, 'Hey, motherfuckers . . . How the hell are ya?'"

Gunner doesn't say anything.

After a few minutes, I start to worry that he walked off and left me high and dry. But by the time I reach the road and glance back behind me, I see him following me up the hill, shaking his head in disbelief.

"Fine," he grumbles as he passes me. "Let's go."

Under any other circumstances, I can't imagine feeling grateful that a shrimpy little punk agreed to accompany me on a suicide mission. But right now Gunner is all I've got, and I desperately need his help.

When we reach the restaurant parking lot, Gunner heads straight for the cluster of abandoned vehicles, and I start picking through the rubble in the hope of finding a weapon.

I'm terrified I'm going to find the body of another dead Recon cadet, but I don't. The ground is littered with bullet casings and three dead drifters, but I don't see any gray fatigues.

I finally manage to get my hands on one automatic rifle and a handgun. Then, off in the distance, I hear the reluctant sputter of an engine. Gunner must be trying to hot-wire one of the abandoned trucks, but it sounds as though the vehicle is putting up a fight.

The engine roars to life, filling the parking lot with a high-pitched whistling sound. I look around to see what vehicle he managed to resurrect, and my mouth falls open.

Gunner is driving a battered blue Crown Victoria. It's missing one of its doors and three of its hubcaps, and it sounds as though it's got a wild animal stuck under the hood. I groan.

I can't imagine how we're going to creep up to the compound in this old junker, but right now it's our only option.

Moving like a zombie, I bend down to give my head room to clear the door and slowly lower myself into the passenger seat.

"Here," I say, sliding the handgun across the center console.

"Thanks," murmurs Gunner, giving the dashboard a reassuring pat and glancing over at me. "What do you think?"

"I think it's a miracle it still runs," I say, taking in the duct tape holding the driver-side door together and the mess of wires dangling from the steering wheel column.

"I know, right?"

Gunner hits the gas, and the handgun slides off the console onto the floor.

Gunner never even picked it up to check if it was loaded, and I realize with a start that I've never actually seen him shoot a gun.

"You ready?" he asks, looking as though he'd rather be *anywhere* but here.

"Just drive."

Right now, I'm not worrying about the Desperados. I'm not worrying about the car or how we're going to get to the compound without being seen. I just have one thing propelling me forward: saving my brother and escaping the compound alive.

The drive back to 112 is the most miserable car ride I've ever experienced. The Crown Victoria wasn't built for off-roading in the desert, and the car must have taken some hits in the shootout at the restaurant.

The engine sputters and smokes as we push farther into the desert, and when the sun hits the dirty old upholstery, the smell of animal urine nearly bowls me over. Even with all the windows rolled down, the stench is overwhelming, and the heat makes everything worse.

Within five minutes, my T-shirt is soaked with sweat, and my damp jeans are stuck to my skin. Looking down at our dirty drifter clothes, I realize that the only way we're going to get inside the compound is if we're dressed as Recon operatives.

I left my uniform back at camp, so I direct Gunner toward one of the checkpoints on the edge of town. Stopping will add a few minutes to our journey, but it's the only way we're going to get within a mile of the compound without being shot or blown up.

To distract myself from the pee smell, I yank down the battered sun visor to survey the damage from Malcolm's men.

Now I understand why Gunner thought I was crazy for wanting to follow the Desperados. My face looks as though someone shoved my head in a blender with a handful of gravel and rusty nails. My lip is split, both eyes are black, and all the fleshy parts of my face are the color and texture of raw hamburger.

"How do you feel?" Gunner asks.

"Better than I look, I guess," I say, giving my nose a tender poke.

"Well, that's good . . . because you look like shit."

"I shouldn't have stopped," I mutter, thinking of the drifter shootout and the moment I signed Kindra's death certificate.

"What?"

"Back at the restaurant . . . Malcolm asked me to cover him. I didn't."

"*Yeeeeah.* I didn't think that was an accident."

"He yelled at me to shoot, but then I saw Kindra and I . . . I just froze."

"What happened to her wasn't your fault," says Gunner in a sympathetic voice.

I shake my head. "Malcolm saw the whole thing. He must have figured I knew her somehow. That's why he killed her."

"Maybe," says Gunner. "But you can't blame yourself, man. Malcolm's fucking nuts. You can never predict what he's gonna do."

Of course Gunner is right, but my mind keeps spinning out of control. If I hadn't stopped in that parking lot — if I'd covered Malcolm like he asked — he never would have turned that truck around to hunt down Kindra. She would have escaped with nothing more than a few scrapes and bruises, and I might be at the compound by now.

"Stop it," says Gunner, correctly interpreting my silence. "You're gonna drive yourself crazy. I know you're thinkin' about what you could've done different to save that girl, but it's not doin' nobody any good."

I don't say anything. I keep my gaze focused on the horizon to avoid betraying my tangled mess of emotions.

"I've been there, ya know," he continues. "When my moms died . . . and when they shot my cousin . . ."

I swallow uncomfortably and breathe through my mouth. I wish he wouldn't have said anything. Hearing Gunner's sad story isn't going to make me feel any better. Everyone alive today has some kind of sad story, but no matter how many you listen to, you still have to live through your own.

Gunner falls silent, but the awkward weight of his confession hangs in the air. I don't want to know what happened to his family, but it seems cruel not to ask.

"What happened to them? Your mom and your cousin."

"My cousin Barry was shot by someone from the compounds," says Gunner in a rush. "My moms lived through all the radiation and shit after Death Storm, but then winter came and she ended up dyin' from pneumonia."

He shakes his head. I can tell not many people have bothered to ask Gunner about his life before now, and he's starved for someone to talk to.

"It's fuckin' crazy . . ." he continues. "I guess you never know what's gonna get you."

"Yeah . . ."

"I keep thinkin' I should've died a long time ago," he says brightly. "But like my step-dad used to say, you can't kill lazy and stupid."

"I don't think you're lazy and stupid," I mutter. "Anyone who's survived this long can't be *that* stupid."

Gunner quirks both eyebrows and lets out a snort of laughter. "Nah. The only reason I'm still alive is 'cause I joined up with Malcolm's crew." He gives me a serious look. "That's the way he is, you know? He'd take a bullet for you today . . . turn around and shoot ya tomorrow."

"I have to stop him."

"Yeah . . . You and what army?"

I don't know what to say to that. Gunner's no battle strategist, but he's right about Malcolm. The Desperados outnumber Recon eight to one. Unless we can somehow get the rest of the sections to stand with us to defend the compound, we won't be able to keep Malcolm's men at bay for long.

I've only visited this particular checkpoint a couple times in my life, so it takes lots of circling to find it without an interface. The entire area is overgrown with sage and stubby little cacti, but I find the spigot protruding from the brush. The drifters already sealed the checkpoint on the other side of town, but this one is still operational.

I pry open the trapdoor without much trouble and lower myself into the hole to retrieve a couple of fresh Recon uniforms. They smell a little musty from being buried so long, but at least they'll provide some camouflage.

"Uh-uh," says Gunner when I try to hand him the smaller one. "I'm not wearin' that."

"It's the only way we're getting anywhere near the compound," I say, giving the wad of fabric an impatient shake.

"I'm not wearin' that shit," he repeats, more emphatically this time. "No, sir. I'll die first."

Frustrated, I toss the uniform on the ground and use both hands to pull myself out of the trench.

"Have it your way," I growl. "But don't blame me when you get a hot piece of lead in your ass just because you were too proud to put on a damn uniform."

Turning away, I strip off my sweat-soaked T-shirt and pull on the fresh black one. The fatigue pants are much lighter than my jeans, and even the gray overshirt isn't bad.

I'd be ashamed to admit it to Gunner, but I instantly feel more like myself. There's no love lost between me and Recon, but it's all I've ever known. I'm Lieutenant Parker through and through, whether I'm in uniform or not.

With a pang of regret, I ball up my old pair of jeans and toss them into the hole. Then I close up the hatch, and we get back into the car to continue our journey to the compound.

Before we're even a mile out, I hear the rapid volley of gunfire and the rumble of destruction. If I squint, I can just barely see the blurred outline of vehicles fanning out around the perimeter.

The Crown Vic coasts to a stop, and I look over at Gunner.

"Wasn't me," he says, holding up his hands and staring at the dash. "We're out of fuel."

"Doesn't matter," I mumble. "We can't exactly drive up to the fence."

"So what's our move?" asks Gunner, getting out and slamming the creaky door behind him.

I sigh. "We wait."

"What?"

"It's too late to warn them now. The Desperados are already at the perimeter. We'll go when it's dark. That's the only way we're gonna make it without getting ourselves killed."

Gunner nods but doesn't say anything. I know he thinks we're going to die anyway. What I don't know is why he's going along with my plan. I barely know this kid, but he's resigned himself to die by my side.

As the sounds of grenades and gunfire echo in the distance,

a deep sense of dread takes root in the pit of my stomach. We're too far away to tell who's winning or how many of my friends have died, and it kills me to be standing on the wrong side of the battle lines while Miles, Lenny, and Bear fight for their lives.

The only thing that soothes my anxiety is the knowledge that Harper is hundreds of miles away, safe from the bullets and the bombs. If she were with me right now, I'd be out of my mind with worry.

As the afternoon sun beats down, I clench my jaw and turn my thoughts to Owen.

I have one chance to save my brother — one chance to make things right. To do so, I'll have to get past the Desperados, over the fence, into the compound, and up to Constance.

I know it's going to take everything I have — maybe more — but I've already made up my mind: I'm leaving the compound with my brother, or I'm leaving in a body bag.

fourteen

Celdon

A hard shiver rocks through me as I take the stairs from Systems to Information. Nearly every Systems worker is at home, yet the long white tunnels are practically empty.

Since the outbreak, they've all locked themselves in their compartments to avoid exposure. They're probably glued to their interfaces, watching the rate of infection tick steadily upward as the virus takes hold in tier two.

Information is like a different world. Frenzied reporters sprint from one room to the next, gathering information and comparing figures before running back to the bullpen to put together more news footage.

Information is the one section besides Health and Rehab where viral outbreaks and drifter attacks are good for business.

I've never visited the retiree wing before. The walls are the same uniform shade of black, and each door is marked with a silver placard with the name of the person who lives there.

I walk all the way down to the end of the tunnel and stop in front of the last door. This plaque doesn't have a name. It just says "Founder Suite." If I weren't looking for it, my eyes would have skimmed over it without a second thought. But if Devon's instructions are correct, I'm about to enter the compartment of Constance's leader, Ozias Pirro.

I've never met Ozias. I've only ever heard his voice coming through a speaker — once during a meeting and once before

Devon killed Jayden. I'm not sure why Ozias wants to see me, but you don't ignore a summons from Constance's leader.

Swallowing down my nerves, I give the door two good knocks. At first I hear nothing, but a moment later, I'm greeted with a raspy "come in."

I half expect to step into a top-secret office hidden behind a false wall, but when I turn the silver door handle and step inside, I realize that this really is Ozias's home.

I'm standing in a narrow hallway with a black-and-white tile floor and a towering nine-foot ceiling. The foyer is lined with buttery wood trim the color of dark chocolate, which has been buffed and polished to a perfect shine. On one side hangs a five-foot mirror in an ornate silver frame. On the other, a ceiling-to-floor glass case displays a collection of pre–Death Storm memorabilia.

"Come in," repeats Ozias, much more forcefully this time.

I swallow and snap the door closed behind me.

My footsteps echo loudly in the cramped hallway, but when I reach the end, I see that Ozias's study is decked out in the same pre–Death Storm style: lush burgundy carpet, enormous leather armchairs, and bookshelves constructed from identical dark wood.

Ozias is sitting in a high-backed chair holding a glass of scotch in one hand and a vape pen in the other. He has ancient-looking skin the color of rust and a white beard that frames his face like a lion's mane. His long gray eyebrows jut out from his temples in sharp peaks, adding to his vaguely feline appearance.

"Are they . . .?" I gesture to the bookcases.

"Real?"

I nod.

"Why, yes. Yes, they are," says Ozias proudly. "The books and the shelves."

"Wow." I've never even held a physical book before, and all furniture manufactured in the compound is made from vegetable fiber or recycled plastic.

"Trees are too valuable to be made into books and furniture," he continues. "But back when the compound was first built . . ."

"You're really one of the original founders?"

"Yes," says Ozias. "I came here when I was twenty-eight years old. Back then I was an out-of-work reporter with a very expensive college education and too much time on my hands." He laughs. "I suppose that must sound like a very long time ago, but to me it seems like it was only yesterday."

I raise an eyebrow. If Ozias helped establish the compound in his late twenties, he has to be pushing ninety.

"See those papers over there?" He points over to the fireplace, where three skinny golden frames are hanging over the hearth. Inside each frame is an old print newspaper. "Take a look."

I hesitate. I didn't come here for a history lesson, but I can't deny that I'm curious.

Padding over to the mantel, I see that the frames do contain old news articles, carefully preserved behind glass and arranged in chronological order.

The first is a *Salt Lake Tribune* article with a photo showing a group of young men and women smiling coyly at the camera. It's a piece about a group of preppers, survivalists, and New-Age nuts constructing a utopian megaplex out in the desert with the headline "Doomsday Enthusiasts Expand Operation."

The paper in the middle was a front-page story titled "Failed Experiment or Post-Apocalyptic Safe Haven?" It has a picture of the completed compound and a smaller photo of the founders gathered in a laboratory. I recognize Ozias by his crazy eyebrows, but he's got shaggy brown hair and a soul patch.

Finally, my eyes drift over to the last clipping, which is another front-page story dated smack dab in the middle of Death Storm: "Survivalists Shut Out Desperate Civilians."

"It took an epic disaster for those morons to take us seriously," says Ozias.

I jump. He's standing right behind me, reading the news stories over my shoulder. I hold back a shudder and try to breathe normally as he points his vape pen at the very first clipping.

"When I told my old colleagues that I was testing to be one of the compound's starter citizens, they laughed in my face." He raises one wiry eyebrow. "People thought I'd gone off the deep end."

I turn to look at him, trying to picture a twentysomething Ozias as a young, idealistic reporter trying to make history.

"*I* was the crazy one . . . even though we were already in the lead-up to full-scale nuclear war. U.S. relations with the rest of the world were as tense as they'd been since the Cold War. We were headed for annihilation, but people refused to *believe*."

I don't say anything. I'm too fascinated to interrupt.

"My friends stopped returning my calls. I was disinvited from professional events. My own *brother* called to tell me that I shouldn't come to Thanksgiving that year because it would upset my parents."

He shakes his head. "Years later, my brother sent me a message *begging* to be admitted to the compound. They'd just bombed Salt Lake City, and he and my sister-in-law had nowhere else to go. Of course, by that point, my hands were tied. We were restricting admittance to only the best the world had to offer." Ozias shrugs. "We could take our pick."

I swallow down the sick feeling rising up in my throat. He actually sounds *happy* about it. He's proud of what he's done.

"I won't bore you with any more ancient history," he says, waving a dismissive hand. "I did not invite you here to listen to an old man's stories."

"Why *did* you ask me to come?"

Ozias takes a deep breath and meets my gaze with fiery eyes. "Mr. Reynolds, you are one of our newest members, and yet I see a level of devotion in you that I wish I could elicit from all our members." He smiles. "You remind me of my younger self."

That comment causes a kick of discomfort in my gut, but I concentrate on keeping my expression neutral.

"Because of the dedication you've shown so far, I feel I can trust you."

"Okay . . ."

"Can I be frank with you, Mr. Reynolds?"

I nod quickly, too numb to refuse.

"When we first got wind of the outbreak at 119, we did everything we could to ensure that the virus would never reach us here. We had a front-row seat to the devastation, and we knew we were unprepared for an outbreak of that scale."

My heart sinks. I can't help but think of Sawyer, curled up in bed and slipping closer and closer to death.

"Now that the virus has reached critical mass, we have no way of stopping it. We have some experimental treatments in the works, but a cure won't come fast enough to help some of the infected."

He sighs. "It's no accident that the drifters chose *now* to launch their attack. They've seen this virus progress before, and they know we are weak right now."

Ozias falls silent for a moment, and I sense he's deciding whether to tell me everything or soften the edges of what he's about to say.

"So far we've been able to keep this under our hats, but you should know . . . We're all that is left of civilized society in the Southwest."

"What are you saying?"

"I'm saying that all our neighbors to the south and east have already fallen. If we don't act now, the drifters will destroy everything we have worked so hard to preserve. And they won't stop with us. They'll continue moving west until they've demolished all the compounds along the coast."

"What does that have to do with me?" I ask.

Ozias runs one gnarled hand over the edge of the mantel and feels for dust between his fingers. "Recon can't hold them off forever. There are too many of them. Our only hope now is to persuade our enemies to lay down their weapons before we're forced to surrender . . . And the only way to do that is through psychological warfare."

"I don't understand," I murmur. "They have us right where they want us. They aren't going to give up their position — not now."

"You're right," says Ozias, raising an eyebrow. "But there's one big problem everyone faces when they find themselves in the position of advantage."

If speaking in cryptic sentences was a sport, Ozias would be the undefeated champion. I raise both eyebrows and lean forward, waiting for him to spit it out.

"When you have everything to lose, you will always face a threat from those who have *nothing* to lose."

There's a long, drawn-out silence. I'm starting to see where he's going with this, but he still hasn't given me any sort of to-do list. It all just sounds like the enigmatic rambling of a crazy old man.

"So what do they have to lose?" I ask.

"*That* is an excellent question."

Ozias begins to pace, stopping every once in a while to admire the artwork hanging on his walls. I'm starting to think he just invited me here so he would have someone to talk to, but then he stops and turns around excitedly.

"Drifters are like cockroaches. Kill one, and two more spring up to take its place. The leaders don't care how many of their people die, but if the people lost one of their leaders . . . If they saw that we had the ability to capture and kill them at will . . . It could have a chilling effect on their campaign of violence."

"Sir?"

Ozias's eyes flash in excitement, and I get a pang of dread.

"We may not have Malcolm Martinez, but we do have the next best thing."

I stumble out of Ozias's compartment in a daze.

As long and drawn out as his diabolical plan seemed in the moment, the logistics are incredibly straightforward. Ozias's idea is just as sick as I expected, but I'm still a little stunned as I make my way back up to Systems.

What he's asking me to do isn't the worst part. I'm just the messenger, really — a single performer in Constance's circus of human suffering. Still, I'm crucial to Ozias's plan, and I have a plan of my own.

To pull it off, I'll have to go along with this sick charade, which will destroy any chance I might have had of putting this nightmare behind me.

As soon as I do my part, a whole new nightmare will begin. I'll be a hunted man — hated by the people I love and notorious in Constance. Harper will never forgive me, but if I succeed, Constance will be crippled.

Ozias was right about one thing: Those with everything to lose will always face a threat from those who have nothing to lose, and right now I have no life, no best friend, and no real future.

Lucky for me, Ozias's part of the plan is already in motion. All I have to do is show up and hit "record."

To quiet my nerves, I keep replaying the conversation I had with Remy Chaplin: *The only way to take down Constance is from the outside.*

There's a reason Ozias has been able to live like a king for decades. There's a reason Constance can torture and kill without consequence: No one knows what's happening.

Sullivan Taylor's murder was never solved. Control made a few arrests to quell public panic after the bombing, but no one was ever charged. Constance simply dug up new distractions and used Information to bury the story.

When people started dying at 119, Constance kept it quiet. And when Jayden failed, Ozias had her killed.

Broadcasting the truth is a death sentence, but going public is the only way to ensure that Constance can't cover up its crimes. And to make my accusations stick, I need incontrovertible proof.

I'm out of breath by the time I reach my compartment. I head straight for my computer, pound in my password, and fumble around on the underside of my desk for the tiny blue chip I've kept hidden for months. It's no bigger than the thumbnail of my pinkie, but it's probably the most dangerous thing in the entire compound.

The chip is filled with thousands of vocational aptitude results and copies of the board members' private messages about Constance-subsidized bids. I saved the files from the Systems server after I uncovered the truth about Harper's bid. It's not the sort of thing I'd dare keep on my hard drive — not with Harper and me being watched so closely — and I get a little thrill as I copy the files over to my desktop and upload them to the compound's public server.

Hands tingling, I draft a new message and copy the entire compound directory into the "to" field. I include a link to the new repository I just created and schedule the message to go out in a few hours, which should buy me some time.

I collapse against the back of my chair and let out a long breath. The VocAps scandal alone will be an enormous wake-up call for the compound. It draws attention to the corrupted bid system and highlights the suspicious circumstances surrounding Sullivan Taylor's death.

The evidence raises a lot of questions, but it doesn't tell the full story. It doesn't show how Constance deals with people who pose a threat to their mission or all the suffering they've inflicted.

To tell that part of the story — to force people to understand — I have to let Ozias's plan unfold. It's undoubtedly one of the worst things I've ever done, but it's the only way to stop dozens more people from suffering the same way.

My heart is beating in my throat as I watch the time change in the corner of my desktop. There's no going back after today.

For better or for worse, my old life is over.

fifteen

Harper

Robin's words wash over me, but it takes several seconds for their full meaning to sink in.

"Malcolm never . . . There's . . . There's no cure?" I choke.

She shakes her head slowly, deep layers of distress etched in her quivering blue eyes.

"How . . . How can that be? Malcolm had ex-Recon operatives deliver the virus. The people who joined the Desperados . . . Why would they agree to deliver it if there wasn't any —"

"Malcolm has unbelievable powers of persuasion," says Robin, a clear tone of disgust in her voice. "There are Desperados who would do *anything* for the cause — including give up their lives."

"But what if the virus spreads?" I ask. "What if it infects Malcolm's whole gang? He has to have some kind of a backup plan."

"This isn't the compounds," says Robin gently. "Malcolm has no reverence for life — not even his own. The way he sees it, we all should have died a long time ago. He and the others only survived because they were the most aggressive, most feared gang on the Fringe."

I don't hear what Robin says next. My head is spinning, and my mouth has gone dry. I can't accept the reality of Malcolm's scorched-earth strategy. I just can't imagine how someone could be so careless.

"There's no cure?" I repeat.

"I'm sorry," says Robin. "I've scoured every place those files might be. As far as I can tell, there's no contingency plan for a widespread outbreak."

I sink down in the chair behind me before my legs give out. I know I can't stay here. I shouldn't even be talking to Robin.

Sage is still killing time for us back at the loading bay, and Jackson is busy fending off drifters. They could be in danger, but right now all my thoughts are consumed by Sawyer.

I'm never going to see her again.

"Oh my god," Robin murmurs.

I look up. Robin's gaze has drifted to the computer just over my shoulder, and her eyes are locked on the upper left-hand corner of the screen.

"It's him," she breathes, looking as though she might faint. "He's trying to make contact."

"Who?" I ask, wheeling around to look at the screen.

My heart skips a beat when I see a dialogue box blinking in the corner of the monitor.

An unknown user is trying to video message Robin, so she bends over my shoulder and types in a password to accept the call.

A moment later, Celdon's pale face appears on-screen. I wait to feel the surge of fury I got when I first learned Celdon was working with Constance, but my grief seems to have crowded out all other emotions.

"I'm so glad to see you," says Robin.

Celdon doesn't respond. He doesn't even look at her. It's as if he's staring right through her, but I can tell from his darting eyes that he's focused on his computer screen.

Judging from the background, Celdon is sitting in his Systems cube. Old boxes of takeout are just visible in the bottom corner of the screen, and his face is pale in the harsh electronic glow.

"Celdon?" I say, leaning forward to get a better look at him.

Celdon doesn't react to my voice. He doesn't even blink.

"*That's* Celdon?" chokes Robin, looking up at me with an amazed expression.

"Yeah . . ." I say, too perplexed to wonder why Robin seems surprised.

"Celdon!" I yell, trying and failing to get his attention.

Now I'm *really* annoyed. Why would he go to the trouble of slipping through the drifters' network to reach his mother only to ignore her when the video chat connects?

Then another window appears off to the side. It's black with white scrolling text, but Robin isn't even touching the computer.

She shakes her head. "Celdon?"

Robin's eyes flicker over to the secondary window, and I realize that Celdon is running a script.

Suddenly, the video feed cuts out, and Robin's cursor shoots across the screen.

"No!" she cries, slamming back to reality. Her fingers fly across the keys, trying to stop whatever Celdon is doing. But he seems to be three steps ahead of her, and a moment later, all the sleeping monitors flicker to life.

"He's hacking the network," she murmurs, sounding simultaneously horrified and astonished by her son's ability.

I don't say anything. I don't know whether I should be rooting for Celdon or trying to intervene. I have no idea what he's doing, and neither, it seems, does Robin.

"I . . . I can't stop him," she says in a dumbfounded voice as all the screens around the room change to mirror Robin's. "He's taking over all our computers."

As I watch, Celdon's face reappears on screen. Then he cuts out, and the video feed switches to another camera.

It's focused on a sterile-looking room with padded tan walls. The harsh florescent lights are beaming down on a single slumped figure. He has short dark hair, heavy black eyebrows, and a hard, unforgiving jaw. His blue eyes are sunken into two pits of fatigue, and his mouth is twisted in pain.

As he raises his head to look at the camera, I realize with a flutter of relief that I'm looking at Owen, not Eli. But that feeling is cut short as I take in his battered body.

Owen's hands are bound behind him, and he's naked except for a pair of navy-blue shorts. His tattooed chest is covered in chemical burns, and his neck is marred by angry red probe marks.

"Oh my god," mutters Robin. That's when I remember that she knows Owen, too.

As the older Parker brother shivers on the floor, an ominous feeling settles over me. There has to be a reason Celdon wanted the drifters to see this. I just don't know what that could be.

Before I can put the pieces together, a tall figure steps into the frame wearing a dark-green hazmat suit. I can't see the man's face through the condensation on his mask, but his voice is cold and familiar as he orders Owen to give up Malcolm's location.

Owen says nothing. He just stares at the man with a look of cool indifference.

"Do you know what this is?" asks the man, holding up a tube of clear liquid. His voice sounds canned and muffled, but I know I've heard it before.

Owen doesn't answer.

"This vial contains a live sample of the virus that your friends introduced to our people. When airborne, the normal incubation period is around seventy-two hours, but injecting it directly into your bloodstream will make the magic happen much faster."

I can't pull my eyes away from the screen. I have to *do* something. My limbs burn as I fight the urge to hurl myself into the screen and slap the vial out of the man's fingers.

I watch in horror as he fills a syringe with the contents of the vial. Then he bends down on one knee, preparing to inject Owen with the virus.

There's a heart-wrenching scuffle as Owen bends his knees and tries to escape. But there's nowhere for him to go.

The camera flickers and readjusts, zooming in on Owen trapped in the corner. The man bends over, grab's Owen by the arm, and drives the needle into his flesh.

There's a brief struggle, but then the man presses the plunger — sending the virus straight into Owen's bloodstream. Tears blur my vision as Owen yells and thrashes on the ground, trying and failing to get away.

Finally, Owen stops fighting, and the man straightens up and turns toward the camera.

"Your soldiers may be pounding at our gates, but we welcome the attack," he says. "Every hour you make us wait for the cure, five more of your men will be captured and injected with this virus." He pauses for dramatic effect. "Our people may bleed. Our people may suffer. But as long as we draw breath, your people will suffer with us."

The broadcast cuts out, and Robin and I are left staring in horror at the place where the man's face disappeared.

Celdon is in Constance. Celdon stood there and watched while they injected Owen with that virus. Celdon hacked into the drifters' network so that every Desperado would see it and report back to Malcolm on the battlefield.

My mind races, and soon my disgust is replaced with panic.

Owen is infected. Eli is looking for Owen. He's breaking back into the compound to rescue his brother, and he has no idea what he's walking into.

"I have to go," I say in a shaky voice, getting up and grabbing my rifle off the desk. "I have to warn Eli before he —"

I pause briefly with my hand on the knob, glancing back over my shoulder.

Robin is still standing in front of the computer, staring at the blank screen where her son's feed disappeared. There are no words to describe the crushing heartbreak written all over her face.

"Robin?" I call, unsure how she's going to respond.

"What is it?" she murmurs, finally tearing her eyes away long enough to look at me.

"I have to get out of here and get back to the compound . . . before it's too late."

Robin looks at me with a mixture of confusion and despair. She probably thinks it's already too late, but I can't think like that.

"I need your help," I say in a rush, thinking of the drifters in the lobby. "I need you to help me get out of here alive."

sixteen

Harper

To my amazement, Robin doesn't hesitate or put up a fight. I'm not sure if she's helping me because she wants to or because she feels guilty for her part in Malcolm's crimes.

Either way, I'm happy to have her by my side as we exit the control room and check around the corner for any sign of lurking drifters.

Jackson is nowhere in sight, but I'm not sure if that's a good thing or not. It's possible he was killed or captured by the Desperados, or he might have headed back to the loading bay to help Sage.

My mind races as we dart across the lobby back toward the storage room. After watching Owen get injected with the virus in the cold, clinical cell, the pre–Death Storm opulence of the casino seems like a whole other world. I find it hard to believe that the entire country was once filled with places just like it — enormous palaces designed for nothing but gaming and fun.

I get a shiver when we reach the middle of the lobby. There's no sign of a struggle — no indication that Jackson was ever here.

Robin leads me around a bank of gambling machines and starts heading in a different direction than the corridor Jackson and I came through.

"Wait!" I hiss, stopping and pointing back toward the employees-only hallway.

Robin shakes her head. "It's too dangerous."

"But my friend —"

"If he went back to the loading bay, we'll find him," she says, jerking her head toward a much larger, festive-looking hallway.

I hesitate, glancing down in the direction we came. As much as I hate deviating from our original path, I can't argue with Robin. If a drifter jumped out of one of those rooms, we'd have no choice but to shoot. The noise would send every drifter in the building running, and we'd never get out of the casino alive.

Reluctantly, I follow her down the wide, ambling corridor. We pass a themed bar, a bronze statue of a Navajo Indian, three restaurants, and several gift shops. All the stores have anti-theft cages drawn over their entrances, but I can see the dusty remains of souvenir T-shirts, novelty shot glasses, stuffed animals, and knickknacks with the casino's logo on them.

We wind around another small bank of machines, and I stop in my tracks.

A man's body is lying facedown on the carpet, blood fanning out over the ugly floral pattern and staining his sandy-blond hair.

"Oh my god!" I gasp, running past Robin and collapsing next to the body.

I grip the man by the shoulder and tug, dreading the sight of Jackson's boyish dimpled face. Then the man's head flops to the side, and I'm filled with relief and disgust.

It isn't Jackson.

The dead drifter is blond and a similar height and build, but he's got a large nose and a sparse mustache that tickles his pale, lifeless lips. A bloody hole in the side of his head tells me everything I need to know about the way he died, but I feel strangely empty as I turn him faceup on the carpet.

Then I look at Robin. Her eyes are brimming with tears, and I'm reminded that every drifter is a friend to someone.

"Did you . . . Did you know him?" I ask quietly.

"Yes," she chokes, bending down and touching his chest. "I knew him."

She closes her eyes and shakes her head, and I wonder if she's having second thoughts about teaming up with someone like me.

"I'm sorry," I murmur, knowing as I say it that no apology can undo what's been done.

Robin nods and bites her lip, fighting back tears and getting to her feet.

When she meets my gaze, I brace myself for the inevitable. I wait for her to say that I'm on my own or maybe pull a gun on me.

Instead, she lets out a sigh, and her gaze softens. "I'm coming with you," she whispers.

"What?"

"I'm coming back to the compound," she says. "I need to see my son."

"Are you sure?" I ask, trying to think of a tactful way to state the obvious.

Robin returning to the compound after she fled isn't just foolish; it's a death sentence. No one leaves the compound and comes back — especially now with the drifters waging war on 112.

"I understand the risks," she says, reading the concern in my gaze. "But I can't run from my past forever."

Robin starts walking again, and I fall into step behind her with my gun trained up ahead.

"I need to face what I left behind. That includes Celdon."

I swallow down the sick feeling rising up in my throat. I can't believe Celdon stood by and recorded as someone tortured and infected Owen with the virus.

A few days ago, I never would have believed that Celdon would even consider getting involved with Constance. But learning that he allowed himself to be drawn in makes me think that I don't know him as well as I thought I did.

"Don't be too hard on him," says Robin, correctly interpreting my silence.

"How can you say that?" I ask, stopping in the middle of the tunnel and staring at her in disbelief.

"Because of the choices I've made, I never got the chance to know him," she says. "I have no idea what kind of person my son is or what he's done, but if he's friends with someone like you . . ." She smiles. "He can't be all bad."

"He's not, but —"

"He's made mistakes," Robin says in a firm voice. "But we all have."

"Why didn't he tell you who he was?" I ask.

"I don't know," she says. "I'm sure he had his reasons."

I shake my head. I don't understand how Robin could forgive Celdon so easily, but I admire her for it.

As we approach the rear of the building, Robin takes the lead to ensure we don't walk into an ambush. I wait while she ducks around the corner, but before she gives me the all-clear signal, I hear a stifled yelp and the sounds of a struggle.

My heart stutters wildly, and I leap around the corner with my rifle raised.

"Don't!" I cry, pointing my gun at her attacker.

Jackson's face appears behind Robin, and I freeze.

He's sweaty, shaken, and covered in blood, and he's got Robin in a headlock. The muzzle of his gun is pointed directly at her skull, and judging by the stunned look on Robin's face, Jackson caught her by surprise.

His eyes flit from me to Robin and back to me — clearly confused. "What?"

"She's on our side!" I cry, glancing behind Jackson to make sure no Desperados get the drop on us.

"No," he growls, grinding his gun into her head. "She's one of them."

Robin doesn't move.

Judging from the wild gleam in Jackson's eyes, he's been through hell in the past thirty minutes. He's looking at me as though I've lost my mind, and I can tell he's seconds away from pulling the trigger.

"She used to live in the compound," I say in a rush. "She's coming with us."

Jackson is still staring at me as though I've gone insane. He releases Robin but keeps his gun pointed at her chest. "You're from one of the compounds?"

"Yes," she pants. "I escaped when I was twenty-eight — after they had my husband killed."

Jackson lets out a low breath and looks at her suspiciously. "If that's true . . . why would you want to go back?"

"My son is there," she says. "I *have* to go back."

"But you did work for Malcolm."

"So did you," I say, giving Jackson a pointed look.

He doesn't respond. He hasn't taken his eyes off Robin once.

"Whatever Malcolm is planning, I don't want to be a part of it anymore," she says.

Jackson still doesn't look convinced, but I can tell that the pressure of the situation is forcing him to make a quick decision.

I understand Jackson's reservations. I had plenty of my own

when Eli asked for Sage and Jackson's help. But with Malcolm looking to take over every compound in the Southwest, none of us can afford to turn down allies.

"Fine," he sighs, lowering his gun and gesturing down the hall. "Let's go."

Robin nods and turns down the hallway, and Jackson shoots me a look that says, "You better keep an eye on her."

We round another corner, and my heart speeds up as the opulent wallpaper fades into plain beige paint. The flooring changes from carpet to tile, and the smell of disinfectant stings my nostrils.

Robin leads us to a door at the end of the hallway with a glowing red "exit" sign, and I get a familiar whiff of grain and cardboard. This must lead to the storage area where we left Sage.

I nod at Robin. She pushes the door open slowly and leads us into the room, where stacks of crates and boxes throw shadows over every corner.

We move slowly toward the center of the room, and the muffled drone of male voices drifts back to us through an open door. It must be the office where the drifters take inventory of incoming supplies.

I glance past the office to the loading bay. The door is closed, and Jackson's Explorer is nowhere in sight.

There goes any chance of a smooth exit. Raising up that noisy door is going to bring every drifter on this floor running.

I swallow. If the clock on the wall is correct, we left Sage here more than forty minutes ago.

We still don't know if the Desperados bought her story. They might have inventoried her supplies and sent her on her way, or they might have realized that she wasn't there to deliver a shipment after all.

If Sage's cover was blown, there's no telling what they've been doing to her or if she's even still alive.

Creeping around an island of crates, we slowly make our way toward the office. The voices grow louder with every step, and I'm able to pick out two speakers.

"You're saying *Malcolm* sent you to deliver these supplies?" asks a drifter with a low, macho voice.

"*Yeah*," says Sage. "He's been a little busy planning the attack on 112."

Relief floods through me at the sound of Sage's voice. She's alive, but she's trapped in that room with two men who wouldn't hesitate to kill her.

"Why didn't he send Craig or Trent?"

"He needed boots on the ground. So he sent me instead."

Sage's other interrogator scoffs. "He sent you . . . by yourself."

"Yeah, he did."

"He sent you by yourself through no-man's land north of 119?" He scoffs. "Yeah, right."

"Believe what you want," snaps Sage. "Look, I don't have time for this shit. I'm supposed to be back later tonight, and I'm fucking starving. Are we *done* here?"

"We'll be done when I say we're done," says the macho guy.

There's a long, drawn-out pause, and I can sense the tension in the room rising.

"Funny thing is . . . we weren't expecting no supplies. We never got word from Malcolm or nobody."

There's a brief silence, and I picture Sage giving the man an impatient shrug and tossing her long ebony mane over her shoulder.

"I'm sorry," she says in a calm voice. "That's all I know. If you guys got your wires crossed —"

"Nobody here got no wires crossed, missy. Nah. You're *hiding* somethin'."

"What would I be hiding?" cries Sage with a note of indignation. I can tell she's trying to play off her panic with impatience, but the waver of her voice gives away her guilt.

"Maybe Malcolm didn't send you," says the macho one. "Maybe Jackson Mills got wind of Malcolm's plan to clean out the compounds. Maybe he's hopin' to snap up 112 for himself."

"Oh *yeah*," snarls Sage, going from lightly pissed off to *really* pissed off in two seconds flat. "Jackson Mills wanted me to fuck up your whole operation, so he sent fifty boxes of ammo and a whole bunch of other shit your people need to throw you off the trail. Use some fucking common sense."

I raise my eyebrows at Sage's gutsiness, torn between admiration and panic. She doesn't take shit from anybody, but now might not be the best time to lash out at the drifters.

"You fucking bitch!"

I hear a sharp slap, followed by a gasp.

Jackson lunges forward, gun drawn, but Robin steps in front of him and shakes her head.

The look on Jackson's face is downright terrifying. He's ready to shoot his way into that office to get to Sage, but we all know that the second he does, it's going to destroy any chance of making a clean escape.

Robin is still standing in front of Jackson, holding him back with a hand on his chest. He's breathing hard, but Robin gives him a pointed look and moves her hand to her waist. She pulls an old-fashioned handheld radio off her belt and shuffles back the way we came.

Jackson and I exchange a puzzled look, but a few seconds later, we hear a blast of static coming from the office and Robin's garbled voice.

"Hey! Is anybody down there? This is Reynolds. I need backup on the fifth floor. Over."

The men questioning Sage fall silent, and then one of them picks up. "What seems to be the problem?"

"I've got an armed intruder on the fifth floor," says Robin. "I need backup ASAP. Over."

The alpha male swears loudly and punches his radio again. "Ten-four, Reynolds. Jameson and I are on our way. Just hang tight. Over."

Suddenly, Sage's interrogators are frantic. Something heavy scrapes across the floor, and I hear a light *click* and the grumble of a threat.

One of the men shoots out of the office, and I pull Jackson down behind a teetering stack of fuel containers.

We wait breathlessly for the sound of the interrogators' footsteps, and as soon as they pass our hiding place, Jackson flies around the corner to get to Sage.

Then a gunshot cracks the air.

I duck down behind the crates, and my lungs seize in panic. A second shooter returns fire, and somebody yells my name.

Bracing myself for the worst, I tear out from behind the crates and head for the office. I almost run straight into a bald man in an army jacket, but I point my gun and shoot.

The man cries out and stumbles, and I nearly drop my gun in shock. I clipped his shoulder, but he's still on the move.

When the man disappears through the doorway, I turn my attention back to the others. Jackson seems shaken but unharmed, and Sage is sprawled on the ground as if someone pushed her down.

"We gotta go," says Jackson, reaching down to help Sage to her feet.

As she turns, I see the red mark on her cheek from where

the drifter struck her, and a surge of anger rises up in my chest. I want to chase down those men and beat them with a shovel, but there's no time.

I follow Jackson and Sage out toward the loading bay, and a second later, Robin flies around a pile of old clothes.

Sage's eyes widen in fear, but I mutter a quick "She's with us," thinking I can explain on the way.

I help Jackson raise up the door to the loading bay, and the four of us sprint toward the SUV.

Jackson and Sage pile in the front, while Robin and I squeeze into the middle. I slam my door closed, and Jackson hits the gas.

We peel away from the casino in a cloud of dust, and the sound of sirens follows us into the desert.

seventeen

Eli

As darkness descends over the desert, the shadowy figures on the battlefield seem to melt into the earth.

Clouds are swirling rapidly overhead, but it's hard to tell if the weather system is moving on or if the desert is gearing up for a violent storm. The purple-tinged sky could be beautiful, but the crack of gunfire and the blast of grenades offer a harsh reminder of the battle waging up ahead.

"It's time to go," I say to Gunner, grabbing my rifle and getting to my feet.

"Okay," he chokes, deep lines of concern etched all over his sunburned face.

We both know how risky the approach will be, but every second we wait is a second Owen doesn't have.

Gunner and I approach the compound slowly, following the drifters' tire tracks to avoid getting blown up by a buried land mine. It makes me uneasy to think how the drifters navigated this area without triggering any explosions. The only logical explanation is that they used a stolen interface to render our first line of defense useless.

The blasts of gunfire grow deafening as we approach the perimeter. We pass several bodies sprawled on the ground, but I don't look down at them. Every dead drifter is a harsh reminder that we could be next.

With each step, every nerve in my body stretches a little thinner. I keep waiting to catch a stray bullet or set off a buried land mine, but miraculously, it never happens.

Once we're just a few hundred yards from the fence, I see dozens of makeshift barriers erected on either side. Malcolm's men are using cars, scrap metal, and old pieces of furniture to shield themselves from the bullets; Recon operatives are using sandbags on the other side of the fence.

Enormous searchlights pan out along the perimeter, offering a limited view of the encroaching drifters. Every so often, a head pops up over a barricade long enough to aim and fire, and each shot is returned with another violent blast.

I knew breaking through the front lines would be tough, but getting past the drifters and over the fence without being shot will be nearly impossible. To do it, we'll have to attract the attention of someone who trusts me enough to disable the electric fence so we can climb up and over.

It's a long shot.

While some older officers might respect me enough to break the rules, most cadets only know me as the lieutenant-turned-deserter they've been ordered to kill. And if the wrong people spot us first, we're as good as dead.

My spiraling thoughts are cut short by the unwelcome hum of an approaching vehicle. I freeze and throw out an arm to stop Gunner.

Another truckload of drifters has arrived, and it's headed straight for us.

I watch the pair of headlights grow larger in the distance and then whip back around to face the fence.

I'm not the only one who's noticed the truck. A cluster of officers on the Recon side have seen it, too, and they're moving out one by one to get a better shot at the vehicle.

"Fuck," Gunner whispers. "Fuck, fuck, fuck, fuck, fuck."

"Shut up!" I hiss, grabbing his shoulder and yanking him

down low.

My mind is spinning. If we don't move, there's a chance the vehicle might pass in the dark without noticing us. There's also a good chance we'll get run over or shot.

But before I can make a decision, I'm blinded by a bright white light shining from the opposite side of the fence.

We're exposed.

"Run!" I yell, taking off toward the area where the drifters are thinnest on the ground.

Gunner doesn't hesitate. We sprint toward the place where the fence begins to curve, ignoring the threat of land mines buried underfoot. My bruised legs feel like jelly, and my injured ribs ache each time my lungs fill with air, but I push my body harder, and it obeys.

The truck swerves to the left, and suddenly it's blazing right behind us. The engine drowns out the sounds of gunfire, and I know I won't hear the quiet *click* of a land mine before we're blown to smithereens. I can't hear Gunner's footfalls, either, but his dancing shadow tells me he's right on my heels.

The truck slows as we draw closer to the fence, rolling to a stop a hundred yards from the perimeter.

Suddenly, a gunshot cracks the air, and I throw myself to the ground. My ribs and back scream in agony, but I block out the pain and focus on flattening myself against the earth.

A tortured yelp pierces the night, followed by another blast.

Ears ringing, I look up in time to see a shadowy figure flail helplessly before collapsing on the ground.

"Gunner!" I yell. But I can't even hear my own voice. Another volley of gunfire stutters nearby, followed by a scream.

Fifty yards away, the big red Chevy that chased us groans, and its enormous off-road tires spray up a cloud of dirt. The driver hits the accelerator, and I watch in disbelief as the truck plows forward — straight toward the fence.

Shouts erupt on the other side, and several Recon people dart out from their barricades. I wait for the truck to stop, but it never does.

Four tons of steel and rubber collide with the chain-link fence, and sparks erupt like tiny fireworks. They rain down on the truck, bouncing off the hood and disappearing into the dirt.

The engine groans as the driver grinds the accelerator into the floor, and I hear the high-pitched *creak* of the chain-link panels being ripped from their posts. There's another bright spark of electricity, and then the fence shorts out.

Drifters jump down from the truck, and a hot, choking dread seeps into my stomach.

The fence is down. The drifters are coming. It's open season on the compound.

"Gunner!" I yell, army-crawling across the ground in the direction he went down. My hand brushes what feels like an ankle, and I continue to pull myself forward until I'm right beside him.

Gunner is lying face down in the dirt, thrashing and shaking like a fish out of water.

"Gunner!" I hiss. "You hit?"

He doesn't respond. He just lets out a pained gargling noise and continues to tremble.

My heart is racing. I can't think straight. All I know is that we're out in the open, and Gunner is hurt too badly to move.

Fumbling along his back and shoulder blades, I don't feel blood or an exit wound. That's not a good sign. If the bullet had gone straight through, he'd probably be okay. But the fact that it's still inside him means it might have broken into pieces or ricocheted off a bone.

Slowly, carefully, I roll Gunner onto his back, and he lets

out an agonized cry. I slap a hand over his mouth to muffle the sound and do a quick scan of his body.

Gunner's face is pale and silvery in the moonlight, and I know before I even look that the wound is bad. I run my hands down his chest, and something hot and sticky coats my hands.

The bullet is lodged in his chest — just above his heart.

Blood is gushing everywhere, so I bend down and press my palms over the wound. Gunner whimpers loudly, but I continue to apply pressure.

Deep down, I know it's useless. I know there's no way in hell I can save this kid or even extend his life. But a force beyond reason keeps me kneeling there beside him, holding him together as blood seeps out from under my palms.

"Hang on," I choke, pressing down harder.

Gunner coughs and meets my gaze with wild eyes.

I know that look. He's scared, and he's in pain. He knows he's going to die, and there's nothing I can do to save him.

"It's okay," I gasp against the tide of tears streaming down my face.

My hands shake as I press Gunner into the earth, trying to stop an uncontrollable flood through sheer force of will. He convulses violently under my weight, and then his body goes limp.

I don't immediately recognize the signs of death. Instead I give him a hard shake that makes his head flop to the side.

"Hey!" I cry, giving his ridiculous blond mane a tug.

Gunner doesn't move.

"No," I choke, my voice disappearing on the air.

Slowly, my senses reawaken to the distant sounds of gunfire. I lower my head to Gunner's chest, but all I hear is the tremor of the ground as war wages all around us.

There's no gentle thud — no rise and fall of his chest. The

kid I captured as a hostage — the only one willing to go along on my mission — is dead because of me.

I back away on my hands and knees and slowly rise into a standing position. I don't want to leave him here, but I don't have a choice.

Drifters are plowing toward the hole in the fence, and a dozen more pairs of headlights are already glowing on the horizon. Malcolm is bringing in reinforcements, and the drifters have breached the perimeter.

This is the best chance I'm going to get — maybe my only chance — to scale the fence and find my brother.

Sending a silent apology to Gunner, I trip away from his body and start limping toward the fence inside a fresh set of tire tracks. By now my ribs are howling in protest, and my legs feel beaten and battered.

I head for a portion of the fence that's still standing to avoid the hoard of Desperados pouring into the cleared zone. Recon is focused on the encroaching mob, emptying their magazines to keep more drifters from crossing into compound territory.

I reach the fence without anyone seeing me and throw out my hands to touch the cold metal. The fence isn't live.

Peeling off my overshirt, I throw it over my shoulder and start to climb the chain-link panel, blood pounding in my ears.

It takes longer than it should and drains all the energy I have left. My body is completely spent, and the toes of my boots keep slipping out of the gaps in the fence.

I slide down a few inches every time, but I finally reach the top and look out across the battlefield.

Dozens of solar panels have been destroyed, and the ground is littered with shrapnel and bodies. It's only a matter of time before the drifters break through Recon's ranks.

Throwing my overshirt around the barbed wire, I push

down and hoist myself up to clear the top. I shimmy over the fence without any trouble, but as I fumble for a foothold, my weight shifts too far forward.

I make a grab for the fence to try to stop my fall, but as I reach for the chain-link panel, I let go of the razor wire. As I pitch forward, the barbs pierce my flesh, tearing into my leg as I fall toward the ground.

I reach for the fence again, but there's no stopping my momentum.

I hit the ground in a burst of pain and cringe as my bloody leg gives out. I collapse in the dirt, scraping my face, but there's no time to take stock of my injuries.

I clamber up into a standing position and begin to limp toward the compound. I keep my rifle up and my ears piqued for any sound of movement. If I run into someone from Recon, there's no guarantee they'll hold their fire. I never thought I'd have to shoot a fellow officer, but if it's me or them, I'm prepared to pull the trigger.

By now the pain in my leg is too strong to ignore. I feel every step along the entire left side of my body, but instead of growing numb to the pain, I feel myself getting weaker.

Finally, when I can't take it anymore, I duck behind a battered tent and pull up my ripped pant leg to assess the damage.

In the low light, I can see two distinct gashes about ten inches long wrapping around my ankle and calf. The cuts are deep, and my blood isn't clotting. I have more than a mile and a half of ground to cover before I reach the compound, and I'll never make it that far if I can't move at a decent pace. My leg really needs stitches, but the best I can hope for around here is some coagulant and dressing.

Glancing around, I spot the supply tent about three hundred yards to my left. It seems to be unmanned, and it's my best chance to get my hands on some first-aid supplies.

Hobbling from tent to tent, I reach the supply area without incident and scan the tables for what I need. Most of the tent is occupied by crates of ammunition, weapons, and explosives, but I spot a few crates from Health and Rehab and rip into a package of gauze.

Swabbing the worst of the blood away, I grab a brown bottle from the first-aid supplies and douse my leg in hydrogen peroxide. I grit my teeth as it bubbles in my cuts and fumble with a package of clotting powder. My hands are shaking too badly to open it, so I tear into it with my teeth and dump the contents over my leg.

Someone yells a few yards away, and I hurry to cocoon my calf in clean dressing. Blood soaks through faster than I can layer the gauze, but soon the coagulant will kick in and stop the bleeding.

Checking to make sure I don't have an audience, I open a crate marked "uniforms" in search of an air mask to cover my face. There's nothing in here except women's fatigue pants, so I shove it off the top of the stack and open the next one.

This time, I hit the jackpot. There's a brand-new black mask calling my name, so I pull off the plastic and strap it over my face.

If anyone looks too closely, they may be able to recognize me. But with the battle waging inside the perimeter, I have a shot at reaching the compound undetected.

Behind me, one of the hanging lanterns goes out, throwing the tent into total darkness. I turn to go, but my path is blocked by an enormous round chest.

"Sorry!" I mumble, my heart beating loud enough to give me away.

I back away from the stranger as fast as I can, hoping he

doesn't recognize me.

"Who's there?" he asks.

Panic flashes through me. That voice is startlingly familiar, but I can't quite place it.

Before I can answer, the stranger flips on his interface and blinds me with its bright blue light. I throw up an arm to shield my face, but not before he gets a good look.

Suddenly I realize that I'm completely unarmed. As I rushed to patch up my leg, I threw my rifle down on the ground and never bothered to retrieve it. It's lying four or five feet away — completely useless.

"Eli?" says the stranger.

I don't answer. I'm completely frozen.

"Holy shit!"

I don't move, but a second later, the lantern flickers back on, throwing light over his face.

Recognition and relief flare through me. It's Bear.

With the shadows playing over his enormous frame, he looks uncharacteristically imposing. After months of training, Bear's managed to fill out his extra-large uniform with more muscle than blubber, and he's wearing his short hair high and tight. He looks like a real soldier. He looks badass.

"What happened to you?" he asks, staring at my face with a look of pity mixed with disgust.

"Long story."

Bear raises both his eyebrows and shakes his head in confusion. "I saw you guys running off with that drifter, but I almost didn't believe it. He looked *just* like you. I thought I'd gone insane, and now they won't tell me —"

"That's my brother," I say in a rush, hoping Bear harbors enough loyalty to let me go without alerting everyone in camp.

"No way," he breathes, looking as though I just blew his

mind. "Shit, man. I-I'm sorry . . ."

He trails off, and I brace myself for bad news.

"What the hell were you doing?" he asks, his anger catching up to his initial enthusiasm. "They're saying you and Harper are deserters."

"I don't have time to explain," I say quickly. "Listen. You know us. We're not deserters."

"But that drifter . . ."

"Do you know where he is?" I ask, trying to mask the desperation in my voice with my old lieutenant forcefulness. "What *happened* to him?"

Bear falls silent, and my heart sinks.

Owen is dead.

I knew I shouldn't have run that night. I should have listened to Harper and gone back for him while we still had the chance. If I'd doubled back for my brother then, he might still be alive.

"I don't know," says Bear.

"*You don't know*?" I repeat, fighting the flutter of hope in my chest.

"They dragged him in for questioning, but . . ." Bear shakes his head. "It's weird."

"What do you mean?"

"It hasn't been on the news. I mean, they said you and Harper had been caught fleeing with a drifter and that the drifter was in custody, but I haven't heard anything since."

"You don't know if he's dead?" I croak.

Bear shakes his head with a grimace. I have no idea what's running through his mind right now, but I'm just grateful he hasn't turned me in.

Bear, like Kindra, was one of the least capable cadets I'd ever been assigned to train. But Bear worked like a motherfucker, and he got better. It would kill me if I had to put a bullet in his brain to get to Owen.

"Listen," I say, throwing caution to the wind. "I know you don't have any reason to trust me. I know this looks really bad. But you have to believe that I'd *never* help the drifters bring down the compound."

Bear scrutinizes me for a long moment but doesn't say anything.

"We don't choose our family," I continue in a desperate voice. "Yes, my brother is a drifter. But if I hadn't been brought here when I was a kid, I'd be a drifter, too." I sigh. "I can't just leave him — not like this."

Bear is silent for a long moment, studying me with serious eyes. "You're a lot of things, Eli . . ."

I hold my breath.

"But a traitor isn't one of them."

I open my mouth to speak but abruptly close it again. I want to ask Bear if he'll help me get into the compound, but I worry I may be pushing my luck.

"I'm sorry I shot your brother," he mumbles, lowering his head in shame.

"So . . . you're not going to turn me in?" I ask, a little thrown off by his apology.

Bear lifts his chin, a look of resolve blazing in his eyes. "Fuck no," he rumbles, retrieving my gun and pushing it into my hands. "Whatever you need, I'm your man."

eighteen

Eli

It takes less than a minute for Bear to come up with a plan to get me into the compound.

With the cleared zone under siege and the virus spreading like wildfire, the only people being allowed back inside are the wounded and the dying. The only way I'm getting through those airlock doors is if I'm coming in on a stretcher, which means Bear needs help.

He runs off to the front lines to find reinforcements, but the second he leaves, I get a sharp twinge of panic.

What if Bear has a change of heart and decides to turn me in? What if his reinforcements aren't as receptive to my story as he was? What if someone overhears and decides to sound the alarm?

My first instinct is to get the hell out of there, but I'm in no shape to run. The adrenaline from the battlefield is fading fast, and I'm becoming painfully aware of all my injuries.

My ripped pant leg is soaked with blood, my ribs are cracked, and I'm pretty sure I sprained my ankle falling over the fence. Still, I need to be ready for a fight, so I numb my leg with painkillers and load my pockets with ammunition.

A few minutes later, I hear the sound of approaching voices. I stiffen and back into the corner of the tent, bracing myself for a fight. The voices could belong to Bear and his partner in crime, but they could also belong to Seamus and another officer.

A flash of light from a nearby explosion trickles in through the tent flap, and the voices seem to grow louder. The first speaker is definitely Bear, and the second sounds like a woman.

"I don't see what could possibly be so important," she huffs, stomping in behind him.

Their silhouettes appear outside the tent, and relief floods through me. Bear's shadow is large and meaty, while the second belongs to a diminutive girl with a slight limp.

Lenny.

Her hair is falling out of its neat French braid, and her face is streaked with dirt, but it's definitely Lenny.

"Son of a —" The part of her face I can see drains of color, and her bright-green eyes grow wide with shock. "What're you *doing* here?"

"There's no time to explain," I huff, too anxious to unload the full story.

Lenny turns from me to Bear and back to me with a half-crazed look in her eyes. For a second I think she might raise her rifle and shoot me on the spot, but then she lets out a sigh of relief.

"Where's Harper?"

I hesitate, wondering how much I should tell them about Harper's mission. I don't want to get their hopes up, but they deserve to know what's going on.

"Harper's fine," I say, hoping that it's the truth. "She's out looking for a cure."

"She's . . . You're not with her?"

I shake my head, feeling shitty. Even Lenny knows we should be together.

Then she glances up at Bear. Judging from the look in their eyes, they think I'm delusional. Neither one of them thinks a cure is even possible, but I don't have time to dwell on that now.

"So . . . what's the plan?" asks Lenny.

"Right," says Bear, nodding as if he just remembered why he brought Lenny here in the first place. He grabs one of the flimsy stretchers propped against the side of the tent and lays it on the ground. "Get on."

Feeling ridiculous, I kneel down and lower myself onto the stretcher. I hide my rifle under a scratchy brown blanket, and Lenny and Bear hoist me off the ground.

"At least — you'll pass — for someone — who's injured," pants Bear.

"Yeah," says Lenny. "What the hell happened to you anyway?"

My mind goes to Kindra and the drifters who attacked me, and a sick feeling rises up in my throat. I don't want to tell them what happened — not after Lenny watched Blaze get shot. Not when they're fighting a losing battle and men are dying left and right.

"I had a run-in with some Desperados," I say, hoping my vague explanation will be enough to make Lenny drop it.

"*Desperados*? It looks like you had a run-in with a brick wall . . . and a herd of angry cats."

"Funny," I mutter.

My heart speeds up as we draw closer to the compound. I can't see exactly where we're going, but I can tell we're walking through the solar fields.

"Are you sure about this?" I ask after a moment, thinking through my plan. "You'll be in serious trouble for helping me."

"Fuck," Lenny grunts. "We'll be lucky if this place is still standing tomorrow. Getting court-martialed is the least of our problems."

Bear grunts in agreement, and I grin despite myself.

I almost feel bad about being so hard on Bear and Lenny in

training, but if I hadn't been tough on them, I'm not sure they'd still be alive. They're a far cry from the whiny, incompetent recruits that walked into the training center six months ago. They're soldiers now.

Tilting my head back, I see that we're just a few hundred yards from the compound. Coming back here should feel like returning home, but this place hasn't felt like home in quite a while. I've learned things I can't forget and seen things I wish I hadn't. I gave my life to a uniform that could never love me back and pledged my loyalty to a place that was ultimately indifferent.

It's that indifference that got Blaze killed and allowed Kindra to be sent out onto the Fringe before she was battle ready. It's the reason the compound is using its workers as human shields.

I can practically feel the nerves pouring off Bear as we approach the entrance. The two of them lower my stretcher to the ground, and Bear bangs loudly on the door.

"Hey! Heeeeey!" he yells, his voice cracking in desperation. "We need a doctor out here!"

Nothing.

A second later, Lenny joins in the banging. They shout and beat on the door for several minutes, and the anger inside me intensifies.

The compound leaders are so afraid that they've completely shut us out. They don't care if another Recon operative dies on the battlefield. We're all disposable to them.

I don't know what I'm going to do now. I hadn't planned on this. There are only two ways into the compound that I know of, and the other entrance is on full lockdown.

Then, finally, I hear the low *hiss* of the doors being released, and Bear bends down to pick up the stretcher.

They rush me into the radiation chamber, and I'm momentarily blinded by the harsh blue light. Lenny and Bear struggle to maneuver the stretcher in the cramped, stuffy space and slowly lower me to the ground.

The first set of airlock doors close with a hiss, and a pale masked face appears overhead: a man in his late fifties with thinning gray hair, glasses, and a beard.

"What happened to him?" the doctor asks, shining a flashlight in my eyes.

Bear mumbles something about a land mine, and at the same time Lenny squeaks that I was attacked.

The doctor looks from one to the other, confusion and suspicion competing for dominance.

"He's bleeding out!" Lenny gasps in an overdramatic voice. "Hurry!"

The doctor lets out a breath of annoyance, and I feel his gloved hands fumble to remove my mask.

"I don't see —"

Before he can finish that sentence, I jump to my feet and jab my rifle into his chest.

"Hey!" he shouts, raising his hands in surrender. "Take it easy."

But then recognition dawns on the doctor's face, and the eyes behind his mask grow wide. "You're the —"

I don't give him a chance to finish. In one jerky motion, I shove my rifle against his windpipe and slam him into the side of the chamber.

"Thanks," I pant at Bear and Lenny, who are crammed against the wall on the other side of the stretcher.

To their credit, they don't look surprised to see me going apeshit on the good doctor, and I get an undeniable urge to laugh when I imagine them slinking sideways out the door as though they didn't see a thing.

When I turn back to the doctor, I see him groping along

the wall behind him, and I realize too late that he's pressed the call button. The doors to the postexposure chamber slide open, and two med interns I don't recognize appear in the doorway.

"Shit," I whisper.

Both kids look completely unprepared for a patient gone rogue, but they recover almost immediately and start pushing their way into the chamber to pry me off the doctor.

As I push forward, they shove me back, and I end up sandwiched between the doctor and the doorframe. One of the interns tries to wrestle my rifle away from me, but I catch him with a hard elbow to the mouth.

The momentum throws me into the postexposure chamber, and then there's only one intern standing between me and the exit. The door leading back to the radiation chamber has sealed, and we're trapped in there together.

The kid's eyes grow wide with panic, and he hits the button for decontamination. Freezing-cold water spurts out automatically, spraying my eyes and blurring my vision. The door to the tunnel opens with a *beep*, and the intern takes off at a sprint.

I start to follow him, but then the door to the radiation chamber opens again, and the first intern charges out like a bull.

He pushes me against the wall, so I knee him in the gut and sweep his legs out from under him. He hits the ground flat on his back, and I get a twinge of guilt for beating up on an intern.

Meanwhile, the old doctor is hacking in the corner of the radiation chamber, looking as though I just took ten years off his life. I feel bad, but I can't worry about them right now. I'm in.

I take off down the tunnel at a limp, and my footsteps echo loudly in the large, empty space. I realize too late that I left my mask back in the chamber, which means anyone watching the security feeds could recognize me.

It's only a matter of time before someone shows up to make the arrest, so I drag in a fortifying breath and hobble straight for the emergency stairwell. I throw open the door, limp up the first flight of stairs, and almost smack face-first into the plastic barricade.

I swear loudly. I'd forgotten that Operations blocked off the mid-levels to keep the virus contained in tier two.

Feeling flustered, I lean against the barricade to take some of the weight off my leg while my mind races to come up with an alternate plan.

I'll never get past tier two looking like a deranged Recon zombie. Any tier-three worker wandering around on the ground level would attract attention, but I'm a wanted man covered in blood.

The only way I'm going to get past the barricade is if I can somehow disguise myself as an Operations worker.

Swearing and panting, I hobble back down to the main tunnel and head toward the canteen. Lights flicker on in the unused portion of the tunnel, and I glance nervously up at the security cameras mounted near the ceiling. If anyone from Constance is monitoring the feeds, I won't have more than a few minutes.

Luckily, the lobby outside the canteen is completely deserted. The enormous cafeteria area is dark except for a few emergency lights around the perimeter, and the metal doors are rolled down over the serving lines.

The only sign of life is the enormous LED screen mounted in the far corner of the lobby. The feed is oddly fuzzy, as if it's stuck between two channels.

Then, suddenly, the screen goes blank, and a grainy shot of a pale Systems worker overtakes the screen. His golden-blond hair is in complete disarray, and his thin face is marred by deep dark circles.

It's Celdon.

"Hello," he says, looking straight into the camera. "My name is Celdon Reynolds. I'm a penetration tester in Systems." He swallows and takes a deep breath. "You probably don't know who I am, but I have an important message for you . . ."

Celdon's brow is damp with sweat, and I can tell that whatever he's about to say is making him extremely nervous.

"For the past few months . . . I've been involved with something horrible."

"Don't do it," I murmur, staring at the screen in disbelief.

"I know everybody likes to pretend that Constance doesn't exist, but I'm here to tell you that it's very real, and it poses a serious threat to this compound. As I sit here, someone from Constance is trying to interrupt this broadcast."

He cocks one eyebrow in a smug expression, as if to say he's ten steps ahead of them.

"The footage you just saw was recorded earlier today. That sort of horrific torture is an everyday reality here, and it's not just a method reserved for our enemies. Constance routinely violates human rights to extract information from people they consider dangerous, and that could be just about anyone . . . people from the Fringe, people who know too much about them, people who have outlived their usefulness . . ."

At the mention of drifters, my mind goes to Owen. *Was he the torture victim Celdon was referring to?*

"During my time in Constance, I've witnessed the torture of innocent tier-three workers, politicians, and EnComm leaders. As a new recruit, I've been ordered to hijack dozens of interfaces without a warrant and help cover up the murder of Recon Commander Jayden Pierce."

My stomach drops to my knees, and it feels as though all the air has been sucked out of the room.

Jayden is dead? Constance killed Jayden?

Jayden made my life a living hell. I should feel relieved that she's gone — grateful, even — but all I feel is helplessness. Jayden was the most evil, conniving woman I ever knew, and still Constance disposed of her.

Celdon glances down at his desk, and I realize he's reading off a sheet of paper. "Commander Pierce was killed because she failed to eradicate the leaders of the Fringe survivors and silence two Recon operatives who knew the truth about Constance. Smoke and mirrors is how Constance survives, which is why I'm sharing this with you today."

My breath catches in my chest. What Celdon is doing is completely insane. He isn't going to survive this. But as foolish as his broadcast may be, I can't help but think that no one has ever done anything so important for the compound.

"We've been told since birth that we're the only survivors," he says. "That everyone else died from the radiation. I thought we were, too." He takes a deep breath. "Our leaders want us to believe that we're the victims in all this . . . that the people out there are the enemy. But what's happening today is the result of *years* of systematic murder."

Celdon pauses.

"Ever since Death Storm, Recon's job has been to destroy any evidence of the people we left behind — the people we left to die. But it's not Recon's fault. They're just following orders . . . trying to make the best of the hand they've been dealt."

He stops and cracks a bitter smile. "See, most of us like to think we got where we are today because we *deserved* it — because we were smarter or worked harder than everybody else. But the truth is that I got into Systems because of my genes, and you got to where you are because of yours."

I watch in utter horror as Celdon unloads the truth about the VocAps test and the infighting on the board that led to Sullivan Taylor's murder. He reveals what we learned about the Fringe Program and how Harper's parents were killed upon arrival. He talks about his mother — the Systems worker who married a Recon operative — and his father who was killed and virtually erased from public record.

In less than ten minutes, he deconstructs every lie the board has worked so hard to contain, and I can almost picture Constance frantically trying to kick Celdon off the air.

"I've sent each one of you a zip file with documents that back up everything I just said," he continues. "It contains the true scores of everyone who's taken the VocAps test in the past ten years, along with very personal data on their health history and genetic outlook. I've thought long and hard about the consequences of this information, but I've decided that the injustice of keeping it in the dark is more than I can live with. I hope that someday —"

The screen sputters again, and Celdon's feed cuts in and out. A second later, the screen goes dark, and the normal news feed flickers back on.

Constance must have succeeded in disrupting Celdon's broadcast, and it's only a matter of time before they show up at his door.

Even though his confessional has ended, I can't tear my eyes away from the screen.

I can't believe he just did that. He just exposed Constance's most carefully guarded secrets and blew the lid off of lies that have been repeated for decades.

At this moment, shockwaves are fanning out across the compound. Anyone watching is probably still staring at their screens in disbelief, unable to fathom a story so different from the one they've been told their entire lives.

As reality sinks in, I realize that Owen isn't the only one I need to save. Celdon is probably minutes away from a fate worse than Jayden's, and there's no way he'll survive if he stays in the compound.

There's no time to try to con my way past the tier-two barricade. I have to get a message to Celdon and get him to override the locks. To do that, I just need to get my hands on an interface, and I know where I can find one.

Heading back the way I came, I see lights flicker on in the main tunnel. I hear the sound of approaching footsteps, but I can't see around the corner.

I freeze. There's no reason for anyone to be coming this way, which means they must be after me.

I'd been so caught up in Celdon's broadcast that I completely forgot about the cameras mounted along the walls outside the canteen. Someone from Constance must have spotted me.

I wheel around to find a place to hide and duck down behind a thick concrete pillar. I'm prepared to shoot my way out of here, but then the footsteps stop.

I wait several seconds, my breathing low and ragged. I don't hear the footsteps retreating, which means the intruders must be lurking nearby.

Slowly, I poke my head around the pillar and aim my gun at the entrance to the tunnel.

Swallowing down my nerves, I step out from behind the pillar and creep slowly toward the tunnel with my gun drawn.

I hold my breath and move with care to avoid triggering the motion-activated lights, but before I reach the edge of the lobby, a dark shape leaps around the corner.

I whip my rifle up to shoot, but the intruder fires first.

Tiny sparks crackle off the weapon, sending a powerful electric shock through my entire body.

I let out a yell and look down. A hot pair of prongs have latched on to my chest. They're attached to some sort of wire, which is sending powerful jolts of electricity through my entire body.

The pain and surprise immediately scrambles my thoughts, and I feel myself losing control of my body. My rifle clatters to the ground, and my injured leg gives out. I hit the ground hard, and my head bounces off the tile. Lights flicker on all across the lobby, and a familiar face appears overhead.

I recognize Seamus's smug, pathetic mug instantly. He's sneering down at me with a triumphant expression, looking as though he can't believe his luck.

"Nice to see you, Parker," he croons.

"Go fuck yourself," I choke, still shaking from the electric shock.

I get a faint prickle of satisfaction, but that feeling is short lived. Before I can move or jump to my feet, Seamus brings his boot down onto my head, and everything goes dark.

nineteen

Sawyer

It's impossible to tell if the immunotherapy is working the way it should. Angela hasn't returned since Caleb and I started treatment, and none of the nurses will let me read our charts.

One thing is for certain: Our symptoms have definitely gotten worse.

In less than twenty-four hours, the lookalike virus raging through my system has sapped my energy and left me feeling weak and dizzy. I can't walk to the bathroom without wheezing, and even my sleep is hijacked by powerful coughing fits. All the hacking leaves my throat achy and raw, but whenever I look over at Caleb, my inner whining stops.

Caleb is terrifyingly pale. He sleeps most of the day, and yet the purplish circles under his eyes grow more and more pronounced.

We hardly talk at all now. Even a few words can trigger a horrendous coughing fit, and those steal away energy when there's already none to spare.

After hours of begging, I persuade the nurse on duty to bring in a portable monitor and an interface so we can watch the news.

A look of relief spreads across Caleb's face when she reappears with the borrowed equipment. Even though the news is sure to be grim, it will at least provide a temporary distraction from our misery.

I don't bother asking the nurse about the tier-two workers who were infected in the commissary. They weren't given the experimental treatment, which means that they'll all soon be dead.

I glance over at Caleb and tap the news icon to turn on the feeds. Instantly, the screen is overtaken by an enormous picture of Celdon — probably his ID photo — along with a caption giving his name.

My mouth falls open in shock, and I hoist myself into an upright position to get a better look.

"My sources tell me that Control has confirmed the whistle-blower's identity," says the reporter. "The leak broadcasted earlier this evening came from twenty-two-year-old Celdon Reynolds. Reynolds has worked in Systems for less than a year as a penetration tester, whose job it is to identify network vulnerabilities and secure compound computer systems.

"According to Chief Operating Officer Tobias Brown, Systems will convene a panel later this week to determine if Mr. Reynolds's actions could be grounds for dismissal.

"'Whatever Mr. Reynolds's motives may have been, the release of the private VocAps data is in direct violation of Systems's confidentiality agreement,' Brown said. 'Systems does not condone these extreme breaches of privacy — no matter what the reason — and we're working around the clock to ensure that all compound data is secure.'"

"What did he *do*?" I hiss, staring at Celdon's picture in disbelief.

The reporter continues. "Reynolds may be standing on shaky legal ground with Systems, but allegations that the bid system could be rigged has led to a storm of public outcry. A cursory examination of the leaked data confirms Reynolds's accusations, and our analysts say that all VocAps scores evaluated so far were weighed heavily to favor those with good health history and exceptional genes."

As a blown-up image of a VocAps spreadsheet fills the screen, I suck in a panicked burst of air that sets off another coughing fit.

"One-Twelve News Today is working tirelessly to determine the authenticity of the leaked documents," says the reporter. "If they are legitimate, the so-called 'Bidgate Scandal' could have major consequences for compound workers and the board."

"What the hell?" chokes Caleb, dissolving into a series of wheezes. "Somebody released the VocAps data?"

"Not just someone," I whisper. "My friend, Celdon."

Caleb whips around to look at me before turning back to the screen. "They think the bid system is *rigged*?"

"Yeah."

"Along with the VocAps records, Reynolds also leaked a graphic video of a man being infected with the virus," says the reporter. "Reynolds alleges that the infamous compound espionage unit Constance is responsible. The man in the video has yet to be identified, but several sources say he could be Lieutenant Eli Parker."

My stomach drops, and the screen flashes to a shirtless man lying on the floor of the psych ward. The footage is too grainy to know for sure, but the man does look a lot like Eli.

"Oh my god," murmurs Caleb.

I forgot he knows Eli.

We watch in horror as someone in a hazmat suit bends down and struggles to subdue the shirtless man on the floor. As he does, I'm able to get a closer look at the captive.

The man *looks* like Eli, but it isn't Eli. His jaw is much too square, and his eyebrows don't look quite right. The resemblance is uncanny, yet somehow I know it isn't him.

Then it hits me: The man in the video is Eli's brother, Owen.

There's a brief scuffle on the floor as Eli's brother fights to put some distance between himself and the man in the hazmat suit, but then the stooped figure traps Owen and plunges a syringe of clear liquid into his arm.

I cringe, suddenly feeling lightheaded. Then the screen changes, and a different news story starts to play.

"Sorry," says Caleb. "I couldn't watch any more of that."

I'm too stunned to speak. I just watch in numb silence as the news anchor analyzes the fighting going on out on the Fringe. His commentary is playing over an animated graphic of the compound and the surrounding territory. By the looks of it, the drifters have already breached the perimeter and are pushing Recon back toward the solar fields.

"Holy shit," mutters Caleb.

The screen shifts back to live footage, and we watch in horror as a battered tent goes up in flames. Recon is unloading a stream of bullets on the encroaching drifters, but it doesn't seem to be slowing down the hoard of people pushing toward the compound.

"I can't believe this," I breathe.

"I know. A couple days in here, and the whole compound goes to hell."

"I can't believe Celdon did that," I murmur.

"How did he even get ahold of that video?"

I swallow. "He was recruited by Constance."

"No way," says Caleb, leaning forward and staring at me with wide bloodshot eyes. "You've got to be *shitting* me."

"I wish," I say, shaking my head. "He's as good as dead now."

My dark train of thought is mercifully interrupted by a dull knock at the door.

Caleb sits up and mutes the screen, and a second later, Angela Starks walks in wearing a full-body hazmat suit. I can see what looks like our charts projecting against her face shield, but she isn't wheeling the heavy lab cart.

My heart sinks.

"How are you feeling?" asks Angela, stopping at the foot of our beds to give us a good once-over.

"Like hell," croaks Caleb.

Angela nods. "That could be a good sign. It could mean the treatment is working."

"Or it could mean we're just going to die faster from a different virus," I add bitterly.

Angela purses her lips. "Sawyer, can we talk?" She glances nervously at Caleb. "Privately?"

I feel like shit, which is pushing my ultra-bitchy alter ego front and center. "Whatever you have to say to me, you can say in front of Caleb."

"All right, then," says Angela. She takes a step closer to the foot of my bed. "May I?"

I give her a stiff nod, feeling incredibly worried. If she needs to sit down to deliver this news, it can't be good.

"Sawyer . . . were you aware that your parents designated you as their power of attorney?"

I shake my head. Of all the scenarios I'd been expecting, that opener takes me by surprise.

For the past two and a half years, my parents have been completely immersed in their latest project for Progressive Research: testing out an extended virtual hiatus.

Life support has been sustaining them throughout their mental vacation, and since they are completely detached from reality, they have no idea that a deadly virus is sweeping through the compound or that their only daughter could be dead within days.

"Well, as their power of attorney, you are in the unique position of being able to revive them at any time during the experiment," says Angela gently.

"So?"

Her face grows serious. "So, you and you alone have the power to put their project on pause."

"Why would I do that?" I ask. "Pulling them out would ruin the whole experiment. It would render any of their findings invalid."

"That's true," says Angela slowly. "But Sawyer . . . no one would think badly of you if you wanted to put the project on hold so that you could see them before you . . . get any worse."

"What's *that* supposed to mean?"

Angela sighs. "It means you could have a chance to say goodbye."

Rage and terror flash through me, and tears well up in my eyes before I can stop them. "Are you saying that I *should*?"

"No," says Angela. "I'm just saying you should think about it."

"You think I'm going to die."

"Sawyer . . . you and I both know that there's a strong possibility you may not respond to treatment."

"What about Caleb's parents?" I cry, turning to him. "Why aren't you badgering *him* to say his goodbyes?"

Angela gives Caleb a sympathetic look.

"My parents are tier two," he says in a husky voice. "They were in the commissary when the virus was released." He shakes his head. "They aren't undergoing treatment."

My heart contracts painfully, and I feel a fresh kick of guilt. Surely Caleb would have mentioned his parents' sections in all the time we've worked together. I must have just forgotten.

"We have no way of knowing how effective this treatment will be," Angela continues. "We can't try it out on people until we understand the potential risks and benefits."

"*Potential risks*? Who cares about the risks if they're going to die anyway?" I yell.

Angela doesn't answer, and I know I'm fighting a losing battle.

"Would you like me to put in an order for your parents to be revived?" she asks, smoothly steering the topic back to her original inquiry.

"I . . . I don't know," I say. "This project was their life. If I pull them out early . . . the last two years will have been a complete waste."

"That's true," says Angela evenly. "But no one would blame you for wanting to see your parents again."

I fall silent for a moment, imagining what it would be like to see them, talk to them, hug them after all this time.

"There is one thing you should know," says Angela.

"What?"

Judging by the look on her face, she's debating whether or not she should tell me at all.

Finally, she says, "Constance put in an official request."

I glance at Caleb, utterly confused. "A request for what?"

Angela's face goes dark, and she glances around to make sure we can't be overheard. "A request to release all our research data — including the information we've gathered on the Fringe kids and their radiation resistance."

"What does that have to do with my parents?"

"Progressive Research answers to a higher ethical obligation," she says in a low voice. "We require a unanimous vote from all our members to release confidential patient data, and we can't vote on the issue without your parents or their proxy."

"Who's their proxy?"

Angela raises an eyebrow, fighting a triumphant grin. "They didn't select one. Constance has been trying to get their hands on the Fringe Program data for years. Your parents didn't want to risk their proxy being compromised while they were immersed, so . . ."

"They've voted on this before?"

Angela shakes her head. "We were preparing for an official vote just before your parents entered their hiatus. Plenty of us thought the timing wasn't an accident."

"What do you mean?"

"If your parents had been forced to vote, it would have put them and you in incredible danger."

"I had no idea," I say, my mind still reeling from the shock of it all.

It's no surprise that Constance has been working to get their hands on that data. If they had proof that the Fringe kids were resistant to radiation, they'd know exactly whom to send out into the desert, and those people would be sentenced to life on the Fringe.

There'd be no bidding ceremony — no choice whatsoever. For the people with those specific genetic mutations, there wouldn't even be the illusion of a meritocracy.

What surprises me is how far my parents went to protect that data. Both of them were at the top of their class in higher ed, and they received huge bids from Health and Rehab when they were my age. They never struck me as the rebellious type — certainly not the type of people to put their careers or their lives on the line.

Maybe I didn't know my parents as well as I thought.

"I can come back later," says Angela. "Give you some time

to think it over."

"You don't need to," I say, stopping her as she gets up to leave.

Angela freezes, and Caleb's eyes snap onto me.

"My answer is no," I say. "I don't want you to revive my parents."

Angela looks pleasantly surprised by my answer — maybe even a little relieved. She never came out and said how she would have voted on the issue, but I have a feeling that Constance wouldn't be happy with her decision.

"That's very good to hear, Sawyer," she says. "I'm glad to know you would put the good of our patients over your personal comfort. That's one of the reasons we were going to ask you to join us in Progressive Research next spring."

For a second, I'm struck completely speechless.

"You too, Caleb," she says. "You both have all the qualities we look for in our recruits," Angela continues. "You're smart, you work hard, and you're curious. Sawyer, you uncovered a pattern in the Fringe Program data that took our people *years* to discover."

I shake my head. I can't believe it. I know I should feel elated that the thing I've been working toward is finally within reach, but all I feel is despair.

I worked my ass off for years to get into Health and Rehab and then to be considered for Progressive Research. I did that thinking that there would always be time to enjoy myself, but I'm probably going to be dead soon.

"Stay strong," says Angela. "If you make it through this, you'll always have a future here."

"Thanks," I say, feeling a little woozy.

"But I should warn you . . . We haven't heard the end of this."

I nod.

"They want that data, Sawyer," she says. "They could come after you."

"I know."

"And you're okay with that?" Caleb asks, looking from me to Angela with clear panic in his eyes.

I tilt my head to the side. "Look at me." I raise an eyebrow. "Look at us."

"This could mean the treatment is *working*."

I shake my head. "Tell Constance I said no," I repeat. "My answer is final."

Angela gives my leg a quick squeeze. She gets up to leave, and I feel an unexpected pang of regret in my stomach.

Even though I know I made the right decision, some small childish part of me really wishes I could see my parents again. And right now, the only way that's going to happen is if I survive the virus.

twenty

Celdon

I feel strangely numb as I watch Constance's goons fan out from Information. The manhunt is officially underway, and they're headed straight for my compartment.

Amateurs. Like I would really record an illegal broadcast from my own compartment and then wait around for someone to come murder me.

I knew they'd be trying to shut me down the second I hacked into the news feeds. The only reason I was able to stay online as long as I did was because I was three steps ahead of Devon Reid.

I hunkered down in Harper's compartment and logged in under a fake user name. Then I onion-routed my traffic through about a dozen different relays so he wouldn't be able to pinpoint my IP address.

When Devon finally grew tired of playing router whack-a-mole, he cut the power to end my broadcast — which is exactly what I would have done. By the time he sent someone to my compartment to finish me off, I'd already bypassed three Operations barricades and made my way up to Systems to watch the drama unfold over the security feeds.

Ozias must be pissed. He'd only intended for me to broadcast Watson's sick experiment to the drifters' network, but I took it one step further. I replayed the entire recording on all the compound's news feeds and added my own color commentary.

As I watch the security feeds, Devon and an old controller I don't recognize appear in one of the Information tunnels. They're headed for the megalift, which means they're probably on their way to find me.

I'm just about to log out and make a run for it when another feed captures my attention. It's one of the cameras mounted inside the perimeter.

The Fringe is dark and smoky, but the infrared shows warm bodies pushing forward and a dozen clusters of Recon workers struggling to hold them back. Panning out, I can see several dozen more dots approaching the compound. Each of those dots represents a drifter toting enough firepower to take out an entire squad of Recon operatives.

We aren't just under siege as Information would have us believe — we're seriously outnumbered. Even with every Recon operative fighting Malcolm's men, we aren't going to be able to hold them off for long.

Shaking with nerves, I click back to the internal security feeds and do another scan for Constance. Devon and the controller are no longer in Information. They've already reached the main Systems tunnel, and they're headed my way.

I need to get out of here. I'm a dead man walking. But as my gaze drifts over the honeycomb configuration of computers to the emergency exit, I feel an unfamiliar tug of hesitation.

The bullpen is completely silent except for the quiet hum of sleeping computers and the soft hiss of the air conditioner. It's beautiful in its own weird way, and for the first time I understand why Harper loves this place.

She should have earned a spot in here — no doubt about it. She kicked my ass on the Vocational Aptitude test, and she's smarter than anyone in here. Instead she got stuck doing the most dangerous job the compound has to offer.

She doesn't owe these people shit, but she gave everything to the same system that fucked her over. She isn't like me. She doesn't take the easy way out.

I decide in that moment that I'd rather die doing some good than spend the rest of my life wishing I were dead. I'm going to do what Harper would do. I'm going to fight for the compound.

Just then, the door to headquarters bursts open and bangs into the adjacent wall. A shot cracks through the air and shatters the front wall of my cube.

I duck under my desk as shards of glass rain down. Sharp little fragments slide over my keyboard and get lodged in my hair, but somehow I'm not dead yet.

Another shot rings out, but the bullet pings off my monitor and plunges my cube into darkness.

"Fuck off!" I yell at Devon.

That asshole can mess with me all he wants, but you don't fuck with a man's computer.

Gasping and shaking, I reach into my waistband for the stolen handgun.

"Boy, you really fucked up good!" comes Devon's silky, infuriating voice.

Another bullet shatters the cube next to mine, and I wonder briefly how Constance will explain the destruction to Systems administration.

"Come out, come out, wherever you are!"

I hear Devon's footsteps crunching over glass and know he must be close. The controller hasn't said a word, but I'd bet he's covering the other end of the room, waiting for me to make a break for the exit.

"You think you can make a home movie like that and get away with it?" Devon calls.

There's a long pause as he listens for me to give up my

position. "You just gave Ozias carte blanche to have you terminated."

As irritating and off-putting as Devon's speech may be, it's giving me a chance to gather my thoughts and make a plan. I'm still shaky and out of breath, but I feel a renewed sense of strength as his footsteps draw closer.

I only have one chance to get out of here — one shot at reaching the door without getting a bullet in the back of the head.

My only option is to shoot them before they shoot me. Of course, one of them is a trained controller, but what have I got to lose?

Suddenly, I hear a crunch of glass a few yards to my right.

In one violent motion, I spring to my feet and aim for the blurry shape just outside my cube. I fire off three rounds — two at Devon and one at the controller approaching from my left — and the controller cries out in pain.

I hit him, I think. *I can't believe I hit the motherfucker.*

Devon doesn't even bother to check on his fallen comrade. He's too busy weighing his options and deciding what to do.

He could kill me, but that would draw even more attention to Constance. On the other hand, I just shot a controller, and he's probably considering how he can sell me to the media as a violent criminal with drug-induced hallucinations.

Devon's hesitation costs him. While he's scheming, I shoot forward like a linebacker and slam my head into the center of his chest.

His feet fly out from under him, and we hit the ground in a tangle of limbs. I come out on top and use my position to lay into him with a painful right-handed punch.

Devon groans as my fist smashes into his jaw. He immediately tries to reverse our positions, but I hunker down and throw my weight onto his belly, swinging down at him as if my life depended on it.

A couple yards away, the controller is regaining consciousness. I only have a few seconds to end this fight, and Devon is tougher than he looks.

I tear my eyes away from the controller in time to see Devon grab something shiny off the ground. I can't tell what it is, but a second later I feel a burn of pain. I slap my hand over my neck, and a hot trickle of blood spurts out from under my fingers.

The asshole stabbed me with a piece of broken glass. He didn't manage to clip my carotid, but he did plenty of damage.

He's still flailing around underneath me with his improvised weapon, so I make a grab for his wrist. I get it pinned, but somehow Devon manages to slice my arm open in the process. The cut burns for a second, but the pain only adds fuel to my fury.

Grabbing a fistful of Devon's perfect hair, I yank his head to the side and drive his skull into the ground. It bounces off the floor with a heavy thud, and he tries to buck me off him again.

This time, he manages to toss me to the side. I feel the weight of his body on my chest, and a second later he slams his arm down across my windpipe. I claw at his face — aiming for his eyes — but he doesn't release the pressure.

My body rebels as Devon slowly cuts off my air supply. My legs convulse on the ground, and my arms flail uselessly at my sides. I'm about to pass out when my fingers brush something cold and solid, and my tired brain flickers back to life.

Devon shifts on top of me to get a stronger grip, and I taste blood in the back of my throat.

In one powerful, desperate motion, I throw my hips to the left. Devon struggles to regain his balance, and I make a grab for the gun. It's just barely out of reach, but I stretch my arm as far as it will go, and my fingers close on the cold metal handle.

As my brain sucks up the last delicious gulps of oxygen, I pull the gun up and aim it between me and Devon. I release the safety and pull the trigger, and the gunshot shatters my eardrums.

Devon's body goes limp on top of me. His chest crushes my lungs, but the pressure on my windpipe eases slightly.

I gasp and choke for air, sloughing Devon off me like a sweaty comforter. It's tough to get my first arm free, but once I do, I'm able to pull myself out from under him and get to my feet.

The controller I shot is pulling himself along on his hands and knees, so I take careful aim and shoot him in the back. He collapses onto his chest like a worm, and I kick him in the ribs until I'm sure he's dead.

Crunching over shards of broken glass, I limp toward the exit and let myself out of headquarters. I squeak down the tunnel, hands still shaking, listening to the sound of my own ragged breathing.

Finally, reality comes charging back: I just killed two Constance goons, and the rest of them are still after me.

Quickening my pace, I head straight for the emergency stairwell and take each flight of steps two leaps at a time. I reach a landing and round the corner, almost colliding with a harried reporter.

He's too shocked to respond, but one look at the gun in my hand is enough to make him shrink back against the wall.

I'm sure that will make the news later — "Crazed Constance Whistle-Blower Threatens Reporter With Gun" — but I can't think about that right now.

I reach the clear plastic partition blocking off the medical ward and swipe the master key I created. I'm dying to stop in to check on Sawyer, but there's no time. Constance may have already put out an order for my arrest, and every second counts.

By the time I reach the lower tunnels, I'm sweaty, out of breath, and bleeding profusely.

Recon is deserted, so I head straight for the supply room. I bust out my master key to let myself in, but the door is already propped open with a cinder block.

Rows of ceiling-to-floor shelving units occupy almost the entire room. There are shelves devoted to stacks of gray uniforms, black combat boots sorted by size, bins of ration packets, first-aid supplies, and hundreds of water bags piled near the back.

Thinking fast, I grab a pack of bandages out of one of the first-aid bins and rip it open with my teeth. I slap one of the bandages over my neck to soak up the blood and continue my search for weapons.

The food and uniforms look largely untouched, but the bins dedicated to ammunition are almost empty. There are a few hand grenades left in a bin toward the back, so I put one in each pocket of my blazer and head for the armory.

To my surprise, the heavy-duty cage door is already rolled up, but as soon as I step inside, I see why. All the M-16s and M-4s are gone. All that's left are a couple of dusty old handguns and a rocket-propelled grenade launcher.

I load up on ammo for my stolen handgun and then hesitate. The grenade launcher is calling my name, so I sling it over my shoulder and run back up to the ground level.

I'm so amped up about making my escape that I don't stop to listen for the sound of voices. I just throw open the door leading to the main tunnel and emerge into complete chaos.

Several dozen controllers are packed into the tunnel, loading their guns and preparing for something big. Their low, panicked voices bounce off the high ceiling, and as soon as I emerge from the stairwell, several swivel around to look at me.

Shit.

Constance probably already put out an order for my arrest, and I must look like a fucking maniac. My white Systems uniform is covered in blood, my face is bruised, and my pockets are bulging with stolen ammo. Oh, and I've got a fucking grenade launcher slung over my shoulder.

Before the controllers can draw their weapons, I turn to the right and make a break for the airlock doors at the end of the tunnel.

"Hey!" shouts an older controller. "Stop him!"

I push harder, not pausing to look back at the controller who spoke. I'm sure he's got a gun pointed at my back, but he probably hasn't held a real weapon in years. Controllers use electric nightsticks inside the compound, and this guy looks like someone they pulled out of retirement as a last line of defense.

He shoots.

People scream, but the bullet whizzes over my shoulder. I'm too surprised to feel real panic.

"Stop! You're not allowed —"

I don't hear whatever he says next. An enormous explosion erupts outside the compound, shaking the ground and rattling the interior walls. I grab on to a door handle to stop myself from falling, and a bunch of the controllers behind me hit the deck.

Staring down at the keypad, I realize with a jolt of horror that I never bothered to override the exterior door codes. I search the door for a card reader, but this one will only open with a code.

I take a step back. From the looks of it, this door is mostly ornamental. It's made of frosted glass and designed to hide the heavy steel monstrosity on the other side.

Taking a deep breath, I pull out my gun. I take aim, close my eyes, and pull the trigger.

The entire door shatters, sending shards of glass in every direction.

Behind me, a female controller screams. I'm not sure if she's worried about the radiation or the lunatic blasting down doors, but I don't have time to care.

I step over the useless steel frame and into the radiation chamber. I feel as if I'm standing in a giant tin can, and I'm staring down at another keypad that unlocks the last set of doors.

Suddenly, it occurs to me that I might have finally snapped. In the past hour, I've exposed all of the compound's secrets, killed two Constance creeps, stolen a grenade launcher, and shot out a door on my way to the radiation-soaked desert.

What — the — fuck.

I'm about to turn around, drop to my knees, and blurt out some desperate plea of insanity when the double doors slide open with a loud *hiss*.

A flurry of orange dust blows into the chamber, and I hear the frantic scurry of controllers sprinting toward the canteen. Gunshots crackle in the distance, and the smell of smoke and burned plastic hits my nostrils.

A tall, muscular black guy steps into the chamber hauling a pale blond girl over his shoulder.

Strangely enough, I know this guy. It's Eli's fighter friend, Miles, and he looks pissed. He's sporting a nasty cut over his left eye, and his black T-shirt is torn from flying shrapnel.

"What — the fuck — are you doing?" booms Miles.

I shake my head, shocked into silence by the pool of blood

spreading from the girl's abdomen. She's sweaty and exhausted and much too pale, and suddenly I feel my own selfish worries evaporate.

"I-I wanna help," I choke.

"Good for you," he groans, making eye contact with someone behind me. I whip around — expecting to see controllers at my back — but it's just two Health and Rehab workers waiting to take the injured girl.

Miles helps them transfer her to a stretcher, and the doctors gently remove her mask and hand it to Miles.

I watch them wheel the girl into the postexposure chamber, and then I turn to face the Fringe.

"Damn," I breathe to no one in particular.

The wind feels strong and harsh against my face, and the flying sand stings my eyes. Yet I can't look away.

I've seen the outside before, of course. I've looked out at that same desert my entire life from behind six inches of glass. But *feeling* it? That's an entirely new experience.

"What the fuck are you waiting for?" barks Miles.

My heart practically jumps out of my chest, and I whip around to look at him. But as soon as I open my mouth to speak, a strong blast shakes the ground and illuminates the entire night sky.

I stumble into Miles, but he shoves me away — straight out the airlock doors. I hit the dirt on my hands and knees, and my grenade launcher rolls a few feet away.

"Shit!" says Miles, ducking out of the chamber behind me. "Are you fucking *kidding* me?"

He's staring down at me with a mixture of irritation and disbelief, but a second later, a look of recognition flares in his eyes.

"Ho-ly shit."

"What?" I splutter, scrambling to pick up my grenade launcher.

"You're *him*!" he yells. "*You're* the guy who leaked all that shit about Constance."

"Yeah, that's me," I say, thinking it's probably a miracle that I made it this far.

He lets out a hollow burst of laughter. "Man, you really fucked yourself releasing that video."

"Well, as long as we're all fucked," I grumble, getting to my feet. "Say . . . you need a below-average shot with balls of steel and a death wish?"

"Not really, no."

"I'd be another moving target . . . someone else for those fuckwads to shoot at . . ."

Miles scrutinizes me carefully, and I feel myself shrink about three inches under his gaze.

"You've got some fucking nerve showing your face out here after what your people did to Eli's brother."

"There was nothing I could have done to stop that," I say quietly. "Constance was hungry for blood, and Owen was at the top of their hit list. If I'd gotten in their way, they would have killed me, too, and no one would have ever known the truth."

Miles lets out an aggravated sigh, but then he shakes his head and starts walking toward the battlefield. I'm not sure if he wants me to follow him or not, but I have nowhere else to go.

"As you can see, we can't afford to be picky right now," he calls, tossing the injured girl's mask over his shoulder.

I catch it and pull it over my head, trembling with anticipation.

Suddenly, a bullet pings off a solar module three feet to my left, scattering bits of blue silicon all over the ground. I let out a panicked gasp, but Miles doesn't even seem to notice. He's already jogging back to the front lines, so I duck my head and follow.

A strange mix of panic and awe swamps me as I leave the compound behind. I feel as if the endless navy-blue sky might swallow me whole, but somehow I remain attached to the earth.

Shadowy figures shoot past us in the distance, and a small explosion up ahead causes me to freeze.

"Come on!" yells Miles.

I trip along behind him, my heart speeding up as I try to absorb all the information assaulting my senses.

I've never experienced so many . . . smells. Dirt and decay, burnt hair, melted plastic, sulfur, smoke, and fire. The stench of war is harsh and horrible and exhilarating — all at the same time.

"Do you even know how to shoot that thing?" Miles yells, referring to my grenade launcher.

"Uh . . ."

We stop near a bullet-ridden tent labeled "supplies," and he snatches it out of my hands.

"Fucking hell."

"I —"

"Take this," he says, grabbing a rifle off the table that looks much more manageable. "The mag goes here," he says. "Safety here. Scope . . . find your target . . . shoot. Got it?"

I nod wordlessly, my eyes still tracking the silhouettes of people and trucks approaching from the desert.

"Don't shoot any of our guys, and don't shoot yourself," he says, shoving the gun into my chest.

"Yessir."

Fumbling around in the crates, Miles fishes out a few extra boxes of ammunition. "We're rationing these, so don't go crazy."

"Okay."

"Let's go!" he yells.

I'm still fiddling with my new rifle, but Miles is already several yards away — headed for the front line of Recon operatives.

Shots echo over the cleared zone, and a sudden blind panic flashes through me. My heart is pounding in my throat, and I feel as though I might throw up. The smoke and dust make it impossible to see what's happening five feet in front of me, but the horizon is glowing with the charred remains of burning trucks and makeshift barricades.

Miles ducks behind a low wall of sandbags and pulls me down next to him. A girl with a red braid whips around, and when she sees me, she swears.

"Holy shit! You're the —"

"He's with us," says Miles, redirecting her gaze to the line of drifters on the other side of the fence. "Eyes up."

"Fuck," she breathes.

At first I think she's still talking about me, but when I follow her gaze to the nearest drifter convoy, I see what got her attention.

A line of trucks is approaching the perimeter, but instead of breaking off into groups of two to pass through the hole in the fence, they fan off to the side and keep driving forward.

As I watch, they press their grills against the chain-link panels and hit the gas. I hear a heavy groan of metal, and then the fence shudders. Several more panels collapse at once, hitting the ground in a cloud of dust.

"Brace yourselves, motherfuckers!" Miles yells, unloading his entire magazine on the line of encroaching vehicles.

The window of a white pickup shatters, and several bullets ricochet off the hood. Blood splatters the windshield of the truck farthest to the left, and that vehicle slows to a halt.

The redhead blows out the tires of the Jeep on the right,

and somebody finally takes out the driver of the center truck.

But the damage is already done. The fallen fence has opened the floodgates, and an entire fleet of Desperado vehicles are blazing across the border.

People scream as barricades catch fire and bullets hit their targets. Through the haze, I see Recon people running and yelling — retreating to the compound.

"Holy shit," mutters the redhead.

Nobody in our little group has taken a hit, but I can read the desperation on all their faces.

For the first time, I notice that it isn't just Recon fighting. The broken front line is a mishmash of gray, orange, and green uniforms. The ExCon and Waste Management people probably have less experience holding a gun than I do, and still they're joining in the fight.

But even with every tier-three worker defending the compound, I don't know how much longer we can possibly hold them off. Malcolm seems to have an endless supply of men willing to die for him, and judging by the devastation they've caused so far, they've been stockpiling weapons and ammunition for years.

Suddenly, I hear the low hum of a vehicle coming up behind us.

I whip around and aim my rifle in that direction, but Miles pushes it down.

Three sets of headlights appear in the distance, approaching the fence from the south side of the compound. They're driving at a rapid clip and growing larger every second.

"What the fuck?" Miles mutters.

The redhead wheels around and slowly lowers her weapon. "Are those . . .?"

We watch in astonishment as the headlights grow nearer.

But as soon as the enormous tires and aerodynamic profile of the front car comes into view, I know exactly what they are.

In broad daylight, the pearly finish of the vehicles would appear burnt orange. At dusk, the paint might take on a slightly rosy hue. But in the dark, the cars reflect the deep blue of the desert sky.

The rovers are one fixture of the compound that everyone has heard of but few have ever seen. The fleet was designed to whisk the board away in an emergency, but the compound has never faced a threat great enough to warrant the board's relocation.

If the Secretary of Security made the call to relocate the board this time, that must mean they think we're fighting a losing battle.

"They're *leaving*?"

"Those fucking cowards," growls Miles.

We watch with sinking hearts as the rovers drive over the downed fence, past the drifter convoy, and out into the open desert. A dark cloud of despair settles over the battlefield, and then a burst of flames erupts in the distance.

The momentary flare is bright enough to illuminate the frame of the front rover as it's blown to smithereens. A second later, two more explosions follow in quick succession.

"Oh my god!" chokes the redhead, staring at the fiery remains of the three rovers.

"They blew them up!" yelps another girl. "They blew up the board!"

"How in the *hell* did they do that?" whispers Miles in horror.

My stomach drops to my knees. I know exactly how they did it, but I'd give anything for it not to be true.

When the drifters hacked into our network, they gained access to the compound's security plans. Those plans included our emergency quarantine protocol, mine maps, and a host of other top-secret defensive strategies.

They must also have included the board's evacuation protocol.

The Desperados must have known that someone would sound the alarm for the board to flee once they breached the perimeter. And if my mom told the Desperados the exact route the board would take, it wouldn't be hard to plant mines along that path to ensure no compound leaders survived.

"I can't believe it," murmurs the redhead, staring out at the wreckage. "*They're all dead.*"

twenty-one

Harper

The tension hangs thick in the SUV as we speed north toward the compound.

Sage spends the first hour interrogating Robin, glaring at me in the side mirror every so often as if I made a massive error in judgment bringing her along. Sage seems pretty shaken up from her ordeal, which is probably why she's lashing out.

To Robin's credit, she fields all of Sage's questions calmly and clearly. She doesn't get defensive when Sage implies that she could be one of Malcolm's spies, and she doesn't take offense when Sage asks why she abandoned her son in the first place. Robin recounts the same story she told me, and by the end of it, Sage seems convinced that Robin isn't a threat after all.

Jackson hasn't said more than two words since we left the casino. He's probably replaying the past hour in his mind, wondering what he could have done differently and picturing the looks on the drifters' faces the moment before they died.

The longer we drive, the more my anxiety grows. I know I have to tell Sage and Jackson what I learned, but finding the words seems impossible.

Owen is as good as dead, and Eli might be infected, too. There is no cure. There never was one. I dragged Sage and Jackson into a hotbed of drifters, only to come up empty-handed. I failed Sawyer, I failed Owen, and I failed Eli by abandoning him when it counted.

"I take it you didn't find a cure," says Sage, drawing me back to the present.

"What?"

"That's why we came here, isn't it?" she snaps. "To find a cure that could put a stop to all this?"

There's a heavy, bitter pause as reality sinks in.

"Well?" she prompts.

I shake my head.

"There never was any cure," says Robin quietly. "I looked everywhere for it, but . . . Malcolm never had any intention of stopping this."

Sage shakes her head, trembling with rage. I know she isn't really angry with me. She's angry at herself because she didn't intervene, but she couldn't have stopped this if she tried.

"There's more," I say, summoning up the courage to tell her what we saw on the feed.

"How can there be *more*?" Jackson asks.

"Someone from the compound sent a message to Malcolm," I murmur. "They wanted him to know that they'd captured Owen . . . and that they were going to make the Desperados suffer."

"What?" gasps Sage, twisting around in her seat to look at me. "What do you mean?"

I swallow to wet my parched throat and take a deep breath before answering. "They . . . infected Owen with the virus."

Tears erupt in Sage's eyes, and a heavy tide of despair washes over my entire body. I lean forward and place a hand on her shoulder, but Sage jerks it off and starts to shake, rocking back and forth in a silent wave of tears.

"I'm sorry," I say, trying to keep my voice steady.

"Are you . . . Are you sure?"

"Yeah," I choke. "We saw them inject him."

Sage pulls her hand away, staring over my shoulder with shimmering eyes. “How long does he have?”

“I don’t know . . . Maybe a few days.”

I hesitate, watching Sage’s face in the side mirror to gauge her reaction. It’s a horrible moment to ask for a favor, but I’m running out of time. Once Sage and Jackson accept the likelihood that Owen is going to die, they may lose all interest in helping me break into the compound.

“Listen . . . I need your help.”

Sage and Jackson don’t say anything, but I know they’re listening.

“Eli doesn’t know Owen’s been infected yet. If he makes it inside the compound —” I break off, struggling to keep my emotions in check. “He’s going to go straight for Owen. I need to stop him before it’s too late.”

“It might already be too late,” says Jackson.

“I know. But I can’t just leave him,” I say. “I have to try to stop him.”

Sage is still rocking back and forth in her seat, trying to hold herself together.

“*Please*,” I beg, catching Jackson’s eye in the rearview mirror. “Just get me close to the compound. I’ll go in alone, but I —”

“You won’t be alone,” says Robin.

I pause, too shocked to react with an appropriate amount of gratitude. “I won’t?”

Sage shakes her head. “No, you won’t be.”

“You’ll come with me?”

“Yes,” she says, her voice quivering with resolve. “I-I want to see Owen.”

I nod hastily, but my stomach is squirming with guilt. I don’t want to give Sage any false hope that she’ll get to see Owen one last time. There’s no guarantee we’ll even be able to get her inside the compound — let alone find the place where Constance is keeping him.

"Listen," I say, choosing my words carefully. "You don't have to come. It's really dangerous, and —"

Sage wipes her tears away and sniffs, summoning some of that inner toughness I've grown to love about her. "I don't care. I'm in."

I sigh and shoot her an appreciative look. I wish I could tell her how glad I am to have her on my side, but my throat is already burning with emotion.

I don't want to talk anymore. I don't want to think. I just want this all to be over.

The wind howls as it blasts through the open windows and out the back hatch. It turns my hair into a tangled mess and makes my eyes feel dry and itchy.

Within a couple hours, the sun sinks below the horizon, and the only sources of light are the anemic glow of our headlights, an endless blanket of stars, and the delicate silver moon. It's unnerving.

Every shape that appears in the shadows makes my hand inch toward my gun. My brain is always convinced that the shadow belongs to a drifter, but it just turns out to be a scrubby little bush or a misshapen boulder along the side of the road.

We haven't seen any sign of the Desperados since we left the base, but I'm not convinced that we've lost them completely. We could be driving straight into an ambush. We could wander into the territory of another gang or get a flat and be stranded out in the middle of nowhere.

But after several hours, we hit a patch of desert air that smells like smoke. It isn't the organic scent of burned wood. It's acrid and chemical like melting plastic.

"We're getting close," Jackson mutters, slowing the Explorer to a crawl.

I flip on the borrowed interface to scan for mines, and Jackson follows a pair of tire treads to avoid explosives the Desperados might have planted.

Sage and Robin haven't said a word in hours, but I can tell from their posture that they're wide awake. The sounds of gunfire and grenades are unmistakable, growing louder every second.

Suddenly, a flare of light erupts in the distance. It has to be at least two miles away, but it illuminates the entire landscape like a spotlight. For a split second, the shadow of the compound appears on the horizon. Then darkness envelops the desert once again.

"What the hell was that?" asks Sage.

"That was a land mine," says Robin.

I swallow. A land mine being triggered could mean any number of things. It could mean a drifter blew himself up or that one of our people tripped one of the Desperados' reburied mines.

But as we watch, a secondary explosion seems to swallow the first. It erupts with blinding intensity, sending a plume of noxious smoke billowing into the air. Then a third ball of flame explodes, and the stench of sulfur drifts toward us on the wind.

"Were those mines, too?" whispers Sage.

Robin nods, looking deeply troubled.

As we draw closer, the fragmented outline of the compound begins to take shape. Judging by the pattern of light emanating from the upper levels, it must be experiencing a partial power outage. A volley of mini explosions makes the sides of the SUV rattle, and Sage passes me a box of ammunition.

I check my rifle and the spare magazines on my belt, and we follow a line of drifter trucks rolling toward the compound.

My eyes scan the darkness for the twelve-foot electric fence, but we never reach it. Then our tires bump over something rough, and my heart sinks.

Several sections of the fence have been completely torn away, and dozens of drifter trucks are rolling unimpeded into compound territory.

"What now?" asks Jackson.

I don't know what to say. Up ahead, I spot the outline of several makeshift Recon barricades. By the looks of it, the Desperados have already pushed our people back, and Recon is vastly outnumbered.

Suddenly, a Desperado rears up from the bed of a truck and launches a grenade toward a sandbag barrier. Three or four people dart out, and the Desperados open fire.

"No!" I yell, watching in horror as one man goes down.

Before I have time to formulate a plan, I'm fumbling with the door handle and jumping out of the SUV. I whip my gun around to aim at the truckload of drifters, but then I hear a strangled yell and the sound of another door opening.

"Harper, wait!" yells Sage.

I don't listen. I take aim and fire, hitting the drifter who launched the grenade. He lets out a moan of anguish and then topples backward out of the truck bed.

"What are you doing?" yells Sage, pushing down my rifle. "They'll see you!"

"Those are my friends!" I shout. "I can't just *stand* here and do nothing!"

"It won't do any good to bring the Desperados down on us now," says Robin, materializing on my right.

"This is my home!" I cry, fighting the swell of anguish rising up inside me.

"How can you say that?" yells Sage.

The glow of a nearby fire throws deep shadows over her face, making her look downright terrifying.

"Those people took Owen!" she screams, pointing up at the looming glass tower with a shaky hand. "They're *killing* him, and they might be killing Eli, too!"

"I still have friends in there!"

"News flash!" yells Jackson, getting out of the SUV and slamming the door. "We don't give a fuck about your friends."

We all turn to stare at him.

"I'm sorry, but someone needed to say it."

Sage takes a deep breath. "I think what he means is that —"

"Don't try to tell me what I mean," he snaps. "This whole thing has gone far enough."

"What are you saying?" I ask.

"I'm saying that this was supposed to be about saving Owen, but obviously it's too late." He shrugs. "You're all right, Harper. I really wish I could help you. And I'm sorry about Eli, but you need to give this up. This isn't our fight."

A rusted-out old truck explodes nearby, illuminating Jackson's cold expression and shaking the ground beneath our feet.

I wait for Sage to say something, but she doesn't. Tears are streaming silently down her face, and I know she thinks I'm holding on to hope for a rescue that just isn't possible. The only reason she's going along with it is so she can see Owen one last time.

Jackson turns to go, and I feel a tide of hateful words bubbling up in my throat. I try to swallow them down and think of something better to say, but they burst out of my mouth before I have a chance to censor myself.

"This is what you do, isn't it?" I shout.

"What?" he barks in surprise.

"As soon as things get a little dangerous, you pack up your shit and leave."

Jackson freezes.

"You gave up Nuclear Nation to the Desperados," I yell, my voice quivering with rage. "Then you realized you'd made a huge mistake, so you ran away and hid."

Sage's eyes grow wide, but I keep on rolling.

"You *left* Owen, and he covered for you! He almost got *killed* because of you. And now that Malcolm is winning this fight, you're just gonna run away again."

Jackson still has his back to me, but judging from the look on Sage's face, I know I've struck a nerve.

"You don't know anything," he growls.

"I know you were only too happy to run off with me instead of going through the Desperados to get to Owen."

Finally, Jackson seems to have had enough. He wheels around, eyes blazing with fury, and I take an automatic step back.

"Shut up!" he yells. "Shut — up! You think you know what it's like out here just because you ran away from the compound?" He shakes his head. "You don't know *shit*! You don't know shit about the Desperados, and you don't know shit about me!"

"I know that if we don't do something, the Desperados are going to take over the compounds — just like they took over Nuclear Nation," I fire back.

"Well, I'm sorry, but that's not my fucking problem anymore!"

"It's everybody's problem!" I shout. "Do you really think anybody will be safe once Malcolm takes over the compounds? You think things will get *better* for you?"

"It's not like things can get much worse."

"Oh, that's bullshit."

Jackson's lip curls in anger. He's staring at me as though he wants to slap me, but then he seems to deflate. "What do you want from me, Harper?"

I open my mouth wordlessly, a little taken aback by his question.

"I didn't ask for this."

"None of us did," I say, annoyed by his sudden cowardice.

Jackson hesitates, looking down at his shoes. For a second, I think he might cave to the pressure and man up, but then he turns around and climbs back into the driver's seat.

"What are you *doing*?" yells Sage.

"I'm sorry," he calls down, tossing Robin his handgun.

"You're sorry?" Sage splutters.

Jackson slams the door, and Sage's eyes narrow in confusion.

"You don't need me anyway," he mutters. "You need a goddamn army."

"Jackson!"

It takes me several seconds to realize what's happening, and once I do, it's already too late.

Jackson throws the Explorer into reverse and starts backing away the way we came.

"No!" I shout, following the truck for several yards. "You can't leave! Not *now*."

But Jackson doesn't stop. Instead, he spins the truck around to face the open desert. His foot hits the gas, and he speeds off into the night — leaving the three of us standing out in the desert, completely exposed.

I look around hopelessly. During our shouting match, another convoy of Desperados materialized on the horizon, and they're headed right toward us. If we wait around, we're going to get caught in the crossfire.

"We have to go," I say, glancing around for a clear path forward.

Sage nods numbly, and Robin looks down at the gun in her hands.

Just then, one of the trucks speeds up, blinding us with its headlights.

"Run!" I yell.

We take off at a sprint — Sage and me leading the way with Robin bringing up the rear. I keep my feet inside the drifters' tire treads, and my lungs burn as we race across the dusty battlefield.

Suddenly, Robin cries out in alarm, and I look back in time to see a Desperado launch a grenade into the air. It flies toward us in a graceful arch and lands less than fifteen feet away.

I scramble to put as much distance between me and the grenade as possible. My legs feel heavy and gelatinous, so I throw myself onto the ground and cover my head with my hands.

A second later, the grenade explodes, sending razor-sharp splinters and fragments flying in every direction. A few slice over the tops of my hands and the backs of my legs, but I just lie there and wait for it to end.

Breathing hard, I rise into a crouch and search the ground frantically for Robin and Sage.

Robin moans a few feet away, and I feel her fingers curl around my wrist. We help each other into a standing position, and I do a quick scan for wounds.

Robin is shaken and a little scratched up, but she seems otherwise unharmed.

Sage is nowhere to be found.

"Sage!" I yell, squinting through the shadows for any signs of life.

Nothing.

I drag Robin through the dust, coughing and shaking.

"Sage!"

Somebody chokes nearby, and my heart speeds up.

"Sage!"

"Here!" she calls.

Judging by the sound of her voice, Sage is several yards away. She must have seen the grenade coming before we did and gotten herself out of harm's way.

Struggling through the thick veil of dust, we locate Sage and start running toward the line of trucks inching closer to the compound. People are running in every direction, and I don't have time to wonder whether they're Recon, Desperados, or tier-three workers fleeing the compound.

We reach a smoking black sedan littered with bullet holes and duck behind it to catch our breath. Positioning my rifle on the top of the car, I squint into the darkness for a safe path through the wreckage.

Several yards ahead is a large Recon barricade made out of sandbags, old crates, and what look like metal doors ripped from the ExCon latrines. Peering through my scope, I spot a mane of fiery-red hair pulled up into a disheveled braid.

Lenny's milky-white skin is smeared with dirt, but when she rises over the barricade to shoot, I know it has to be her.

"On my mark!" she yells. "One . . . two . . . three!"

A deafening blast shakes the ground we're standing on, and an enormous white van goes up in flames.

"Where are you going?" yells Sage as I inch toward the nose of the car.

"That's my friend!" I shout, pointing over at the barricade. "She's our ticket inside."

Sage peers over the hood of the car to get a look at Lenny, and I see reluctant acceptance flash across her face.

"Stay low," I say, glancing over at Robin to make sure she's ready.

Judging by her horrified expression, all her days out on the Fringe never prepared her for a battle like this.

"You still with us?" I yell.

She swallows and nods, and I lock eyes with Sage. "Let's go."

Heart pounding, I shoot out from our hiding place and make a beeline for Lenny. There's no cover between here and the barricade, but Lenny's squad is focused on a truckload of Desperados.

As soon as we're within earshot, I call out to her, waving my arms to get her attention.

Lenny doesn't look over. She's too busy shooting at the Desperados, but we're getting close.

I call again.

This time, I see her braid whip over her shoulder as she searches for the source of my voice.

"Lenny!"

Finally, her eyes latch on to mine. Confusion, recognition, and relief dawn on her face, and I glance over my shoulder to make sure Robin and Sage are still with me.

When I look back, Lenny has opened her mouth to say something, but I can't hear what it is. I see my name form on her lips, but then a look of horror washes over her face. Her gaze is fixated on something behind me, but I don't have time to turn around.

The ground shudders beneath my feet, and I feel a flash of heat spread across my back.

An unstoppable force throws me to the ground, and my head hits the earth. Somebody screams. It could have been me. Then something sharp slices through my flesh, and my shoulder burns in agony.

Hot scraps of metal and rock rain down all over my body, but I'm too stunned to move or even shield myself from the debris.

When I open my eyes, all I see is a thick wall of smoke and flames lapping at the ground around me. The air smells like melted plastic and burned flesh, but I have no idea what just happened.

I think I yell, but I don't hear my own voice. The only thing I'm aware of is a white-hot pain in my shoulder and a dull ringing in my ears.

Twisting around in the dirt, I see nothing but an endless wall of fire. I call out for Robin, Sage, Lenny — anyone — but my voice is drowned out by the deafening *whoosh* of flames.

My eyes are watering, my skin is burning, and my mouth is too dry to speak. But then I see a flash of white pierce the thick veil of smoke, and hope flutters in my chest.

Somebody yells my name, but it can't be who I think it is.

My head is spinning, and I can feel myself slipping away. Through the haze of smoke, I see a man in white fighting through the flames.

At first I think I must be hallucinating, but then I hear my name again. I open my mouth to call back to him, but my reply is stifled by a painful, choking cough.

Fighting to stay conscious, I stare through the flames, but my rescuer never appears. I call back in desperation, but my weak, raspy voice disappears on the air.

Blackness is pressing in on the edges of my vision, and my limbs feel as though they're made of lead.

As my head grows heavy and the flames start to thicken, I realize that no one is coming to save me. There isn't anyone calling my name — there never was.

I'm alone.

twenty-two

Eli

I'm awoken slowly by deep, burning pains all over my body. My ribs ache from my earlier beating, my leg is shredded, and my back is bruised. I'm lying on a cold hard floor, but the harsh light trickling through my eyelids tells me I'm no longer in the canteen.

As I regain consciousness, memories of the last few hours set off a chain reaction of slowly building dread.

I managed to break through Malcolm's army, scale a twelve-foot fence, and persuade Bear to smuggle me back into the compound, but somewhere along the way I was captured by Constance.

I peel my crusty eyelids open with a wince and wait for my vision to adjust. Bright white light is beating down with blinding intensity, and it takes me a moment to realize that part of the brightness has to do with the cream-colored walls and ugly white tile. It's speckled with gray, yellow, and puke-brown flecks of paint — the sort of tile they might use in the medical ward to hide traces of dirt and blood.

Upon closer inspection, I see that the walls are no ordinary walls. They're padded with a thick plastic material that's probably soundproof as well as suicide-proof.

"Heeeeey, brother . . ." croaks a low, familiar voice.

I blink, too depleted to be truly startled. I can't see anything in my peripheral vision, so I turn my head slowly to one side and then the other.

Owen is slumped against the wall to my left — pale, shirtless, and covered in chemical burns. His eye sockets look like two purplish pits, and his chest is shining with beads of sweat.

I never noticed Owen's tattoos before, but now I see that he's got an intricate sugar skull design inked in black over his heart. Three skulls are clustered together in a radiating geometric design: two larger ones flanking a child-sized skull.

"Is that me?" I ask in a delirious voice, not expecting him to know what I'm referring to.

He nods. "You . . . Dad and Mom," he mumbles. "I never thought I'd see you again."

"Where are we?" I ask.

"You tell me."

He doesn't say it, but his meaning is clear: This is my home, and these are *my* people.

I drag in a labored breath and focus on the details of the room I can see. We're surrounded by four padded walls. One has a door handle cut into the padding. Another has a large streaky mirror positioned at chest level, but it could very well be hiding an observation window.

We aren't in Constance headquarters, and we're not in the cages. It's too clean to be Recon and too dated to be Systems. They wouldn't dare take us up to the medical ward — not since the virus put the entire section on lockdown. I have no clue where we are.

"You shouldn't have come back," says Owen, his voice ragged and uneven as if he's struggling for air.

"I had to," I say.

"Why?" he snaps, speaking so harshly that it launches him into a brutal coughing fit.

I wait for it to stop, trying to decide how to tell him the truth without getting my ass beat.

"You were in the clear," he continues. "You and Harper could have kept going and never had to —"

"It wouldn't have been right," I say. "It's my fault you were captured. I'm the reason you came back."

"And I'm the reason you left," he says, silently daring me to contradict him.

"I lied," I mumble, cringing as I pull myself up against the wall.

There's a long, heavy pause.

"I know."

"You *know*?"

"I knew you couldn't stand what Malcolm had done. You'd have found a way to fuck everything up."

I shake my head, utterly confused. "If you knew, why didn't you say something?"

Owen shrugs. "I didn't say I knew it at the time. I *should* have, but I didn't. I guess I just wanted to believe you so badly that —"

He breaks off in another coughing fit, and something about the wet hacking sound triggers a deeper concern.

"How long have you been coughing like that?" I ask, taking in his pale skin and feverish eyes with renewed worry.

Owen doesn't say anything. He doesn't shrug it off, either, which is what I would expect from a hard-ass like my brother.

"What aren't you telling me?"

Owen is silent for so long that I think he might be ignoring me. But when he finally looks up and meets my gaze, the dread in his eyes is unmistakable. "I'm infected."

"*What*?"

"Ironic, isn't it?"

I shake my head. "No. You can't be . . . How is that possible?"

"The fucking psycho who's been giving me the runaround

injected me with the virus to put on a show for Malcolm's crew — one last pathetic attempt to force him into giving up the cure." He flashes a dark sneer. "Joke's on them, I guess."

"Why do you say that?"

Owen narrows his eyes and cocks his head to the side. "Think about it."

I don't say anything. I'm still having trouble accepting the fact that my brother is infected. And if I'm sitting here with him, that must mean I'm infected, too.

"What?" I bark.

He seems awfully fucking chill about the fact that a deadly virus is ripping through his veins and that I'm cooking in the same shit stew.

"There isn't any cure," says Owen, looking at me as though my hopefulness is the real tragedy.

I open my mouth to speak, but no words come out.

There are no words for what I'm feeling. I'm trapped in a room with the brother I thought I'd lost forever. Both of us are going to die, and it's all my fault.

"You shouldn't have come back," Owen repeats.

I shake my head. I don't want to hear it.

"I'm sorry," he murmurs.

That takes me by surprise. I can't remember Owen ever saying he was sorry — even when we were kids. He could be a real dick sometimes, and he was never sorry.

"It's fucked up what Malcolm did," he continues. "I never should have been a part of it . . . I never should have let myself get sucked in."

I should feel gratified to hear Owen admit that Malcolm is an evil son of a bitch, but it all just seems so fucking pointless.

"I don't blame you for any of this," Owen adds. "We've all done so much terrible shit . . . I can't blame anybody else anymore."

"You should," I mutter. "This is all my fault."

"No," he says. "I did this. I may as well have infected myself."

Suddenly, a crack of static breaks through our pathetic conversation. I whip my head around for the source of the noise, but before I can locate the speaker, a sickeningly familiar voice booms out in our tiny chamber.

"Welcome, Parker . . . or should I say *welcome back*."

I swallow once to wet my parched throat.

"I guess trouble runs in the family," says the Answer Man, his voice crackling over the speakers.

"What do you want?" I ask, staring up at the ceiling in search of a camera.

"Your time for negotiation has passed, Eli," he replies swiftly. "You are only here as a tool."

I don't say anything. I don't know what that could possibly mean, but I won't give him the satisfaction of asking.

"Your brother is just as stubborn as you were."

"I already told you," growls Owen. "There's no — fucking — cure!"

"I have no way to know whether or not you're being truthful with me, Owen. But fortunately, we don't need your cure anymore."

Apprehension flashes in Owen's eyes. He probably thought that the possibility of a cure was the only thing keeping him alive.

"That's right," says the Answer Man. "Our medical personnel are seeing great progress with an innovative application of immunotherapy. We have several infected patients undergoing treatment as we speak."

This has taken an unexpected turn. I know the Answer Man isn't telling us about a new treatment to give us hope. He's telling us so that he can use the treatment as leverage. Or maybe he's just fucking with us.

"As I'm sure you know . . . Malcolm Martinez has distinguished himself as the compound's number one enemy . . ."

"Aww," mutters Owen. "And I thought *I* was your number one enemy."

"Don't flatter yourself. You are merely an annoyance . . . a tick on the compound's back. But I believe we could turn that parasitic relationship into a . . . *symbiotic* one."

"How's that?"

"Just give us the location of the Desperados' other base."

I glance over at Owen, trying to gauge his reaction, but his expression is unreadable.

"What other base?"

"The base that serves as the true center of drifter operations. The base where the Desperados have been stockpiling food and ammunition to prepare for this attack."

"There is no other base," says Owen.

"That's too bad."

I have no way to see the Answer Man's face, but I can tell he's working hard to avoid betraying even the slightest frustration so we don't think he's losing control.

"Sorry to disappoint," says Owen, his voice dripping with sarcasm.

"I know you worked closely with Malcolm Martinez over the past few months," says the Answer Man. "You must have some idea of how this virus progresses."

Owen swallows, unable to hide the tremor of rage that flits over his sweaty, bloodless face.

"The difference is we were able to isolate the virus and inject a sample directly into your bloodstream. The coughing . .

. the wheezing . . . the slow suffocation . . . the hallucinations . . . All those wonderful symptoms will soon be yours, but at an accelerated rate."

Owen drags in a breath that looks as though it costs him great effort, and I begin to panic. If what the Answer Man says is true, then Owen could only have a day or two — not the week most patients get.

"We've already offered you an out, and you've refused."

"What does it matter?" yells Owen. "You're just gonna kill me anyway."

The Answer Man lets out a harsh laugh. "And here I thought you were refusing help on purely *moral* grounds."

Owen lets out a disgusted scoff.

The Answer Man pauses. "No matter . . . You're well within your rights to refuse treatment for yourself. But I wonder . . . Would you refuse treatment for Eli as well?"

Owen is fighting to keep his expression neutral, but I can tell from the flare of his nostrils that the Answer Man has struck a nerve.

"What kind of man — what kind of *brother* — would allow his younger sibling to die a slow, painful, wholly preventable death?"

"No," I say aloud, locking eyes with Owen and shaking my head.

The second Owen gives up the one card he has to play, Constance will have no reason to keep either one of us alive.

"Don't be a martyr, Eli," the Answer Man simpers. "Why should you die to save the gang that has been killing your cadets in cold blood for years? Why should you die when you can live?"

"You're just gonna let me live, huh?" I snarl. "Yeah, right. If you'd had your way, I'd have been dead a long time ago. No one knows I'm here! What's to stop you from killing me the second he tells you what you want to know?"

"Nothing," says the Answer Man. "You're just going to have to trust me."

"Fuck off."

"It's live or die, Eli."

"I'm not afraid to die," I growl.

"No?"

"Don't tell him shit," I say to Owen, glaring up at the ceiling.

"Your choice, Owen," says the Answer Man.

Owen doesn't say anything, but I can read the fear and regret in his eyes. Thirteen years' worth of guilt is weighing on his soul, and it's clouding his judgment.

"You might not want him to save you now," the Answer Man croons. "But when your lungs are so full of fluid that you're drowning . . . When you can no longer breathe from the pain of it all . . . When the hallucinations bring back every horrible thing you've ever done . . . You'll be *begging* me —"

"Okay!" Owen barks.

"Don't!" I yell, whipping my head around.

A fiercely protective expression dawns on Owen's face, and he looks so much like our dad that it gives me chills.

"What are you *doing*?" I hiss.

"Saving your ass."

"Are you crazy?" I shake my head in frustration. "We don't even know if he's telling the truth!"

"It doesn't matter," says Owen.

"Yes, it does!" I lower my voice to barely above a whisper. "As soon as you tell him what he wants to know, he's not gonna have any reason to keep you around."

"Don't worry about me," says Owen. "I'm gonna get us out of this."

"I'm waiting," says the Answer Man.

I hold Owen's gaze for several seconds, wishing he would listen to me just this once.

"I'll tell you whatever you want to know," he says, tearing his eyes away from me. "Just leave my brother out of this."

twenty-three

Harper

Slowly, painfully, I emerge from the undertow. I wasn't quite asleep, and I'm not dead, either. I'm in way too much pain to be dead.

By now the adrenaline has faded away, and the burning sensation in my shoulder is excruciating. My head feels fuzzy, and my arms and legs are cocooned in a thin, scratchy blanket.

Voices bounce off the walls around me, and I can detect movement dancing over my eyelids.

Peeling my eyes open a fraction of an inch, I'm instantly blinded by artificial light. I blink several times to force my eyes to adjust, and Celdon's pale, anxious face swims into view.

"Hey, Riles," he croaks.

His voice sounds so familiar and so normal that I wonder briefly if I *am* dead. I don't know how else Celdon could be sitting beside me.

"Why are you here?" I ask, surprised by the effort it takes to force out those words.

"You got blown up."

"*What?*"

"Yeah. One of the drifters had a pipe bomb. You're lucky to be alive."

That would explain the blast and my singed hair, but it doesn't explain where I am. It's loud and echoey and very bright. I'm not in the medical ward, and I'm not in Recon.

"You're in the multipurpose room off the main tunnel,"

says Celdon.

I start to sit up, but he pushes me back down.

"Don't worry — you're safe," he says, correctly interpreting my alarmed expression. "They set up a temporary med station here to take care of the wounded. We managed to convince everybody that you're on our side."

"We?" I repeat. "Wait . . . What happened to me?" I ask, feeling the thick pad of gauze taped over my shoulder blade.

"Shrapnel," says another familiar voice. "And you hit your head pretty hard."

Lenny's worried face appears over mine. Her fiery hair is tumbling out of its braid, and her peaches-and-cream complexion is marred by dirt and blood. She looks as though she's been through hell, but the sight of her gives me a surge of relief.

"Oh my god," I mutter, letting out a grateful laugh. "You're alive."

Lenny nods and leans over to give me an awkward half hug.

"Oh, god. I thought . . ."

"I know," Lenny murmurs.

"What about the people I was with?"

"We made it," says a voice to my left.

"Robin?" I choke.

"I'm here," she says, leaning in so I don't have to strain to look at her.

Robin's face and chest are covered in burns, and she's got a thick bandage wrapped around one side of her neck. At first I think those are her only injuries, but then I see that her arm is wrapped in a thick layer of gauze.

"It's all right," she says. "It looks worse than it is."

I shake my head, pushing down the lump in my throat. "And Sage?"

Robin purses her lip and glances away, and a sick feeling rises up in my stomach.

"No," I whisper.

"It's okay," says Robin. "She's alive."

"Where is she?" I ask, my voice coming out much louder than I intended.

I try to sit up again to look for her, but Celdon puts a hand on my good shoulder to hold me down. "Easy."

"She's still in surgery," says Robin carefully.

"What?" I cry. "Why? What's wrong with her?"

Robin sighs. "She saw the man throw the pipe bomb before I did. She pushed me out of the way in time, but she got the worst of the blast." Robin closes her eyes and swallows before continuing. "A piece of shrapnel got lodged in her head. They're trying to remove it now."

"Oh my god."

I can't believe this is happening. We survived a bomb blast, but Sage is in surgery.

Then it hits me: Sage is here because of me.

"I shouldn't have asked her to come," I whisper, more to myself than to Robin.

"Harper, this isn't your fault."

"Yes, it is."

"No," says Robin.

"Sage wouldn't even *be* here if I hadn't asked her to come."

"That's ridiculous."

"I asked for her help!"

"You also told her that her boyfriend was infected," Robin reasons. "It wouldn't have mattered if you'd told her *not* to come. There's nothing in the world that could have prevented her from trying to see him one last time."

I pause, turning this idea over in my head. Deep down, I

know that Robin is right, but it doesn't make me feel any better.

"Help me up," I say finally, reaching for Lenny's hand and using it to pull myself into a seated position. A burst of pain erupts in my shoulder, and I have to squeeze my lips together to keep myself from screaming.

"What're you —"

"I have to go," I grunt, swinging my legs over the edge of my cot and preparing to stand.

"What? Harper, no."

"I *have* to," I say, dragging in a deep breath to keep the pain at bay. "I have to find Eli before he gets to Owen."

But Celdon is already shaking his head. "Harper, you can't. You just had a two-inch piece of metal taken out of your shoulder. You probably have a concussion. And if you get caught —"

"It doesn't matter!" I cry. "Look. I tried to find a cure for this virus, and I failed. If Eli gets to Owen, he's as good as dead. I'm not gonna let that happen."

"Harper! Listen!" yells Celdon, losing all composure and putting a hand on my uninjured shoulder. "You can't help him. It's too late. Lenny just told me she helped Eli break into the compound *hours* ago."

"Was there anybody with him?" I ask.

Celdon and Lenny exchange a puzzled look.

"No," says Lenny. "He was alone."

My stomach drops. If Gunner wasn't with him, it must mean he deserted Eli or got killed along the way.

"I have to go," I repeat.

"Harper, no," says Celdon. "Either Eli already made it to Owen, or he's been caught."

"You don't know that."

"Yes, I do. And I'm not going to let you run off and get

yourself killed."

"I'm not giving up on him."

"I know you don't want to," says Celdon. "But you have to be realistic."

"That's what I told Eli," I whisper, my stomach aching with regret. "I told him we'd never get past Recon *and* the Desperados, and I was wrong. I left him to go look for a cure, and if I hadn't —"

"If you hadn't, you would have gotten captured or infected right along with him."

I shake my head. "I'm not going to leave him again. I won't do it."

Celdon and Lenny exchange a serious look. Robin has been strangely silent throughout this whole conversation, but she's wearing an expression that tells me she thinks that Eli is a lost cause.

Suddenly, a surge of anger rises up inside of me, and I turn to glare at Celdon. "If Eli gets infected, I swear to god —"

"I'm sorry, Harper!"

"You're *sorry*?" I repeat, my whole body thrumming with indignation. "You let Constance infect Owen for some sick public service announcement. Do you have *any* idea how fucked up that is?"

"There was no stopping them!" he snaps. "I didn't know Eli was trying to get to Owen, but even if I had, there was nothing I could have done to protect him. Owen is a drifter."

"God! You're so full of shit."

"Believe whatever you want," snaps Celdon. "I knew you'd hate my fucking guts, but I had no choice."

"Yeah, keep telling yourself that."

"People had to know!"

I roll my eyes and glance away, too disgusted even to look

at him.

"Listen, I know I've done some super shitty things lately, and I can't take those things back. But telling people the truth? Exposing Constance? That's *worth* something."

"What are you talking about?"

Celdon nods over to one of the video screens along the wall. Each one is playing the news, and to my astonishment, I see Celdon's face stretched across two of the screens.

"You didn't," I breathe.

Celdon nods.

"You went public?"

He swallows and nods again.

"What did you tell them?"

He shrugs. "Everything. I leaked the VocAps records . . . private messages about Constance subsidizing bids . . . I even told them about Jayden and Sullivan Taylor."

"Jayden?"

Celdon raises his eyebrows. "Jayden's dead."

"*What*?"

"Constance had her killed."

"*Shit*."

I don't know what shocks me more: hearing that Jayden is dead or that Celdon went public about Constance.

Singlehandedly taking on the most dangerous organization within the compound is probably both the bravest and stupidest thing he's ever done. But rather than looking pleased with himself, Celdon keeps glancing nervously at the door.

At the moment, the only people milling around are doctors and nurses in red scrubs, but we both know he's in danger.

"You shouldn't be here," I say. "It's only a matter of time before they come after you."

"They already have."

"What?"

"They sent Devon to Systems to kill me," he whispers.

"Oh my god. What *happened*?"

Celdon glances off into the distance, and I catch a glimpse of the deep seed of darkness that's taken root in his soul. "It doesn't matter."

I don't know what to say to that, but then Celdon sighs. "Unbelievably, I'm not Constance's biggest problem right now."

"What are you talking about?"

"The drifters took out the board," he says. "They were trying to flee the compound, and Malcolm blew their asses up. The compound's gonna have to hold an emergency election, and you can bet Constance —"

"They blew up the whole board?"

Celdon and Lenny nod, and suddenly I remember the explosions Robin, Sage, and I saw in the distance.

"Oh my god."

My mind is spinning. I can't believe the board is gone. The compound has never had a president die in office, and losing all our leaders in one fell swoop is incomprehensible.

But I can't think about the board right now. I can't think about the drifters or Celdon or Sage lying on the operating table.

Eli is here, which means he's in danger.

"I have to get back out there," says Lenny after a moment. "I'm sorry, Harper."

"It's okay," I murmur, swallowing down my fear. Everywhere I look, people I love are throwing themselves into peril.

"Please be careful," she whispers, bending down to give me a gentle hug. "If you *do* find Eli . . . tell him he owes me one."

I grin and give her hand a grateful squeeze. I can't quite put my feelings into words, but I'm so damn proud of her. I'm also terrified I might lose her.

Never in a million years would I have imagined that the drifters would march on the compound and break through the perimeter. I never thought that the people I trained beside for months would be falling left and right on the battlefield. It feels like a nightmare that none of us can wake up from.

I watch Lenny go with a tight feeling in my chest and then round on Celdon.

"Tell me where he is," I say.

"Riles —"

"I'm going with or without your help, Celdon. Not telling me will only slow me down."

Celdon sighs and turns to Robin. "Will you tell her she should just stay here and rest?"

Robin looks startled at being dragged into this argument, but she fixes her son with a serious look. "I think you should tell her what she wants to know."

"*What*?"

"She can't just walk away," she says softly. "Take it from someone who knows: Even when it seems like the most sensible thing . . . once you walk away, that decision will haunt you for the rest of your life."

Celdon just stares at Robin as though he can't believe what he's hearing.

"I'll give you two some time," she says, getting up and looking over toward the area that's been partitioned off for surgery. "I'm going to see if there's any news on Sage."

"Thank you," I say, shooting Robin a grateful look.

Celdon watches her walk off with a stunned expression on his face, and when he turns back to me, he looks as though he forgot what we were arguing over in the first place.

"I have to get back out there," he says.

"Out where?"

"The Fringe."

"The . . . *What?*"

"I'm playing Recon today," he says with a shrug. "They need all the help they can get right now."

"Are you serious?"

He nods.

"You are such a hypocrite."

"How am *I* a hypocrite?" he splutters.

"You don't want me going after Eli, and yet you're throwing yourself into battle?"

"It's not the same," says Celdon. "Going after Eli is a suicide mission."

"And running into a war zone without any training *isn't?*"

"It's not the same!" Celdon cries, his voice torn by pain and frustration. "You don't deserve to die."

"Neither do you!"

Celdon's eyebrows shoot up in surprise, and I feel my iron veil of resentment lift enough to see the pain and self-loathing written all over his face.

"You don't deserve to die," I repeat in a low voice. "You aren't a bad person."

"You don't know all the things I've done."

"You don't know all the things I've done either," I say. "I've killed people, Celdon. I helped start a war that we don't know how to end. I let Eli come here alone because I was so sure I could find a cure for this virus, and I failed."

Celdon is staring at me as though his heart is breaking, and I feel all my anger evaporate.

"I'm going to find him," I say quietly. "And you should try to fix things with your mom."

Celdon's expression hardens. "I don't have anything to say to her."

"Yes, you do."

Celdon doesn't respond right away, but he looks extremely uncomfortable. It's a strange experience. I can't ever recall a time when Celdon said anything less than exactly what was on his mind.

"She did what she did because she *loves* you," I add.

"That's not an excuse."

"I know it's not, but she wants to fix it. And she's risking her life just by *being* here."

Celdon lets out a long sigh, and I see all the fight drain out of him in an instant.

"Owen's being held in the medical ward," he murmurs, looking as though he already regrets his decision to tell me.

"What?"

"He's in the psych ward. If Eli's on the right track, that's where he'll be."

My mind flashes to the video of Owen in the sterile, padded room, and I wonder how I missed it before. I've *been* in the psych ward. I spent a week there after my first deployment.

As I mentally map the path I'll have to take, Celdon reaches into his back pocket and fishes out a blank key card.

"This is the master key I made to get through all the barricades," he says. "It should get you through just about any door in the compound."

"Thanks," I say in surprise, taking the card reverently. "But what about you? Don't you need it?"

Celdon shrugs. "I always make doubles."

I take a deep breath. I don't want to think that this could be the last time I see Celdon, but the odds that we're both going to live until tomorrow are slim.

"Promise me you'll be careful," I whisper.

"Riles, come on," he says with an echo of his old carefree

self. "You know some of the cray-cray shit I've done." He cracks a grin. "I ain't dead yet."

"This is different."

"Yeah, I know . . ." he says, bending down to look at me at eye level. "This is the first crazy thing I've done that actually *means* something."

That statement nearly cracks me in two. A choked sob works its way up my throat, and I throw my arms around his neck. Celdon lets out a surprised burst of air and then wraps his long, skinny arms around my waist.

"I love you," I murmur into his blood-stained blazer. "You know that, right?"

"Yeah, I know," he says. "You have to love me . . . You're the only real family I've got."

I pull back with a sigh and straighten his lapel. "Not anymore," I whisper. "Go talk to your mom. And be careful."

Celdon nods once and gives me a chaste kiss on the side of the head. "Good luck, Riles. I hope you find what you're looking for."

twenty-four

Celdon

I watch Harper go with a sick feeling in the pit of my stomach. Her gait is slow and stiff as if every movement pains her, but she crosses the room with a look of such determination that I know she'll die before she walks away from Eli.

Along the edge of the room, medical ward personnel have rolled a dozen white privacy dividers in front of the ceiling-to-floor windows, blocking the Fringe from view. I suppose it's to keep the wounded from having to see their friends get slaughtered on the battlefield, but I can still see the flashes of exploding cars and burning barricades in the distance.

Here goes nothing, I think, picking up my rifle and heading for the door. But then I hear Harper's nagging voice in my head, and I turn toward the surgical station instead.

The area is blocked off by more white partitions, but I see Robin pacing back and forth outside the makeshift operating room, waiting for news about a drifter girl she hardly knows.

I walk toward her slowly, drawn by a mixture of longing and resentment.

"You seem awfully dedicated," I call as soon as I'm within earshot.

Robin turns to look at me, and a million weird expressions flit across her face: surprise, guilt, hope, and . . . something else.

"I think they can sew her up without your help."

"Sage saved my life," she says. "I wouldn't be here if it

weren't for her."

I nod. "That's what it takes to get you to stick around, huh?"

A pained look flits across Robin's face, and I instantly feel guilty for being such an asshole.

"I made a mistake," she whispers, her eyes burning into mine. "I can't ever take it back, but I'm here now."

"You didn't need to come back for me, you know," I say in a cold voice. "I've survived this long without you."

A glimmer of tears flicker in Robin's eyes, but she doesn't break down and cry. She just stares at me with a mixture of pity and regret. "I know you have," she murmurs. "And I'm proud of you."

My insides squirm uncomfortably. I don't know how to respond. I'm sure she's just saying that to win me over, because I certainly haven't done a lot to be proud of lately.

"You shouldn't be," I say. "But thanks for, uh . . . showing up, I guess."

Robin opens her mouth to say something, but I turn to go before she can get a word out. It's not exactly the tearful reunion Harper had in mind when she told me to talk to my mom, but I just can't stand there and pretend that everything is fine.

No matter how pure Robin's intentions may have been when she left me outside the compound, I still spent the past twenty years of my life without a mother. We're practically strangers.

I stride purposefully toward the exit, but before I get halfway across the room, a familiar weasel-y face appears in the doorway.

Paxton Dellwood is standing just inside the double doors, blocking my path with his stocky frame. His eyes are flashing with smug satisfaction, and his shit-eating grin says he's ready to rumble.

I whip up my rifle and point it at his head, but Dellwood reacts just as quickly. He raises his gun, and several nearby nurses scream. Two med interns throw themselves to the ground, and even the wounded Recon operatives look panicked.

"Drop it, Reynolds!" Dellwood barks. Despite his serious controller voice, I can tell he's secretly delighted that he may have cause to shoot me before the day is over.

"You first," I call.

My gut is screaming at me to pull the trigger, but my rational self knows I can't get away with shooting a controller — at least not in a room full of witnesses.

The board may be dead, but murder is murder. And as far as anyone knows, Dellwood is a law-abiding controller trying to keep the compound safe, while I'm facing charges for leaking confidential records.

"Drop your weapon!" yells another voice.

Paxton's eyes grow wide, staring at a spot just behind me. I don't move or look around, but several more Health and Rehab workers hunker down under tables and cots.

I hear careful footsteps coming up behind me, and then I see a flash of white in my peripheral vision.

Robin is standing a few feet to my left, holding her gun on Dellwood, too.

"You stay out of this," he calls, not taking his gun off me. "This doesn't involve you."

"Oh, but it does," says Robin in a cool, deadly voice. "That's my son you've got your gun pointed at, so if you plan to shoot him, you better shoot me, too."

I chance a glance at Robin, simultaneously shocked and impressed by her behavior. It's not what I'd consider mom-like, but I suppose it could be the Fringe equivalent of milk and cookies.

I don't know what my next move should be. Dellwood is blocking the nearest door, and the emergency exit is a good twenty or thirty yards away. I could put down my rifle and shoot Dellwood with the handgun tucked into my waistband, but there are too many innocent people who might catch a stray bullet — including Robin.

"I *said* drop it!" Dellwood yells, releasing his safety and preparing to shoot. "I'm not gonna tell you again!"

"And I'm not gonna tell *you* again," I say, managing to sound way more confident than I feel.

"Go fuck yourself, Reynolds," Dellwood snarls. "You know what the penalty is for drawing on a controller?"

"It might be worth it to get rid of you," I growl.

Dellwood scoffs, but I see a flicker of concern in his eyes. "Funny . . . I was thinking the exact same thing . . ."

"You're not gonna shoot me, Dellwood," I call, flashing a sardonic grin.

"Oh, yeah?" He's trying to sound tough, but his voice betrays his anxiety.

"Yeah."

At first I think I've scored a partial victory, but then Dellwood crosses over from anxious to reckless. He takes a step forward, licks his lips, and points his gun at Robin.

"How about I shoot your mom instead?"

Rage like I've never known flares through me. My blood begins to boil, and my vision narrows to a point. I'm half a second from blowing Dellwood away when another voice booms out from behind him.

"That is enough!"

My brain lurches, and I look around in confusion. I was so focused on the gun in Dellwood's hands that I never saw anyone coming up behind him. But when the newcomer's stern face appears over his shoulder, I feel my jaw drop.

Remy Chaplin is standing in the doorway, dressed in his crisp taupe suit. His shoes are shined, his pants are wrinkle free, and he's pointing a Recon-issued handgun at the back of Dellwood's head.

Judging from the glimmer of perspiration collecting on his upper lip, it's been a while since Remy held a weapon. But his stance is strong and confident, and the way he's holding the gun tells me he's had legit training. Not all the board members used to belong to the sections they oversee, but Remy *must* have been in Recon.

"Lower your weapon, son," he says in a low, commanding voice.

"Not before you identify yourself."

"Remy Chaplin, Undersecretary of Reconnaissance and acting president of compound 112."

Dellwood's face drains of color, but he doesn't put down his gun. "Sir, I've been authorized to detain Celdon Reynolds, using force if necessary."

"Detain him?"

"Reynolds is wanted for the theft of official compound property."

"Officer Dellwood, according to compound bylaws, you are now under my command, and I am ordering you to release Mr. Reynolds."

"With all due respect, sir, this is a Control matter. I've been authorized to —"

"I'm only going to ask you one more time, Mr. Dellwood," says Remy. "Lower your weapon — immediately."

Dellwood blinks furiously, looking as though he's about to explode. His lip twitches once, but then he lowers his gun.

"Place your weapon on the ground, and step away *slowly*,"

says Remy.

Dellwood is still staring at me with a murderous expression on his face, but he follows orders.

Once the weapon is on the ground, Remy approaches Dellwood from behind and stows his own gun in its holster.

"Paxton Dellwood, you're under arrest for assault, use of excessive force, participating in illegal espionage, and conspiracy against the compound."

"*What?*"

"Handcuffs, please," says Remy.

Dellwood lets out an angry huff of air but reaches into his utility belt and withdraws his handcuffs.

I gape openmouthed at Remy as he strips Dellwood of his electric nightstick and cuffs his hands behind his back. Two more controllers appear in the doorway, and Remy sends Dellwood away.

Once the danger has passed, I lower my own weapon and turn toward Robin. She's breathing hard and fast, but she's lowered her gun and looks relieved that she didn't have to shoot anyone.

"Thanks," I say, still reeling from the shock of it all.

"You don't need to thank me," she says, staring at me with the same expression she had before. "I did what any mother would do."

This time, I recognize the look she's giving me. It's love.

I clear my throat and shuffle uncomfortably, unsure how I should respond.

"Well . . . thanks," I say finally.

"You're welcome," she murmurs, glancing anxiously behind me. "Um . . . I think the undersecretary wants to have a word with you."

I follow her gaze back to the doorway, where Remy is

beckoning me into the tunnel.

"Please be careful," she says, reaching out to give my arm a quick squeeze. "You never know whom you can trust."

"Tell me about it," I mumble, still a little dazed from Remy's display of power.

I throw Robin one more perplexed look and then follow Remy out into the tunnel.

The area just outside the makeshift medical center is bustling with activity. Controllers have formed a human wall just inside the airlock doors, Operations workers are hauling supplies down from Manufacturing, and interns in red scrubs are frantically shuffling wounded workers in from the Fringe.

Remy leads me down the tunnel and beckons me into a quiet little alcove where Operations stores its janitorial supplies.

"I thought the board all fled," I stammer, staring at him in disbelief.

"Most of them did," he says. His tone is short and clipped, but his face betrays his barely subdued anger. "Undersecretaries Mayweather, Griffin, and myself are the only board members who elected to stay behind."

Those names ring a bell. Natasha Mayweather is the Undersecretary of Health and Rehab, and Undersecretary Griffin is the outspoken populist leader of Exterior Maintenance and Construction.

"That was a close call," Remy adds, glancing up and down the tunnel to make sure we can't be overheard. The only person within earshot is a controller guarding the multipurpose room, but Remy doesn't seem concerned.

"You're telling me," I breathe. "What the hell was that all about?"

"Beg pardon?"

I shake my head in disbelief. "How did you know to come

after Dellwood? How did you know he was in Constance?"

"I didn't," he says. "But after your stunt out on the Fringe, I asked Officer Finley there to keep an eye on you." He nods at the controller standing outside the multipurpose room.

"Why?" I ask. It sure would have been nice to have a secret bodyguard when Devon was trying to kill me earlier.

"I suspected Constance would try to keep you from doing any more damage to their organization, and I was right," says Remy. "Officer Dellwood was the first person to come after you following your little broadcast, and so I knew."

"He wasn't the first person to come after me."

Remy's brows scrunch together in confusion, but he keeps talking. "I asked Officer Finley to check the Control feed. There was no official warrant for your arrest, so I knew Dellwood had to be working with Constance."

I raise an eyebrow, unable to hide how impressed I am.

"For the next twenty-four hours, we need to focus on keeping you safe."

"Hang on," I say. "Why do you suddenly care about me? I already went to Ferguson with this information, and he didn't want to hear it. You were ready to let me die for this. Why are you helping me *now*?"

Remy's eyes smolder in a way that tells me I'm dancing on the edge of insubordination.

"Mr. Reynolds, I'm not usually inclined to speak ill of the dead, but it may have been Ferguson's unwillingness to confront reality that got him killed."

I swallow. I hadn't expected Remy to be so frank with me, but he seems to have realized that there's no time to waste being politically correct.

"With most of the board gone, Constance is going to make a grab for power. In the past, they've chosen to remain separate from the board, but I fear that with everything that's happened, they may decide to secure their position in the compound by corrupting our leadership."

"What does that have to do with me?"

"You dealt a serious blow to Constance with that video, Mr. Reynolds. There's no doubt about that. But I'm afraid you made one crucial mistake."

"What's that?"

"You didn't name names. Right now, you're the only one in the compound who knows the identity of every single member of Constance. And with you out of the picture, who's to stop them from gaining seats on the board when we hold emergency elections?"

I don't say anything, but Remy puts a firm hand on my shoulder and leans in closer. "We need to keep you alive until we can pull Constance out of hiding."

For a second, I just stare at him. Remy's got the commanding presence of a man who's used to giving orders but the quiet impotence of an elected official who's spent his career following the letter of the law. I want to trust him, but I have my doubts.

Remy is all piss and fire when the drifters are pounding at our door and a virus has incapacitated a quarter of the population, but I have a feeling he'd be much more restrained in his approach if Recon defeated the Desperados tomorrow and the compound was once again operating in a state of peace.

"You think you can identify the bulk of Constance's members?" Remy asks.

"I can do better than that," I say, watching his face carefully. "I can take you to their leader."

Remy's expression turns serious, and his gaze flickers down the tunnel once again. "Tell me," he whispers, keeping his eyes fixated on the door to the makeshift medical center.

"Ozias Pirro."

Remy finally looks at me and takes a big step back. I expect him to act surprised — maybe even a little excited — but instead, he lets out a breath of frustration and massages the bridge of his nose between his thumb and index finger.

"What?" I ask, waiting for Remy to march up to Officer Finley and order his arrest.

"I know Ozias," he says in a low voice. "He's one of the original founders."

"Yeah, I know. And he's fucking psycho."

"Ozias Pirro is one of the most respected members of this community," says Remy. "He's the godfather of Information and a respected philanthropist. He's the reason the compound dedicates so many resources to preserving our history and disseminating information."

"Yeah," I say with an eye roll. "He's also the man who ordered the murder of Jayden Pierce. He's probably the mastermind behind all of Constance's illegal espionage and the one who ordered the hit on Sullivan Taylor. He's fucking evil."

"It doesn't matter."

"What do you mean it doesn't matter? He's the one behind all this. You arrest Ozias, and Constance will crumble from the inside out."

"Will you lower your voice?" growls Remy.

"What is your *deal*?"

"I do not want this information leaking out before I've had a chance to get ahead of it," he says.

"What?"

Remy sighs. "Did you think crucifying a man like Ozias Pirro would be easy?" he asks. "Ozias has an *army* of First-Gen supporters . . . not to mention respect from the entire tier-one community."

"He's a murderer!" I cry.

"Says *you*," Remy snaps. "But where is your proof?"

"*What*?"

"I can't accuse one of the most respected men in the compound of murder and conspiracy without any evidence!"

"I know it was him!"

"So it's your word against his," says Remy. "The word of a drug-addled party boy against a founder."

"You fucking —"

"I'm sorry. But that's just the way it is."

I scoff, my face burning with rage.

I always knew people thought I was a worthless, overpaid piece of shit, but I never thought it would matter. I just went about my life, did what I wanted, and said fuck everybody else. But for the first time, it does matter, and it bothers me more than I'd like to admit.

"So what's your plan?" I ask, my voice trembling with fury. "You're just gonna round up the members of Constance who aren't that important? The people who no one will defend? You're going to nail the tier-three traitors to the wall and let the doctors and founders and Control captains *walk*?"

Remy's eyes are wide and serious. "I will do the very best I can to bring them all to justice."

I shake my head. "No. That's not good enough."

Suddenly I realize I was right to doubt Remy. He never had any intention of prosecuting all of Constance. There's no trusting any board member, no matter how honorable he may seem. They're all the same, really — all more concerned with perception than reality.

If the compound survives the drifter attack and recovers from the virus, Remy will be a shoo-in to take Ferguson's seat as president. Everyone would throw their support behind the man who stayed when things were at their worst.

The only thing that could stop him would be a threat from Constance — a hidden scandal, real or imagined, that they could use to buy his silence. If Remy is elected, those with enough power and influence will be left alone, and Constance will continue to operate in the shadows.

"What would you have me do?" asks Remy. "Haul in the most powerful people in the compound on nothing but your word?"

"No," I say in a resigned voice. "I'm not asking you to do anything. I'm done asking. From now on . . . I'm the one calling the shots."

Remy looks confused and irritated, but he also looks concerned.

"Here's what's going to happen . . ." I say, reaching into my jacket pocket and pulling out the tiny blue microchip. "This chip contains a list of every member of Constance I ever saw, along with their crimes. You'll also find a map to their headquarters in Information. You'll find all the evidence you need."

I place the chip in Remy's smooth, manicured hand, and he stares at it as though it might combust.

"When the battle is over and the dead are buried, you're going to hold a press conference where you announce that every known member of Constance has been brought into custody."

Remy opens his mouth to speak, but I hold up a hand to cut him off.

"You're going to publish the list I gave you to the news feeds." I pause to glare at him. "The *entire* list."

Remy swallows once, staring at me with a mixture of wariness and resentment. "And if I don't?"

"You will," I say. "Because if you don't, I'll make sure the rest of those names are released."

I point at the chip in his hand without taking my eyes off his. "There are plenty more copies of that list floating around. Right now, they're in the hands of people I trust. But if anything happens to me, that list *will* go public. The only question is . . .What side of history do you want to be on, Mr. President?"

twenty-five

Harper

Miraculously, I don't encounter a single controller or Operations worker as I jog from the multipurpose room to the emergency stairwell branching off the main tunnel. I swipe my way through the first barricade with Celdon's magic key card and pray that the virus has been contained in tier two.

My shoulder burns as I climb the stairs to the medical ward, but the pain is not nearly as bad as it was when I first woke up. The painkillers must be kicking in, because my brain feels oddly fuzzy as I tear up the steps and blaze past the first few landings.

The cinder-block walls blur in and out of focus as my tired body struggles to carry me up the last five flights, and I stop for a moment to catch my breath and check my dressing. I can see the faint hint of pink coming through the thick layer of gauze taped to my shoulder, but I can't worry about that now. I have to get to Eli before it's too late.

Finally, I reach the landing with the distinct red crosses. I'm a little unnerved to see that the barricade is unmanned, but I suppose all Operations workers must be busy running medical supplies down to the ground level and briefing people on emergency protocol.

I managed to swipe a mask from one of the nurses stations in the multipurpose room, but I couldn't get my hands on a full-body hazmat suit. I didn't think I'd be needing one at the time, but the second I emerge into the brightly lit medical ward,

I realize it might have been worth the effort to find one.

Every nurse and doctor I can see is covered head to toe in one of the hunter-green suits. Meanwhile, I'm dressed in ripped denim shorts, a tank top, and a hoodie, with dirt and blood all over my face.

I cross the waiting area at a brisk walk and turn down a narrow tunnel branching off the main corridor. But just a few seconds later, I hear a frantic voice coming from behind me.

"Hey! Stop!"

Whipping around, I see a petite nurse in a hazmat suit rushing toward me. I turn around and quicken my pace, but she doesn't give up.

"Hey! You! Stop right there!"

I don't know what to do, so I run.

Behind me, I hear the comical squeak of rubber on tile as the nurse tries to run in the cumbersome suit. "Security!"

I break into a sprint. With the compound under siege, I highly doubt that Control can spare any men to guard the medical ward, but I don't want to stick around to find out.

Clutching my injured arm to my chest, I push my legs harder and tear around the corner. I cut down another side tunnel to lose her, but she probably knows this place a hell of a lot better than I do.

I don't have much time. Even if I'm right about the controllers, all her running and yelling will definitely attract attention. I can't afford to bring Constance down on me before I've even found Owen.

But my anxious line of "what ifs" is cut short when the psych ward comes into view. Since I spent days in there wondering if and when I would be released, I know those steel doors better than anyone.

Each operational patient room has a tiny safety-glass

window cut into the top, and it doesn't take a genius to figure out which room they're holding Owen in. The window at the top of one of the doors is completely blacked out. There's no sign of Eli anywhere, but that doesn't mean he hasn't been here.

I crank down on the handle, but of course it's locked. I swipe Celdon's master key card through the reader, but the red light on the keypad just blinks angrily.

I yank on the handle again and swear.

I wasn't prepared for this. Celdon said his card would work on just about any lock, but Constance must have put extra measures in place to ensure that no one — not even Celdon — could access this room without authorization.

I pause for half a second, my mind flying through all of my options. I could try to shoot out the lock, but that would definitely attract the sort of attention I want to avoid. For all I know, Constance could be watching me right now.

I look up and immediately spot three security cameras directly in my line of sight.

Shit. If Constance isn't on their way to get me yet, they will be soon.

I study the row of doors desperately, trying to remember the exact layout of the rooms in the psych ward. In the room I stayed in, there were no windows and no other doors. There were just four padded walls, a bed, a nightstand, and a closet. All the furniture was bolted to the floor, and all the vents were reinforced to prevent escape.

Suddenly, I hear the slap of approaching footsteps and the sound of labored breathing. I freeze, and the nurse who was chasing me flies around the corner. She's sweaty and out of breath, but damn she is determined.

"You can't be in here!" she pants, looking as though she might collapse.

Her face mask is almost completely fogged up, but I can tell she's a mousey woman in her midforties with short brown curls and thin-rimmed glasses.

In that instant, I know what I have to do. Hating myself, I whip my gun up with my good arm and point it at her head.

She yelps and throws her hands in the air, breaking into uncontrollable whimpers.

"Shut up!" I hiss, taking a step forward. I have no intention of shooting her, but desperate times call for desperate measures.

"I need to get into this room!" I say, working hard to keep my voice as cold and emotionless as possible.

I have no idea what I'm going to find in there: Owen dead, Owen alive, Owen *and* Eli, or no one at all. The only thing I do know is that if Eli and Owen are being kept behind those doors, I can't just leave them.

"Y-you can't," she stammers.

"Why not?"

"I-I d-don't kn-know!" she blubbers. "I have orders n-not to let anyone in there."

"Orders from who?" I yell.

"D-Dr. Watson," she blubbers, clearly torn between her sense of duty and fear for her life.

"I don't care," I say, releasing the safety on my gun. "If you don't let me in, you are going to die. Do you understand?"

"I . . . c-can't." She sniffs, dissolving into a puddle of tears. "I don't even have a k-k-key!"

"There has to be *some* way in there," I snap. "Isn't there some master key that only the doctors —"

"That's only for regular patient rooms," she squeaks.

"That's not a patient room?"

She shakes her head, unable to speak over her dramatic wave of tears.

"What's in there?" I bark.

"I d-don't know!" she cries. "It used to be an observation room for psych patients. I think it's just an office now."

"How can I get in there?" I demand.

At first I think she's completely checked out, but then she raises her arm and points to the door next to it. This one doesn't have a window at the top, and on first inspection, it looks as though it might be a supply closet or a bathroom.

"It's connected," she chokes.

Without another word, I leap in front of the door and tug down on the handle. Of course it's locked, too, but I have one more trick up my sleeve.

Hands trembling with anticipation, I shove Celdon's so-called master key through the card reader. There's a soft *beep*, and the light blinks green.

Crying out in relief, I turn the handle and pull the door wide open. I bound inside, whip my gun into the air, and immediately scan the room for threats.

My heart sinks. The room is completely deserted.

I'm standing in a small stuffy observation area that's been converted into an administrative office. There are a couple dusty old computers, two chairs, and what used to be a two-way mirror. The large rectangular hole in the wall is covered in chipboard, and there's a closed door to the left leading into the next room.

I move toward the door on instinct, but then I hear a sharp crackle of noise coming through the speakers on the desk. The first voice is angry and familiar, and the second is cool and acidic.

"I've told you everything you wanted to know. Now it's time for you to keep your end of the deal."

"You're absolutely right, Mr. Parker. You're absolutely

right." The second man pauses for dramatic effect. "We did have a deal."

There's another long pause as one man savors his moment of power over the other and considers how to proceed.

"But you know . . . deals are funny things . . . especially deals struck under duress."

"What the fuck is *that* supposed to mean?"

The second man chuckles, his footsteps echoing off the tile. "When in doubt, always get it in writing."

"You son of a bitch!"

There's a heavy *clang* of metal on tile, and I imagine somebody lunging across the room.

I see my window of opportunity, and I take it.

In an uncoordinated rush of movement, I throw myself against the door and pull down on the handle. It turns immediately, the door flies open, and I'm suddenly blinded by a bright strip of florescent lighting.

I turn my gun in search of a target, and my drug-addled brain takes a hazy inventory of the people in the room.

I see a tall, skinny man in a lab coat pointing a gun at the man on the floor. I follow the gun's trajectory to the doctor's victim, and my gaze locks on a familiar pair of eyes.

The man on the floor meets my gaze, and the doctor's shoulders ripple as he prepares to shoot. I take aim at the man in white, and my gun goes off in my hands.

twenty-six

Harper

As the butt of my rifle slams into my shoulder, the unforgiving blast mixes with a burst of agony from my wound.

Two pairs of eyes snap onto mine.

At first I think I'm seeing double, but then I notice two distinct sets of features framing identical pairs of eyes.

The first eyes I saw are framed by thick black eyebrows and a jaw that's too hard and square to be familiar. Those eyes weren't full of love, but I did see a flicker of relief, maybe even gratitude, as I pulled the trigger.

The second set of eyes only appeared when the doctor fell to the ground. I like those eyes best when they're crinkled in one of Eli's rare smiles. But right now, Eli's face is battered beyond recognition, and his eyes are wide with horror.

Eli's lips move, but I can't hear what he's saying. I'm too busy taking inventory of his wounds and trying to piece together what happened.

The doctor is lying on the ground in a pool of his own blood, which is spreading across the flecked white tile at an alarming rate. Owen is slumped against the wall, but I can tell immediately that something is wrong. He's got a fresh wound spouting blood from his chest, and his eyes are watery and unfocused.

Eli's hands are still bound behind his back, but that doesn't stop him from pushing his way across the floor toward his brother.

I shake my head in disbelief, trying to understand the scene in front of me.

I saw the doctor shoot, but I didn't hear the blast of his gun. I only heard one shot, and that shot came from my rifle.

My eyes flicker to the doctor's weapon, which is lying on the ground a few feet away. The muzzle is longer than a normal handgun, and I realize that it was equipped with a silencer.

I look back at Owen, who's much too pale and fading fast. He slips down the wall and onto his back, and I see Eli struggling to free himself from his restraints.

"Harper!" Eli chokes. "Help me!"

Moving in a trance, I lay down my weapon and step around the pool of blood. I yank my knife out of my boot and cut Eli's hands free. Then I run to the door and stick my head out into the tunnel.

The woman I held at gunpoint is nowhere to be found, but I can hear the sound of approaching footsteps.

"Help!" I yell. "We need some help in here! A man has been shot!"

Eli calls my name, and I tear back into the room. He's staring down at his brother with a mixture of horror and disbelief.

I've never seen Eli freeze up in an emergency, but when I kneel down beside him, he seems to come back to life.

Working on autopilot, Eli pulls his shirt over his head and applies pressure to Owen's chest. It's standard procedure for treating a bullet wound in the field, hardwired into Eli's brain from years of training.

But when Owen's eyes roll back and Eli's hands begin to shake, I can tell the battle is already lost.

I want to save Owen, but I don't know what more we can do. Tears are streaming silently down Eli's face, and he's staring up at me like a scared child.

"Help me with him!" he cries in a strangled voice.

I shake my head, utterly lost for words. Owen's eyes are already fluttering closed, and his lower lip is trembling in pain.

Suddenly, I hear a small commotion outside the observation room. There are several people standing outside in the tunnel, and at least one of them is trying to get in.

"We need to get through here," says a sharp female voice. "Someone's been shot."

"I'm sorry, ma'am. I can't let you go in there," says a man — probably one of Constance's controllers.

"Didn't you hear me? Somebody's been *shot*!"

"Stand down, ma'am. We can't let you in there until we secure the prisoner."

"Prisoner?"

I can't stand it anymore. I'm not going to let Constance disrupt Eli's last moments with his brother. I get to my feet, snatch a chair from inside the observation room, and use it to wedge our door shut. With the barricade and the automatic lock, we can't get out, but they can't get in.

Eli sinks back on his heels. He's abandoned first-aid procedure but keeps one hand resting on his brother's chest. I sink down beside him and take his other hand in my own, trying to ignore the warm blood between our fingers.

I see the life fading from Owen's eyes, but he takes one last look at Eli and murmurs something indiscernible. I can't imagine Owen uttering anything that could put Eli's tortured soul at peace. I just hope he said something kind.

Eli's face is frozen in anguish, and the look in his eyes tells me he can't believe that a single bullet could bring down his brother.

Neither of us sees Owen's dying breath. One moment he's breathing, and the next, he isn't. There's nothing to mark his final attempt at life, but I feel it the second Eli realizes he's gone.

He lets out a horrible, gut-wrenching sob and collapses over his brother's limp body. He grips his chest in a crushing hold, as if he can somehow pull him back from the brink of death. But the light has already drained from Owen's eyes, leaving only an empty body behind.

Eli trembles in silence, and a fresh wave of horror washes over me when I realize what this all means. Owen was infected before he died, and Eli was imprisoned here — breathing Owen's air for who knows how long.

Eli's face is still healthy and flushed, but I know the virus must be coursing through his veins. Once those people outside break down my barricade, we'll only have a few seconds before they take him away.

Eli seems to realize this, too, and he doesn't put up a fight when I lift his head off Owen's chest and pull it into my lap. Grief hits me like a runaway train as I run my hands through his dark hair.

After everything we've been through together, Eli is going to die from a fucking virus. He fought so hard to get here, and in the end it didn't matter. He dodged the drifters' bullets, scaled a twelve-foot fence, talked his way back into Recon's ranks, and sneaked into the compound — only to lose his brother and his own life at the hands of Constance.

With Eli's face pressed against my stomach, I can't tell which one of us is shaking. Tears are trickling out of my eyes, and my arms are trembling with the effort of holding on to him.

"You . . . You shouldn't be here," he murmurs finally.

"I'm not leaving you."

"Harper . . . I don't want you to get infected."

I shake my head even though he can't see me. All I want is to peel off this stupid mask and kiss him senseless, but a second later, we're interrupted by a loud pounding on the door.

I hold Eli tighter and squeeze my eyes shut, knowing that our time together is almost at an end.

There's a brief pause as the people outside reconsider their strategy, and then the banging gets louder and more violent.

Suddenly the door crashes open and bangs against the wall. People in hazmat suits flood into the room, and I hear a woman shriek.

"He's been shot!" someone screams. "Watson's been shot!"

Voices trickle in from the office next door, and then someone shouts for a crash cart.

Squinting up through a fog of tears, I see two nurses in hazmat suits sobbing as they stare down at Owen's and Watson's limp bodies.

"What the hell happened?" one of the nurses blubbers.

I stare up at them with a furious expression, incensed that they expect me to explain myself when Constance has been purposely infecting people right under their noses.

"He infected them," I spit, glaring over at Watson's corpse. "He *tortured* them, and then he killed Owen. That's what he did."

The younger nurse's eyes bug out in horror as the full reality of the situation sinks in. A second later, she tears out of the room, and the other nurse crouches down to feel for Watson's nonexistent pulse.

There's a long pause, and the room is completely silent except for the sound of the young nurse's retreating footsteps. The older nurse searches Watson's body for signs of life, her face shifting slowly from panicked to crestfallen.

By the time her colleague returns, she's already determined that Watson is dead.

They dutifully record Watson's time of death and move over to examine Owen's body. I feel Eli stiffen in my arms, but he doesn't make a move to shield his brother. He knows Owen is beyond saving.

The nurse feels for Owen's pulse and quickly decides that he too is a lost cause. She shakes her head slowly and then turns to look at me. "You need to come with us."

"No," I snarl, gripping Eli's shoulders tighter.

"Please, ma'am," she says, more impatiently this time. "I don't know how you got in here, but this ward is off-limits for non-medical personnel. Every patient here is highly infectious, and you being here puts everyone in this compound at risk."

"How could you let this happen?" I ask, staring over at Watson's prone body. "You *knew* what they were doing in here, and you just let them torture and kill an innocent man."

"Innocent" may be a bit of a stretch for Owen, but judging from the look on the nurse's face, she knows they fucked up big time.

"This ward was under strict orders to —"

"I don't give a fuck!" I yell. "Constance — tortured — Owen Parker. They purposely infected him under *your watch*. And now *he* might be infected," I finish, looking down at Eli.

"Ma'am, I understand that you're upset," says the nurse, clearly trying to pacify me so I don't do anything crazy.

"You don't understand a goddamned thing!" I yell. "You just *stood* there and allowed this to happen!"

The nurse is starting to look uneasy. "Ma'am, I'm going to have to ask you to lower your voice and let him go. Your friend has been exposed to the virus, and he needs to be contained."

"Whose fault is that?" I snap. "I think they should lock *you* up with someone who's infected and see how you come out of it."

At that, the nurse touches her interface and swipes the panic button to call for backup.

"We need to move him to a secure location," she says.

"No!" I scream.

"Harper," Eli croaks, turning his head to look at me. "She's right."

"No," I repeat, trying and failing to fend off the tears welling up in my eyes.

"Harper . . ."

"I won't leave you," I squeak, sounding just as pathetic as I feel. "We're partners."

"I might be contagious," he says.

By now, half a dozen more nurses and doctors have congregated outside the observation room. Two controllers are trying to hold back the crowd, but I can hear them whispering that Dr. Watson has been shot.

I feel utterly disgusted. Nobody cares that Watson tortured, infected, and killed Owen for his own sick gains. Nobody knew him as anything other than a brilliant doctor.

In all the commotion, I hardly notice the two burly male techs push their way into the room. One of them grabs my arm, and the other tries to pull me up by the waist.

Eli is beginning to return to his senses, and he shoves one of the techs away with a venomous look in his eyes.

"Stay calm," says the tech. "We're gonna have someone —"

I don't hear what he says next. One of the men yanks on my arm, and a flash of pain rips through my shoulder. I cry out in agony, and Eli launches himself at the offending tech, tackling him to the ground.

While I'm distracted, a bigger doctor appears to assist the second tech, and the two of them lift me up and drag me bodily out of the room.

"No!" I cry, throwing back an elbow into the doctor's fat stomach and earning a low grunt of pain.

It doesn't stop the tech's momentum, though. He's strong enough to get me halfway across the room on his own, but I thrash violently in his arms and swing out the elbow of my uninjured arm. It hits him square on the side of the head, and I take the opportunity to wriggle out of his grip.

Eli gets to his feet, and I pull him toward the door. A tight knot of people are blocking our path, but as soon as they see Eli, they practically trip over themselves to get away.

Only the controllers put up a fight. We keep running and pushing our way through the crowd, but then I feel the sharp shock of an electric nightstick between my lower ribs.

I drop to the ground as the spasms rock through me, and somebody tackles Eli from behind. I look back in time to see them hit the ground, but then somebody shocks me again. Suddenly I'm writhing in a ball on the floor, crying out in pain as my body convulses.

Somebody strong pins my arms to my sides, and my brain flashes back to the time Eli and I were arrested. The prospect of a more permanent separation is enough to overwhelm me with panic, and I lash out like a lunatic, kicking and screaming.

As I struggle to free myself, I'm overcome by the grim realization that no matter how hard I fight, there's no way to save Eli. The virus will take him just as it takes everyone else, and no amount of strength or resistance will be enough to stop it.

The sound of a familiar voice is the only thing that calls me back to reality.

"Harper! Hey — Harper! Stop! It's okay!"

I look up and do a quick scan of the tunnel. Two controllers have managed to subdue Eli, but it wasn't his voice that I heard.

Suddenly, Sawyer materializes from the crowd, and my heart almost breaks in two.

Sawyer's face is pale and sickly. Her eyes are drooping with bags of fatigue, and her voice is feeble and ragged. Instead of her usual crisp red scrubs, she's wearing simple white pants and a boxy V-neck shirt.

"Oh my god," I wail, peeling my good arm out of the tech's grip and stumbling toward her with tears in my eyes.

"Hey," she says weakly, managing a small smile.

I let out a strange little sob, and Sawyer doesn't resist when I throw my arms around her neck.

"It's so good to see you," she whispers. "I never thought I'd see you again."

"I'm so sorry," I blubber, squeezing her tighter.

At that moment, a dam breaks somewhere inside me, and a flood of tears comes pouring out. "I'm sorry!" I cry. "I c-couldn't f-find it."

"You couldn't find what?"

"The cure!" I sob. "I'm s-s-sorry. I l-left the compound to try to find it, but M-Malcolm never had one."

"What?"

"I did everything I could, but I f-f-f-failed."

"No, Harper, no!" Sawyer says, rubbing my back in a very motherly way. "You didn't *have* to. It's okay."

"It's n-not okay," I cough, suddenly overwhelmed by grief and disappointment. "I was supposed to *fix* this."

"No . . ."

"I did everything I could, but I . . . don't know what to do anymore . . ."

"Shhh," says Sawyer, rubbing my back and squeezing my torso. "You didn't fail," she whispers. "This wasn't your problem to fix."

"I tried," I say, drawing back to look her in the eye. "You're sick, and now Eli's sick . . ."

"It's okay," says Sawyer, staring at the dressing sticking out from under my hoodie with doctor-like concern in her eyes. "Don't worry about us, okay? Eli and I are going to be fine."

"What?"

Sawyer's face brightens visibly. "They've developed an experimental new treatment," she says. "It's a type of immunotherapy."

"Experimental . . . Immuno . . . What?"

"They tried it on me and a few other Health and Rehab workers who got sick," says Sawyer, her eyes lighting up with a familiar nerdy excitement. "Harper . . . it's working."

I shake my head, unable to believe what she's telling me. "Are you . . . Are you sure?"

Sawyer nods. "I mean, I still feel like shit because my body has been fighting off another virus, but my test results look good."

"That's . . . That's great," I stammer, my eyes itching with happy tears. I turn to look at Eli. "Oh my god."

"A lot of people are still going to die," she says in a somber voice. "They only administered treatment to a small group of people at first. But now that they know it works . . ."

Despite the fact that Owen is lying dead in the next room and our friends are perishing out on the Fringe, I feel an overwhelming surge of gratitude.

Eli isn't going to die.

"Harper . . . you shouldn't be here," says Sawyer.

"I know," I sigh, glancing sheepishly at all the Health and

Rehab workers I punched and kicked while trying to make my escape.

"I promise I'll look after him," says Sawyer. "But you have to go."

I nod. At first I think she's just being overly protective — worrying that I'll catch the virus. But then my eyes drift to the window at the end of the tunnel, and the full meaning of her warning sinks in.

I feel myself propelled toward the window by an unknown force, and my stomach curdles with dread.

The crack of bullets drifts through the six-inch glass, and I press my face against the window to get a closer look at the Fringe.

A fire is blazing about a mile and a half in the distance, and dark shapes are moving in every direction. The compound is surrounded by a convoy of vehicles, and Desperados are mowing down our people one by one.

Suddenly, a ball of flame erupts against the velvety night sky, and once my eyes adjust to the light, I see that the supply tent is on fire.

"Oh my god," I mutter, backing away from the window and nearly bumping into Sawyer.

She's standing right behind me, watching the scene unfold with barely concealed terror.

Malcolm's men just broke through Recon's front line, which means there's nothing but a few of our people standing between them and the compound.

twenty-seven

Celdon

Power corrupts — plain and simple. I want to believe that Remy is one of the good guys, but I just don't trust him.

If we survive this attack, he'll use the chaos and tragedy as a springboard to launch his presidential campaign, but he won't want a media war over Constance muddling his message.

If Remy won't hold Constance accountable, I will. Even if he tries to have me killed, the names of Constance's elite and powerful won't die with me.

When I broke into Harper's compartment, I sent a message to her and Sawyer containing the same list of names I gave to Remy. The truth will come out no matter what happens, but there's one member of Constance I want to handle myself.

Ozias Pirro represents everything that's wrong with this place. He built the compound on elitism and tyranny, and he has to be stopped.

But even with my duplicate key card, getting from the ground level to Information won't be easy. The main tunnel is clogged with people: Health and Rehab interns, Operations workers, and controllers preparing a last line of defense against the Desperados.

I'm sure shooting out the airlock door didn't earn me any friends in Control, so I duck down a side tunnel and wrack my brain for a good diversion.

Luckily, two guys carrying a stretcher walk in almost immediately, giving me a chance to slink around to the emergency stairwell unnoticed. I ditch my rifle and pull out my stolen handgun, counting my rounds and formulating a plan.

As I approach EnComm, a faint hum of activity drifts down the stairwell. With all the voices echoing off the cinder-block walls, it's impossible to tell what they're saying, but they sound angry.

The voices grow louder with every step I take, but I don't hear the sound of approaching footsteps. When I round the corner, I see why.

At least a dozen people are crammed onto the landing behind the EnComm barricade, pounding on the plastic and trying to pry it away from the wall. Most are men in their twenties and thirties, and they all look extremely pissed off.

Four controllers are standing on my side of the barricade, dressed in full riot gear and air filtration masks. They're armed with pepper spray and electric nightsticks, but they still look nervous.

"We want answers!" one of the men yells, his voice muffled by the thick plastic wall.

"You can't lock us in here with the infected to die!" yells another.

"Let us out!"

The men on the other side of the barricade appear healthy, but there's no way to tell whether they're infected or not.

Now that the first wave of sickness has taken hold, they're fighting back against the quarantine. They're armed with bats and pipes, and they're pushing and prying at the plastic barricade.

I watch apprehensively, trying to think of an alternate route that would allow me to bypass the angry mob.

Before I have a chance to come up with a plan, something

or someone seems to disrupt the crowd. The men erupt into wild cheers, and the controllers shift to see what's causing the commotion.

A little piece of orange machinery materializes on the landing, and the EnComm people shuffle back to make room. It's a vehicle from the commissary designed for hauling heavy loads, and when I hear the shrill *beep, beep, beep*, I realize the driver is backing up — driving straight into the plastic wall.

As I watch, the brackets holding the barricade to the wall groan, and the airtight seal along the edges starts to tear. The nearest controller glances at his colleagues, and they seem to reach a consensus.

The protestors either don't notice or don't care. They just keep cheering until the driver pops the airtight seal and tears the corner of the barricade away from the wall.

The men surge forward and lift the corner of the barricade, and a skinny guy with a red mohawk slides on through.

Mohawk dude launches himself at the nearest controller, and everything goes to hell. He and the controller tumble down the stairs, and several more rioters wriggle through the gap.

The controllers back down the stairwell, practically tripping over each other to get away from the mob, and one of them launches a metal can into the air. I watch it soar toward the protestors and hit the step just before the barricade.

Suddenly, a cloud of white gas swallows the stairwell. My eyes and lungs start to burn, and a bitter taste hits my tongue.

I cough hard to try to clear my throat, but it's no use. I hold my breath, but the burning only intensifies as the fog thickens. Snot and tears are streaming down my face, and my eyes are stinging so badly I want to rip them out of their sockets.

Half a dozen protestors managed to break into the stairwell, but now they're gasping and choking and trying to escape the fumes. A couple people try to squeeze back through the barricade, but it just widens the gap and fills the other side of the stairwell with gas.

People all around me are yelling and retching, and I nearly tear my leg off trying to follow the protestors through the plastic barricade.

I blindly feel my way forward, gasping like a dying man, and collapse halfway up the next flight of stairs. Crawling on my hands and knees, I finally reach air that's more oxygen than tear gas, and my lungs seize violently as they try to fill themselves with clean air.

My eyes are still burning like crazy, so I stagger through the doorway to the nearest drinking fountain and stick my face under the stream of water.

Slowly but surely, the stinging subsides. I continue up the stairs at a limp, stopping every now and then to mop the snot off my face. I'm still focused on my mission, but I can't get the image of the trapped workers out of my head.

Breaking through the barricade was incredibly stupid. For all they know, they could be infected, which would put everyone in the lower levels at risk. But if I'd been trapped behind that barricade, I'd have done the same thing.

Thankfully, I don't encounter any more obstacles on my way to Information. Even the journalism wing is eerily quiet. Nearly every reporter is gathered at the windows, staring down at the battlefield and counting corpses.

As I cut down the residential tunnel toward the founder's suite, my dread and resolve begin to mount. Everything Constance has done has been leading up to this moment, and Ozias deserves to die a thousand deaths.

Still, a terrified voice in the back of my mind whispers that I could just walk away. I could turn around, make a run for those airlock doors, and live out the rest of my miserable life on the Fringe. It would be a brief and violent existence, but the old me makes a persuasive argument.

The old me doesn't want to fight. He just wants to get burned and forget everything he's ever done.

I'm fucking sick of the old me.

Before I have a chance to talk myself out of what I'm about to do, I make the last turn down the tunnel, and Ozias's compartment comes into view.

I'm unsurprised to see the tall bald man in a suit standing guard outside Ozias's suite. His gaze swivels in my direction, and I nervously raise my right hand to try to look friendly.

The guard hesitates and then nods in greeting, but I know he's watching me carefully.

As soon as I'm within earshot, his mouth twitches, and he takes a step forward. "I'm sorry, Mr. Reynolds. I can't let you go any farther."

I drag in a deep breath and give the guard a quick once-over. He's big and beefy like a power lifter, but he moves with the grace of a three-legged elephant. He's got a wedding-ring tan line, which means he's either separated or he just doesn't wear his ring to work. Maybe it's a distraction, or maybe he thinks it makes him look weak.

Either way, this guy is a person with a life. And to make matters worse, I feel as though I've seen him before.

Then I realize how I know him: Constance.

I stop and swallow. The guard slouches in relief. He thinks I'm obeying. He thinks I'm going to turn around and walk away.

Instead, I reach behind my back and pull the stolen handgun out of my waistband. I see the realization flash across his face and a calm, collected negotiation form on his lips.

I don't stop to hear what he has to say. I just shoot.

The guard winces, but he doesn't go down.

I missed.

I'm about to shoot again, but he reacts as any trained bodyguard should. He goes for his gun, and I fire off two more rounds.

My first bullet zings past his head and shatters a modern-looking glass sconce. Sparks erupt, throwing the tunnel into shadow, but my second bullet hits him squarely in the chest.

The guard goes down, but he isn't dead. The bullet hit him in his protective vest, knocking him back. His big round face is screwed up in pain, and he's clutching his chest where the bullet struck him. He's too consumed by his own agony to realize what's about to happen — an unfortunate side effect of getting shot in the chest.

Shoving down the darkness rising up inside me, I walk forward until I'm hovering right above him and shoot him in the head. My shot echoes down the tunnel, and his eyes go blank.

I stare at him for several seconds as blood oozes out of the hole in his skull. Then I bend down, rip the special access card off his belt loop, and swipe into Ozias's compartment.

Once inside, I take a second to focus on my breathing. My shooting is amateur at best, but I've learned that the faster my heart is pounding, the worse my aim gets. I only have a few rounds left in my clip, and I can't afford to waste them on any more sloppy shots.

After being surrounded by the sounds of death, the silence of Ozias's compartment is downright chilling. My footsteps echo off the pristine tile floor, and I catch a glimpse of my reflection in the tall glass case. I hardly recognize myself.

My face is pale and sunken, with twin black pits where my eyes used to be. I'm thin and haggard with dull, greasy hair, and my face is wrecked with misery.

As I draw closer to Ozias's study, I hear the loud chime of an antique clock and the rumble of Ozias's calm, commanding voice. He's on a conference call — too cowardly to step outside his compartment — and by the sound of it, things aren't going well.

When I round the corner, my loud, ragged breathing draws his attention. He pauses mid-sentence and glances up, but he doesn't seem surprised to find me standing there.

Ozias pauses and says, "I'll be in touch shortly." Then he reaches up with a gnarled hand and taps his interface to end the call.

"Hello, Mr. Reynolds," he says. "I thought I might be seeing you."

"Oh yeah?" I choke, too amped up to stick to my original strategy of pause, point, and shoot.

I know I shouldn't stop to listen to anything the old man has to say. Ozias is a master manipulator, and I can't risk getting sucked into his bullshit.

Filling my lungs with a shaky breath, I raise the gun and point it at his head.

"That's it?"

Ozias's tone is colored by surprise — maybe even *amusement* — and his lighthearted demeanor is enough to make me pause.

"I really thought my death would have a little more weight," he muses. "But I guess we all do, don't we? Even those poor souls out on the Fringe . . ."

"Don't talk about them," I growl.

"I seem to have struck a nerve . . ."

"You don't give a shit about the people out there."

"Quite the contrary," says Ozias. "I'm very grateful for

everything our workers have done to protect this compound."

"Bullshit."

"But I am. Recon has put up a good fight. But I suppose all good things must come to an end . . ."

I don't really know what to say to that. Ozias's quiet, thoughtful demeanor is off-putting to say the least.

I expected him to fight me. I expected him to break down and beg for his life, yell for security, or maybe try to strangle me with those arthritic old-man hands. I just didn't expect him to be calm.

"Aren't you going to kill me?" he asks pleasantly.

I pause. "Do you *want* to die?"

"Oh . . . heavens no. I don't expect any of us ever really *wants* to die, but it seems inevitable, doesn't it?"

I stare at him, completely dumbfounded.

How did a man like Ozias become one of the most powerful men in the compound? It just doesn't make any sense.

"I take full responsibility for this," he says suddenly. "Even the best of us can sometimes make errors in judgment."

He nods once in my direction.

"Me?"

"Why, yes, Mr. Reynolds. You're one of the smartest, most promising young people Constance has ever recruited. You hacked into the Institute's housing portal by the time you were nine . . . started editing your grades by the time you were twelve . . . scored a ninety-five on your VocAps exam . . ."

"You've been spying on me this whole time?"

Ozias smirks. "We make it a point to get to know *all* juvenile delinquents with special talents who come through the system. I had high hopes for you, too." His smile fades. "But all of us were so enamored with your abilities — and your, shall we say, *inability* to connect — that we overlooked one fatal flaw."

I glare at him, my finger poised over the trigger. I don't know why I haven't pulled it yet. I have no reason to listen to this sadistic asshole, but I can't deny that I'm curious what the most evil man in the compound perceives as my fatal flaw.

"Well?" I snarl. "What is it?"

"You don't have any instinct for self-preservation. You value your own life so little that you were willing to throw it away just to expose our organization."

"That's rich," I grumble. "You lecturing *me* on the value of human life."

"Does that surprise you?" he asks. "It shouldn't, you know. I don't underestimate the value of human life. I'm just not burdened with delusions like most people are."

"Delusions?" I repeat.

"Perhaps I should say *wishful thinking*. You see, people like to tell themselves that all men are created equal. It's easier to get along in polite society that way. But the barbaric truth is that some lives are more valuable than others. It's a simple fact."

I feel as though I need to be sick. This old bastard is unreal. He truly believes his own bullshit.

"What?" he asks, correctly interpreting my silence. "You think some Recon grunt could have done what I've done? You think one of those ExCon monkeys could have built all of this?" He holds out his arms to represent the weight of everything he's accomplished. "No. They couldn't have."

I don't say anything. I just continue to glare at him.

"It's not their fault," he adds. "They aren't bad people. Most of them are very good people who simply don't have the God-given ability —"

"Look around you!" I snap, cutting him off. "Everything you *built* is falling apart. Everything you worked so hard to control is out of control."

I point out toward the Fringe. "All those people you see as inferior are out there fighting so you can stay locked up in your precious little prison." I shake my head in disgust. "You might be the last one standing, but you *failed*."

"I didn't fail. My life's mission has been to preserve the human race, and that mission doesn't end with me," he says. "People rely on Constance to do what needs to be done. Your little stunt won't change that. It's men like us who make the unpopular but necessary decisions."

He breaks into a condescending smile. "Equality is a delicious myth, Mr. Reynolds, but it's humankind's most destructive one. People fighting for an equal share in our splendor is what led us here in the first place. There will always be people trying to take more than they're worth. And it makes —"

The blast of my gun surprises even me.

I pressed down lightly, and my aim was true. The bullet hits home just behind Ozias's wilted boutonnière, and he smiles an eerie smile as he teeters on the edge of life and death.

His blue eyes bore into mine, and blood bubbles from his mouth as he chokes. Then his eyes droop closed, and he slumps in his chair like a forgotten marionette.

"Fuck you," I whisper.

Ears ringing from the blast, I drop the stolen gun and slide down the wall to the floor. The stench of gunpowder stings my nostrils, but it isn't strong enough to overpower the scent of old books and cigar smoke — smells too rare and luxurious for Ozias to share with the rest of the compound.

A heavy sob works its way up my chest, burning my already tender throat. A dry wail shakes my whole body, and I pull my knees up to my ribcage to hold myself together.

Now that I've completed my mission, I feel drained, exhausted, and completely hopeless.

Ozias may be gone, but I can't get him out of my head. Killing him did nothing to erase the problems and ideals that made it possible for Constance to survive.

As much as I hate him, Ozias was right: Everybody wants what we have, but there will never be enough.

twenty-eight

Harper

Heart pounding, I double back to retrieve my rifle from the room where Owen was kept prisoner. Both of the bodies have been removed, but the pools of blood on the floor are a grim reminder of what transpired.

Ordinarily this room would be considered a crime scene, but with all the controversy surrounding the kidnapping and torture of a drifter, no one has erected a barricade to keep people from destroying evidence. I doubt there will be any investigation. According to Sawyer, Celdon's announcement threw suspicion onto Control, so all criminal proceedings have been put on hold pending a formal section audit.

I should feel relieved — god knows I've broken more laws than I can count — but it makes me sick to think that Watson's crimes will go unpunished.

After a hasty goodbye with Eli, I head for the emergency stairwell and take the steps down to the ground level. The barricade blocking off EnComm has been partially dismantled, but other than that, I don't encounter any surprises until I reach the main tunnel.

When I hit the last landing and burst through the door, I nearly run straight into a wall of armed controllers. They're dressed in full riot gear, complete with masks and shields, and are staring at the main entrance to the compound.

They must be waiting for Recon to fall. If the drifters break through the last line of Recon's defenses and force their way into the compound, Control will be the only thing standing between the Desperados and our people.

Unfortunately, if it comes to that, the compound is probably doomed. While some of the younger controllers are fit and competent, most are chubby desk jockeys whose greatest challenge in the field is running up a flight of stairs.

None of them have seen real battle. Most have probably never fired a gun at anything but a stationary target.

Luckily, nobody pays me any attention as I push my way through the sea of navy. They're all thinking about what's going to happen if the Desperados reach the compound.

I'm shocked to discover that the first set of airlock doors has been completely destroyed. Bits of glass are strewn all over the shiny white tile and are sticking out of the metal frame.

An older lieutenant I don't recognize is stationed in the radiation chamber, waiting behind the second set of doors for a signal that Recon has fallen.

"Hey!" he yells, wheeling around and pointing his gun at my chest.

I realize belatedly that I'm still dressed like a drifter, and the only thing keeping him from shooting me is a vague familiarity.

"Cadet Harper Riley!" I say quickly, raising one hand in surrender. "I'm in Recon. I'm on your side."

The lieutenant blinks in surprise but doesn't lower his gun. "You're the girl who deserted the compound with Parker."

"I didn't desert!"

"They said you did."

"I know what they *said*," I snap. "But I'm here now. Do you want to stand here arguing or let me out there to shoot some drifters?"

"Watch your tone, Cadet."

"Sorry, sir."

"I have explicit orders to detain you pending a formal hearing."

I let out an exasperated sigh. "With all due respect, sir, I think we have bigger problems right now."

He stares at me for a long moment and then lets out an exasperated breath. "Fine. But I didn't see you."

"What?"

"And you didn't see me either."

I pause, utterly bewildered. Then the doors open with a loud *hiss*, and I realize he's letting me go.

"Move!" he barks as a cloud of radioactive dust billows into the tiny chamber.

"Yes, sir!" I yell.

He pushes me out into the Fringe, and the doors slide closed behind me. I'm immediately engulfed in dirt and smoke, but I crouch down, raise my rifle, and follow the blasts of gunfire.

I can't see more than a few feet ahead, and I nearly stumble right into one of our barricades.

Two ExCon workers and a Recon private are hunkered down behind the sandbags, and they hardly seem to notice as I duck down beside them.

The private is a guy with a goatee I've never spoken to who's got a bloody bandage wrapped around his leg. One of the ExCon workers is a sunburned ginger with a spiderweb tattoo inked across his neck, and the other is a woman with thick chestnut cornrows.

When the ginger moves, a fourth person comes into view: a tall man with a violet-tinged mullet, ostrich-skin boots, and pieces of silver in his teeth.

Shane.

While the tier-three workers are dressed in fatigues and jumpsuits, Shane is wearing a pair of expensive slacks streaked with dirt, a black silk shirt, and a bolo tie. He's hunkered down behind the barricade, shooting at the drifters with one eye closed.

"*Well* . . . look who the cat dragged in," he drawls.

"Why are you here?" I ask, instantly repelled by his slimy tone.

Shane doesn't stop shooting, but he cracks a smile that makes my stomach crawl. "I could ask you the same question, sweetheart."

I open my mouth to tell Shane that I did what he asked and that our debt is square, but suddenly a powerful set of headlights cuts through the smoke, and two shadowy figures come into view. I shoot at the drifter on the right and miss, but Shane unloads a torrent of bullets in his chest.

"Funny, isn't it?" Shane yells over the din.

I don't say anything. Just because we're united against a common enemy doesn't mean I have to play Shane's games.

"What's funny?" yells the private.

"That all the people the compound has shit on are the people out here killing themselves to protect it."

I don't say a word. Shane isn't wrong, but before he was banished to the Fringe, he had the system so rigged that he lived better than most tier-one workers. He can hardly put himself in the same category as the Recon, ExCon, and Waste Management workers who've been mistreated all their lives.

Between the five of us, we manage to take out the entire truck of drifters, but a minute later, I see three more pairs of headlights bumping toward us over the uneven ground.

"Shit!"

"I'm out," says the woman, dropping her empty clip.

"Yeah, fuck this," says the ginger, rising into a crouch and preparing to flee.

The woman follows him, and together they fall back toward the compound.

Anxiety sweeps over me as our little group shrinks. I take aim at the nearest truck, and the private postures up to shoot at a drifter who's pushing forward on foot. A bullet whizzes between us — or so I thought — but suddenly the private yells out in pain and collapses beside me.

I look down. The side of his head is covered in blood, gushing from a spot above his right ear.

"Oh my god!" I yelp, ducking down to help him.

My heart is pounding in my throat, my ribcage is vibrating from the incessant gunfire, and my ears feel as if they're bleeding from the noise.

"It's okay," I choke, tugging off my hoodie to make a bandage. "It's just a scratch."

"It feels like — fuck!" yells the private, squeezing his eyes shut.

Hands shaking, I start a rip in the seam near the shoulder of my hoodie and tear the entire sleeve away. I scrunch it up and press it to the side of the private's head, glancing back at the compound to see if the path is clear.

"You need to get to a doctor," I yell.

"Geez . . . ya *think*?" Shane quips, not taking his eyes off the enemy line.

The private swallows in pain. "I'm not leaving. There are too many of them."

I let out a breath of frustration. "You really don't have a choice."

The private continues to gasp for several seconds, glancing back toward the battlefield and then up at the compound.

I can tell he doesn't want to abandon his post, but we both know the fight is over for him. Blood is soaking through the makeshift bandage at an alarming rate, and we haven't even made a dent in the hoard of advancing drifters.

Finally, he lets out a stream of curses and pulls himself into a crouched position.

"Go!" I growl, grabbing my rifle and opening fire on the closest truck.

The private hesitates for one more second and then sprints toward the airlock doors.

"Looks like it's just you and me now," Shane calls over the racket.

"Lucky me," I growl, hunkering down next to him and blasting the Desperado who shot the private.

"Fuck," he mutters suddenly. "I'm low."

"Me too."

"Well, it was nice knowing ya, kid," yells Shane, looking over at me with a mischievous gleam in his eye. "I guess I'm never gonna get a rematch from you and Marta . . ."

"I guess not."

"It's too bad," he muses, shooting repeatedly at the same drifter until he collapses. "You are a *scrappy* little thing."

"Thanks," I mutter, not really knowing how to respond.

There's something strange about Shane's tone. He doesn't sound like the slippery, scheming operator I've come to hate. He sounds almost wistful.

"My son was fond of you, Miss Riley," he yells, gritting his teeth and shooting another Desperado in the face.

I get a pang in my gut at his mention of Blaze, followed by a trickle of sympathy. Blaze was Shane's only son — probably the only real connection he had in this world.

"And if he liked you . . . you must be pretty special."

I stop shooting for several seconds and turn to look at Shane. He's pulling back from the barricade and straightening his bolo tie.

He sniffs loudly, wipes a hand over his greasy mane, and steps around the wall of sandbags.

"Shane, don't!" I yell, glancing over at the nearest truckload of drifters.

A rusty old pickup truck is barreling through the dirt less than twenty yards away. Three Desperados are riding in the bed, armed to the teeth with automatic weapons.

But Shane keeps going — walking straight toward the drifters with his gun in the air. He tucks his chin as he aims and shoots, unloading a stream of bullets in the side of the truck. The drifters return fire, but Shane keeps walking as if propelled by some greater force.

After a few seconds, he lowers his gun, and I know it's all over. One of the drifters in the back leans out with an AK-47 and unleashes a hailstorm of bullets into Shane's chest.

His body convulses as the bullets tear through him, and then the drifter throws something into the air.

For a moment, everything slows down. I dive into the dirt and cover my head with my hands, and another pipe bomb hits the ground.

It detonates several yards away, but I still feel the blast of heat as the flames incinerate a nearby row of solar panels. The ground trembles beneath my chest, and a cloud of dust covers everything within a thirty-foot radius.

My skin is prickling and my heart is racing, but I just keep my head covered and wait for it to end.

Finally the heat subsides, and I rise up onto my knees and squint through the haze of smoke.

Shane is gone — his body incinerated by the blast — but the looming shadows of drifter vehicles are less than ten yards away.

I roll back into a crouched position, shooting whomever I can hit, and my injured shoulder screams from the kickback.

Suddenly my rifle clicks instead of fires.

I pull the trigger again, but nothing happens.

I'm out of ammo.

As the dust settles, I see two drifters in black bandanas running toward me — dirty, sweaty, and hungry for blood. I scramble to my feet, still unsteady from the blast, but then the men freeze and fall to the ground.

"That was a close one!" yells a voice from behind me.

I wheel around to get a look at my savior and see a familiar pair of beady eyes protruding over his mask.

"Bear!" I yell.

"You out?"

I nod, and he tosses me a new mag.

"Good to see you again!" he booms over the gunfire. "I wasn't sure I would."

I grin and slam the clip into my rifle while he unloads on the nearest cluster of Desperados.

Once I'm locked and loaded, we tag team the last truckload of drifters preparing to run us over. I want to feel relief, but there's an even bigger convoy moving toward us at an alarming clip.

Then, out of nowhere, somebody flings herself behind our barricade, drops a satchel on the ground, and rolls onto her stomach to shoot.

"That's the last of it," Lenny yells. "The main supply tent is toast."

I dig into the satchel and see just a couple boxes of ammunition. My heart sinks.

Without more ammo, we'll be forced to retreat. There will be no one defending this section of land, and Malcolm's men will reach the compound.

As I squeeze the last round out of my rifle, my shoulder burns in protest. I can feel the warmth of blood soaking through my dressing, but even if we had a truckload of ammo and I had a brand-new shoulder, it wouldn't make a difference. We're overrun and outgunned, and we've sustained devastating casualties.

Lenny misses her next shot, and so does Bear, allowing a Jeep full of Desperados to continue its slow roll toward us.

Suddenly, another section of the compound loses power, throwing us into total darkness. As the next convoy materializes on the horizon, an overwhelming sense of dread rises up in my throat.

I glance to my right and then to my left.

Bear's eyes are scrunched in concentration as he fires at a battered green Jeep. Lenny's face is flushed and dirty, but she's never looked more powerful.

Then the Jeep hits the gas.

"Oh, shit," groans Bear.

The truck Lenny was shooting at speeds up, too, and I'm blinded by two pairs of headlights.

Lenny grabs my good arm and yanks me to my feet. She starts pulling me back to the compound before my brain can register what's happening, but I follow her purely on instinct. My feet struggle to find footing on the uneven ground, and I trip and stumble several times.

Then my sweaty hand slips out of Lenny's grip, and I pitch forward and slam into the earth.

The entire right side of my body throbs in protest, and I scramble to get back on my feet. Bear grabs my hand to pull me up, and we keep running toward the compound at a dead sprint.

When we reach the glow of emergency lights shining up

from the ground, I realize it's just me and Bear. I thought Lenny was a few steps ahead, but she's nowhere in sight.

Wheeling around, I search the darkness for a glimpse of her fiery red hair, and I finally spot her several yards back.

I call out her name, but she doesn't answer. Lenny isn't running anymore. She isn't taking cover. She's yelling like a maniac and shooting at the nearest drifter truck.

Bear and I watch transfixed as one of its tires blows. The truck spins out and crashes into a solar module, but Lenny keeps firing.

I start running back for her, calling out her name, but Bear is two steps ahead of me and gaining speed.

"It's done!" he yells.

Lenny doesn't move.

"Lenny! Run!" screams Bear, moving faster than I've ever seen him run.

With a creak and a groan, the driver-side door of the truck swings open, and two large boots hit the ground.

It's too dark to make out the driver's features, but Lenny has a clear shot.

I wait for her to fire, but she never does. Lenny steps back, and I realize why she stopped: She's out of ammo.

I call her name, but Lenny doesn't answer. Then a blurry shape flies through the air and tackles her to the ground. A gun goes off in the dark, and I scream.

By the time I reach the spot where Lenny went down, two figures in gray are lying in a tangled heap. Lenny is sprawled flat on her stomach, and Bear is lying across her legs.

My breath catches in my throat. The gun I heard belonged to a drifter, and that bullet was meant for Lenny.

A high-pitched wail cuts through the darkness. At first I think Lenny has been shot, but then I realize what happened.

The drifter's bullet was meant for her, but it hit Bear instead.

A crimson pool of blood is spreading quickly over his oversized gray shirt. He mumbles something indiscernible, and I feel an animalistic sob work its way up my throat.

"Fuck! I had him!" Lenny blubbers, pulling herself out from under Bear and shaking his shoulder in misery.

"You didn't," he croaks, eyes fluttering closed.

Hot tears are streaming down my face, but I don't bother wiping them away.

My breaths are coming hard and fast, and my lungs are working overtime. The battlefield is a total blur, but one figure stands out clear as day.

Bear's shooter is still firing at a nearby Recon barricade from behind his smoking truck. In the red glow of his taillights, I can just make out a narrow, pointed face, pronounced cheekbones, and severe black eyebrows.

It's Malcolm.

In a cry of rage, I snatch up Bear's weapon and stagger to my feet. My shoulder is throbbing and my body is deteriorated, but I don't feel any pain as I plant my feet and fire at Malcolm's head.

My first shot misses by at least a foot, and I let out a cry of frustration. I shoot again and again, but then I hear a *click*.

Bear's gun is out of ammo.

Throwing the rifle down on the ground, I reach into my boot and withdraw my knife. I sprint toward Malcolm — not caring that I'm exposed — and he disappears behind his truck.

My legs burn as I carve a path outside the range of Malcolm's headlights. I see the flicker of a shadow, and suddenly a dark figure tackles me to the ground. We hit the dirt, and my shoulder burns as Malcolm slams me onto my back.

Two strong hands press down on my windpipe, and I start

to panic as he cuts off my airways. I claw at his hands, choking and gasping, and in the reddish glow of Malcolm's taillights, I see two dispassionate black eyes.

Malcolm is choking me as if I'm just a nuisance, and that's when I realize he doesn't know who I am. He doesn't care that he just shot my friend. He doesn't care how many men die in his quest for control. He's just like Constance — the killing is routine to him.

Malcolm may not know me, but I know him. I know all the lives he's taken. I know what he has planned for my home.

My vision starts to blur as he cuts off the flow of oxygen to my brain, and at some point I stop trying to peel his hands off my throat.

Malcolm sneers. He thinks he's winning. But my hand is still curled around my knife.

My arm is sore and heavy, but my body moves as if it knows what I have to do. In one desperate motion, I throw my arm up and slash my knife across Malcolm's wrist.

Hot blood spurts out, soaking my neck and spraying into my mouth. Malcolm cries out in pain as I cut his tendon, and I gulp in a burst of air as the pressure on my windpipe dissipates.

While Malcolm is distracted, I buck my hips and dump him onto his side. I scramble to get on top of him, but he rolls onto his hands and knees.

I can't let him get away. This is my only chance.

With a primal yell, I throw all my weight onto Malcolm's hips and grab a fistful of his hair. I yank his head back with vicious force and slice my blade across his throat.

Blood gushes out all over my arm, and Malcolm chokes in agony. I release my grip, and he falls to the ground, blood spewing from his wound.

My stomach turns as I watch Malcolm fight for air. Blood

continues to spurt from his severed artery, and he curls into a ball as his brain shuts down.

As I watch him die, I don't feel relief or vindication or even remorse. All I feel is ugliness.

After a minute or two, Malcolm's body goes still. War is raging all around me, but my legs feel like lead as I stumble back to the spot where Bear collapsed.

Lenny is curled around his torso, trying to stop the bleeding with her overshirt.

"What the hell happened to you?" she squeaks.

I look down. My arms and chest are coated with blood, but I feel strangely numb as I bend down to check Bear's pulse.

It's faint and weak, but it's still there.

"We have to move him," I say.

Lenny nods, and I glance around nervously. People are shooting and screaming all around us, but we can't save them.

Hunkering down on one knee, I scoop up Bear's enormous arm and fling it over my shoulder. I post up one of my legs and push, but I only manage to lift his right side a few inches off the ground.

He's *so* heavy, and I only have the full strength of one of my arms. Lenny is struggling under the weight of his left side, but she's too small to lift even half his body.

I don't know what to do. My ears are ringing, Lenny is crying, and we're both seconds from getting shot.

"I'm sorry," she wails, looking up at me with devastated eyes. "I'm sorry. I c-can't."

"We have to," I moan, fighting to heave Bear more securely over my good shoulder.

But I can't move him alone, and Lenny is falling apart. A bullet whizzes past my head, and a grim reality sinks in: We aren't going to make it.

The Desperados are picking us off one by one. Our ranks have been torn apart, and there's no one left to keep Malcolm's men at bay.

"Wh-who's shooting?" mumbles Bear, his eyes drooping under the weight of his lids.

"What?" Lenny squeaks.

But I heard him.

At first I think it's just a hallucination brought on by the sudden loss of blood. But then I listen, and I hear the sound of distant gunfire.

I look up. Where there should be a horde of Desperados barreling down on us, I see nothing but Malcolm's abandoned truck and a thin haze of smoke. There are still carloads of Desperados about fifty yards away, but they don't seem to be getting any closer.

People are shooting in the distance, but they sound farther away than they did before.

I squint out into the desert and see *more* headlights approaching. But instead of moving in formation with Malcolm's men, these people are shooting at the Desperados.

Malcolm's men are yelling and screaming. Some of them are still trying to reach the compound, but most seem to be retreating.

"What the —?"

Then I see a familiar vehicle pass under a searchlight. It's a black Ford Explorer with the license plate taped over.

"It's Jackson," I murmur in disbelief, watching the Explorer cut off a carload of Desperados.

Suddenly the car stops, and several people jump out. Three of them stand and shoot, while the other two sprint back toward town. The gunman in Jackson's SUV fires back, and two of Malcolm's men collapse. The last Desperado standing empties his clip and then turns on his heel and runs.

"Who *are* those people?" shouts Lenny.

I shake my head in disbelief. It has to be Nuclear Nation — or what's left of it, anyway.

When Malcolm absorbed Jackson's gang, anyone who was too young or too old to fight was simply left to fend for themselves. Other members abandoned Malcolm's crew and fled because they were too disgusted to stay.

"Allies," I murmur, turning my attention back to Bear.

When I look down, I get a fresh jolt of alarm. The front of Bear's uniform is soaked with blood, and his face is pale and lifeless.

"Shit! Bear! Stay with me!" I yell, shaking his beefy shoulder and trying once more to get under his weight.

This time Lenny grabs him under the armpits from behind, and the two of us manage to get him into an upright position. Pushing my legs as hard as I can, I rest his armpit over my good shoulder while Lenny wraps an arm around his waist.

I glance up toward the compound, and my stomach drops. It looked so close a few moments ago, but now it seems miles away. My back screams with every step, and spots appear on the edges of my vision. I feel lightheaded and dizzy, and my injured shoulder has gone completely numb.

As Bear's weight presses me harder into the earth, every muscle in my body cries for relief. I want nothing more than to collapse onto the ground and let the desert take me, but then I think of Bear leaping in front of that bullet.

He would have done the same thing for me — the same for any of us. He shot Owen to protect the compound, and he put his own life at risk to help Eli.

Bear was the cadet who didn't belong, but he quietly proved himself over and over.

My renewed surge of strength lasts as long as it takes for a stronger set of arms to lift most of Bear's weight off my shoulder.

I look up in a daze and see Miles's dirty, exhausted face above me. I want to cry out in relief, but I don't have the energy.

Miles takes over for Lenny, and between the two of us, we manage to drag Bear the rest of the distance to the compound.

I stagger through the airlock doors and am instantly blinded by the unearthly blue light of the radiation chamber. Two burly men heave Bear onto a stretcher, and a couple of interns whisk him away to the makeshift medical center.

I limp after them, and a concerned voice calls me back. I don't listen. I trip after Bear's runaway gurney and push past the wall of controllers.

The interns bank right into the multipurpose room, and I follow them into the sea of cots. Suddenly I'm surrounded by people in red. There are too many sounds and smells for my brain to process, but I manage to locate Bear's gurney.

Then someone steps in front of me, blocking my path. It's another nurse, and she's telling me I have to wait to be seen. I mumble something about my friend, and her mouth sags in sorrow. I read the word "surgery" on her lips, but I don't hear what I'm supposed to do now.

The woman holds out a hand to stop me, and I can only follow Bear with my eyes.

Someone places a mask over his pale, bloodless face, and a nurse begins cutting his uniform down the middle. A man in scrubs moves a partition to block Bear from view, and machines beep frantically as they hook him up to the monitors.

The last thing I hear is the incessant trill of a flatline, followed by crushing silence.

twenty-nine

Celdon

The second the bullet leaves my gun, all the fight drains out of me at once. My legs go weak, and suddenly simple things like breathing and standing seem to require great effort.

With the power on the fritz, it's about a thousand degrees in the old man's compartment. I'm sweating like a motherfucker, so I peel off my filthy blazer and toss it over my head. It lands on the back of Ozias's armchair, and the sleeve falls over his lifeless face. I can still see the wet spot on his black shirt where the blood poured out of him, but without a beating heart to pump it through his body, it seeps slowly across the fabric and dries where it lands.

I mop my face with a shaky hand and try to figure out what to do next. It's only a matter of time before someone wanders down the tunnel and sees the dead guard's carcass.

The stiff slam of the front door drags me back to reality. Soft footsteps echo down the entryway, and I sense a cautious presence in the room before a familiar scent reaches my nose.

It's soft and clean — almost like baby powder, but with soft floral undertones. It's how moms smell.

"Celdon, it's time to go."

Robin's voice is warm yet firm, but I'm not in a place to talk to anyone right now.

"Why? You got somewhere to be?" I snap.

I don't know why I'm still being a dick to her. Less than two hours ago, she pulled a gun on Paxton Dellwood. That has to count for something.

"How did you find me?" I ask.

"Remy's not the only one watching out for you," she says, crossing the room and rummaging around in Ozias's huge mahogany desk.

"You followed me?"

"At a distance," she concedes with a shrug. "I thought you might need my help."

I feel a bratty retort forming on my lips. But as I watch Robin move around the room, all the animosity I felt toward her evaporates, leaving only this weird ache behind.

I don't want to fight with Robin, I realize. I want to know her. More than anything, I want someone to tell me that I can come back from this, and that's something only a mother can do. Nobody else could love a person who's done the things I've done.

Robin moves around Ozias's study at a slow pace, but she doesn't handle his belongings delicately. She tosses what's probably a priceless antique book aside and tips a stack of papers over to see what's hiding underneath.

I don't ask her what she's looking for, but a moment later, she holds up a shallow brown box with a golden clasp and walks over to where I'm sitting. She sinks down onto the ground beside me, and I study her carefully out of the corner of my eye.

Robin is a head shorter than me and much more compact. Her hair is blond like mine but lighter from the sun, and when she frowns, her mouth fits comfortably into two deep divots — as though she's worn that expression for most of her life.

Robin opens the box and pulls out two fat cigars. She hands one to me and then flicks open a silver lighter. She puffs on the cigar as if she knows what to do, and a moment later, fragrant smoke wafts out and drifts up over our heads.

I take the lighter when she offers it, but I don't light the cigar. My throat is still on fire from the fucking tear gas, but holding the cigar between my thumb and two fingers is comforting all on its own. I don't know how to smoke the thing, but an authentic pre–Death Storm cigar like this is probably worth more than my entire annual stipend.

Somewhere in the study, I hear the rhythmic beeping sound that means breaking news is about to play over every device in the compound. An expensive screen tucked away in an antique wooden cabinet switches on of its own accord, and a Vietnamese woman with long shiny hair appears.

"Good morning," she says. "We interrupt this broadcast for a special announcement. Interim President Remy Chaplin has announced that the violence on the Fringe has come to a halt. At least two hundred compound citizens died in the battle, and dozens more are being treated for serious injuries.

"Compound personnel managed to drive off the hostile intruders with the help of another faction of Fringe survivors. Our source inside Recon tells us that the friendly survivors arrived at a crucial point of the engagement, forcing the intruders to retreat. No word yet on who these survivors are or why they came to help, but all remaining board members will be holding a summit with the survivors' leaders to negotiate a peaceful resolution.

"In other news, Undersecretary of Health and Rehab and Interim Vice President Natasha Mayweather has announced that the viral outbreak is officially under control. Those infected have received a groundbreaking new treatment, which will render them noninfectious within twenty-four hours. This treatment has come after nearly six hundred fell ill and died. A group service for the dead will be held in the coming days. I'm Kim Nguyen. Goodnight."

The screen goes dark as the broadcast ends, and I'm left with the sinking feeling that business within the compound will continue as usual.

"What happens now?" I croak.

"Now we rebuild," Robin breathes, sounding nearly as exhausted as I feel.

"Rebuild *what*?" I snap. "Eight hundred people are dead. Most of the board was blown up." I shake my head. "Those drifters who jumped in to help us . . . They didn't do it out of the goodness of their hearts. What's going to happen when they start making demands?"

Robin whips her head around and fixes me with a sharp look. After learning about her history with the compound, I began to think of her as one of us. But based on the look she's giving me now, she doesn't see herself the same way.

"If they didn't do it out of the goodness of their hearts, then why do you think they helped?" she asks.

"I don't know," I mumble. "But they're gonna want *something* . . . a stake in all this . . ."

"Maybe," says Robin. "But that's not what you're really worried about, is it?"

I let out a dismissive scoff, but she's right. There's a painful lump expanding in my throat that's making it difficult to talk. My eyes are stinging with tears, but I don't let them fall.

"What the fuck am I supposed to do?" I whisper.

"You move forward."

I shake my head. "I've hurt so many people."

"We all have blood on our hands."

I let out a harsh laugh that sounds pretty fucked up. "Yeah, but I have, like, *literal* blood on my hands." I swallow. "They're not just gonna let me walk away from this."

Robin stares at me for a long time, as if she's trying to figure out what to say. "Well, would you do any of it differently?"

I shrug. "I don't know."

"It doesn't matter," she says. "You can't go back." She glances down at the hand holding her cigar. "None of us can."

"So what should I do?"

I look into her eyes, expecting to see disappointment or maybe pity. Instead, I'm startled to see that her gaze is full of pride.

"You finish what you started," she murmurs. "You go back to Systems and make sure the people responsible for this are exposed — including me."

"You?"

She nods. "I may not have brought that virus in here, and I may not have blown up those board members, but I still played a role in all of this — no matter how much I'd like to pretend otherwise."

"You can't seriously —"

"Maybe he would have found a way without my help," she says. "But that doesn't absolve me from responsibility. Just as finding you now doesn't erase what happened twenty years ago."

"We've been through all that," I sigh.

"No, we haven't."

"I don't want to talk about it," I say firmly. And I mean it. It's too fucking painful.

"All right. We won't talk about it today. But someday we're going to have to."

I nod.

"You have to know . . . Everything I did, I did it for you."

"I know, Mom."

It's the first time I've said that out loud, and it surprises even me. A hopeful smile flickers across her face, lighting up the entire room and momentarily making me forget about the dead man sitting ten feet in front of me.

Then reality comes rushing back. "What about him?" I croak, nodding at Ozias.

Robin's face goes dark. "Ozias Pirro was an evil man," she says. "He did a lot of bad things to a lot of people." She pauses. "Ending his reign of tyranny was the right thing to do."

"Yeah, but . . ." I roll my eyes and jerk my head back toward the tunnel. "It's still murder. I'm pretty sure Control isn't going to care that I chose to murder an asshole."

Robin nods and meets my gaze with a stern but compassionate look. "After everything that's happened . . . I can't imagine there's a single person in your position who would have done anything differently."

"Still . . . I'm gonna pay for this."

"Trust me. We're *all* going to pay for this. The lives that have been lost . . . The trust that's been broken . . . These are things that can't be fixed overnight." She sighs. "But people knowing you did this . . ." She nods at Ozias. "That isn't going to help anybody."

"What are you saying?"

Her eyes zero in on the weapon lying a few feet in front of me. "Where did you get that gun?"

"I stole it," I mutter sheepishly.

"Good," she says, getting to her feet and grabbing it off the floor. "That means it's not checked out in your name."

She walks over to Ozias's dead body and plucks the handkerchief out of his breast pocket. I watch transfixed as she wipes down the gun and lays it carefully in the middle of the desk. Then she makes her way around the room, wiping every surface we touched and erasing all evidence that we were ever here.

"Do you still have access to the security feeds?" she asks.

I nod, too stunned to speak.

"As soon as we leave here, go straight to Information and wipe all the footage." She gives her head a slight shake. "Hopefully they don't look into this too hard."

"Are you kidding?" I cry. "Ozias was a founder!"

"And Remy Chaplin knows he was involved with Constance."

"Because I told him."

"Trust me," she says. "He's going to want to put all this ugliness behind him."

I stare at her in disbelief. "You're saying I should just *walk away*? What happened to people taking responsibility for their crimes?"

"You did take responsibility," says Robin. "It's a burden you never should have had to bear, but you did the right thing."

I shake my head, utterly dumbfounded that my mom is helping me cover up a double homicide.

"People need you, Celdon," she says in a serious voice. "They need you to help rebuild this place."

"What about you?" I ask.

"I don't know what's going to happen to me," she says slowly. "I may not be welcome here once people find out —" She breaks off and smiles. "But you . . . You're a hero. People will be looking to you."

"Why?" I scoff. "Because I'm some Systems douchebag who Constance singled out to brainwash?" I shake my head. "It wasn't talent that got me here. Systems wanted me because of *your* genes — not because I'm good with computers."

"But you *are* good with computers," says Robin. "You've proven that you belong."

I shake my head. "No. People's sections . . . What they've done . . . All that's irrelevant now."

"It's not," she says. "We are who we are, and the things people have done *do* matter. There's no doubt in my mind that you belong in Systems, regardless of how you got there."

I squirm under the compliment. It still weirds me out that my mom is the sort of hacker who could give me a run for my money.

"Sweetheart, the bid system may be flawed, but that doesn't mean it made a mistake with you."

She's still staring at me with love in her eyes, but I don't say anything. I just want to sit here and enjoy it.

"None of us can change the past," she whispers. "None of us can fix everything. All you can do is take the talents you've been given and use them to start cleaning up this mess."

thirty

Harper

I awake slowly to the incessant shuffle of feet and the intrusive beep of machines. I don't know where I am, but it feels as though I'm cocooned in some sort of sling.

I'm not wearing my regular clothes. I'm draped in a baggy hospital gown with a scratchy blanket covering my legs. I can feel a needle sticking out of my arm and a long thin tube running along the side of my body. My head is throbbing dully, but other than that, I feel all right.

Groaning at the bright lights overhead, I peel my eyelids open and take in my surroundings. I'm lying on a cot in a room full of wounded people. Men and women in red scrubs are milling between the rows of cots, checking patients' vital signs and adjusting the meds flowing from plastic tubes.

I listen intently for the sound of gunshots or explosions in the distance, but the Fringe is unnervingly quiet.

Reaching across my chest, I feel a brand-new cotton bandage that's been taped over my shoulder. I should be in agony, but instead I just feel fuzzy and a little nauseated. It must be the painkillers.

"You're awake," says a weak, scratchy voice beside me.

I turn my head to the left. Lenny is curled up in a folding chair beside my bed, wearing a clean pair of pants and a baggy sweatshirt. She looks as though she's had a shower, but her hair is an angry nest of curls. She must have been sitting there for a while.

"Yeah," I groan. "What's *happening* out there?"

"It's been quiet," she says with a sniff, glancing nervously toward the crisp white partitions blocking the Fringe from view. "I think they drove them off."

"Who's *they*?" I ask.

My memories of the battle are still intact, but they feel strangely distant, like a half-forgotten dream.

Lenny sniffs again and wipes her nose with a crumpled tissue. "The other drifters. They call themselves Nuclear Nation. It's been a whole day since they showed up, and the Desperados have been gone ever since."

"A whole *day*?" I cry. "How long have I been asleep?"

Lenny frowns. "Since yesterday. You passed out on the floor. They think you have a concussion. The doctor sedated you to run some tests and so you could recover."

"They kept me *unconscious*?" I spit, shaking my head with rage.

"Sorry," says Lenny. "I tried to stop them, but I'm not family, so . . ."

Suddenly, my memory of what I was doing before I passed out comes roaring back. "Oh my god," I whisper. "Where's Bear?"

Lenny looks over at me with tears in her eyes and shakes her head slowly. "He didn't make it."

"*What*?" I cry. "No. No. That doesn't . . ." I shake my head in disbelief. "He was still alive when we brought him in, wasn't he?"

Lenny opens her mouth, but no words come out.

I wrack my brain, thinking back to everything that happened after Bear was shot. If I hadn't gone after Malcolm . . .

"If he'd had more time . . ." I begin in a shaky voice. "If we'd gotten him here sooner . . ."

Lenny shakes her head, and when she finally speaks, her voice cracks with emotion. "No. They said there was too much damage to his heart. Even if he'd gone straight into surgery . . . a wound like that wouldn't be survivable."

I suck in a shaky breath of air. Bear is dead — gone forever.

Yesterday I was fighting beside him on the battlefield, and now he's lying under a sheet waiting to be transferred to the dead level.

It doesn't seem real.

A horrible choking wave of sobs works its way up my throat and bursts out in a pathetic gargle. Hot tears gush out of my eyes and run down the sides of my face, stinging the myriad of cuts and burns on my cheeks.

Soon my tears escalate to full-body sobs, and fresh tears spring into Lenny's eyes. My lungs are heaving — struggling for air — but no one even turns to look at us.

Everyone in here knows what we're feeling. They've all lost someone.

"Wh-what about Sage?" I ask, almost afraid to put the question into words.

"She made it out of surgery," says Lenny. "She's resting now."

I nod. "Has she said anything?"

Lenny shakes her head. "The surgeon said everything went well, but we won't know for sure until she wakes up."

"What about Eli?" I ask.

"I haven't heard anything," Lenny whispers.

I let out another blubbering sob. The last time I saw Eli, he was in the medical ward about to undergo some new type of immunotherapy. It's been a whole day since he was admitted. We should have heard by now if he was responding to treatment.

I have to get out of here.

"What are you doing?" asks Lenny when I pull myself into a seated position.

"I have to go," I murmur, looking around for my clothes.

"Go where?"

"I have to see Eli," I say, feeling a little dizzy as I swing my legs over the side of my cot. "I need to know he's okay."

"Harper, wait."

But I'm done waiting. Eli's all alone in the medical ward, and if he isn't responding to treatment, he doesn't have much time.

"I'm going," I say, more to myself than to Lenny.

"They said they wanted to monitor you for a few more days."

"*A few more days*?" I repeat, ripping off the plastic tape holding my IV needle in place. "I can't stay here that long."

Lenny looks around anxiously, torn between what the doctors told her and my desperation to see Eli.

"Okay," she whispers. "I'll go find your clothes."

Lenny gets up and walks around the edge of the room toward the storage bins stacked along the perimeter. She returns a few minutes later carrying a plastic laundry bag and my dusty combat boots.

Glancing around to make sure none of the nurses are watching me, I rip open the bag and pull out my bundle of clothes. As I shake out my shorts and bra, I get a strong whiff of detergent, and I'm amazed to see that my tank top is spotless.

There's no evidence of the wounds I sustained or the blood that poured out when I slit Malcolm's throat. Only my boots tell the full story. They're coated with dirt and blood, and there are tiny blue silicon fragments embedded in the soles.

I pull the scratchy brown blanket over my body to dress, wincing as the fabric disturbs my bandage. I shove my feet into my boots, and Lenny helps me up.

I feel weak and a tad lightheaded, but my legs work fine.

"Thanks," I say.

"Any time," she whispers, wrapping her skinny arms around my waist. "Now go find Eli."

I nod and return her hug with my good arm, wishing there was something I could do to bring back Bear.

I pull away with a sniff and look around again to make sure none of the nurses are paying attention. I toss Lenny one last look and then slip down the outer aisle between the beds and the windows.

Halfway across the room, a burst of dizziness swamps me. I'm not sure if the lightheaded feeling is due to the medication or the concussion, but I can't afford to faint and end up handcuffed to my bed.

I duck around a partition to ride out the spell, and all the air leaves my lungs.

I'm staring out the window at the desert, which is almost unrecognizable.

The Fringe is no longer the eerily beautiful place from my nightmares. The desolate, burnt-orange terrain is singed and destroyed — blackened by bombs and fire.

The ground is littered with blue silicon, bullet casings, and scraps of metal. Burnt skeletons of trucks and vans litter the dusky landscape, and the smoldering remains of barricades show where our people fought and died.

Suddenly I wish I could have seen the Desperados retreat. I wish I could talk to Jackson and the other members of Nuclear Nation and thank them for coming to our rescue.

We never would have survived without their help, and we'll be indebted to them forever.

I'm almost to the door when a familiar face catches my eye.

She's lying on a cot far removed from the other patients with cloth dividers surrounding her on three sides. She's got smooth coppery skin, long black hair, and a thick cotton bandage wrapped around her head. Half her face is badly burned, and she has a drip of IV fluids running into her arm.

"Sage," I whisper, stumbling toward her in a daze.

Trembling with apprehension, I kneel down beside her cot and gently squeeze her arm. She looks so small lying there asleep. But then she opens her eyes, and I see a shadow of the strength that emerged when we were ambushed on the Fringe.

"H-Harper?" she whispers hoarsely, her eyes searching my face in confusion.

"Yeah . . . It's me."

She glances around, looking lost and a little scared. "Where . . . Where am I?"

"You're in the compound," I say quietly. "You were hurt in the explosion, but our doctors are taking care of you."

That doesn't seem to put her mind at ease. She drags in a worried breath and tries to move, but tears of pain spring into her eyes.

"It's okay," I whisper, finding her hand and giving it a gentle squeeze. "They know you were helping us. Nobody's going to hurt you. It's gonna be okay."

"My head hurts," she murmurs, raising her arm to touch the bandage.

"Yeah. You had surgery to remove a piece of shrapnel. Do you remember what happened?"

She thinks for a minute and then gives her head a slow shake. "The last thing I remember is Jackson driving off."

"He came back!" I whisper. "And he brought a whole *army* with him."

"He did?"

"*Yeah.* He drove off the Desperados! He's the only reason we're all still alive."

Sage manages a small smile, but it fades almost instantly. "What about Owen?" she asks. "Did you find him?"

I nod wordlessly, swallowing down the lump in my throat and trying to think of a way to tell her what happened. She already knows that Owen was infected, but she must be holding on to some small shred of hope that he's going to be all right.

"Is he . . . Is he alive?"

I shake my head, squeezing her hand and wracking my brain for some way to take the sting out of what I'm about to say. Tears are welling up in my eyes, blurring my vision and scrambling my brain.

"He . . . He didn't make it," I choke. "I'm so sorry."

At those words, Sage's face falls, and her eyes fill abruptly with tears. She sniffs loudly to hold them in, but several manage to escape.

"Did he . . . Did he suffer?"

"No," I manage, shaking off the image of Owen slumped against the wall, battered, bruised, and burned. "It was . . . It was quick."

"How did it happen?"

I hesitate. "He was shot," I say. "Eli and I were with him when he died."

Sage sniffs, staring up at the ceiling. "Good. That's good. I'm glad he didn't have to die alone."

Sage's voice peters out on the last couple words, and my heart contracts painfully. I know she would have given anything to see Owen one last time — even just to tell him goodbye.

"What about Eli?"

"He's alive," I gasp, hardly able to believe it myself.

"Good," she squeaks, closing her eyes as she succumbs to

tears.

I don't say anything else. I just hold her hand while she cries.

Once Sage lets herself go, the tears flow heavy and fast. They stream down her face, soak into her pillow, and get lost in her long black hair. She cries the way I would cry if I'd lost Eli, and that makes it feel so much worse.

When Sage's tears intensify, I squeeze her hand tighter, wishing there was something I could do. But there's nothing I can say to alleviate her pain — nothing I can do to bring Owen back.

"You should go," she says finally, her tears morphing into shakes and sniffles.

"I can stay," I whisper. "I don't mind."

"No," says Sage, dabbing under her eyes with the back of her hand. "I . . . I think I just need to be alone for a while."

I hesitate. Sage is a drifter inside the compound — a soldier behind enemy lines. She doesn't know anyone, and she just lost the love of her life. I don't want to leave her on her own, but she seems adamant.

"Please," she says, meeting my gaze with those intense brown eyes. "I'm fine."

"Are you *sure*?"

"Yeah," she says. "I'm sure."

I sigh. She really wants to be left alone. I give her hand one last squeeze and slowly get up to leave. I watch her until I'm all the way to the door and then slip out of the med center as quietly as I can.

I nod casually at the controller stationed at the entrance so he thinks I was just discharged and walk down the main tunnel at a leisurely pace. My heart is fluttering with anticipation, but I don't want to arouse suspicion and get sent back to the medical center.

The wall of controllers has finally disbanded, but the tunnel is still crowded with people. Tier-three workers are standing around waiting to be admitted as nurses assess their injuries. No one pays me any attention as I walk toward the emergency stairwell.

Along the way, I pass a tunnel I rarely use, and a strange odor hits my nostrils. It's foreign and familiar at the same time, and I find myself pulled forward by my own curiosity.

I walk a hundred yards down the tunnel, and the smell grows stronger until it's nearly overwhelming.

I hold my breath as I round the corner, and my heart drops to my knees.

Dozens of bodies are laid out side by side in the adjacent tunnel. They're shrouded in white sheets, and I have to cover my mouth to stop myself from vomiting.

Normally people are given a simple funeral and buried in the dead level so their bodies can return nutrients to the soil. But the number of people we lost in the battle is staggering, and that many corpses would overwhelm the ecosystem.

With this many dead, I don't know how we'll ever be able to lay them all to rest. There isn't enough time or space to hold individual funerals, and we can't bury them all inside the compound.

Ironically, Recon has probably put a hundred times this many drifters in the ground, but seeing so many of our own people slaughtered — people who were running and fighting just a few hours ago — makes me feel sick to my stomach.

Fighting the overwhelming tide of despair rising up inside me, I stumble back to the main tunnel and head up the emergency stairwell. I clutch the railing for dear life as I climb, stopping every now and then to ward off the dizziness threatening to pull me under.

Celdon's master key must have gotten lost when my clothes went through the laundry, because when I reach into my back pocket, all I feel is denim.

Luckily, I manage to get through tier two and reach Health and Rehab without using it at all. With all the infected undergoing treatment, the compound must have lifted lockdown.

Sure enough, when I push the door to the medical ward open, I see that all the doctors and nurses have ditched their hazmat suits. They're dressed in normal red scrubs and lab coats, and a few visitors are milling around the waiting area.

I catch several wary looks as I make my way down the main tunnel toward the patient rooms, but nobody stops me or asks me to leave.

"Harper?" calls a familiar voice.

I turn.

Sawyer is standing behind me wearing a pair of gray slacks, a white camisole, and a yellow cardigan. She looks as though she's lost a few pounds, but the color is starting to return to her cheeks.

"H-hey," I stammer, slightly taken aback to see her standing there. "What are you —?"

"I'm officially noninfectious, so they sent me home to recover," she says, taking in my dirty boots and tangled hair with a concerned look on her face. "What are you doing out of bed?"

"I got out," I say, feeling suddenly nervous.

"Harper, you got blown up," says Sawyer, taking a step forward to examine the bandage sticking out from under my tank top.

"Yeah . . ."

"I messaged the ground annex last night. They said it would be a few days before you were discharged."

"Well, I . . ."

Sawyer's eyes grow wide. "You left without being discharged, didn't you?"

I roll my eyes. "It's no big deal."

"No big deal?" Sawyer splutters. "You could have an infection! You could have a concussion. You could —"

"I have to see Eli," I break in. "I couldn't wait any longer."

Sawyer sighs, and a sudden warmth washes over her stern exterior. "Harper, he's fine. He's still undergoing treatment, but he's officially noninfectious."

Relief as I've never known floods through my entire body, sending an unexpected surge of lightness through my chest and limbs. Suddenly my knees feel weak, and I wobble on the spot.

"Easy!" says Sawyer, jumping forward to steady me.

"I'm fine."

"You're *not* fine."

"Stop it, Sawyer. I need to see him!" I cry, thinking of all the bodies lined up on the ground level.

"Okay, okay," she says, pulling me in for a hug. "I'll show you where his room is. Just . . . take it easy. I don't want to lose you."

"I don't want to lose you either," I mumble, giving in to her embrace and letting a few stray tears trickle down my nose. "I was so scared, Sawyer. I thought you were going to die."

"Yeah . . . Me, too."

"I don't know what I would do without you."

Sawyer shrugs her shoulders. "You'd be sad for a while . . . Then you'd find some other intern to corrupt."

"I'm serious," I snap, pulling away so I can study her face. I was so wrapped up in finding Eli that I never even considered everything she's been through. "Is Caleb okay?"

She nods and closes her eyes in relief. "As far as I know,

everyone who received treatment in time is going to be all right."

I sigh and pull Sawyer in for one more hug. Then she links her arm through mine and leads me silently down the tunnel to the room where Eli is staying. Two tunnels we pass have bold red signs indicating that the patients in those rooms are still infectious, but other than that, the ward looks just as it did before.

After what feels like an eternity, Sawyer stops outside a room at the end of the tunnel and gives my arm a squeeze. The door is closed, but I can see the glow of a single light emanating through the frosted-glass walls.

"I'll give you guys some time," she whispers, cracking a small smile. "Caleb should be released soon. I'm gonna go wait for him."

"'Kay."

I watch her walk down the tunnel with an overwhelming feeling of gratitude. I came so close to losing Sawyer forever, but she's still here. Eli is still here.

Dragging in a deep breath, I turn the handle and open the door slowly.

At first, I'm not sure Sawyer brought me to the right room. There is a man lying in bed, but his eyes are closed, and his face is so badly beaten that he's almost unrecognizable. If it weren't for the strong set of his jaw and the body I know so well, I wouldn't believe it was him.

Eli's got little round sensors all over his chest and an IV drip going into his arm. His torso is covered in cuts and contusions, and his eyes look like two black pits. His soft dark hair is damp with sweat, and he doesn't stir when the door snaps shut.

Swallowing down my tears, I cross to the bed and watch for the slow rise and fall of his chest. His monitors are blinking with numbers I don't understand, but he seems to be stable.

Once I'm just a few inches away, I reach out and skim my finger along his jaw, smiling at the slight prick of stubble.

At my touch, Eli exhales and shifts slightly in bed. I want nothing more than to bend over and kiss him, but he looks so fragile that I'm afraid I'll hurt him.

Shaking slightly, I sink down beside him and lower my head to his pillow. I know I shouldn't be this close. I'm filthy and gross and covered in radioactive dust. My boots still have blood from the battle caked along the soles, but I have to be near him.

Tears continue to fall down my cheeks as I curl up beside Eli. His body seems too hot — as if he's fighting a fever — but every rise and fall of his chest helps convince me that he really is going to be all right.

Slowly, my breathing falls into a rhythm with his, and I feel myself sink deeper into the pillow. I snuggle closer to Eli, press my nose against his shoulder, and drift into an almost peaceful sleep.

thirty-one

Harper

For the first time in days, I wake up in my old compartment. There are no trains blazing through the Underground tunnel, and the cadet wing is eerily quiet. My computer is hidden under a thin layer of dust, but everything else is exactly how I left it.

I take a fresh uniform off the stack in my closet and pull on my fatigues with restrained anticipation. All Recon operations have been suspended since the Desperados' retreat, but today we'll hear the results of the election, and there's a rumor that the new president will announce what's going to happen to Recon.

I take a deep breath and run my hand over the embroidered hawk on my uniform, remembering a conversation I had with Eli months before: *The hawk will fight until he dies or wins.*

Staring at my tired reflection in the mirror, I can't help but think that we got it all wrong.

We didn't die fighting the drifters, but we didn't win either. You can't ever really win a war; you just live to fight another day.

Once I've summoned the strength to greet the world, I take the megalift up to the canteen for breakfast. Since the Desperados destroyed a large chunk of the solar fields, the compound is still conserving energy. Only emergency lights illuminate the tunnels, and the canteen seems oddly bright in comparison.

For the first time, my Recon uniform doesn't make me feel invisible or despised. Those who fought in the battle are being treated like heroes, and I receive several polite nods as I walk toward the serving line.

With all the casualties Recon sustained, our tables are pitifully empty. Most of the survivors have squeezed in with their friends from other sections, and instead of throwing the newcomers scornful looks, people are leaning in eagerly to hear their stories and bombard them with questions about the drifters.

I glance up at the enormous screen on the wall and catch a glimpse of the headline: "Former Undersecretary of Reconnaissance Remy Chaplin Wins in a Landslide."

It doesn't surprise me one bit. The official election was just a formality, and judging from the snippets of chatter I hear, most people are happy about Remy's victory.

In the days he served as interim president, Remy signed a warrant for the arrest of every member of Constance. He invited Jackson Mills into the compound to negotiate a treaty with Nuclear Nation, and he sat down with all high-ranking section officials to discuss reform of the dirty bid system. He even pardoned Celdon's mom and invited her to stay in the compound.

As I go through the line, I catch several people staring at me for far too long. I'm getting used to the attention, but it still makes me squirm.

After Celdon leaked the VocAps scores, a bunch of tier-one workers were outed as genetic freeloaders, while others like me gained reputations as secret prodigies.

Then there's the rumor that I slit Malcolm Martinez's throat and watched him bleed out on the battlefield. Nobody has any proof I did that, but people will believe anything.

I'm relieved when I spot Celdon sitting alone at the end of a Systems table. He's got his interface tuned to the news feeds and appears to be deep in concentration. I slide onto the bench across from him and playfully bump my tray into his. Celdon's eyes flicker behind the projection, and a look of warm relief spreads across his face.

"Hey, Riles."

"Hey."

"Good to see you decided to return to the land of the living."

"They ran out of chocolate pudding in the medical ward."

Celdon grins and flips off his interface. "You look like hell, by the way."

"Thanks a lot, asshole," I mutter, ramming my fork into my maple-glazed sweet potatoes.

"I mean it," he says, making a big circular gesture around my face. "When's the last time you slept?"

"Last night."

It's no secret that I've barely slept at all since the battle. No matter how hard I try, I just can't stop thinking about Bear and Owen or the look on Malcolm's face as he died.

I worry about Eli being sent out onto the Fringe without me, and I worry about Celdon being tried for murder. But last night my body couldn't take it anymore, and I passed out on top of my covers for a good three hours.

"I had a meeting with Remy," says Celdon in an offhand voice.

"*What?*"

"Relax," he says, correctly interpreting the panic in my voice. "He just wanted more information about Constance. They're still building a case against the members, and they need my testimony."

"What about" — I lower my voice and glance around — "Ozias?"

Celdon and I haven't talked about it openly, but I'm pretty sure he murdered Ozias Pirro and his bodyguard. The news coverage of the case has been suspiciously slim, but the other day Control announced that they would be looking into former members of Constance as suspects.

Celdon waves a dismissive hand. "One of the conditions for my testimony was immunity. Even if they managed to pin it on me, they wouldn't be able to do anything about it."

"What about Devon Reid and that controller?" I whisper, raising an eyebrow.

He shakes his head and pushes a clump of rolled oats around on his tray. "That was purely self-defense. And as far as the public is concerned, Devon Reid was just another member of Constance. I'm the guy who blew the lid off the whole thing." He tilts his head to the side. "Remy just got elected president, Riles. He doesn't want to hold a criminal trial for a hero. He needs the public on his side to push this new drifter resolution through."

I shake my head, my body tingling with nerves. On the one hand, I'm beyond relieved that the board won't be pressing charges against Celdon. On the other, I'm a little put off that they're already covering up murders to advance their political agendas.

"What's gonna happen to them?" I ask quietly. "Constance?"

Celdon shrugs. "They won't be walking around the compound anymore, that's for sure. I'm guessing most of them will be sentenced to life in the cages."

"Just watch your back, okay? As long as they're still alive —"

"Riles, you don't have to worry about me anymore," says Celdon. "I'm a bigwig now."

In addition to the compound-wide notoriety Celdon earned

with his Constance broadcast, he was also just asked to head up a special Systems task force to expose illegal espionage within the compound.

"I'm proud of you, you know," I say. And I mean it.

In the past week, Celdon has been more focused and motivated than I've ever seen him. He hasn't gone down to Neverland once, and he's been hanging out with his mom while she undergoes cancer treatment.

"How's Robin feeling?" I ask.

"Better, I think. The doctors say her prognosis is good. It helps that she'll have something to keep her busy . . ." Celdon rolls his eyes. "A purpose in life and whatnot."

I can tell Celdon is extremely proud of himself about something, but he's trying to play it off.

"I talked to my supervisor about bringing her back into Systems once she's recovered," he adds. "She said we could use an 'outside perspective' in penetration testing, so . . ."

"That's great!"

I'm glad to see Celdon patching things up with his mom. After everything he's been through, he needs her now more than ever.

I glance at the clock and get a tingle of excitement when I realize it's almost oh-nine hundred.

"I gotta go," I say, shoving the last pile of oatmeal into my mouth and getting up from the table.

"Gotta go get your *man*," chuckles Celdon.

I roll my eyes, but I can't help smiling. Eli is being discharged today, and we planned on going to see the president's inaugural address together.

My heart speeds up as I climb the stairs to the medical ward. It's still at capacity with all the wounded tier-three workers, and people in red scrubs are rushing up and down the frosted-glass tunnels.

The girl working the front desk doesn't say a word as I make my way back to Eli's room. I've spent practically every waking hour in the medical ward since he was admitted, and almost every intern knows me by name.

Eli's door is open when I get there, but I stop just outside the room to take in the sight of him.

He's sitting on the edge of his bed dressed in his old lieutenant's uniform, lacing up one of his freshly shined boots. I can tell the motion pains him, so I bend down to tie it for him.

"Thanks," he murmurs, giving me a small smile.

"Any time," I choke, a little taken aback.

Eli hasn't smiled once since Owen was killed. And ever since he woke up in the medical ward, despair has hung over him like a storm cloud.

I know that sitting helpless as his brother died will haunt him for the rest of his life, but today is a good day. Today, he's a lieutenant again.

Reinstating Eli was one of Remy's first actions when he stepped in to do damage control in Recon after the battle. We haven't talked about it, but I know a return to the gray fatigues is a big deal for Eli. As much pain as his position brought him, being a lieutenant meant everything to Eli. And when Jayden demoted him to ExCon, she robbed him of his identity.

When I finish tying Eli's boot, I get to my feet and give him a quick once-over. I know his injured ribs still bother him and the scars on his leg won't ever go away, but his coloring has returned to normal, and the bruises have started to fade.

His neat hair and crisp uniform give him the quiet dignity of an officer, and the fiery look in his eyes tells me he's ready to get back to work. So am I.

The battle might be over, but the war is still going on outside the compound. The Desperados are still at large, and the Fringe is just as deadly.

In the end, Eli's warning from our first day of training turned out to be true. Only, it didn't take two years for Recon to claim three of our people — it took less than six months.

No matter how grateful I am to have survived the battle, I don't know if I'll ever feel whole again.

But when Eli gets to his feet and holds out his hand, all that darkness recedes enough for me to breathe. No matter how much we've lost, all we can do is push forward.

We walk out of the medical ward hand in hand and make our way down to the main hall for Remy's speech. Now that the outbreak is over, the hall has been returned to its original purpose, but it seems a little less grand than it did on Bid Day.

The banners hanging over the raised platform look faded and tattered, and the workers filtering into the amphitheater are subdued.

Miles is already sitting alone near the front of the hall. Eli puts a hand on his shoulder to greet him, and Miles gets to his feet and throws an arm around Eli.

They give each other a couple of affectionate backslaps, and then Miles turns to hug me. I'm a little surprised, but I just give into it. Miles's girlfriend died in the outbreak, and I suspect he just needs to feel connected to someone.

As the hall fills with people, the light chatter fills me with a quiet sense of hope. Everybody lost friends and loved ones to the virus and the battle, but life is slowly returning to normal.

"Hey," says a voice over my shoulder. I turn around.

Lenny is standing right behind me wearing a fresh set of fatigues and combat boots. Her face is sunburned and covered in scratches, but otherwise she looks good.

The sight of her in her cadet uniform gives me a sharp pang

of sadness. Lenny and I are all that's left of our squad, and the thought of reporting to training without Bear, Kindra, or Blaze makes me want to cry.

I reach out to give her a hug, and she squeezes me as though her life depends on it.

She doesn't vocalize it, but I know what she's thinking. We're both wondering how we managed to survive.

When she pulls away, Lenny turns to Eli, and I'm shocked when she straightens up and salutes him in the aisle.

Eli's eyebrows shoot into his hairline, and for a moment, he looks as if he's forgotten what to do. The sting of every cadet's death is written all over his face, but I know what that display of respect must mean to him.

Eli clears his throat, returns Lenny's salute, and then chokes out a quick "at ease." But when Lenny lowers her arm, Eli cracks a sideways smile and pulls her in for a hug.

At ten hundred, Remy Chaplin takes the stage, and the hall erupts into applause. Several people near the front jump to their feet, and soon he's getting a standing ovation.

The message is clear: Remy was one of the few board members who chose to stay when things were at their worst, and that's not something people forget.

Remy's mouth twitches into a smile, and he gives the crowd a gracious nod. Judging from the slight bend to his back, Remy isn't completely comfortable in the spotlight. His previous position was relatively low profile — not the sort that required speeches and public broadcasts.

"Thank you," he says, his smooth voice booming out over the crowd. "Thank you very much."

He takes a deep breath as the noise subsides. "Today I stand before you with perhaps the most daunting undertaking our compound has faced since Death Storm."

The crowd falls silent.

"Just a few days ago, our home was facing a war on three fronts. As we battled a deadly epidemic inside these walls, the brave men and women in Recon, Waste Management, and Exterior Maintenance and Construction were fighting an enemy most of us never knew existed." He pauses and glances down at the lectern. "Meanwhile, a hotbed of evil had been growing unchecked for generations, quietly undermining the values we worked so hard to build into our society.

"In the past two weeks, we have lost hundreds of friends and loved ones. Our home has been damaged . . . and so has our trust in mankind."

Remy takes a long pause, and the tension in the hall seems to build.

"I am incredibly moved that you have trusted me with the honor of the highest office in this compound. And for that honor, I promise to repay you with everything I have.

"For the past three days, I have been working closely with section leadership to determine our best course of action, both in terms of our relationship with the outside world and our responsibilities within 112.

"As most of you know, several of our neighboring compounds were wiped out by the same virus that took the lives of so many here. Meanwhile, our brothers and sisters out on the Fringe have been fighting for their very survival."

A ripple of murmurs fan out across the hall, and several people shift uncomfortably in their seats.

"Many of these people are not war mongers as we once believed, but people with families . . . people with hopes and dreams just like us. Despite the horrendous war we've been waging against them for years, a brave coalition known as Nuclear Nation came to our aid in our darkest hour.

"Since the Desperados' retreat, I have been working closely with Nuclear Nation's leader, Jackson Mills, to determine how we can coexist peacefully in the future. Those talks are still ongoing, and I suspect they will continue for months, if not years."

The murmurs grow louder, and several people get up at once. At first I think they're standing to show their support, but then they start walking toward the door.

A few more people get up and join them, and I realize they're leaving to protest the peace talks.

Eli and I exchange a wary glance. To most people, drifters are drifters. Only those who were on the ground can really grasp what Jackson and his people did for us.

Remy's eyes follow two waves of people out of the hall, but then he continues as though they never left.

"Then there's the issue of our own citizens," he says, "many of whom have been denied the opportunities they deserve due to systematic bias built into the bid system."

There's a renewed flurry of chatter — both from tier three and tier one.

"After many exhaustive talks and negotiations, we have come up with a solution . . . one that I hope will appease those who have been discriminated against."

There's a collective intake of breath in the crowd.

"With 116 and 119 standing empty, we are in need of a workforce that can produce many of the imports on which our economy relies. This presents both a problem and a potential solution. From now on, citizens of 112 may apply for any position in compounds 116 and 119 — regardless of their current section. Candidates will be selected based on both their true aptitude scores and their performance in their current position."

At these words, there's an uproar of noise from the crowd. Some people seem angry, while others are nodding in approval.

Remy pauses to acknowledge the shock and excitement and then continues in a slightly louder voice.

"Those who choose to relocate won't just be faced with the responsibilities of their new position. They'll serve as a test case for compounds around the country and become ambassadors to our Nuclear Nation allies. The survivors who helped us defend 112 will also have the option of taking shelter in our neighboring compounds."

Suddenly, the voices in the crowd rise to an almost deafening level. Another wave of people get up to leave. Several more shout out questions and protests, but their voices are lost in the deafening storm of noise.

"I realize this will be an adjustment," Remy yells, looking out over the crowd in a way that makes me think he's going off script. "But we can no longer ignore reality. There are innocent survivors suffering on the Fringe — children, the elderly, the sick. Turning them away now while entire compounds stand vacant wouldn't just be a gross violation of human rights. It would be incredibly *foolish*."

He waits for the flurry of noise to die down, but it doesn't. He looks over to the cluster of gray and orange uniforms off to his left and continues his speech at a yell.

"The way we've treated our brothers and sisters in tier three is appalling. For that reason, I'm issuing an executive order to relieve Recon and ExCon workers of their current duties."

At those words, several rows of workers stand up and cheer, while others continue their angry shouts.

"I understand that we are in the midst of an energy crisis, but as long as I am president, no compound citizen will be forced to endure conditions which are hazardous to their health.

"Instead, we'll be asking for volunteers to test for radiation resistance. Those who are unaffected by the radiation may choose to be part of teams that will rebuild the rest of the solar fields and perform a new kind of reconnaissance out on the Fringe. These are still dangerous jobs, but rest assured: You will be well compensated for your sacrifice."

Suddenly, an alert silence falls over the crowd of tier-three workers, and I don't know whether to feel panic or relief.

Remy continues. "I've proposed that we devote twenty thousand man hours over the next year to locating Fringe survivors and extending humanitarian aid. We will do all we can to find these people homes and offer them the help they so desperately need. In return, I hope that we can find peace with the outside world."

A fresh wave of chatter ripples through Recon. I glance at Eli. His expression mirrors my thoughts exactly. To shift from hunting drifters to saving them is such a drastic change that it almost sounds absurd.

But to my immense surprise, the cadets and privates seated nearby don't look angry. They aren't tuning Remy out or getting up to leave in protest. They're listening with rapt attention.

It suddenly occurs to me that these people watched the Desperados slaughter their friends, but they also fought side by side with Nuclear Nation to defend the compound.

"These measures I've proposed won't fix everything," Remy admits. "But they are steps toward solutions that I believe will help sustain us for generations to come.

"Believe me when I say that I don't take this opportunity lightly. And I swear that I will never stop fighting to keep us moving in the right direction. Thank you."

At Remy's final nod, the hall bursts into raucous applause. People jump up, cheer, and whoop, and Eli and I get to our feet in a daze.

For a first speech, Remy certainly didn't hold back. It might not be realistic to think he can accomplish all those things while he's in office, but it's impressive that he wants to try.

As soon as he climbs down from the platform, people start trickling out for an early lunch. I hang back and look for Sawyer, anxious to see what she thinks of the proposed new measures.

As the crowd thins out, I spot her sitting toward the back with Caleb. They're both dressed in their red scrubs, and my heart beats a little stronger when I see that they're holding hands.

Caleb is still pale and drawn from his ordeal, but Sawyer looks much better than she did the last time I saw her. She smiles shyly when she sees me wandering over, and Caleb pulls her in for a quick kiss.

He grins and sidles off to give us a minute, and Sawyer raises her eyebrows in a "Can you believe it?" sort of way.

"Wow," I say, grinning after Caleb.

"I know!" she squeals in a very un-Sawyer-like way.

My smile broadens as she pulls me in for a hug, and it hits me how lucky I am to have made it through the outbreak with both of my best friends alive.

"You two look happy," I murmur into her hair.

"*Yeah.*"

"Is today the day?"

Sawyer pulls away and gives me a wide-eyed nod.

"Are you nervous?"

"A little."

"Don't worry," I say. "This is a *good* thing."

"I don't know."

"It *is.*"

Today is the day Sawyer revives her parents from their virtual hiatus. Exercising her right as power of attorney will put an end to her parents' landmark three-year study, but it also means she'll have a chance to rekindle her bizarre relationship with them.

"What if they hate me for it?" she asks in a small voice.

"They won't," I say, squeezing her arm. "You're their *daughter*."

Sawyer shakes her head as if this is an irrelevant detail, and I hold back an exasperated sigh. Sawyer wants to see her parents again so badly, but that isn't why she's reviving them.

With so many doctors killed in the outbreak, Natasha Mayweather asked Sawyer to pull the plug on her parents' study. Constance no longer poses a threat to them or anyone else, so Sawyer agreed on the condition that Progressive Research greenlight her parents' next project.

"They're going to be so proud of you," I murmur. "If it weren't for you, they never would have been able to roll out the treatment on time."

"It's not like I *discovered* the treatment," she says bitterly.

I can't help it. I laugh. Leave it to Sawyer, the chronic overachiever, to feel as though she hasn't done enough.

"Trust me," I say. "They're gonna be amazed. How many first-year med interns have offers to join Progressive Research?"

"Just two," she admits.

"Exactly. And what have your parents been doing? Lying on a virtual beach somewhere."

Sawyer laughs. I can see the pride fighting to break through her self-critical nature, and that makes me smile. "We're proud of you" are the four words Sawyer has always wanted to hear from her parents, but they've been the most elusive throughout her life. Seeing that Sawyer is proud of *herself* shows just how much she's grown.

I feel a soft brush against my arm and sense Eli's reassuring presence. Sawyer flashes him a grin, and I lean in for one more hug. She squeezes me tightly and then rushes off to the medical ward.

Eli snakes his arm around my waist, and I lean into him. But instead of going for a quick peck on the lips, Eli pulls my body flush against his and brings his mouth down for a long, passionate kiss. He threads his fingers through my hair and squeezes my hip lightly.

I quickly lose myself in his warm smell and fold myself tighter into his arms. I don't even think about the fact that we're in the middle of the main hall or that there are hundreds of people who could be watching.

As we stand there kissing by the window, a strange sense of déjà vu creeps over me.

Six months ago, I sat next to Eli in this very hall thinking that I'd just lost everything. I'd lost my only chance to be recruited for Systems. I'd lost my shot at wealth and status and the life I'd planned for myself.

But as Eli's fingers brush against my cheek, I realize just how much I've gained.

It's not just that I found Eli. I learned how to survive. I found the truth, I found purpose, and I found myself.

I don't want the same things that I did back then, which is why I'm not applying to be a programmer in 119.

Systems just isn't me anymore. My place is in Recon. I know I can survive out there. I've already faced the worst the Fringe has to offer. If Eli will agree to be my partner, I'm going to volunteer for the new Recon team.

For better or for worse, Recon is who we are. And in a way, our job is no different from Celdon's or Sawyer's or Remy's.

From now on, everyone's job is the same. Our job is to rebuild.

epilogue

Eli

One month later.

After a war, all people want is for things to go back to normal. Trouble is the old normal isn't an option.

"Normal" used to mean killing in secret and putting the good of the many over the good of a few. But to have peace, we have to rethink everything we've done for the past three generations — starting with the drifters.

Right now, nobody is asking the hard questions — at least not in public. Instead of wringing their hands about how we're going to merge two very different groups of people, the compound's new leaders have reacted with an outpouring of generosity and support.

Their speeches are heavy on words like "solidarity" and light on solutions. In other words, they're opting for denial.

After years of fighting and killing to maintain the illusion of peace, I'm done with denial. And when you can't pretend to be happy with the status quo, the only option is to start over.

I first saw this place about a year and a half ago when Recon was still sending out operatives to refill our most far-flung checkpoints. Back then, I was so dead to the world that hardly anything could pull me back, but this place made me feel as if I'd finally woken up from a long sleep.

Fifteen dusty miles from the compound, I found an abandoned adobe house nestled in a pocket of overgrown sagebrush. The door must have fallen off its hinges decades ago and had lain undisturbed for years on the old wooden porch. The windows were framed with chipped teal paint, and inside were the remnants of life before Death Storm: a rickety wooden chair, an earthen fireplace, and several empty clay pots drying on the window sill.

I never asked Harper to move out here with me, but she was sitting in the passenger seat the day I drove out to bury Owen and Gunner in the desert.

I knew Gunner probably wouldn't have cared where I buried him, but Owen would've balked at being laid to rest in the dead level. If it were up to Owen, he would have died in the desert and simply rotted away, but I wanted to give him and Gunner a proper burial.

The spot just over the hill from the old house seemed as good a place as any. Jackson lent me one of his guys' pickup trucks, and Miles helped me load up the bodies. Harper and I dug the graves, laid them in the earth, and stacked mounds of desert rock over their heads to mark each plot.

We sat on the hill together and watched the sun sink over the distant rock formations. When the sandstone turned red and the sky faded to a muted violet, we walked slowly up the narrow dirt path and stopped outside the broken-down house.

Harper said she wished we could stay there forever, and I realized it could be the best thing for both of us.

Neither of us had said it out loud, but the past few weeks had been torture.

In the fallout from the battle, Remy had forged an alliance with Nuclear Nation, and the board was in the process of drafting a resolution for peace. With Constance gone and the old bid system abolished, it appeared that the compound was turning over a new leaf. But Harper and I had been holding our breath — waiting for the day we'd be asked to start killing again.

After all the deception and bad memories, staying at the compound just wasn't an option. It didn't matter that the new Recon commander wanted to promote me to captain or that Harper could have gone to work for Systems. Neither of us had the stomach for it.

That's how we came to stay at the desert house. The change of scenery hasn't put all our nightmares to rest, but it's a start. We just take it day by day — one sunrise, one meal, one worry at a time.

Once I get the fire started, I put a pot of water on our homemade rocket stove and go inside to wake up Harper. The door still doesn't hang straight on its hinges, and it squeaks loudly when I push it open. A light breeze is fluttering through the curtains Harper made out of an old tablecloth, and the weak morning light illuminates her sleeping form on our lumpy pallet.

Harper stirs as I climb up beside her. I hover over her body with my weight on my elbows and really take her in. Her dark hair is lying in a messy puddle under her head, and her skin is flushed with a delicate tan.

She cracks one eye open and lets out a groggy little moan. I bend down and kiss her softly, and she returns with a gentle nip.

After a moment, she reaches up and threads her fingers through my hair, pulling me toward her for a *real* morning kiss.

I work my tongue in between her lips, and she sighs against me as my hands push up the hem of her tank top.

I get lost exploring her silky skin, pausing to taste each new freckle.

Soon we've exhausted all our time, and Harper's hands slow to trace gentle circles on my back. I roll off her with a groan, grab my shorts, and go back outside to cook us some oatmeal before we have to leave.

Harper and I are doing recon again, but with a few crucial differences. We go dressed in drifter clothes instead of our fatigues, and the handgun tucked into my waistband is just a precaution. We won't be going alone this time, and instead of looking for drifters to shoot, we're hoping to get close enough to talk.

With Malcolm dead, the Desperados have been limping along on the verge of extinction. There are dozens — maybe hundreds — who survived the battle, but most of them have gone underground or moved west toward the coast.

The smaller Desperado cells left in the area are the only real threat, and our job is to protect peaceful survivors and invite them to take shelter in the compounds. It's a tough sell to drifters who've lost loved ones to Recon, but to those who need food, clean water, and medical care, going to live in the compounds is a no-brainer.

By the time we reach Crazy Horse Saddle & Tack, Sage and Jackson are already waiting outside the workshop. We chose this old Western store to rendezvous because it's about a mile outside the town we're scouting. We need to meet up beforehand to formulate a plan so we don't spook the survivors.

Jackson greets me with a big grin and a warm handshake. For him, things have only gotten better since the battle, and the members of Nuclear Nation who'd been cast out by Malcolm are now living safely at 119. He still wears his frayed khaki shorts and a sun-faded polo, but with his fresh haircut and clean-shaven face, he looks almost too polished to pass as a drifter.

Sage hugs Harper and smiles at me over her shoulder, but it doesn't quite meet her eyes. She still has a long pinkish line running from her temple to her forehead where the shrapnel was removed, but her scars run deeper than that. Looking into her eyes, it's impossible to forget that she recently lost the love of her life.

Sage was inconsolable after Owen died. She didn't want to see his body, and she wasn't there when we buried him.

While I'm glad she didn't have to see Owen beaten and broken, part of me thinks the closure would have done her good.

Unlike Jackson, Sage hasn't assimilated to the compounds. She's still living out on the Fringe, but she made a deal to help Recon in exchange for food and supplies.

I clear my throat. "What have we got?"

"Just a routine escort," says Jackson. "We found nine unaffiliated survivors in hiding at an old motel."

"You've already made contact?"

Sage nods. "We found them yesterday and briefed them on 119. They lost two in a Desperado shooting last month, so they're pretty nervous about relocating. They have two kids in their group, and one of the women is pregnant. We told them we'd make sure they made it safely."

"All right," I say, clapping my hands together. "Let's get the show on the road."

Jackson's SUV is parked behind the shop, so we all pile in and drive down the road to greet the survivors. Sunlight shines through bullet holes in the door and something under the hood rattles, but miraculously the Explorer still runs.

We drive through the abandoned town, and Jackson kills the engine outside an old motel. The natural stone masonry mixed with yellow siding gives the place a retro look, and the decommissioned "No Vacancy" sign adds to the fleabag motel feel.

We're parked in the shelter of several mature juniper trees, but I still feel exposed. All the windows are boarded over, but there's a rusted-out pickup and an old Subaru parked around back.

"I don't like this," I mutter as Sage and Jackson get out.

"Just relax," says Harper. "They know what they're doing."

The plan is for me and Harper to hang back so Sage and Jackson can greet the survivors first, but I don't like splitting up. It always feels like walking into an ambush.

Jackson knocks on the third door down from the entrance, and for a moment, I don't think anyone is going to answer. But then a piece of cardboard rustles in a window, and the door opens a crack.

A pale skinny guy sticks his head out, and I can see that he's in his late twenties with messy black hair and a scruffy beard. Jackson says something, and the man's gaze drifts over to the SUV. I stiffen as his eyes dart from me to Harper, but then he nods, and Jackson waves us over.

I let out the breath I was holding, open the door, and stow my handgun under my T-shirt. The guy looks harmless enough, but I still position myself between him and Harper as we make our approach. I'm wary of anyone who's spent too much time on the Fringe.

But as soon as the scruffy guy gives us the once-over and opens the door, I realize my fears were completely unfounded.

These people aren't like the Desperados. They aren't fighters, and they aren't survivalists. They're just people with the genes to withstand radiation who hunkered down and hid rather than engage with the nearby gangs.

All the survivors are thin and haggard. They're dressed in tattered clothes and look like a bunch of scared animals. Among the group is an older couple, a bearded guy in his midforties, a kid who can't be older than eighteen, and two women in their midthirties. One of the women is in fact pregnant — probably seven or eight months along — and when we crowd into the front room, I spot two little kids watching from around the corner.

After a round of strained introductions, we go over the plan and explain how they'll be integrated into compound 119. Fifty or sixty members of Nuclear Nation have already taken up residence there, which seems to put the survivors at ease.

It's a long journey to the Arizona border, so we fill our tanks with all the fuel the group has and plan to stop at a former Desperado base. There we'll be able to refuel and stretch our legs before making the last dangerous push through Desperado territory.

All we have to do is deliver them to the border, where a group of Recon workers will be waiting to guide them the rest of the way.

Jackson and Sage take a few of the survivors in the Explorer, and the scruffy guy agrees to let Harper and me drive their truck. The remaining group members pile into the Subaru, and we caravan south toward 119.

Harper sits in the bed of the truck to scan for drifters while I drive. I'm supposed to be watching the road, but I keep glancing up into the rearview mirror to reassure myself that Harper is safe. Sure enough, she's still sitting with her back against the cab and her long hair blowing in the wind.

We don't encounter any Desperados the entire drive, but my eyes are heavy and tired by the time we make it to the border. We do the handoff at an old truck stop, and the scruffy guy gives my hand a hearty shake as we say goodbye. All the survivors look nervous, but their eyes are full of hope that makes the entire drive feel worth it.

It's nearly midnight by the time Sage and Jackson drop us off at the Crazy Horse. I climb into our borrowed truck, and we drive off into the darkness.

I never really appreciated it before, but the stars on the Fringe are unreal. This far from the compound, they fill the whole sky like a billion silver coins, and I can still see them long after I close my eyes at night.

"Do you think it'll last?" Harper asks in a groggy voice, calling me back to reality.

"Hmm?"

She's staring out the window at the desert, taking in the Fringe as if she's never really seen it before.

"This drifter treaty . . . bringing them into the compounds."

"I don't know," I murmur. "We've been fighting them for a long time."

"What's going to happen when the compounds are full again?" she whispers. "Do you think we'll just shut them out?"

I shrug. "I don't know. I hope not."

"I mean . . . when does it end?"

It sounds like a rhetorical question, but I answer anyway.

"I guess . . . I guess it ends once people see that the Fringe is livable . . . when people like us outnumber the Desperados and the world isn't so dangerous."

Harper yawns and nods slowly. "Maybe."

She's abandoning her worries for tonight, but I can tell these questions have weighed on her mind for the past several weeks. They weigh on mine, too, if I'm being honest. It's impossible *not* to consider the worst-case scenario when we've been through hell and emerged on the other side.

Within minutes, Harper drifts off in the front seat, and her head falls against the window. She's worrying a hole in her jeans in her sleep, and I'm struck by sudden inspiration — followed by a quiet tingle of panic.

Ignoring my tired eyes and rumbling stomach, I turn abruptly and head for a checkpoint I haven't visited in weeks.

It's pitch black, and my flashlight batteries are dying, but I manage to find the spot I visited the day Gunner was shot.

By now the brush has grown up around the checkpoint, hiding the trapdoor from view. But after a few minutes of poking and stomping, I find exactly what I'm looking for.

Heaving the trapdoor open, I shine my light down into the hole and squint at the hodgepodge of supplies. Judging from the looks of the place, Recon hasn't been here in ages. The rations, fuel, and water bags look virtually untouched, and to my amazement, my old pair of jeans is still lying in the corner next to a first aid kit.

Tingling with anticipation, I jump into the hole and snatch them up. They smell like damp earth and sweat, but they're mine.

Harper is still asleep when I get back to the truck, and she doesn't wake up when we reach the house. I close the truck door quietly and leave her there while I start dinner. We haven't eaten since lunch, and I know she's going to be hungry.

Once the stew is heating on the stove, I go out behind the house to wash off the dust and grime from the ride. We had a good rain the day before, so there's enough water in the collection drums for us each to take a desert shower with a bucket and a cup.

I walk around the side of the house to get some clean clothes, and when I look back out through the open door, I see Harper sitting by the stove.

I pull on my old jeans that I retrieved from the checkpoint, marveling that they still fit after all these years. I found them on one of my first deployments and paid off a guy in decontamination so I could keep them. These jeans followed me from the Fringe to the compound and back out here, and when I stick my hands in my pockets, I feel a surge of relief.

I wasn't sure if they'd still be there, but I hoped they would be. Owen's treasures are all I have left of my family, and I almost lost them for good.

Luckily, the old photo of the four of us is still folded in the back left pocket, and when I put my hand in the front, something light and cool wraps around my fingers.

Slowly, carefully, I withdraw my mother's necklace on its delicate braided chain. A lump forms in my throat at the sight of the tiny silver hare and the well-worn piece of turquoise hanging beside it.

I'd all but forgotten that I put this in my pocket, and it feels as though it's reappeared now for a reason.

Rubbing the smooth stone between my thumb and middle finger, I let the warmth in my chest rise up to calm the grief that's been threatening to suffocate me for years.

I'm not alone after all. I don't have to be.

Emboldened by the sudden lightness in my soul, I pull on a long-sleeve T-shirt and make my way out to the stove. Harper is sitting on an old bench we found at the Crazy Horse, wrapped in a sweater and a thick wool blanket. Her windblown hair is hanging wild around her shoulders, and her cheeks are pink with sunburn.

"Hey," she says, giving me a tired smile. "Stew's almost ready."

"That's good," I murmur.

There's a slight chill in the air, so I sit down beside her and drape an arm over her shoulders. Holding her close, I follow her gaze up over the hill to the spot where we buried Owen and Gunner.

"Can I ask you something?" Harper whispers.

"Anything."

She hesitates. "What did Owen say to you?"

"When?"

"Before he died . . . He muttered something. What did he say?"

I look down at my hands, feeling the memory of Owen's death threatening to swallow me whole. "That we'd always be family."

Harper drags in a breath and lets it out slowly. "Those are good last words."

I nod, thinking back to those horrible final moments in the psych ward.

"Owen loved you, you know," says Harper, looking up at the endless blanket of stars fanning out over the sandstone formations. "He may not have known how to show it, but he did."

"Yeah, I know," I sigh, fighting down the lump in my throat. "It didn't save him from Constance, but maybe it saved him from himself."

Harper looks over at me, and I feel a little self-conscious all of a sudden.

"What do you mean?"

"Maybe having someone — someone to care about . . . Maybe that saved him from turning out just like Malcolm."

Harper seems to consider this for a moment but doesn't say anything right away.

"You saved me," I add, feeling my face heat up. "If it weren't for loving you . . ." I shake my head. "I don't know that

I'd be able to feel anything anymore — not after everything I've done."

Harper's gaze softens. She's looking at me in a way she never has before. It's as if she's finally seeing me — truly *seeing* me for the first time. It's a magical feeling.

A coyote howls somewhere in the distance, and another joins in. Soon the desert is echoing with their unruly cries, and Harper takes both of my hands in hers.

"For what it's worth . . . you saved me, too."

My heart thumps loudly in my chest, and I take a deep breath to gather up the courage for what I'm about to say.

Slowly, carefully, I tilt her chin up toward my face and brush my lips against hers. She returns my kiss with a sweet sigh of satisfaction, and when she pulls away, I can see the stars winking back at me in her eyes.

"It's what we do, isn't it?" I say. "Save each other?"

She smiles. "Yeah. It's what we do."

"No matter what happens, you'll always have me," I whisper, giving her knee a light squeeze.

Harper leans back to study my face, and her smile widens. Her expression is light, but I can tell from the warmth in her eyes that it means a lot to her.

"Thanks," she says in a tender voice. "I'm not going anywhere either."

"Good," I say, shifting to one side so I can pull the silver chain out of my pocket. The flash of metal catches Harper's eye, and her expression becomes very serious as I stretch the necklace between my fingers.

She swallows as I lower it over her head and rearrange her hair over the chain. Slowly, gently, I trace the line of braided silver down her collarbone, finally pausing where the charm falls in the valley of her chest.

"We're partners, right?" I murmur.

"Partners," she chokes, looking up with eyes that seem to burn straight through me.

For several seconds we just stare at each other, and then Harper's eyes flutter closed. She kisses me senseless under the desert sky, and I feel as though I've finally come home.

Author's Note

Thank you for reading *Annihilation.* I hope you enjoyed the story and that it left you feeling satisfied and hopeful about the future of your favorite characters.

I took a bit of a hiatus from The Fringe before writing this book because this series is so special to me, and I wanted to do the finale justice. The Fringe is the series that allowed me to quit my day job to write full time, and it's connected me with so many wonderful people all around the world.

It's hard to believe that I've dedicated more than two whole years and nearly half a million words to building this story universe, and yet I feel as though I've only begun to scratch the surface. This story grew and grew, and the characters took on such rich lives that they almost began to feel real to me. I will miss them all so much.

Harper and Eli were enormous fun to write because they're the type of characters who make no apologies for who they are. I loved watching Harper toughen up in Recon and watching Eli progress from a bitter, world-weary lieutenant to a man capable of love and hope.

As Celdon became involved with Constance, I inadvertently turned some of you against him. Deep down, I knew Celdon was still good, and it felt like a personal victory to watch him step up and do the right thing. I had no idea going in that he would become the true hero of the story, but I love it when characters surprise me.

In the original draft of *Annihilation*, Owen refused to give up the location of the Desperados' base. But after he'd made the dangerous journey to the compound to warn Eli about the drifter attack, it just didn't feel right for him to pass up one last chance to show his brother that he cared. No matter how closed off and stubborn Owen may seem, I knew that someone raised with the same unconditional love Eli experienced as a child could never turn his back on family.

I loved writing The Fringe from all these different perspectives because it allowed me to gain greater insight into the characters than I've ever had before. An unexpected benefit of this intimate knowledge was that it helped bring rich secondary characters out of the woodwork and allowed me to explore their unique backstories.

Every time I opened a new storyline, I discovered fascinating new tidbits of information that made the entire series a blast. I couldn't believe how much fun I had coming up with Sawyer's parents' research project, fleshing out Gunner's character, and watching Remy's evolution as a political figure.

When I first created Remy, I saw him as a stodgy, useless bureaucrat who stood passively by as hundreds of Recon people died. But as the story unfolded, I realized it was more complicated than that.

Remy is a person with a strong moral compass, but his position on the board forced him to look the other way until Constance's depravity became too intense to ignore. In the end, it took some serious arm-twisting to keep him honest, which just goes to show how politics can corrupt the best of us.

Another aspect of this book I enjoyed was delving deep into setting to create some vivid new environments for the characters to inhabit. Besides shopping for character names, building new "sets" has become one of my favorite writerly activities.

This past year I had the privilege of traveling to Taos, New Mexico, which gave me a better feel of the desert Southwest and allowed me to add so much more depth to the Fringe itself — especially Eli and Harper's desert house.

After my trip, I developed a minor obsession with adobe architecture and off-the-grid living. The desert has always attracted people who value freedom and self-sufficiency, which makes it the ideal place for people to set up a homestead and withdraw from mainstream society.

An estimated 1,200 to 1,500 people currently live on the Pajarito Mesa — an 18,000-acre plot of land outside Albuquerque without electricity, running water, mail, or paved roads. Meanwhile, Earthships constructed from rammed-earth tires, bottles, and cans are springing up everywhere in and around Taos.

While Eli and Harper's house is in the Utah desert, I drew inspiration from some of these people who have chosen to live independent from public utilities. I've also been following Rob Greenfield, whose extreme challenges in minimalism and off-the-grid living provided several ideas for Eli and Harper's house.

From day one, I knew the two of them would choose to make their home in the desert. Even though they have friends back at 112, I knew they would never again feel truly safe or happy living in the compound after everything they'd experienced. Since society failed them so miserably, they would have no choice but to retreat to the wilderness.

I hope you enjoyed *Annihilation* and that you'll help me spread the word by leaving a review on your favorite retailer's website and Goodreads. Reviews help readers like you discover books by independent authors, and I really appreciate them.

Finally, I couldn't have created The Fringe without the help of my phenomenal team of beta readers. These wonderful people have been reading my books and supporting me since the very beginning, and I literally wouldn't be where I am today without their help. They've given me encouragement, feedback, and brilliant suggestions that have continually elevated the quality of my work.

For now, The Fringe is drawing to a close, but I won't promise that I'm done with this universe forever. Some ideas grow such deep roots that it's impossible to keep new stories from springing up.

In the meantime, you can look forward to more dystopian adventures from me. Be sure to visit my website at **www.tarahbenner.com** and sign up for my mailing list so you can be the first to hear about my next release.

Looking for your next great read?
Check out more books by Tarah Benner:

Bound in Blood
The Defectors
Enemy Inside
The Last Uprising
Recon
Exposure
Outbreak
Lockdown

Follow me on Twitter @TarahBenner.
"Like" the books on Facebook.
Connect at www.tarahbenner.com

Made in the USA
Las Vegas, NV
21 June 2021

25155839R00219